IN MY
FATHER'S
HOUSE

In My

Father's House

THE SHILOH LEGACY SERIES ✶ BOOK ONE

BODIE & BROCK THOENE

TYNDALE HOUSE PUBLISHERS, INC.
CAROL STREAM, ILLINOIS

Visit Tyndale's exciting Web site at www.tyndale.com

TYNDALE and Tyndale's quill logo are registered trademarks of Tyndale House Publishers, Inc.

In My Father's House

Designed by Dean H. Renninger

Edited by Ramona Cramer Tucker

Published in 1992 by Bethany House Publishers under ISBN 1-55661-189-7.

First printing by Tyndale House Publishers, Inc. in 2006.

Library of Congress Cataloging-in-Publication Data

Thoene, Bodie, date.
In my father's house / Bodie & Brock Thoene.
    p. cm. —(The Shiloh legacy ; bk. 1)
ISBN-13: 978-1-4143-0120-4 (pbk.)
ISBN-10: 1-4143-0120-0 (pbk.)
1. Shiloh (Ark. : Imaginary place)—Fiction. 2. Depressions—Fiction. 3. Country life —
Fiction. 4. Arkansas—Fiction. I. Thoene, Brock, date. II. Title.
PS3570.H46I5 2006   2005036675

Printed in the United States of America

11   10   09   08   07   06
 7   6   5   4   3   2   1

All the stories I heard as a kid growing up . . .
a thousand novels could not tell them the way you did.
So with thanks and love I give this little story back to you.

My grandmothers:
Rebecca Rachel Moninger
Trudy Vera Brown

and also
Delpha-Mae Nichols,
who held us chillens in her ebony arms
and sang us songs about Jesus

THE BATTLE OF BRITAIN
SUNDAY, SEPTEMBER 15, 1940

The skies above southeast England were clear this Sunday morning, yet thunder rumbled in the air. The peaceful ringing of church bells had been interrupted by the high wail of the air-raid siren and drowned out by the angry drone of the Luftwaffe bombers and fighter planes swarming above the coast of Kent. While thousands of Londoners scrambled for shelter in underground stations, the first wave of enemy planes cast shadows across the cliffs and the pebbled beaches between Dover and Dungeness. A second wave followed—four hundred German planes in all—on their way to London, blackening the skies like thunderclouds.

Colonel Theo Lindheim thrust his head out the passenger-side window of the wildly careening Austin as his son-in-law, John Murphy, pressed the accelerator to the floorboard. An Austin roadster on a country lane was no match for Messerschmitt fighter planes, which seemed to delight in strafing anything on the road, even bicycles and hay wagons.

The sun glinted on the wing of an approaching fighter. "Pull over, Murphy!" Theo gestured toward a drainage ditch and a tall hedge at the side of the lane.

Murphy braked hard and spun the wheel, sliding the Austin into the brush. Theo leaped from the vehicle and dived to the ground. The guns of the Messerschmitt sent spouts of gravel skyward, tearing through the metal body of the car as though it were cardboard. Murphy rolled into the mud with Theo and huddled beneath the shadow of the hedge as the fighter roared above them and then blasted at some other foolish traveler farther up the lane.

The two men exchanged a look and a thought. Theo's wife, Anna; Murphy's wife, Elisa; Lori Kalner; and the children had been evacuated to the safety of Wales. But not even a one-lane country road was safe these days.

Pulling down the brim of his crushed hat, Murphy peered over the edge of the culvert at the Austin. "Sorry, Theo. The car is done for. I can't get you back to Northolt."

Theo nodded curtly and returned his gaze skyward as a squadron of British Spitfires engaged the horde of German attackers. Those were his boys up there, the men of the Northolt Shooting Star Squadron. Theo had trained them well, and they would do their duty even though their colonel was forced to sit out the battle in a ditch.

So few against so many! Did the German High Command know how thin and fragile this last line of British defense was? Did Hitler and Hermann Göring suspect that if these British planes and pilots were lost, there were no others to be sent up to take their places? All Europe had crumbled before the Nazi Blitzkrieg. Now only Britain remained to fight.

Theo shielded his eyes against the glare and followed the distant dogfights high above him.

Among the brave English pilots was a handful of foreign fliers like Theo Lindheim who had fled to Great Britain as the Nazi juggernaut rolled across their homelands. Each man had come to this island fortress not for refuge but for battle.

Dark-eyed Pasquale had escaped from France with little Fuqua as Dunkirk fell. Cervantes fled from Spain after the slaughter of Barcelona. Falk and Warnock stole a Polish training plane and rattled across the Channel as Danzig fell. They had crash-landed on a beach near Dover and been rounded up by a group of angry civilians who mistook them for the enemy.

And Thoene, the young Dutch pilot, had showed the bravado that earned him the nickname Rock. After Holland fell, he broke the neck of a German SS officer, stole his uniform, and bluffed his way into the cockpit of an ME-109 fighter plane. Within moments he was airborne and headed for England with four Nazi pilots in hot pursuit. His plane full of bullet holes, he barely reached England. Landing in a field beside an insane asylum, he was captured by the inmates and nearly pitchforked by an inmate named Sid who claimed to be Sherlock Holmes. Even after such a welcome, Thoene insisted that English lunatics were far better than the Nazis. Eventually he took his place as a group leader among the other members of the Shooting Star Squadron.

The squadron was fleshed out by American and Canadian volunteers. Barker, Fox, Mooneyham, and Heer came from a flying circus working out of Vancouver. Miller, Hobbs, and Sherrill were part of an American barnstorming troop headed by Wildman McKinney. Last to join the squadron was David Meyer, who had come to England with Theo's sons, Wilhelm and Dieter Lindheim.

These few men formed one of the fiercest fighter squadrons in the air. The British airmen, alone except for a few allies like these, were grateful that the Shooting Stars were fighting with England these days.

"Your boys up there?" Murphy asked.

Theo continued his intense gaze upward. A V formation of Spitfires dived at a massive group of Luftwaffe bombers from upsun at great speed. At such a distance it was difficult to distinguish between planes, and certainly the insignia was not visible. But he had no doubt that he was watching his men attacking the massive swarm of German aircraft moving toward London.

"Yes. Those are my boys." Theo stood up in the ditch and strained to see as the planes momentarily vanished in the sun's glare. He could have replied, *"Those are my sons."* He had come to love them all with the love of a father for his children.

Theo held his breath as the Spitfire piloted by David Meyer, now close enough to identify, led in, striking the formation just to the rear of center. Thoene and Sherrill followed, attacking a Dornier 215, hitting the starboard wing. Massive chunks fell off the wing and engine. The German aircraft tilted crazily, narrowly missing a second Do-215 as it hurled out of formation. Pasquale and Fuqua zoomed in on a lumbering bomber as it maneuvered to avoid the wreckage of the falling plane. Two strong bursts into the cockpit and cannon fire from Mooneyham into the tail section sent the second enemy aircraft flaming toward the earth.

Murphy and Theo cheered their victories from far below. Moments later a vics formation of German fighters regrouped and attacked the Stars from the east, drawing them off the bombers into individual battles for survival. The deadly Luftwaffe bombers droned on toward London with their deadly cargoes, leaving the Spitfires and the Messerschmitts jousting above and behind them.

A Spitfire was hit, falling sideways in a long glide toward the sea.

"Who is it?" Murphy asked.

Theo shook his head. His two sons were also up there. But out of formation, it was almost impossible to tell one plane from another. It all seemed like a fast-moving shell game, with each individual plane shifting places with another, spinning and diving and climbing into the sun at six hundred miles an hour.

"Look!" Murphy cried. A second formation of British fighters had appeared out of the sun to attack the German bombers.

Theo glanced briefly at the new battle. Without fighter cover, the enemy bombers were in trouble. He turned his eyes back to his own men, who fought to keep the Messerschmitts drawn away from the thick cloud of bombers they were meant to protect. It was there that this battle would be won or lost.

"Keep them busy, boys!" Murphy cheered the Shooting Stars on.

Two Messerschmitts spun off, flaming to the earth. Another Star was hit, smoking and coughing away in an attempt to make it back to base at Northolt.

Who is it? Falk? Will he make it to the airfield?

In answer to Theo's unspoken question, the engine choked and stalled. The cockpit opened and the pilot bailed out. An ME-109 spotted his parachute and plummeted after him, as if to shoot the flier and finish the job. A second Spitfire roared after the Messerschmitt, blowing the cockpit canopy off the enemy plane.

Warnock had rushed in to do battle for Falk. Cervantes circled the chute all the way to the ground as Warnock climbed skyward for yet another dogfight. They were family, these boys—looking out for one another. That was what the brass at Northolt said and perhaps why the Shooting Stars had earned such a heroic reputation. These men, Theo knew, had lost everything before the first German bomb had ever fallen on England. They had nothing left to lose but their lives, and they lived only to fight so they might one day return to their own countries in victory. Today, in the cloudless skies beyond Northolt, they did battle one-on-one against the vast powers gathered in the east.

These were the sons of men who had fought in the Great War—the War to End All Wars. Their fathers had fought against one another—some for Germany, others for France or America. A mere twenty-two years earlier, their fathers may have been enemies, but now the Shooting Star Squadron of Northolt bunked together, ate together, and looked out for one another when the battle got rough.

Theo crossed his arms and solemnly gazed up to where a spiral of smoke flooded from a German fighter. David Meyer was on the tail of the Messerschmitt. Theo shook his head in amazement at how things had changed. Twenty-two years before, almost to the day, Theo had been in a plane above no-man's-land in France, and the father of David Meyer had been watching from the other side of the line.

THE
TEMPEST

part one

Nothing except
a battle lost can be
half so melancholy
as a battle won.

THE DUKE
OF WELLINGTON,
1815

CHAPTER ONE

Miracle on the Front

BELLEAU WOOD, FRANCE
AUTUMN, 1918

There was little evidence that this place had ever been a forest. All that remained of the trees were charred, ragged stumps pointing skyward.

Where wildflowers had once bloomed, rolls of barbed concertina wire sprouted from the seared earth like tangled, leafless briars. Across no-man's-land, bomb craters riddled the landscape and caught the rainwater and the blood of felled soldiers. Weary warriors of the German kaiser's army faced the American doughboys and their French and British comrades all along the western front. Fleas and mud and cold and influenza were the common enemies of both armies. This was the Great War in 1918.

Today it was quiet on the western front. Twenty-year-old Private Birch Tucker rested his back against the sandbags of the trench and poked a dirt-caked finger through the slits of a small, square cage containing the pigeons of Company C. The two birds fluttered up and fell back in their confinement. It was too dangerous these days for pigeons to be flying, Birch thought. He lifted his eyes to where two buzzing mechanical birds did battle high above the desolate war zone.

An American-made Curtiss JN-4 was in hot pursuit of a German Fokker. The distant rattle of machine-gun fire drifted down to the trenches. Soldiers on both sides of no-man's-land shielded their eyes against the late-afternoon sun as they cheered their champions on.

The German looped and began a steady, rolling ascent. The American Jenny remained tight on his tail.

"See why I can't let you out?" Birch held up the wooden cage. "The sky ain't a safe place for birds nowadays."

Ellis Warne laughed. "Just don't tell those birds the real reason they're in the trenches with us, Birch m'boy."

Unlike the carrier pigeons trained to carry messages to and from the front lines, Birch kept the birds to detect the presence of deadly mustard gas. If he saw two dead birds, it was time to put on his gas mask. But by the time the birds were gassed, the men would probably have a good dose of the poison as well. So Birch had begun the practice of lowering the cage by a long string into whatever foxhole he intended to make his bed for the night. If the birds came back alive, he knew that it was habitable. He had learned this trick from the coal miners of his native Arkansas, and it had made him popular with his comrades on the battlefield.

Beside him, Max Meyer craned his head back as the *rat-a-tat-tat* of the American machine gun echoed. "We're better off down here," he said without enthusiasm. "Both us and the birds." He grinned. "I paid a dollar for me and my girl to take an airplane ride over New York City last summer." He shook his head with amusement. "Trenches and mud got it beat."

Ellis eyed him curiously, as he always did when Max Meyer began one of his stories. "Yeah? What happened?"

Max followed the slow spiral of the German Fokker. "See that? The pilot did one of those over Coney Island."

"Yeah?" Birch egged him on. Max always left out details until they begged him, and then his stories could go on for hours.

"Irene was on my lap, all strapped in." He patted his knees. "I thought it would be a good way to get her where I wanted her, see?" Max raised a knowing eyebrow to his envious comrades. "Real romantic, I'm thinking."

Ellis had told Birch about one cold winter night, sitting close to his fiancée, Becky Moniger, on a sleigh ride. Birch had once had Thelma Ridgeway fall on top of him at a church social. But Max, with his New York City upbringing, had a different way of going about things where women were concerned.

"So what happened?" Birch urged.

"I started to kiss her. What a place for a kiss, right? Next thing I know, she dumped her dinner all over me and Coney Island both." He jerked a thumb skyward. "Romance. Those fellas are welcome to it!"

As if to make a point, the American Jenny blasted away at the climbing Fokker again. It was only a matter of time now.

"Done for," Birch commented as the German tried and failed to maneuver out of the American gunsights.

"I'll put five on the nose of the Hun," Max said dryly. "Bet he lives to fight another day. Any takers?"

"The Kraut ain't got a chance," Birch scoffed. Another burst of high machine-gun fire punctuated the remark. The German banked left and spun away toward earth in an attempt to shake the American.

Max reached into his tunic and pulled out a leather pouch and a wad of bills and photographs and letters all bound with string. "What do you say, Ellis? Take me on?"

"You cleaned me out last night," Ellis said sadly. "Every cent, or I would." Then Ellis nudged Birch. "Go on. Bet him. You're the only one in the whole platoon who hasn't lost your shirt to this guy in poker. Get a little of it back for me, will you?" The German began a frantic dive, with the American close on his tail. "Bet him, Birch! You can't lose."

"What about it, Birch?" Max held out a fiver and rolled his brown eyes skyward. "I'll even give you odds. Three to one the Kraut lives."

"You know somethin' I ain't heard about, college boy?" Birch glanced at the money distractedly. Then he eyed the photograph of Max's cousin Trudy, who sent Max letters by the dozen and crumbled cookies on a regular basis. For months Max had been reading her letters aloud, and Birch had fallen in love with her right here in the trenches.

"I'll tell you what, Max. You've been keeping that cousin of yours to yourself. If the German lives, I want a real New York City night on the town like you're always talking about. With *her*." Birch pointed to the photograph. The dark eyes stared seriously from the oval face.

"Leave her out of it." Max spat. "She's not your type. Three to one the Hun lives."

Ellis nudged Birch again. "That's fifteen bucks when he loses. Forget the girl. Bet him!"

Birch strained to follow the action.

"What about it?" Max stuck out his hand.

The two great pilots were locked in a duel to the death, with neither willing to break away. Birch felt a moment of hopefulness on behalf of the enemy aviator. Surely any man who flew with such skill deserved to live, but his American counterpart had moved in for the kill. It looked as if this was one bet Birch could not lose.

"Done." Birch shook Max's hand. Then their heads pivoted to follow the dots against the cloudless sky. "You bet on a losin' horse," Birch chided Max. The German was most certainly a doomed man. He was square in the sights of the American, and the sun had sunk too low to be of any help now.

On the far side of no-man's-land, the soldiers of the kaiser shouted encouragement to their unlucky aviator. There was nothing strategic about these aerial dogfights, but the winning side always had a boost in morale when an enemy plane came spinning to the earth in flames.

Max muttered something about cheering for underdogs just as the last burst of the American's gun sounded and the tail of the German Fokker exploded.

A deafening roar of victory rose from the Allied trenches.

There was silence from the German lines.

Max, too, was silent. Birch followed his friend's gaze to the Fokker. It rolled belly-up, then hung suspended for a moment before tilting at a crazy angle to spiral toward the ground in flames.

Ellis thumped Birch on the back in congratulations. "Three to one. That's fifteen bucks you win off the New York City shyster—in fifteen seconds! Ha! I've been trying to beat him at his game for fifteen *months*." He elbowed Max in cheerful derision. "Pay up, Max! Come on, I'm witness. Pay up."

Max kept his eyes riveted to the German plane. "The bet was . . . if he *dies*," he muttered. His darkly handsome features suddenly showed the strain of too much death without any winners. "He's not dead yet."

As Birch's eyes followed the screaming roll of the crippled enemy aircraft, he felt his jubilant expression fade. "Lord," he said dully, realizing that he was about to win a bet at the cost of another man's life. "Lord God." This was more than a horse race.

Fire and smoke streamed from the missing tail of the plane, but the small figure of the German pilot could be seen plainly as he struggled to escape the tremendous force of gravity holding him in the open cockpit of his plane.

Birch stepped forward and craned his neck back, gaping at the life-and-death struggle of the desperate man high above them all. "Live," he whispered. "Come on, fella. I didn't mean it. Get out!"

"Get out of there!" Max echoed.

Ellis cast a sidelong glance at Birch. "If he lives, you lose the bet," he warned.

Birch brushed aside the words with his own sense of shame. He prayed with an urgent hope that the pilot would escape his burning canvas coffin. The German strained to free himself and fell back as fire leaped through the flimsy fuselage. His hands reached up to grasp the wing struts, then slipped. Once again he was held prisoner by the angle of descent.

"LIVE!" Birch urged.

"Come on, Birch," growled Barrett down the line. "No tellin' how many of our own fellows he's murdered. Let him roast, and be glad of it." Barrett was nicknamed Hardboiled Barrett for good reason.

Birch did not reply. Max's jaw was set. It was plain to see that he had bet on behalf of the German more out of hope than thought of gain. Now Ellis, too, took up the cry for life. The three American soldiers stood shoulder to shoulder and cheered the German flier on as though he were one of their own.

Birch willed the doomed man to make one last try. He sent the man imagined strength and silently urged him on. *That's the way, fella. Pull yourself up. Ain't but a few seconds left! Fight it. Come on. Ain't your day to die, mister. Come on! I don't mind losing the bet on this one!*

Beneath his breath, Max muttered in the tongue of his Orchard Street upbringing, "*Schnell! Aussteigen! Bitte . . .*"

Hardboiled Barrett cursed Mac for his lapse. "Dirty Jew. Lousy Kraut college-boy Jew."

But Max did not seem to hear the epithets. He was too engrossed in the death struggle high above.

"Get out!" Ellis cheered.

"That's it!" Max thumped his fist against the sandbags and tossed off his helmet as though its weight were somehow holding back the struggling pilot.

The German grasped the strut of the right wing just as the plane began its final roll. He pulled himself out, kicking against the lip of the cockpit. Then, with one last desperate effort, he launched out into space a mere thousand feet above the ground of no-man's-land. As if outraged by his escape, the wing of the dying plane tilted and slammed hard against him at the instant the parachute opened.

A loud *Ah-h-h-h* swelled from the Allied trenches as the battle ended with the German pilot, certainly dead, floating like a rag doll tied to a handkerchief and flung from a rooftop. All heads pivoted to where the plane flamed low across the cratered field to explode in a tremendous fireball behind German lines.

And so it ended. The wind caught the parachute and rocked the limp and bloody figure to and fro, pushing it toward the heart of no-man's-land. There the body folded down upon itself as it gently touched earth a hundred yards in front of where Birch and the others watched from their trench. The German had a face. A scarf around his neck. Leather gloves. Tall boots. The enemy was a man.

The cheering stopped, and at that instant the first dull whump of German artillery sounded from across the line. The American aviator might have been victorious, but his brief victory had only pushed the Germans to renewed outrage.

"Hit the dirt!" Max urged. "Incoming!"

Birch threw himself against the bottom of the trench and pressed his face against the sandbags. Max huddled against him on one side and Ellis on the other. The shell burst behind them, sending a shower of dirt and rocks into the air.

"What you will do to win a bet!" Max tucked his cousin's photos and cash into his tunic, then passed Birch fifteen dollars.

"Wish I'd lost it," Birch replied as a series of shells exploded in rapid succession. Seconds later artillery from the American lines erupted. This time no one cheered. They were all too scared. Instead they crouched in the mud and kept their eyes on the pigeons and their hands on the gas masks as darkness fell. . . .

Birch lost all track of time since it was dark in the trench. Max and Ellis slumped in the sleep brought on by exhaustion and terror. Far away on the horizon, Birch saw the flashes of the great guns, but he couldn't hear the explosions. Somehow, tonight, the roar of the battle passed over no-man's-land and left an eerie vacuum of silence. The strobelike flares lit the sky at intervals as each side checked to make certain no one crept through the wire or crawled across the forbidden zone in a daring offensive.

Birch stood and stretched as a flare hissed toward the ground. From behind the sandbags, he peered across the desolate landscape of the battle-field. The white-silk parachute of the German flier billowed up from the rim of the bomb crater like a ghost tied to earth by a rope snare.

He stared at the stark reminder of death and again wished silently that he had never made his gruesome bet on this man's life. Then he heard a faint voice from beneath the shrouds of the parachute.

"*Hilf mir, bitte!*"

"Huh?"

"*Wasser . . . wasser. Bitte!*"

A chill swept through Birch. "You're alive?"

"*Wasser . . .*" A low moan—the moan of a man in torment.

A man. Like Birch. Crying for water and for help.

Even as Birch climbed over the lip of the slit trench with his canteen in his hand, he could not say why he was doing what he was doing. He could hear the startled voices of his comrades behind him as another flare cracked the darkness and he threw himself against the scorched earth.

"Birch . . . what are you . . . ? where's he . . . ? he's gone nuts!"

The flare died away, and the cry came again: "*Wasser . . . bitte . . .*"

This time his companions must have heard the voice, too. Birch heard the scramble of other men scaling the wall of sandbags to follow him through the broken concertina, down the scarred slope of a low hill, into a ditch.

Max and Ellis came along. All three of them gone "crackers," as the British would say. "Nuts!"

Steel helmets popped up along the line to follow the progress of three doughboys crawling toward the flapping white silk. Had they heard the cries of the dying man as well? Surely no German soldier could hear the voice of the Luftwaffe pilot half a mile across the open field. It would have to be an American canteen he drank from. An American medic he was carried to.

"You know," Max whispered through clenched teeth, "if we live— and he lives—you lose the bet, Birch."

"I didn't figure you would come along to save him unless there was profit in it for you, Max," Ellis growled.

Max halted his crawl, as if the accusation stung him. "Let me finish, y'dumb mick! So—" he wriggled up beside Birch—"let's call the bet off. What do you say?"

"Hilf mir, bitte . . ."

The three rolled into the crater, where the German pilot lay tangled in the shrouds of the parachute. Max offered the man his canteen, as if this had been his idea in the first place. Ellis began to cut away the lines of the chute. All three responded as if the German were as American as General Pershing.

"Okay, fella. We'll get you outta here. Take it easy."

"Hey," Birch ventured as the German muttered his gratitude for the water. *"Sprechen Sie* English? Name?"

The German gasped as Max carefully straightened the man's twisted leg. Birch and Ellis both hissed, "Easy does it."

Through gritted teeth their patient muttered, *"Danke."* And then he thumped his chest in response to Birch's question. "I am Offizier Theo Lindheim."

Birch gasped. Every soldier knew the name and the reputation of the German ace pilot.

Was there a glint of a weary smile in the darkness? Birch wondered. "Well now, Officer Lindheim," Birch said with authority, "you've been captured by U.S. Infantry privates Tucker, Meyer, and Warne. Company C. That's us, at your service. And we aim to see to it that you ain't gonna die!"

Ellis looked at Birch and shook his head in amazement. Then he stared at Max. Birch could tell what Ellis was thinking: *And Max called off the bet, too? There are miracles, after all, on the western front!*

It was a two-mile walk from the front lines to the field hospital. The German pilot lost consciousness within the first hundred yards. It was merciful. His leg had a compound fracture, and he was bleeding heavily.

He moaned as they laid him beneath the canvas awning. "Anna," he whispered, raising his hand. Then again, louder, "Anna!" A photograph fluttered from his fingers and came to rest on the toe of Max's boot.

The face of a woman and a young girl, who looked about four years old, gazed up from the dog-eared picture. Theo Lindheim opened his eyes. "Anna! *Bitte . . .* Anna!"

Max retrieved the photo and held it out for Birch and Ellis to see. "He has a family." Max frowned at the pool of blood beneath the pilot's leg. "A wife and a little child, see?"

"Well, *they* ain't gonna have *him* if he don't get some attention," Birch insisted as a nurse swept past them.

Ellis reached out and took the woman by the arm. "Hey! This man needs a doctor," he said with uncharacteristic gruffness. "Right now!"

"He's German," the nurse said indignantly. "We have a dozen American boys here—"

Ellis scanned the patients. All were suffering from minor wounds. None were critical except the German pilot. Ellis looked at the picture again, the wife and little girl.

"He'll bleed to death," Ellis said. Then, as if to pull rank, he added, "My father's a doctor."

"Here?" The nurse seemed surprised. She took a second look at the leg of the unconscious man.

"Down the line." Ellis took her arm.

Birch lifted an eyebrow. Ellis didn't mention that "down the line" meant all the way back in Ohio.

"He'll lose that leg," the nurse said in a low voice, then shrugged as if it made little difference to her.

Birch stiffened. He knew that amputation was a quick and easy alternative to spending time on such a wound, especially when the patient was a German.

"No, he won't," Ellis said firmly. "I've seen worse. Now get him in there. My father's saved bones twice as bad as this." He scowled.

At that instant the pilot stirred. He squinted up at the lantern, then into the face of the nurse. "*Bitte.* Please, madame . . ."

She nodded curtly, cast Ellis an unpleasant look, and motioned for the German pilot to be carried into the hospital tent.

Max and Birch nudged each other. "You sure got a way with women, Ellis," Max muttered beneath his breath. "Why didn't we take him to your father's hospital?"

Ellis rolled his eyes. "Ohio's a long way from here. But I'll write Doc that we drew on his reputation as a bonesetter." He watched as Theo Lindheim disappeared behind the flap of the tent. "That will be the first good news he's heard from this war."

CHAPTER TWO

Little Lambs and Soldiers

For thirty-two years, Dr. William Warne and his wife, Molly Grogan Warne, had been following the Lord's command to be fruitful and multiply—first in Belfast, Ireland, and now in Ohio. Doc had planted as well as personally harvested his crop of six living children, ranging between the ages of five and thirty. Once there had been sons enough to field an entire baseball team.

Three Warne babies were buried in the family plot at the Presbyterian church across the road and just up the hill from the white Victorian farmhouse.

The cemetery lay in plain view from Molly's kitchen window. While she kneaded bread or fried bacon or washed the dishes, she could glimpse most of her children. Today, the four oldest Warne sons worked the farm. Two sons had fallen somewhere on a battlefield in France. Even though they were buried in Europe, Doc had erected markers for them beside the three tiny headstones of the babies. Tim had been twenty-one. Jack had been only eighteen. Just boys, really. Just beginning to live . . .

Molly looked across the wide fields to where three stone lambs were flanked by the simple granite memorials to two boys who had rushed off to join the army when the first bugle blew. Spring and summer, fresh flowers were placed regularly on those graves. Come autumn and winter, Molly made wreaths of evergreen and holly and hung them around the necks of the little lambs and on the headstones of their older brothers as well.

No matter how old her other children were, Molly thought, she would forever have three babies—and two boys who had run off to play at being soldiers and now remained forever boys. . . .

A whole world of grief lay in the knowledge of what might have been. For this reason, Molly chose to believe that her babies and boys were only sleeping. One day she would awaken from her own dream and hold them once again. As she gazed out at the three lambs and their soldier brothers, she thought of them as five children now in their Father's house. Forever babies. Forever young men.

In the meantime, there were six remaining children to pray for. Ellis was still in France somewhere, fighting the battles his brothers had not finished. Molly thought of her son a thousand times a day. He, too, had left for France as a boy. She longed to see him come home as a man, marry, and have children of his own—perhaps sons enough for his own baseball team.

He had been born in the medical infirmary at Ellis Island, right off the boat from Ireland. Out of the cramped and stinking steerage deck of a great Cunard steamer, Ellis made his bid for freedom from Molly's Irish womb. He had waited until the gangplank was lowered, waited until his family shuffled down into the shadow of the Statue of Liberty.

"Give me your tired, your poor,

Your huddled masses, yearning to breathe free. . . ."

Through the literacy test and the customs inspectors, he had waited. While others were rejected by the tall, well-fed American inspectors, he was patient. From the womb, he heard the echoing of a thousand hopeful voices in a dozen different languages in the great hall . . . and he waited.

Through the meal line, past the medical inspection. Probing hands checked his mother. She opened her mouth for strangers to peer down her throat. She breathed deeply as they listened to the heart and lungs above his shelter. And he waited, waited until he heard the hard rubber stamp of approval come crashing down on Molly's papers.

"It's all right," she had whispered to his infant soul. "You can come out now."

And so Ellis had been born an American citizen with only a few hours to spare.

Molly had named him after the island where she had first set foot on the Promised Land. Ellis Riley Warne. The first American citizen in the family.

It was a name that spoke of new beginnings, of hope and promise and opportunity. Unlike his rabble of older siblings, he was the first among the Warne family who was not required to earn his American citizenship. He could vote when he was twenty-one, if he lived so long. And when he was eighteen and the whole world trembled on the brink of war, he had proudly declared that if America was thrust into the thick of the brawl, then he would be willing to spill his blood for his homeland.

When the recruiting parades had marched down Main Street in Columbus, Ellis had left his classes and the university baseball field to march among their ranks. He had come home just long enough to tell Rebecca Moniger that their wedding must be postponed. He had walked the furrowed fields of the farm and stood on the rise to watch and remember the last sunset over his father's house.

After one last embrace, Ellis had followed Tim and Jack. His brothers were dead before he ever reached France.

In the quiet of the long night that followed, Doc had whispered that he had not left the suffering of Ireland so that his sons could suffer and die as citizens of a new nation. The violence they had lived through in Belfast the year Ellis was born had pursued them, even to this place, to devour another generation of sons.

At the top of the hill beside the big white frame church, Molly spotted Rebecca Moniger's petite form. Her vibrant red hair was mostly covered by a green woolen scarf tucked into the collar of a long brown tweed coat. She carried her head high, as though she were sensing the wind. Her step was sure as she strode down the hill toward the Warne house.

At seventeen, Rebecca was the mirror image of a photograph of her own mother at that age—except there was no haunting shadow of fear or hardship in her hazel eyes. She seemed to have stepped from the green hills of Tyrone County and into America this morning. Molly watched her coming, and just for a moment it made her homesick for the beauty of her homeland.

Rebecca Moniger seemed to embody all of what had been beautiful and proud in Ireland without the sorrow and hardship of the place. When Ellis had noticed her in the church choir, Molly was glad. She had watched him watch the girl, and she had prayed that the heart of her son might somehow love the child until she grew to womanhood. Now Rebecca was woman enough for marriage, strong enough to fill the weak places in Ellis's life. Molly loved her like one of her own.

She put the kettle on for tea before Rebecca was halfway across the big field. Rebecca hailed Ellis's brothers, Matthew, Mark, Luke, and John, with the precision of a child reciting the Gospels. They raised big hands and nodded in greeting, then continued on with their work. Her arrival at the farm was an ordinary event. She came often to share Ellis's letters with Molly and to hear what news he had written to his own family that he might not have told her. Today she carried a basket over her arm. She swung it through the fence rails and then climbed through after it as the teakettle whistled hello.

Rebecca gave two sharp knocks and came in, kissing Molly and little Julie, slipping off her worn gloves, and hanging up her coat on the rack beside the door. And all the while she never stopped talking. Was there ever anyone so full of news? Molly wondered, serving her tea and sitting across the table from her. The last visit had been only yesterday, yet it seemed as if every minute since then had been filled with something important for her to bring back and report on. This girl would be a wondrous tonic indeed for quiet, shy Ellis. She would draw him out in a thousand ways, filling every room with laughter and the latest news and her interpretation of what it all meant.

Molly smiled as she listened. No doubt the Lord Himself must have looked down from heaven the day Ellis first noticed Rebecca in the choir loft. He must have nodded when He heard Molly's prayer. For here was Rebecca, calling her "Mother Warne" already, and the wedding date still was not set. It was good, Molly thought. Very good.

Rebecca paused long enough to taste the steaming tea, wince, then add a drop of cream. "There just has to be peace soon. They say that Germany is in a shambles. Civil war. Maybe even the Bolsheviks will take over like they did in Russia. If that happens we won't keep fighting, will we, Mother Warne?"

"I suppose that is possible," Molly replied solemnly, although it was difficult to feel solemn even with serious news because Rebecca had a way of describing everything as though it were an exciting novel she was reading.

"I hope not. My sister wrote that she heard we're driving back the Germans all along the front line. What do you think of that? I don't know how she gets the news so quick, even though she does live in Philadelphia. I suppose that has something to do with it. She knows things a whole day before we hear about them out here. I tell her to read all the casualty lists in the morning paper. She starts with the Ws. Even though I know absolutely that Ellis is going to be just fine, Mother Warne." The girl gingerly sipped another swallow of tea. "Still, I told her to check all the same, and she does."

Rebecca moved the basket onto the table and opened it. Out came socks for Ellis, a knitted red muffler, and cookies. Ellis always wrote and praised Rebecca's cookies. At the bottom was a jar of homemade apple butter for the hardtack biscuits he was forced to eat in the trenches. Finally Rebecca placed a photograph of herself on the table. Her expression in the picture was serious, which seemed unusual for Rebecca. Even in the drab photographic tones of black and white and gray, her long hair glistened in the light. Her eyes were clear and deep and beautiful. A sprinkle of freckles still graced her nose. Ellis could imagine all the color when he saw it, Molly told her. He would cherish it, to be sure.

"I keep hoping it will all be over by Christmas." Rebecca looked at her own photograph. "Wouldn't it be the most wonderful thing if it was all over by Christmas and Ellis came home? Home right here in this kitchen to drink a cup of tea with us?" She smiled wistfully and gazed out the window to where the four brothers labored in the fields. "Of course, he wouldn't be in on a day like today, would he? He'd be out there with your four Gospels, wouldn't he? Then you and I would still be sitting here talking about him, only we could see him." She sighed.

Molly patted her hand. "Soon enough, child. Perhaps we could persuade him to have just one cup with us before going to work."

Rebecca took up where she had left off, turning to the subject of Mrs. Metcalf's baby and speculation as to whether it would be a boy or a girl. They would be among the first to know, because Doc Warne would be delivering the baby, wouldn't he?

As Rebecca talked on, Molly silently prayed that her third soldier would indeed come home. That Rebecca Moniger might fill his life with all the gifts of herself—and that it might be soon.

CHAPTER THREE

Orchard Street

The gray skies above Manhattan's Lower East Side threatened snow. Trudy Meyer tucked her muffler tighter around her neck, adjusted her leather schoolbag over her shoulder, and lowered her head against the stiff breeze that whistled around the brick tenements of Orchard Street.

Dozens of pushcarts and horse carts mingled with a few brazen automobiles to choke the thoroughfare. On both sides of the jammed street were open-front dry-goods stores, where men and women warmed their cold hands and backsides around smudge-pot fires.

"Morning, Gertrude. Your grandmother? Is she well? Any news from your cousin Max?"

This morning Trudy was late for school, so she smiled and waved and answered as she passed. Her grandmother, Bubbe Fritz, was fine. No word from Cousin Max at the front in France. But no news was good news, and soon the war would end. The newspapers said so.

Up ahead were the enormous fifty-gallon wooden barrels containing all varieties of Mr. Herzog's pickled herring. Even on such a cold morning the aroma was overpowering. Trudy tugged her muffler over her nose.

Already Trudy had lived with her grandmother and grandfather Fritz for over four years, but she had not gotten used to the acrid smell of the herring vats. Whenever coins from Herzog's fish business would come into Bubbe and Zeyde Fritz's dry-goods store, Trudy could smell herring in the cash register for days afterward. Nobody else seemed to notice much. Trudy's grandfather cast disapproving looks at her when she mentioned the aroma. With a sad shake of his gray head, he would mutter that Trudy had been living in the wilderness too long for her own good and, *Gott sei Dank,* Trudy's mother and father had come to their senses and allowed her to journey to New York to attend Columbia University like Max. Part of that education, apparently, included learning to love the scent of herring of all varieties. Trudy decided she would go to her grave a barbarian before she would learn to like this stuff.

She longed for fresh air. There was Mr. Herzog hanging his head into a barrel of two-cent herring. Trudy quickened her pace and looked away before he emerged and spoke to her and offered her a little herring to taste. Ten long strides and she was practically safe. Once past the candy stand, she gulped the morning air into her starved lungs. She gave a smile and a broad wave to Finkel, the pickleman, who stood outside his store on the corner of Orchard and Rivington. He was shoving the pickles from a barrel into Mrs. Fleischer's big gallon jar with both hands.

Mrs. Fleischer was talking and talking, half in English and half in Yiddish, all about the war in Europe, and when would Kaiser Wilhelm drop dead so everyone could get back to living, anyhow? Mrs. Fleischer always made it a practice to speak to Trudy in Yiddish just to point out how terrible it was that a girl like Trudy had been raised in a home that was practically not even Jewish anymore.

Trudy could make out enough to know that the mood of nearly everyone on Orchard Street was hopeful this morning. Peace was coming. What was left of Germany to fight? The American doughboys of the All-American Division, like Cousin Max, had kicked the kaiser back to Germany. Trudy was proud of Max. On her coat she wore the red, white, and blue ribbon that proclaimed she had a relative fighting in the war. She wore it for pride, but also for her own protection. It was not unusual for some gang of bullies to come into the neighborhood with clubs and pound on anyone who was close by when they heard German spoken.

Of course, Trudy knew that Yiddish was not German, but try and tell that to an Irishman with a brickbat. These days sauerkraut was called "liberty cabbage," and frankfurters were "liberty pups." Thousands of German-born immigrants had been arrested and imprisoned all across America. For this reason, everyone on the Lower East Side who had a relative at the front displayed a placard in their window and pinned the ribbon on each day. Over the months, more and more of those placards were draped in black, and the bright ribbons had been replaced with black mourning armbands. The bullies had few victims on Orchard Street these days.

The real victor of this terrible war, both at home and in France, was the raging epidemic of Spanish influenza. More soldiers on both sides of the front were dying of flu than from bullets. Most everyone on Orchard

Street agreed with what Mrs. Fleischer was telling the pickleman this morning:

"Yankle Schoffer died last week in army camp in Georgia. It is the hand of . . ." Her eyes rolled heavenward, indicating that the hand of God was up there swatting soldiers such as poor Yankle Schoffer like flies. Mrs. Fleischer would not say the name of God, lest the Eternal hear her call and maybe take offense and swat her as well. "He is punishing the whole world for this terrible war business, I'm telling you."

Trudy did not agree. After all, twenty-two children in the neighborhood had died in the last two months. Why should the Eternal punish children for a war that grown men had made? She did not express such thoughts to anyone but her best friend, Henrietta Murphy, whose younger brother, Walter, had died of the flu only three weeks ago. A terrible thing. And it had nothing whatsoever to do with the western front, Trudy thought as she smiled and nodded at Mrs. Fleischer.

"*Guten Morgen*, Gertrude," called the woman.

"English, Missus Fleischer," Trudy replied sweetly. "Remember the kaiser."

A hint of resentment flashed in the heavyset woman's eyes. Trudy remembered the warning of Bubbe Fritz. She must always speak politely to Mrs. Fleischer, even if the woman did have noodles for brains and a tongue like an adder. After all, Mrs. Fleischer was a steady customer. Trudy hurried to redeem herself. "You're looking well, Missus Fleischer."

"And you are feeling full of vinegar this morning," commented the woman. "Overly cheerful on such a day."

"It's the smell of Mister Finkel's pickles." Trudy paused. "It reminds me of Mama setting the cucumbers at home." That was a true statement. It was also true that the scent of spices and brine made her a little homesick. Garlic and cloves and coriander mixed with salt and water did wonderful things to the cucumbers Mama picked fresh by the side of the house. Trudy did not say that even though there was a pickle stand on every corner in New York, nobody made pickles like Mama did back on the farm.

Trudy closed her eyes and inhaled deeply for emphasis.

Mr. Finkel smiled. "Such a pretty face," he said, thrusting a paper-wrapped pickle into her hand. "Here, have a pickle. And write your mama and papa hello from me, eh?"

Trudy thanked him and plugged the giant pickle into her mouth. As she walked away, she could hear Finkel change the subject from death and destruction to the philosophy of pickle making.

". . . You want to make somethin' good, you got to do a lot of work. That's what my customers come here for. You got to age 'em. You age 'em as much or as little as you want. Like you, Missus Fleischer—you like 'em green, but some like 'em a few weeks old or months old maybe, so you got to age 'em, y'know. . . ."

The streets were full of such conversations: business, the condition of kids and brothers and parents, the weather, the street, the flu epidemic, the war. The air buzzed like a beehive with ordinary conversations accompanied by the clop of dray horses' hooves against the cobbles of Orchard Street.

Schoolboys of all nationalities, shapes, and sizes stole their breakfasts from the pushcarts, then dodged and darted around still other loaded wagons and carts. It was a never-ending sport of petty theft, which seemed more pastime than crime in the neighborhood.

Every kid had a name other than the one his parents had put on the birth certificate. On the way to school this morning, Trudy could hear them all calling to one another: "Big Nose. Boots. Bones. Bean Brain. Boomer." And those were only the names beginning with the letter *B*. All of them were thieves, it seemed. Everyone but Trudy.

She was twenty-one years old, and the only thing she had ever stolen was one piece of maple-cream candy from the store back home. She had eaten it and then spent a week sick with remorse. Sick in bed. Sick until Mama phoned the doctor and Trudy finally confessed her sin.

The common practice of stealing from the peddlers was one part of her New York education that she openly denounced. She would not accept gifts from the many young men who offered her their pilfered prizes each day. She turned up her nose and walked away, haughtily condemning the would-be suitor.

"Hey, Boomer! Trudy don't want none of that stuff. Doncha know nothin'? She's a regular George Washington, this one. Never tell a lie."

From this, she had won her Orchard Street nickname. All the gang called her True. At first they had said it with a sneer, but after a year they forgot the origins of the moniker, and now the name was uttered with casual affection.

The kids accepted her odd Midwestern brand of morality. After all, it was a free country, wasn't it? Wasn't that why everybody came to America—so they could believe what they wanted to believe and live where they wanted to live?

Everyone on Orchard Street knew that Trudy's grandparents had come from Germany and settled down right here on the first ledge of the Golden Land where they put their feet. But Trudy's parents had gotten the urge to wander out west. They settled on the very edge of the Indian Territory, a place called Arkansas, to carve out a home in the wilderness, where Trudy and her brother had been born. Now they were hardly even Jews anymore. They blended in with every Irishman and Italian and German—all those who had headed west and left their Jewish identities behind in New York.

Ah, but here in Manhattan, the old country lived on. As a matter of fact, every little neighborhood was a different part of the old country. That was the beauty of New York, America—Italians in their neighborhood across the Manhattan Bridge, Irish in their place, Polish, Russian. Here was a tiny map of Europe, but without the big war. There were some neighborhood brawls, to be sure—mostly the Italians against the Russian Jews, and the Irish against anybody who blocked the sidewalk.

But in the end, every child born here was American. So why did anyone have to go farther west to prove it? Rabbi, priest, gangster, and pickleman were all Americans, just the same as those like Trudy's parents who moved to the West to blend together in a cultural stew.

Trudy remembered the night Mama had begged Papa to let her go back to New York to attend the university and live with Bubbe and Zeyde Fritz. "She has never even met her grandparents. In this place, how can she ever know what it is to be Jewish?"

"Why should we want her to know?" Papa had argued. "Persecution. Poverty. The old ways. We moved here to get away from all that."

Trudy was glad now that her mother's tears had prevailed. She had been allowed to come to New York under solemn oath to her father that she would return home and find a teaching position close by as soon as she graduated from Columbia. And if she kept her promise, then Trudy's younger brother would be allowed to come to school in New York. He would get his chance to spend some time with Bubbe and Zeyde Fritz. To take a brief look into the old way of life and then push ahead into the new way. After four years here, Trudy was convinced that the new path her father had chosen was a better one for her. The world of Orchard Street was very small, indeed.

Back home Papa had forbidden the use of any language but English in the house. Even so, kids at school had noticed the guttural hint of a German accent in Trudy's speech. Here on Orchard Street, however, her conversation and accent struck everyone as tragically Midwestern, without a hint of the Mamaloshen, the mother tongue. She was a shocking example of how quickly the old ways could be forgotten.

On the Lower East Side, Trudy Meyer crossed easily into another neighborhood. A year ago, at a suffrage meeting in the basement of the library, Trudy had struck up a conversation with Henrietta Murphy. Henny, they called her—Irish, plump, dark eyed, also from the Lower East Side and longing to get out of it. The two had become fast friends. Trudy found she had much more in common with this daughter of an Irish florist than she did with the girls Bubbe introduced her to.

Henny Murphy was, to Trudy's way of thinking, one of the best things about living on Orchard Street. Every morning they walked together to the university. Henny talked the whole way—about labor unions and women's suffrage, about the war and the world and God. All by herself, Henny provided True with an unexpected education. And Trudy had found in Henny the sort of friend she had always longed for back home.

The rattle of a motorcar interrupted her reverie as she cut across the intersection and hurried toward the florist shop.

"I was about to leave without you." Henny wrapped her red scarf around her neck and buried her hands in her muffler as the two set out on the long walk to Columbia University. It was cold enough today that Trudy considered paying a nickel to ride the tram, but Henny would have none of it. Henny could afford the nickel much more easily than Trudy, but it was well-known that Henny would walk ten miles to save a nickel. Besides, the two friends got their best talking done during the twenty-five-block stroll to campus.

Columbia University seemed as distant in spirit from Orchard Street as Arkansas was from New York City. Trudy knew in her heart that the real reason her father, Joseph Meyer, had consented to let her come here was Columbia. He despised the thought of Orchard Street and all those things that were confined to that narrow Jewish culture. He did not wish for his daughter to return home spouting wisdom from the Torah or demanding that Arkansas cooking be replaced by kosher dishes. The Orchard Street residence of Bubbe and Zeyde Fritz was only meant to provide free housing and the comfort of family relationships while Trudy broadened her world in a way she could not have done by attending a university in her home state.

As a young man, her father had admired Columbia from afar. He always said that the great alma mater of New York was not aristocratic like Princeton, not sports-minded like Yale. It did not have the old-American history and snobbishness of Harvard. It was, he claimed, an enormous cafeteria of learning. And Trudy had found that to be quite true. With an educational menu to rival even Oxford University in England, it was a small city of brick and marble set in the heart of the great city between the bank of the Hudson River and Amsterdam Avenue. There were schools within the schools for journalism and business and arts and sciences, all built by the donations of various millionaires. Trudy's favorite place on campus was the library, which bore the magnificence of Grand Central Station, cloaked and curtained and lined with books.

The university was run from top to bottom by the dictatorship of President Nicholas Murray Butler, who had turned the place into a center for practical learning. He said quite openly that he aimed to shape men of action, not merely men of learning. President Butler was treated with respect by Oxford and Cambridge. He was courted by presidents and politicians and heaped with honors from Europe—but mostly, he was American. He had only one all-encompassing goal for Columbia in mind: to educate Americans, no matter what their race, heritage, or gender. And so Columbia became an enormous workshop, a factory of culture, the one place in all of New York where a Jewish girl from Arkansas could sit across the aisle from a first-generation Irish girl like Henny Murphy and swap ideas.

In sending his daughter to the confines of little Orchard Street, Joseph Meyer had opened Trudy's life to the bigness of Columbia. He had kissed Trudy good-bye at the Union depot in Fort Smith, and with a wink, he had told her she must learn all about her heritage. But Trudy knew he was speaking of America, not Orchard Street.

In spite of the cold this morning, Trudy was glad Henny had insisted on walking. They talked of all this and more on the way. The walk was always as much of an education as class.

CHAPTER FOUR

Hellfighters

Everyone on both sides of the line knew that the end of the war was drawing near. The kaiser's army was falling back. It was beaten, but still it battled. The questions in the mind of every soldier were: *When will it end? Will I live to see the end? With the end so near, why do men continue to die?*

Those who did not fall from bullets or shell fragments or mustard gas were taken by dysentery or influenza. Farm boys from Bavaria and Saxony perished just like farm boys from Pennsylvania and Kansas. Each one pleaded for Mother or whispered the name of a sweetheart with his dying breath.

Germany had run out of farm boys, while America still had tens of thousands to send to the front. Every man prayed that he would survive to see the end. Yet the generals of both sides still gave the commands, and farm boys still climbed over the top of the sandbags to charge across the cratered fields. They fired their bullets and tumbled together into red ditches. The name *Mother* was sighed out ten thousand times. Fifty thousand times. A million times and more. Still they fought on.

Autumn of 1918 was the worst, simply because the possibility of living seemed so close, while the spectre of death remained so vivid. Men on both sides made their peace with God, then killed one another in the next breath. The souls of enemies flew up side by side from the fields of France, leaving their mortal bodies behind in clouds of gas and pools of blood.

For those who lived, memories of ordinary life became all the more precious. A note from home was shared all around. Memories of one man became the memories of his comrades.

In the gray, colorless world of the battlefield, Ellis described the red hair of Rebecca Moniger. He spoke of his brothers—those who had died in France and those who remained at home. *Home* . . . It had been two weeks since any mail had come to the front. Becky's last letter was soggy and ragged from handling. All Ellis wanted was a letter from home, news of the autumn-harvest baseball game. How had the team done without Ellis as pitcher?

Max Meyer could close his eyes and describe the bustle of Orchard Street in New York down to the last detail of sight and sound and smell. Friends and enemies alike became giants in the telling. He spoke of his Columbia University days, of beautiful Irene and her flock of Irish brothers. The mundane things of everyday life became a source of endless conversation.

Birch Tucker had come to know them all quite well. His farm was a still and beautiful contrast to Max's stories of New York. Shiloh Valley. Not the Shiloh of the Civil War, but a secret little village in Arkansas. He did not have a girl to write him love letters, but his mother wrote each week and filled her notes with news of the neighbors and the church social and new calves in the fields. In her last letter, she had promised to send him a package of warm underclothes and wool socks as he'd asked. She promised to mail it right away, along with the letter.

That letter had arrived a month ago. But to his disappointment, there had been no package along with it. This morning new troops were being sent to the front to relieve the men of Company C. Birch thought about mail call behind the lines. He dreamed of dry socks and maybe even stale cake, or wool underwear that was not saturated with mud and sweat. Mail call was a slice of home. The farm in Shiloh would arrive right here in France. His mother's bright, newsy letter would tell him to be good and stay warm. He would laugh and read her admonition to his friends, and they would read their own letters to him until all the families back home came together to meet here along the border of death.

It was raining today; it had been raining forever, it seemed. The gray sky dissolved into the soggy earth to make rivers of mud. It sucked at the boots of the living and speeded the end of the dying.

Birch huddled beneath a canvas tarp with Ellis and Max. Only one of the pigeons remained alive in the cage. The other had died mysteriously two nights before and had sent up the false alarm of a poison-gas attack all along the line.

"Just the flu," the sergeant had remarked, staring through his gas mask at the single living pigeon.

Rumors of an armistice now swept the ranks with the same excitement brought on by the dead pigeon. Thoughts of home were very close today. Birch chatted on about the mudhole on the bank of the James Fork Creek that had trapped four cattle at once. It had taken two teams of mules to pull them out, and that mudhole was not nearly so bad as this trench.

Ellis countered with his own version of the worst mudhole in Ohio. Max told of being drenched by mud when a taxi splashed around the corner of Broadway and Second Avenue. Such stories made the trenches more unbearable.

It was quiet on the far side of no-man's-land. The Germans, no doubt, also whispered about home and mudholes on their side of the wire. Even mud would be much loved if it was from home.

The men of Company C were ready to go when the announcement was made that replacement troops were moving up to take their positions. Three miles behind the lines waited a hot meal, a small city of tents, and a place to dry off. Most important, the mail from home had been waiting two weeks for them.

Birch held up the birdcage containing his lone pigeon. "Well, what do you say? Think I should hand him over to the new troops?"

"He's been luck to us." Max nodded. "Pass him along, then. Chances are they'll still need a lucky charm here before the war ends."

Ellis nodded agreement and poked a beetle through to the bird for supper. "Can't say I'll miss him much. Or this mud." He scratched his stomach and then his neck. "Or the little critters who live here."

The slosh of boots approaching from the distance awakened the groggiest of soldiers in the trenches. Birch peered back behind the line of cannons as a company of black soldiers marched through.

Down the line they heard Hardboiled Barrett's Louisiana drawl. "Look what's comin'. Either they been in the mud already or they lost their way to the cotton fields."

A few hoots replied to his humorless remark.

"Don't give them darkies your pigeon, Birch," came the call. "Them niggers will eat it up."

Max scowled, then muttered, "Why is it German bullets never find the right targets?"

A soft snicker from Barrett and his friend Cheever floated past. "We oughta leave the Yid here with 'em, too."

"Come on, Max," Birch soothed, taking him by the arm. "Those jokers ain't worth the trouble of bashin'." He shoved the birdcage into Max's hands and nudged him hard to remind him that a fistfight now might mean he would indeed be left in the trenches.

"You see the way he talked to that Kraut flier?" Cheever remarked. "Pretty as you please, like they was old friends."

Max looked as though he would reply with his fists. He glared at Barrett and Cheever, his lips tight with anger.

Ellis stepped between them with his pack as a shield in case something started. "They're trying to set you up, Max," he whispered. "You know Barrett is in good with the sarge. Let it go. *Let it go*, I say. Let's get out of here."

Max clenched and unclenched his fists. Then, with a curt nod, he turned away and retrieved his pack as the Negro platoon marched to the barricade of sandbags. These men had the look of seasoned soldiers. No doubt they had seen their share of action and would likely end their war in the front lines. One way or another, the end would have to come soon.

Captain Honner leaped from the trenches first and was saluted by an enormous black man who wore the uniform of a private.

"Private Jefferson Canfield," said the man.

"Where are your officers?" The captain frowned and scanned the line.

"Dead, sir. Cap'n Smith say I'm in charge now. We took four hundred of them Germans prisoner last night, and now we been told to come on up again. So here we is, sir."

The captain looked uneasily at the weary faces of the soldiers before him. Birch knew what the captain was thinking. *Why were fresh recruits not sent?*

For an instant, Birch feared that the captain would refuse to turn over the line to the Negro troops. Then the officer shrugged. "It's all yours, then," he said grimly.

A cheer arose from the mud-colored men in the trenches. No doubt the enemy thought some news had come that the war was really over. But it was only the prospect of mail call.

Max happily shoved the birdcage into the hands of the leader of the replacement troops. He offered a short word of explanation and then was off down the road without a backward glance. His moment of anger had passed quickly, Birch noted. That was the way with Max.

All the same, Birch could see the relief on Max's face when Barrett and Cheever broke off and headed toward the first mess tent. It was worth the walk of another mile just to eat in peace, Birch thought.

The granddaughter of a former slave and a Cherokee Indian, Willa-Mae Canfield was a tall, strong woman with flashing black eyes and ebony skin. Her shoulders were as broad as a man's, and she could pick four hundred pounds of cotton in a day. She and her husband, Hock Canfield, had birthed and raised fourteen children in all. Four had died.

Three sons were grown and gone. Six daughters remained at home in Mount Pisgah, Arkansas. And one son, Jefferson, was off in the army fighting with the Harlem Hellfighters in France.

Jefferson's full name was Thomas Jefferson Canfield. Willa-Mae had wanted to name him Abraham Lincoln because of freedom and such. She had liked the idea of that, but the Ku Klux Klan got wind of it and put the strap to Hock, beating him badly one night on the road. It seemed sensible to change the baby's name to Jefferson after that. And President Thomas Jefferson had granted his personal slaves freedom. The Klan did not seem to hate Jefferson the way they hated Lincoln. Or maybe they figured the baby had been named for old Jefferson Davis, the Confederate president.

All the same, no matter what the Klan said now, Jefferson was an American soldier, and just as proud as anybody. Since she was his mama, Willa-Mae wore a red, white, and blue ribbon in her buttonhole when she went to church. Some of that congregation thought she was a fool for letting Jefferson go into the white man's army, but she just told them that her own grandpappy had fought in Mr. Lincoln's army, and she was mighty proud of it.

This morning Willa-Mae sat on the porch of the log cabin and braided little Nettie's lamb's-wool hair into nine spiky braids. Nettie sat patiently between her mama's legs and played with the zoop-button toy that Hock had made for her last night. It was nothing more than a button strung on a piece of thread, but Nettie was fascinated by the rhythmic *zoop, zoop, zoop* it made when she stretched the string taut.

Nettie was the last of the girls to be scrubbed, polished, and dressed for church this morning. She was seven years old—probably the last child Willa-Mae would bear unless the Lord did a miracle like the one He had done for Sarah in the Good Book. Willa-Mae fussed a bit more over Nettie since she was the baby. She had raised all her other young'uns with a willow switch in one hand and love in the other. But she scarcely ever had to lay a switch to Nettie. The child was pure sweetness, just as Jefferson had been when he was a small child.

"Mama—" Nettie twanged the string, and the button hummed—"how long till Jeff comes home?"

"Don't know, honey. How come you ask?"

"'Cause we gals doin' all the work since he been gone. Pa say we all got to help slaughter them hogs in the mornin'. I don't want to kill them hogs. I ain't big enough."

"Then you can help me with the sausage and cannin'."

That seemed to satisfy Nettie. "But why ain't Jeff home?" she asked again.

Jeff had always been out in the yard, helping with the tedious and difficult task of the last hog slaughtering. Now there were just Papa and Mama and sisters Lula, Widdie, Angel, Hattie, Pink, and Little Nettie to work the farm. They had to milk the cow, plow the field, plant the cotton, pick it, and tend to the corn and cane. Things had been much easier when Jefferson had been around. He and Hock had managed the hardest work, and now Hock was the only man in a pack of females.

Hock might have been the sole man of the family, but he was a lot smaller than his wife and his three oldest daughters. Jefferson was big. Real big. When Jefferson was home, white folks just tended to look at the Canfield family as they walked to church. Since Jeff was gone, sometimes they said things.

Last week Mr. Folz, the overseer the Canfields worked for, sat on his porch and called out to them in a friendly way. He asked the girls their names, and when Pink told him her name, he laughed so hard he almost fell out of his chair. "Pink! Well, you're the ugliest, blackest pink I ever seen in my born days!"

Chances were if Jefferson had been walking to church, Mr. Folz would not have spoken to them. And he wouldn't have laughed at Pink, either.

"Mama?"

"Yes, honey." Willa-Mae was taking her time with the last braid. There was no reason to hurry, and she liked the feel of the child's hair in her fingers.

"Can we walk to church another way?"

"What do you mean, honey?"

"I don't want to go by ol' Mister Folz."

Willa-Mae laughed. "Is that what's botherin' you, child? What he said about Pink last week?"

Nettie nodded a stiff, jerky yes. "I don't like him laughin'."

"Pay that white man no mind." Willa-Mae kissed Nettie on the head. "He don't mean nothin'. He's just a ugly ol' white man. Look who's talkin'. He never seen such a pretty color pink till he seen a sunrise like the one Pink was born in. Bright, like heaven just split right open. And the color filled up the cabin, so I named your sister Pink to remind me every time I say her name." She raised her eyes heavenward. "Thank You, Jesus!"

Nettie laughed then, like clear water bubbling over the rocks. "He don't know," she repeated. "Ugly ol' white man."

"Ain't his fault. I just name my babies like my Indian gramma— somethin' that sounds happy to me, or a perty vision like Angel."

"Why you call me Nettie?"

"'Cause you my baby girl. My last, I reckon. And I wanted all your names to sound like a song when I call, see?" She raised her chin, and a melody sounded as she sang the names of her girls. "Lu-LAAAA, WID-dieeee, An-GELLLL, Hat-tieeee! PINK! NET-tieeeeee!"

Nettie laughed again. It was a wonderful song. It sounded like love, like singing in church.

Lula poked her head out the door. "What you want, Mama? We all right here."

This made Nettie laugh harder, and Willa-Mae laughed with her until tears rolled down her cheeks. "Praise the Lord!" Willa-Mae slapped her big thigh and held her stomach with the ache from laughing.

Inside the house, Angel asked, "What she want?"

"Nothin'," Lula answered. "She and Nettie just gettin' a head start on church. Big dose of the Holy Ghost, I reckon."

It was a while before Nettie got her breath to ask why poor Jefferson got stuck with such a serious name.

Willa-Mae wiped her eyes with the back of her hand. "Well, mens need serious names. Thomas Jefferson Canfield. A big important name, see? Mister Folz ain't never gonna call Jeff over and call him ugly names unless he think about it real hard first." She finished the last braid. "Besides, Jeff is named after a president, and see where he is? Fightin' like a president would. Like an American." She touched the victory ribbon on her Sunday dress. "It might be why he's fightin' so good."

Nobody moved or spoke along the line of the 369th Infantry Regiment. Probing for the inexperienced or the foolhardy, the fire of the German machine guns whistled across no-man's-land like swarms of vengeful bees looking for soldiers to sting to death. The steady reciprocating rattle of the French automatic weapons was punctuated at intervals by German mortars, but the rounds fell short of the trenches where Jefferson Canfield's company huddled in soggy misery.

"Them Krauts know we're fixin' to attack, and they know whichaway we's comin', too," a soldier to Canfield's left complained bitterly. Despite a general nod of agreement, no one else ventured to comment. It was as if any conversation, however small, might somehow single out the speaker for personal and deadly attention.

A new note of deep-throated noise joined the sounds of the battlefield as the French 155s began to reply to the German fire. The crump of the guns was too ponderously slow to be called a barrage, and Canfield wondered if the French gunners were even bothering to aim or if the answering fire was only for show.

In the early days of the 369th's battles, the sound of the French artillery conversing with the German weapons had brought cheers from Canfield and the others, but the excitement had long since passed. The soldiers of the 369th who had survived this long knew full well that the sound of cannon fire from their own side was nothing to be celebrated. It meant only that the attack was about to begin, and that the word would soon be given: *"Lancez une attaque!* Over the top!*"*

The first black combat unit to arrive in France, the 369th served with distinction while "on loan" to the French 4th Army. It seemed that the American commanders had wanted to use the black regiment for labor battalion duty only, but the French had been eager to bolster their depleted ranks. The black soldiers had been no less eager. To participate in a war to "make the world safe for democracy" seemed tailor-made to erase white misconceptions about black courage and initiative. The opportunity to "prove something" would come only at the front. There was no glory to be gained as stevedores unloading cargo ships or as orderlies carrying bedpans.

The French officers given command of the 369th had been skeptical at first, but they had soon come to admire the bravery and coolness under fire of the men who sometimes went by the name Black Rattlers. The reputation of the 369th was not disputed by the enemy either. The first night assault by the black troops netted over a hundred German prisoners, who came back muttering fearfully about the *Höllenkämpferen*—"hellfighters."

In the clinging mud that followed three solid days of rain, it was difficult to feel like much of a hero. The 369th wore American uniforms, but their helmets were of antiquated French issue and looked like old-style firefighter gear with narrow brims and high-peaked center ridges. The worst thing was they didn't keep the rain off. A soldier had to decide to either lean his head back and let the rain fall in his face or lean it forward and let the drips run down his collar. By now it did not seem to matter. Everyone was soaked completely through anyway.

It may have been the soaking rain that had caused the High Command to order the upcoming attack. Not that the slippery footing or reduced visibility made the Germans any less vigilant. Rather, the rain was melting away the 369th's numbers. Like a child's mud castle disappearing in a thunderstorm, the dysentery and fever sweeping the trenches in the wake of the constant dampness took out soldiers, black and white alike. It had been decided to expend the troops against gunfire rather than against disease. In the latter case, there was no hope; in the former, perhaps some good might be accomplished. The expression of this opinion had been accompanied by a Gallic shrug, meaning, *Who could say?*

CHAPTER FIVE

Love Departed

Army headquarters was an island of canvas tents in a sea of mud. Just over the rise, white crosses sprouted by the thousands in a cemetery that had been a field of grain not long before.

Rain pattered gently on the canvas roof of the mess tent. Birch placed his plate of hot corned beef and mashed potatoes on top of his package as he led Max and Ellis to the plank table closest to the huge coal-burning stove in the center of the room.

Three additional letters were in the pocket of Birch's tunic. Ellis carried two packages and a half dozen letters. Max held a shoebox-sized, paper-wrapped package, which was crushed on one side. He held five letters like playing cards in his still-grimy hand.

Now came the decision: should they eat first or read first? This was their first time in weeks to sit at a real table with a steaming plate in front of them.

"It isn't the Waldorf-Astoria," Max said cheerfully, "but I say we eat first while it's still hot."

Ellis was already tearing open the letter from Rebecca with the oldest postmark. "Speak for yourself," he remarked, inhaling the scent of perfume.

"My mama would want me to eat while it's hot." Birch grinned. "Go on, Ellis; what's new at home?" He filled his mouth and let the hot beef linger on his tongue as if it were the finest meal he had ever tasted. Max dug in likewise, encouraging Ellis to read by a wave of his fork.

Ellis was blushing beneath the mud on his face. He skimmed the first page, then looked up and said, "Not this page, fellas."

A loud groan arose, and a chorus of voices demanded that Ellis read the first page aloud. Forks banged against tin cups of strong coffee. Food-filled mouths shouted up and down the table without regard to propriety. It was only fair that Ellis read the good parts so everyone could enjoy them. And then he must pass the scented paper down the line so everyone could smell it and dream.

"Ah, well . . . er . . . this is private," he said, folding it up.

"Get it from him!" Max said gleefully, and Birch snatched it from Ellis's hands.

Corned beef forgotten, a dozen hands held Ellis in his seat as Max climbed onto the center of the table to read the words of Rebecca Moniger to the waiting mob.

"It's a poem, gents." Max bowed as though he were about to read from Shakespeare.

"All right, Max," Ellis threatened. This was possibly the first time anyone had seen him angry, Birch thought. "You'll *pay* for this, I say!"

A chorus of *boo*s rose up. It was clear that everyone wanted to hear the love poem. After all, for months it had been whispered in the company that Ellis Warne was incapable of anger. To the delight of all, his normally calm and pleasant countenance was red with indignation.

Max cleared his throat, raised his eyebrows suggestively, and over numerous whistles and hoots, he began:

"'Twas one year ago today,
The saddest thing that ever came our way.
Though our hearts were heart to heart . . ."

At this the clamor grew. Ellis tried to rise and was shoved down into place as the corned beef went unheeded.

"*The government bade us part.*
But now those sad days are nearly o'er,
It makes us think all the more
Of those happy, happy days.
Just a short time away,
When we can spend our lives together
Happier, happier as we—"

With a growl, Ellis broke the grip of his captors. He leaped onto the table and hurled himself against Max. Both men came crashing down onto tin plates of corned beef and gravy. Mashed potatoes exploded into the air like clods of earth in an artillery barrage. The joyous cries of Company C rang in the mess tent as Ellis pummeled the handsome face of

Max Meyer, who still held the letter delicately aloft and howled with paralyzing laughter at the blows of his friend.

Birch easily plucked the letter from Max's fingers and skimmed it. A prick of shame stung him at the thought that gentle Ellis would fight for his poem. It was too tender for sharing. He folded it and tucked it into his pocket as Max screamed through gales of laughter, "Get him off me! Ah! Get . . . him . . . off!"

Ellis's dark hair hung over his forehead. He panted like a prizefighter, eager to go at it again. His face was dotted with potatoes, his clothes with corned beef and gravy, which blended with the mud. Two men held each arm as he strained to get at Max again.

Max was bleeding at the nose. Bleeding and hooting. Tears of delight ran down his cheeks. He remained on his back in the plates like an overturned turtle.

A whistle blew from the tent flap. Military police bolted into the mess tent, and everyone stood back, dusting off the combatant. So much for hot meals.

A burly MP circled Max, who stood beside Ellis. Max was clearly trying not to burst out with laughter again. Ellis looked entirely ashamed. He swallowed hard, scanning the rubble for the letter. Birch caught his eye, winked, and patted his pocket. It was safe. The fun was over.

"Haven't you mugs had enough fighting?" asked the MP.

"Not fighting," Max said. "Blowing off steam."

The MP looked at Ellis, who ran fingers through his potato-gooped hair. "Is that so, soldier? All in fun?"

Ellis nodded reluctantly. "Just fun, Officer. Nothing . . . to it."

"Well then. Terrible waste of good corned beef here." He waved his baton over the wreckage. "A dozen plates of mashed potatoes you mugs smashed. Not to mention the beef."

At this realization, the dozen men whose suppers had fallen victim to the poetry reading snatched up their plates and ran off to the chow line for seconds.

Max shrugged. "We've been up front a good while."

Birch wondered if Max was imagining a punishment of peeling heaps of potatoes. KP duty until the war was over and beyond.

The officer batted him gently on the arm with his stick. "Well then. Save this for the Krauts, will you? We've got better things to do." At that, he threatened them with a stay in the brig if they wasted good army-issue food again. Then he was gone.

Birch slipped Ellis the first page of the letter as they moved through the chow line a second time. A sensitive guy, Ellis was—especially where love was concerned. Max had already forgotten about it halfway through the line, but Ellis still had the look of a schoolboy caught in a fight.

Birch leaned forward. "We had it comin'," he remarked to Ellis, who seemed to feel worse about losing his temper than Max felt about getting his face bloodied.

"Well," Ellis said in a low, serious voice, "you know, Birch, I was brought up not to fight."

"Not ever?" Birch was stunned. It was an amazing confession, considering the war.

"Mostly." Ellis frowned. "But I suppose Becky's worth it." A dreamy smile spread across his face as though he could see her standing just over there, in the one empty corner of the place. And without another word, he carried his plate, his packages, and his letters over to that empty space, where he could be alone with the vision of Becky Moniger.

"They want to be alone," Max said with a shake of his head. Then he led the way to the opposite side of the mess tent.

By mutual consent, Birch and Max ate their chow and saved their mail for dessert.

Max's squashed box contained the remains of a pound cake baked by Irene. "It must have been something once," Max said, picking up a handful of stone-hard crumbs and popping them into his mouth. "Now it's Irish hardtack." He grimaced. "Hope I don't break my teeth. Be glad you don't have a girl, Birch, my boy. A mother is plenty to leave back home. I have to eat all this gravel and then write Irene and tell her it was delicious." Another mouthful. A deeper grimace as he urged Birch to open his package.

It was definitely from a mother—firmly wrapped in an uncrushable package. A mother thought of such things; a girlfriend lacked the experience to imagine tons of mail on top of one little pound cake in a shoebox.

"You want . . . ?" Max offered some crumbs.

Birch shook his head.

"Didn't think so." Max sighed.

Birch hesitated to open his package. It was something like Christmas. Or maybe a birthday. Once he opened it, the anticipation of the opening would be over. And so he looked at the knot in the string and imagined his mother tying it on the table in the kitchen. She would have asked his little brother, Bobby, to hold his finger right there in the center while she tied.

"What's wrong?" Max asked.

Birch broke out of his reverie. He must have been grinning stupidly again, thinking of home.

"Open it, will you?" Max insisted. "Your mama always packs such delicious stuff—" He reached out to pluck the string.

Birch slapped his hand. "This is mine," he snapped. He cut the string one strand at a time with his pocketknife. He carefully removed the paper, folding it as if he might save it for something special. The truth was, his mama always sent him extra wrapping paper so he would have it for the latrine. Like Max said, she was a thoughtful woman. Practical and thoughtful.

Inside the box was clean underwear, just as she'd promised. It was folded just as neatly as when she put it in his bureau drawer at home. Socks were tucked in each corner. A jar of wild-currant jam was slipped into one pair of socks, plum jelly in the second pair. Persimmon pudding was in a jar inside the third pair, and rock candy in the fourth. Beneath three pairs of woolen long johns, Birch found a smaller box wrapped in sheets of the local newspaper from Hartford. Names of stores and people and new-baby announcements leaped off the page at him. He did not open the final box but sat and read the news of Hartford and Shiloh from seven weeks ago.

"What's in the box?" Max said through a mouthful of pound cake. "Lend me a pair of those socks, Birch buddy?"

Birch looked up to see Ellis in his corner observing the same holy ritual of mail call. A quiet journey home. News over the back fence. Jams cooking on the enormous Wherle cookstove he had bought for Mama before the war. And now Mama was still using that stove to cook up things for Birch way over here in France.

"What's in there?" Max pointed past socks and jams to that one remaining box.

Birch closed his eyes and imagined what it could be. He thought of all the harvest brought in. Corn in the crib and cotton baled at the gin. The fields would be cleared, and from the kitchen window Mama could look at the birch trees and beyond, where the persimmons would be ripe.

"Bet it's persimmon cookies," he said, and his mouth began to water.

"What's that?"

"Ha!" Birch flipped off the lid. Sure enough. Persimmons and walnuts. Cookies that were almost still fresh. The whole house had smelled wonderful from their baking. He held the box up to his nose and inhaled deeply.

"You going to share, Birch? Why is it that New York City is a thousand miles closer than Arkansas, and all I ever get is—" Max reached out hopefully.

Birch handed him a cookie, still soft in the middle. "Ever had one?"

"Never heard of persimmons." Max bit down and savored the flavor. "But you say they grow right on your place?"

"Like Eden." Birch took a bite. He did not chew. Chewing made things go away too quickly. Max gulped his pulverized pound cake because he did not care if it remained. Ah, but cookies from Mama Tucker . . . they were meant to be considered. They were meant to linger, like crackers from a Communion plate. Something for a fellow to cherish and think about. One bite was enough for now. Birch reckoned that if he only ate one cookie a day, one nibble at a time, he might have enough to last him clear through the end of the war.

Now to the letters. Birch laid them out on the stack of underwear. Another one from Mama. And two without return addresses in handwriting he did not recognize. Sometimes folks from the church wrote him. The postmarks were all from Shiloh—and within days of one another. He decided he would save the letter from Mama for last.

Max was already skimming through his mail. "Love letters from Irene," he announced, then went on to explain the rest. Possible love letters from another female or two. There were three from his cousin Trudy.

Beautiful, dark-eyed Trudy. Birch had come to admire her as much as Max seemed to admire the persimmon cookies.

Birch slit the first envelope, the most recent letter, written in a feminine hand. "It's from my cousin's wife, Maybelle," he muttered with disappointment. Little Maybelle was the gossip of Shiloh. Her news was seldom pleasant, even if it was thorough.

"Go on," Max urged. "Wasn't she the one who wrote about that girl in . . . whatever the place . . . who got in the family way and—"

"Yes."

"Does she tell what happened? Reads like a serial in a dime novel." He finished his cookie and reached for another.

Birch slammed the lid down.

"All right." Max sighed.

Birch began to read silently:

So much has happened here since I last wrote you, Birch. We hear the news that y'all have the Huns on the run. So do our menfolks round here. J.D. and your pa was part of the group that made a call on the German colony. I'm sure your ma writ you about it before she took sick and little Bobby took sick. It is a terrible thing, this flu. Your pa blames the foriners for what he call a plague. He blames the foriners for what happened to your ma and Bobby—

Birch felt the blood drain from his face. What had he missed? He stared at the letters, at the postmarks. What news was in those letters that Maybelle was jabbering so glibly about? His hands started to shake.

"Birch?" Max said solemnly.

Birch looked up at Max.

Max's eyes had darkened, as if he, too, dreaded what was in the letter Birch held. "Birch? You want me to read it for you?"

Birch shook his head and raised the paper to the lantern light again:

It was a shocking thing to all when Bobby took sick. Your pa said he got it from them German kids at school he was playing with. And then when Bobby died, your ma just gave up. So she got it too from nursing your brother. I just couldn't believe it when they come and told us, and then they was ringing the church bell for her as well. The funeral was quite lovely . . . a clear day and we was all——

The letter fluttered from Birch's hand. It seemed the whole mess tent grew silent with the news. He could not hear voices anymore. How could this be? He had just received the long johns she had washed and folded with her own hands . . . the jam and the pudding and the cookies she had made. And she had packed that box with all of her thoughts and prayers directed only toward the safety of her son.

How could this be? Mama gone? But here she was, loving him in the ways she knew best. He had just seen her at the stove . . . just imagined Bobby's finger holding the knot of the string. Bobby was gone, too?

This cannot be so. It cannot be. His thoughts tumbled in disarray as he tore open the letter dated just before Maybelle's. It was from Dr. Brown. . . .

Hours later, the letter from Birch's mother remained unread. Unopened. He could not bring himself to break the seal and spill out her last words to him. Not tonight. If he left it sealed, he reasoned, he would still have it to open one day when he most needed to hear her voice. Perhaps that day would come tomorrow. Maybe it would not come for ten years. But he would save it until some moment when he lacked the courage to take another step. Then she would speak to him.

He wore a fresh pair of long johns. Warm socks. He sank exhausted onto the cot in the vast tent where a thousand other men were bunked. This had been a circus tent, confiscated from some traveling big top months before. The dome rose to a blue-and-white-striped peak, where acrobats had once walked high wires and trapeze artists had launched themselves out over the earth in daring somersaults.

Now the tent was packed with brave men of a different sort. All performers—not a spectator in the bunch. Every man had his own private ache tonight. Birch knew this, and he remained silent about his own grief. There were other men here who had gotten bad news from home. The circus tent was a wide and lonely place. A thousand men, each one alone with thoughts of a faraway place called home.

Max leaned over from his cot. "You okay?"

Ellis propped himself on one elbow. He did not speak, but his eyes questioned Birch. *Okay?*

Birch was not okay, but then, who was? He nodded and rolled over, turning his back to his concerned friends. He closed his eyes and tried to imagine cheering crowds of kids beneath the canvas, tried to think of things like clowns and lion tamers. It was no use at all. He could think of nothing but the wide green fields of Shiloh, swimming with Bobby in the James Fork, of Mama cooking supper and scrubbing the floor with a cornhusk scrub and lye soap.

Strangely, he did not think much of Pa tonight—Pa, who would be alone on the farm now that Birch's two sisters were married. Mama had been like a live oak tree, rooted in her love for the Lord and her desire to raise her sons to serve God and their fellow men. Pa, too, was made of oak, hard and irascible. But he was no live oak. He was more like a fence post, a barrier rooted deep to keep things in and keep other things out, a line of taut barbed wire that crossed his heart and said, *Go no farther.*

Birch could not imagine his father grieving. Or loving. The house would simply be empty now that Mama was gone. Love had departed with her.

This thought at last brought hot tears to sting the corners of his eyes. He pulled his rough wool blanket over his head and pretended to sleep. The house was empty now, and Birch let himself grieve for that. For the first time he knew how much he had drawn from his mother's faith, and tonight he was unsure that he had faith of his own. *Help me pray, Mama,* his heart cried out to her, just as he had as a child at bedtime. *What shall I say? Help me!*

The vast canopy echoed with voices, with the sounds of lonely men. Birch was only one among them all, and he felt very small tonight, indeed.

The flu struck down three daughters at once in the Canfield home. Little Nettie moaned for her mama first in the night, then Widdie, and last of all, Big Hattie.

Willa-Mae lit the lantern and moved Lula, Pink, and Angel over onto her bed as Hock took his quilt to go sleep in the barn.

"This here's that flu they been talkin' 'bout in town," Willa-Mae explained to Hock. "It done took Missus Parker's chil' and Missus Feriby's chil'. Done carried away Miss Trevor, the schoolteacher—"

"Why, they's rich folks . . . and white." Hock scratched his head. He looked at his three daughters, shivering and moaning beneath the heap of quilts. "This time they can't say this plague come from poor niggers." Hock frowned. "Can't blame us sharecroppers and drive us off the land. White folks catched it first. How come it find our chillens, Willa-Mae? We ain't been around Missus Parker's chil' nor Missus Feriby's chil' neither."

"Go on, Hock." Willa-Mae nudged him out the door. "This demon ain't neither black nor white. It come straight from hell, I reckon, lookin' for chillens to swallow up." She closed her eyes and prayed hard with her mother's soul crying out. "Oh, *mighty* Jesus, come heal my babies."

Hock looked once more at his daughters. "Amen. In the name of Jesus!" He shuddered and walked to the barn.

Willa-Mae knew there would be no hog slaughtering for a while, with the pestilence come upon them. She could hear Hock praying as he walked through the darkness of predawn. She knew he would pray as he settled into the hayloft. He would pray as he milked the cow and worked through the day. There was comfort in knowing that.

"Don't make no difference to You, Lord, that we's poor and black," Willa-Mae said as she sponged the fevered bodies of her girls in the dim light of the lantern. "You be here with my babies. Love 'em with an open hand, You say." Then she whispered their names softly with the melody in her voice as she tried to soothe them. "Widdie," she sang. "Big Hattie . . . Little Nettie . . . sweet babies. Sweet honey-babies . . . " From the other bed, Lula, Angel, and Pink watched their mama with wide dark eyes, as if they were watching to see if the unseen thing that made their sisters moan and toss would leap across the room and take hold of them as well.

Willa-Mae turned to Lula, the oldest. "Now you be prayin' for your brother Jeff away in France. The Holy Ghost can see him just as clear as if he was in this cabin with us. And there is somethin' in my heart says Jeff needs prayin' for jest like y'all. Don' think 'bout here in this cabin. Just pray for Jefferson and let the power of Jesus' name save us all."

CHAPTER SIX

Epidemic

This morning Trudy came early to pick up Henny Murphy.

The clamor and the clutter of the street were just as intense here in the Irish Quarter as in the Jewish neighborhood. The poverty of the tenement dwellers was just as harsh. Children worked along with parents. Voices called out to Trudy in soft Irish brogue. Henny had told her that everyone thought she was one of them because she was seen so often in the neighborhood.

"G'mornin', True," said Mrs. O'Halloran from her fruit stand across from the florist shop.

Trudy raised her hand and resisted the urge to reply, "*Guten Morgen. Baruch Hashem.*" Wouldn't that have raised eyebrows? "Good morning. Looks like we're in for rain."

"They're not open today." Mrs. O'Halloran jerked her thumb toward the shop.

Trudy's brow furrowed with concern. Not open? Murphy's florist shop was always open, from seven in the morning until eight o'clock at night. They had closed only once before, three weeks ago when Henny's little brother, Walter, had died from influenza. The family had made the floral arrangements for his funeral and then had pulled the shades and locked the doors for three days.

Once again the green shades were drawn over the windows. Trudy stopped midstride and stared at the window in the flat above the store where Henny's room was. That shade was also drawn. A big block-lettered sign in the window of the shop read CLOSED. The black mourning crepe for little Walter was still in place.

Trudy walked slowly to the door of the shop and stood before it. She loved smelling the flowers inside each morning. The colors reminded her of the gardens back home—of wide fields, a slower-paced way of life. She raised her hand to knock. Then the shade was pulled to the side and the weary face of Mrs. Murphy appeared behind the glass. There were dark circles beneath her eyes. Wisps of dark brown hair tumbled from the bun at the back of her neck. She made no move to open the door. Her breath fogged the window as she spoke through the glass.

"Henny is ill, Trudy."

"Ill?" That meant flu. Trudy simply blinked at her in disbelief. Could it strike so quickly? Henny had been well yesterday. They had stopped together at the candy stand for an egg cream and sipped it and talked about Cousin Max and the end of the war.

"I'll not let you in." Henny's mother seemed near tears. "'Twould not be good for you to come in."

"I'll get her assignments," Trudy blurted out, wishing for some way to make it easier. "I'll bring them by."

When Mrs. Murphy glanced down, fear struck Trudy. Maybe Henny would not need assignments. Maybe not ever.

"That is kind of you, Trudy. . . ."

"Tell her for me—"

Henny's mother gave a curt nod. "I'll tell her." The green fabric fell back, covering the brightness of the flowers, leaving Trudy alone and scared. She did not want to walk all the way to the university this morning. She felt in her pocket for fare for the tram car. Without Henny the walk to Columbia would be too long. Too lonely . . .

Trudy was glad when she finally reached the library. There was a holiness about the Columbia University library. Miles of bookshelves rose from the marbled floors into the dusty light of the cupola. Rows of ink-scarred tables were ringed with scholars feasting on heaps of books. Five million books, to be precise.

Here, more than anyplace else in New York, Trudy felt at home. Although she shared a table with half a dozen strangers, she came here for the solitude and the echoing silence. Hushed whispers seemed like prayers. Here, the squalor of Orchard Street was forgotten for a time. The banter of merchants could be imagined from the pages of Dickens. The thugs of Cherry Street were transformed into pirates and brigands and bandits. In this place there was no Spanish influenza sapping the life of her best friend. There was no war in Europe threatening the life of Max. Trudy had come again to this magic place to forget reality. She was unhappy when reality came to her table and politely asked for a word with her.

She was reading one of Upton Sinclair's novels—*The Jungle*. There were passages in it that reminded her of tragic people and places right around New York. It was not a happy novel, yet it reflected the hearts of characters in a way that made Trudy wish she could sit and talk to them.

"Trudy?"

The whisper pulled Trudy from Sinclair. She lifted her head as though she had awakened from a dream. Irene Dunlap was gazing hopefully at her. *The* Irene, whom Max loved.

"Are you busy?" Irene whispered. "Studying?"

Trudy managed a half smile. A shake of the head. How she hated the interruption. "Just . . . you know . . . reading." She held her thumb to mark her place. "So. Hi, Irene." Too loud. Ten people looked up to hiss her to silence.

"Can we?" Irene inclined her head toward the door of the courtyard. Sunlight, dull and distant, seemed to find its way to Irene's shining blond hair. With her porcelain skin and deep blue eyes, she glowed like the Madonna in the Catholic church back home where Trudy had gone sometimes with Angela Perrelli. Irene was beautiful. It was not surprising that Max adored her. She was not particularly smart, even though she had her teaching credentials and a position.

Such thoughts flitted through Trudy's mind as she followed Irene into the cold courtyard. Piles of leaves lay everywhere. The frigid air was a jolt after the cozy world of the library.

"Where shall we sit?" Trudy waved a hand toward a cold marble bench. Maybe this would not take long. Maybe Irene would go away soon, and Trudy could get back to her novel.

Irene sat solidly on the bench and implored Trudy to also sit. "I need to talk." Irene's face was serious—sad, maybe.

"Sure, Irene." Trudy sat slowly beside her. "What about?"

"Not *what*—" Irene gazed through the leafless branches of the trees— "*who*. Max, that's who." Her eyes filled with tears.

Trudy stared at her, surprised by the emotion, amazed that Irene wanted to tell her anything at all. Why not her own people? Why not her family? Or maybe a girlfriend of the Irish variety? Trudy was merely Max's cousin. Not a friend, really. Not family. "What is it? Is something wrong?"

"I can't tell my family. Not even a friend. No one. I am afraid . . . something . . . *terrible* happened before Max left." Silent tears began to course down her cheeks. Like the weeping Madonna, her expression did not change. Tears simply flowed without strain like words from a song.

"You see . . . I love him so," Irene said. "But, Trudy, I have lost my soul in the bargain. Please don't look at me that way. Please . . . I must tell someone. You will keep the secret because it is also Max's secret." She looked at Trudy's book, at her thumb marking the page. "I have to tell someone. You are the only one I can trust for both of us. For Max and me."

So Irene made her confession. Trudy listened and nodded like a priest in the courtyard. Like the character Ona in Sinclair's novel, Irene shared her deepest soul with Trudy. She expected no advice. Like the character in the story, she only needed to be known.

Little Nettie seemed to have been struck the hardest by the flu. Her eyes were wide and wild with delirium brought on by the high fever. Her body trembled like a fragile leaf in a strong wind that threatened to blow her tiny soul from earth. Willa-Mae held her and rocked her, singing to the rhythmic squeak of the old rocking chair.

Big Hattie lay awake. Beads of sweat stood out across her strong forehead. She sipped the onion-tea remedy that Willa-Mae brewed. Hattie was sixteen years old and strong. She fought the sickness as she would wrestle some mean bully at the school. "You gonna be fine," Willa-Mae told Hattie.

Widdie, ten months younger than Hattie, was tall and slender, and not nearly as strong as her sister. In the first hours of the sickness she had been restless, crying from the terrible ache in her joints. Her fever was also high. She was sleeping peacefully now—maybe too peacefully. Willa-Mae listened to her labored breathing and wondered if she should try to rouse her to sip the concoction of boiled onions, sugar, tallow, and whiskey.

"Mebbe it's better to let them sleep," Willa-Mae said aloud, sensing Little Nettie finally relax in sleep in her arms. "Mebbe they sleep it off and wake up fine."

Five minutes was all the time allotted for a shower and a shave. Birch had not been gone from his bunk more than that length of time, but when he returned, he saw the broad back of Hardboiled Barrett as he passed Cheever the shoebox of persimmon cookies and then hurried to the opposite side of the tent.

"Barrett!" Oblivious to the fact that he was in his skivvies, Birch broke into a run.

Barrett scowled over his shoulder and kept walking.

Ellis and Max must have seen what was happening, for they hurried after Birch.

"Barrett!" Birch roared, and every man looked at him as if he were crazy. Nobody talked to Hardboiled Barrett that way. Not to his face. Not to his back, if he could hear it.

Barrett stopped and slowly turned to face Birch. He had a half-eaten cookie in his big paw. His cheeks were stuffed full. He was smiling, and cookie crumbs dropped from between his lips. "Yeah, Tucker? Birch Tucker? You want somethin'?"

Rage filled Birch as he spotted the empty box lying on the floor. It was sacrilege. It was worse than theft—especially now.

"You're a thief." Birch slowed to a threatening walk. His fists were clenched, his jaw set.

"Yeah? What you call me?" Barrett's eyes narrowed.

Birch could feel Barrett sizing him up. At 175 pounds, Birch knew he was less threat than the solid mass of Barrett's 230. But for once, he didn't care.

Barrett grinned, the smile of a butcher who enjoys his work.

"A lousy thief," Birch added.

The cookies were gone. Ruined. There was no getting them back.

"Right! You Bronx Zoo ape," blurted Max. He looked as angry as Birch.

Cheever stepped up beside Barrett. "We know what *you* are, Max. Max *Meyer*. Ain't nothin' but a stinkin' Jew. Speakin' of thieves." He gave a low, menacing chuckle. The crowd of spectators stepped back. There was going to be a battle right here among the bunks. Two mean-looking bigots from Louisiana sneered and came alongside Barrett and Cheever.

"Thieves!" Ellis spat the word like a curse. "And liars! That's what *I* say you are, Barrett!"

With those words, Birch knew that Ellis, taught not to fight, had committed himself.

Barrett stuffed the remaining cookie into his mouth. He smiled as he chewed and looked from side to side at the serious expressions of the gathering spectators. Then he said, "Did I eat little Birch's cookies?" He swore loudly and spit the chewed remains into Birch's face.

The whole tent exploded as Birch hit him with a roar. Both Ellis and Max threw themselves into the fight. There were no rules in this brawl. Birch's first blow bloodied Barrett's nose and set him back. Barrett coiled and slammed Birch with a hard right to the ear as Max and Ellis pummeled their three opponents. Max was knocked to the floor. He came up with a combat boot on his hand and smashed Cheever's nose with it. Cheever hurled backward, overturning a bunk. One man held Ellis as another pounded his face. Max leaped onto the back of one fighter and beat his head with the boot until he fell away from Ellis.

Now that the odds were temporarily even, Max and Ellis got the better of their opponents.

Birch was in trouble, however. Barrett blasted him with a left hook and then followed with another right. Birch stumbled over a locker and fell to the floor. Barrett was on him in a flash, using his boots to the head and kidneys, kicking and swearing as he increased in fury.

Just then the shrill whistles of the MPs sounded. They struggled to fight their way through the roaring crowd, with little effect.

Seconds later the poison-gas siren howled to life. Men scrambled to their bunks, searching for their gas masks.

Barrett straightened up from his work, leaving Birch half unconscious, wedged between two bunks. The siren continued its wail. The lights blinked on and off. Birch groped for a gas mask. He sat up slowly while the others scrambled around him. Then he saw Captain Honner standing with his revolver pointing at the belly of Hardboiled Barrett.

The scream of the siren ceased. The place was altogether silent now. Men stood, heads bowed in their gas masks, appearing foolish and guilty as the captain asked in a low voice, "Who started it?" He scanned the bloody faces of Birch and Max and Ellis.

Then he looked at the men whom Max and Ellis had whipped and at the bloody nose of Barrett. "Seven of you, from the look of it," he said coolly. "We just had an urgent call for seven men at the front. Germans are mounting an offensive. You want to fight?" He bowed slightly to give his permission. "I'll see you get the opportunity, gents."

Honner scowled at Barrett. "You're a big target, Barrett. I always wondered how long it would take for some German marksman to find you."

Barrett looked genuinely worried by the captain's remark.

"Maybe tonight?" He waved his revolver at the seven of them. "Get your gear. There's a truck leaving in five minutes. Don't miss it, or I will personally see that you face a firing squad."

"Keep this for me." Max held out the photograph of Trudy to Birch as the truck rumbled toward the front line. "My family address is on the back. See?" He turned it over to show the neatly printed Orchard Street address. "You write them if something . . . I mentioned you in my letters. So they'll know."

Birch silenced him. "Nothin's gonna happen . . . but I'll take the picture anyway." He grinned, studying the oval face and the serious eyes. Trudy's dark hair was pulled back to fall gently on her shoulders. "You know I've been wantin' this for quite a while."

Max looked over the wood slats of the truck bed to where flashes of light lit the evening sky. "You gotta promise me you'll write them. I've got this feeling, see?"

Birch cast a wry look toward Hardboiled Barrett, who slouched gloomily against the tailgate. "Same feeling I had when Barrett hit me with his left, I reckon." Birch rubbed his tender jaw. "Look," he said when Max did not smile, "I get that feeling every time. I've got it right now." Dying did not seem so frightening to Birch tonight, however. He unconsciously patted the pocket containing his mother's last letter. Would he see her and Bobby again before this battle ended?

What might lie ahead for all of them?

Ellis raised his head slightly. "It's bad up there."

The whistle of shells and the staccato popping of machine-gun fire sounded over the roar of the line of troop trucks. Ambulances and flat wagons carrying the wounded passed, going the other direction. It was bad, indeed, judging from the number of wounded.

Ellis looked pale. "My dad's a doctor," he said to no one in particular. His eyes followed the progress of a mud-caked ambulance with a red cross painted on every side.

The stench of death hung heavy in the air. Bloated horses lay in ditches alongside smashed German wagons. Such sights spoke of the desperate retreat of the enemy over the last few weeks. This was the last battle. The dying convulsion of the German dream of domination.

Birch looked hard at the face of Trudy Meyer. He wondered what her voice would sound like, if she laughed with the same gusto as her cousin Max. He made himself think about meeting her, about Max introducing them. They would all go together to that Coney Island place Max was always talking about. They would lie on the beach and never think about the war, never talk about it.

Birch slid the photograph into his pocket beneath the letter. "It's almost over, you know," he said to Max. Then he turned to Ellis. "We'll make it. We've made it this far, haven't we?"

"So did they." Ellis gestured toward the ambulance. "This far."

CHAPTER SEVEN

Past Help

That week in New York City there were eight hundred deaths a day from the influenza epidmic. Henrietta Murphy was one of the statistics. Schools and shops closed down. Theatres and churches closed.

There was not a large group of mourners at the graveside of Henny Murphy. It was raining and cold that day, the sort of weather that made almost everyone but family members and the closest friends stay indoors for fear of catching the same flu that had suddenly taken Henny's life.

Like a flock of black crows, the small gathering huddled beneath the protection of their umbrellas. Trudy shivered beneath hers and listened to the drumming of raindrops rather than the echoing voice of the priest. She stared at her shoes, spattered with mud. How odd to think that these same shoes had walked beside Henny every day, and now they stood beside her grave.

Nothing about this day seemed real to Trudy. She raised her eyes to the mounds of flowers covering the coffin. Henny's parents had made the arrangements themselves, just as they had done for every other funeral in the neighborhood. But certainly no king or president had ever had such beautiful flowers as Henny had today.

The air smelled clean and rain-washed. The scent of carnations and roses was sweet. Imagine . . . so many roses this time of year! Henny had told Trudy they were grown in greenhouses on Long Island. Expensive but plentiful.

Henny would have commented on the flowers if she were standing beside Trudy. If it were someone else being buried, Henny would have been irreverent, as usual. There would have been a firm nudge in Trudy's ribs during the prayer. *"You should see the bill for these arrangements. They'll be paying them off for ten years. Papa sure is in the right business these days."*

Yes. Henny would have said it just that way. Trudy smiled. If only Henny were here. Really here . . .

Across the canvas-colored mound of earth, Trudy caught sight of Irene Dunlap as she plucked a rose from the cross-shaped arrangement beside her. She held it to her nose and inhaled, closing her eyes. Then she slipped the flower into the buttonhole of her coat and smiled softly as though remembering something beautiful.

What is she thinking of? Trudy wondered. Maybe that summer night when Max had bought her roses and taken her dancing at the Winter Garden? It was certain that Irene was not thinking about Henny or paying attention to the priest. Beautiful Irene, all dressed in mourning with one red rose in her buttonhole. It was a picture Trudy would always remember.

"Shall we pray?" the priest intoned.

Trudy looked again at her shoes and the wet ground. Raindrops tapped on the umbrella. The sniffles and the voice of the priest seemed very far away. Trudy closed her eyes as the cold air stung her cheeks. She would pretend she was waiting for the tram car. *Out in the cold, waiting for the tram . . .*

She wished the priest would finish, wished she could file past the black-veiled figure of Mrs. Murphy and get it over with. What would she say? What could anyone say to a woman who had lost her only two children within weeks of each other?

Trudy dared to raise her eyes again to look at Henny's mother. She was leaning heavily against her husband, whose round, ruddy face looked exactly the same as it had as Walter's funeral. Mrs. Murphy wore a heavy black veil, and Trudy was glad she could not see her face through it. Henny had looked so much like her mother—a mirror image of what Mrs. Murphy had looked like twenty years earlier, they said. Henny always joked that she had no curiosity about what her future held—she had only to look at her mother's face to see herself in twenty years.

Today had put an end to that, hadn't it? There was no future at all for Henny beyond this cold damp day. The thought made Trudy feel light-headed. *This is real.*

"Dust to dust . . . ," the priest continued.

Trudy steadied herself, grasping the arm of a stranger beside her. She did not want to know her own future, did not want to look into the face of grief. What use was anything—falling in love . . . marriage . . . raising children—if it would all end someday in a place like this?

"Amen."

✳ ✳ ✳

Folks all said this terrible flu took people each in a different way. Willa-Mae Canfield nursed her children and knew that this was true.

Little Nettie awoke from the illness feeling very weak. "Mama, can I have my play-chillens in bed with me?" she asked, eyeing her dolls on the window ledge. That's when Willa-Mae knew her youngest daughter would survive.

Big Hattie swung her legs out of bed. "Mama? Can I have a cup of water? I'm mighty thirsty, Mama. Been thirsty all day and night."

Willa-Mae fetched her the drinking gourd full of cool water. She drank it all down and asked for more. Willa-Mae knew that Hattie would get well.

But thin and fragile Widdie just kept sleeping. She did not open her eyes when her mother tried to rouse her. She did not seem to hear her name.

Willa-Mae propped Widdie up in the bed and managed to spoon a bit of chicken broth down her throat. The child coughed once, and the liquid came back up. The fever subsided, but Widdie did not awaken from her deep and peaceful sleep. Hour by hour she grew cooler. And cooler. And finally cold like ice. She did not utter a sound. There was no fight to remain on earth. Like a spinning willow branch being pulled by the force of a strong river, delicate Widdie finally let go and drifted away, despite the cries of her mother and sisters and poor Hock, who said he saw her spirit rise as he was tending the critters.

✳ ✳ ✳

"Assaut à les baïonnettes!"

The cry echoed up and down the line of the 369th. "Assault with bayonets!" Few of the privates or noncoms of the regiment spoke French, but it did not matter much when the meaning was as clear as this phrase.

Jefferson Canfield cinched up the laces on his leggings and tightened the chin strap on the battered helmet. An image flashed through his mind and brought a grin to his face: his mother fussing over him as a child, checking last-minute preparations for church.

The grin faded as the comparison jarred into collision with the reality of a hundred men removing the leather scabbards from wickedly pointed bayonets thirty inches in length. Their sole use was for skewering men, and the 369th had spent weeks drilling to deadly precision.

When the signal came to launch the attack, Jefferson's squad was already assembled at the foot of the ladder leading up and out of the trench, and he was at the head of the line. "Hey, Canfield," someone taunted, "you buckin' for one of the crows de gare medals?"

"Naw, not this child."

"*Attaque!*" came the cry. This needed no translation either, and a wave of men poured up and over the mushy sandbags and through the sagging barbed wire.

The objective was a mounded area about a mile distant. Two small knobs barely tall enough to qualify as hills rose from an otherwise desolate plain strewn with bomb craters. The Germans were dug in on the tops of both knolls with machine guns and mortars, and the bases of both hills were strung with concertina wire.

Jefferson looked to both right and left along the line of advancing troops. He found himself near the middle of a two-mile-long front of men picking their way over the heaps of earth thrown up by shell fire from what had once been farmland. Curiously, the German machine-gun fire fell silent, as if the gunner were incredulous that anyone would leave behind the relative safety of the trenches and attempt to cross such a barren, exposed stretch of ground.

Jefferson knew that the respite was only temporary. The German officers were undoubtedly studying the advance through field glasses in order to direct their fire against the greatest concentrations of soldiers. Even so, another step, another yard gained without piercing wounds or shattered limbs was a cause for gratitude.

Then it came. Both hilltops exploded in waves of smoke that blotted them out as completely as if a thick gray cloud had suddenly settled there. There was no way the Germans could see through the fog of their own making. But it did not matter. Guns sighted in from weeks of test-firing knew the range to the killing ground. Barrels resting in grooves of sandbags gave the proper elevation: four feet to the height of a man's chest.

The popping sounds of bolt-action rifles reached across the desolation, pruning shears that selected a leg here, a throat there, a life, and then another, lopped off and discarded by friend and foe alike.

The angry buzzing of the machine guns began again . . . scythes to the field of men. Six, eight, ten soldiers in a row threw up their hands in a macabre chorus line. A pause, and the eleventh man hurried on nervously, guiltily, like a misbehaving schoolboy who has only momentarily escaped the punishment meted out to his classmates.

The 369th began to fire back, shooting from the hip. No one stood still to take aim. No one cowered in the craters or hesitated. Rather, they responded in a steady, disciplined flow.

Mortar rounds dropped among the first rank of men, blasting great gaps in the line. At a distance, the shells sounded like thunderclaps. After the first near miss, the small-arms fire could no longer be heard by the deafened soldiers. At a closer distance, one never heard anything again—ever.

A shell exploded behind Jefferson between the first and second waves of men. A piece of shrapnel no bigger than a dime struck his rifle stock between two of his fingers and stuck there. It was burning hot as he plucked it out.

The same mortar round killed the man on Jefferson's right. A small piece of shrapnel struck the soldier's neck. He gave a strangled cry and pitched onto his face, his rifle quivering upside down on the bayonet stuck in the mud, as if the fallen soldier had taken the time to mark his own grave.

Jefferson rushed over to his comrade and knelt beside him. A French officer hurrying along behind the front rank declared, *"Il est perdu! He's past help!"*

Mebbe, Jefferson thought briefly, *we is all past help.*

CHAPTER EIGHT

Night Vigil

It was snowing. Molly Warne sat up in bed and listened to the profound stillness that always came over the world when snow fell.

"What is it?" Doc mumbled.

"Snow," Molly replied, slipping from beneath the down quilts to stand at the window.

When Doc did not answer, she was not surprised. He had been up nearly forty-eight hours straight tending the McNeil family. Six children, and every one of them down with the Spanish influenza. Doc said more folks were dying here at home from the epidemic than could ever be counted in the trenches.

Even so, tonight Molly was thinking about what might be happening on those faraway battlefields. Her heart whispered that beyond the tranquility of the snowbound countryside, momentous things were taking place—things of which her boy Ellis was a part. Where he was, there was no peace. She watched the large flakes swirl down from a windless heaven, and she wondered what might be falling from the sky above the head of her son.

She closed her eyes and saw flashes of light, the screaming of shells tracing across blackness. Something terrible was happening tonight. She knew it, just as she had known the snow had come.

Ellis was in danger. . . .

Molly looked to where the row of lambs and soldiers lay concealed beneath the white blanket. "Not Ellis, Lord," she whispered. The old church was hidden behind the white curtain of snowfall. Just today

Molly had smiled at the building, imagining flowers arriving and guests all dressed up and Ellis in his best suit as a bridegroom.

Had that vision of happiness meant something else? Not a wedding at all?

She frowned and shook her head, not accepting the alternate image. *Men and women in black. Walnut casket. Flowers trailing from the hearse . . .*

"No," she said aloud. "Not Ellis." She reached for his picture and the battered Bible that she kept beside it, opened to Psalm 91.

Molly padded down the stairs to the kitchen. Turning up the oil lamp, she set a kettle on to boil. She had not brought Ellis into the world to die in the muddy trenches of a foreign battlefield. But what could she do to help him now? She closed her eyes, and the image of Ellis came clear in her mind. . . .

Men topple to his right and left, crumpling onto the burning ground. Ellis is crouched low, but moving forward. His face is pale and his lips are moving. Shells explode all around him.

What was he saying? "What is he saying, Lord?" Molly tried to hear Ellis's voice.

"Pray for us, Mama. Pray hard for us." The request sounded as loudly in her heart as if he had been standing right next to her, speaking the words.

The teakettle shrieked unheeded as Molly whispered, "A thousand shall fall at thy side, Ellis. Ten thousand at thy right hand. But, Son, it shall not come nigh thee."

The kettle wailed on, rattling on the hot stove top like distant machine-gun fire. Tonight Molly would not sleep. She knew that, for Ellis, she must stand watch and pray.

✶ ✶ ✶

The lines of attackers surged forward, screaming like madmen. Yelling was supposed to demoralize the enemy, and perhaps it did. But it also served to cover the agonized cry when the man next to Jefferson Canfield got hit, and it masked the pounding of his own heart.

Now the tactics of the assault changed to a bizarre game of leapfrog. On command, the front rank threw itself down behind whatever shelter was at hand. Those fortunate enough to be near a shell hole took cover in the churned heaps of earth. The less fortunate crouched behind the carcasses of battery mules or bloated horses. Some men could only flatten themselves against the mud puddles, as if trying to hide behind their own helmets.

Jefferson hit the ground in back of the shattered hulk of a caisson wagon. The wood was splintered by a hundred bullet holes, and it was clear to Jefferson that the Germans had used it as a mark to sight in their rifles. That realization was not comforting.

Lying on the ground nearby was a discarded French helmet, twin to the one on Jefferson's head. The front of the crest was shot away, leaving a gaping hole. Jefferson prayed that the owner had lost his headgear before the round had struck.

It was amazing to the brawny black soldier that his thoughts could divide so easily, even in the midst of battle. Part of his mind could observe and comment on the useless helmet while another instinct directed him to aim at the crest of the nearer hill and fire his rifle. He worked the bolt and fired again, then again and yet again, until the following wave of the attack swept past him.

Fifty yards ahead, the second rank of soldiers took their turn to burrow in the mud. It was almost magic. One instant there was a line of men racing fiercely as if intent on impaling the hill itself with their bayonets. In the next fraction of a second, mud-colored gophers were doing their best to disappear in the earth.

It was Jefferson's turn to advance again. Just as he jumped up from behind the caisson box, a machine-gun round smacked the lid and blew a fist-sized hole through it. A second's delay and Jefferson's head would have received a wound equal to the one in the shattered helmet. Breathing a silent *Thank You, Jesus,* he ran on toward the hill, now looming just ahead.

Twice more the leapfrog game was played, but each time fewer buddies of the 369th ran by in the second wave, and fewer still got up with Jefferson to charge forward. The last spring carried him to the base of the fortified hill. Outside the thicket of barbed wire was a large crater, made by a round from the French 155s. Jefferson leaped over the rim of the bowl and landed feetfirst in its middle. The shell fire had thrown up a lip of earth that overhung the depression and hid it from the Germans just up the slope.

Canfield turned to wave to his fellows to join him. Here was temporary safety. A chance to catch his breath and reload. He was shocked to see the ragged line of men that responded. So few! A young French officer joined him, then six more soldiers, two of them wounded.

Along the line of concertina wire the remaining members of the 369th struggled to find shelter. Their rifles spoke haltingly in stuttering voices. At such close range, when the German machine guns responded, it no longer sounded like an angry swarm of insects; it was more like the buzz saw in the mill back home that turned sturdy trees into planks of lumber with a single pass.

It was obvious from his prone position that the French officer did not want to be the tree to face that saw blade. He lay on the rim of the crater, peering over it in distress.

"Lieutenant," Jefferson asked the officer, "what is we to do now?"

"Do? What can we do? Where is the colonel? Where is the major? We were supposed to regroup here . . . at least, I think it was here . . . but where is the colonel? I must find him."

One of the other soldiers, a wounded man whose left arm dangled uselessly, spoke up. "I seen him go down. Him and the major both. They was caught by a mortar round."

"Then Captain Reynaud is in command. We must locate him, learn his orders." The lieutenant's voice was high-pitched and panicky. He sounded close to tears.

"'Scuse me, Lieutenant, sir. The captain, he done bought the farm too," said a short stocky man named Harris, who was improvising a sling for the wounded man's arm.

The young French officer grew visibly agitated. "But someone must be in charge!" He was pleading with the air, beseeching a superior officer—anyone at all—to appear and take control of the situation. When he turned from scanning the expanse of no-man's-land, Jefferson and the entire group of soldiers were staring at him.

"What does we do now, sir?" Jefferson repeated.

"No, I cannot lead. Not me!"

"You in charge now, Lieutenant. What we gonna do?"

The lieutenant appeared to think. "Retreat," he said in a flash. "That is it. We must order the retreat."

Jefferson and the stocky soldier looked at each other doubtfully. "Beggin' your pardon, sir," said Jefferson, "but we can't retreat just now. We lost a mess of men comin' this way. If we retreat now, we'd be slaughtered like hogs in a pen."

Skittering, bouncing noises reached the ears of the men huddled in the crater. "That sounds like—," Harris began.

"Ever'body down!" yelled Jefferson, just as the grenades that the Germans were lobbing down the hill exploded like a thunderstorm breaking directly overhead.

The lieutenant jumped straight up and shouted, "Retreat!" just before a burst of machine-gun fire cut him in two.

"Here's how I got it figgered," said Jefferson calmly. "We can't stay here an' we can't go back. I figger we better just finish what we come to do. Harris, snake on over to the right an' find out how many we got that can still fight. I'll do the same on the left."

A few moments of consultations up and down the line produced the information that more of the 369th was intact than they had thought.

But it also confirmed another piece of information: there were no officers left.

"It don't matter none," Jefferson observed. "I can see it plain as day. Them Krauts got their machine guns set up at the head of this here draw." He dug in the ground with the toe of his boot. "An' this hole we's in right below it. They can sweep the battlefield, sure enough, but I'm bettin' they can't lower their aim enough to catch one man sneakin' up that draw."

"What if you wrong?" Harris asked.

Jefferson grinned. "Then it'll be somebody else's turn to go to figgerin'. What I need from y'all is fire to keep them Krauts from droppin' grenades on my neck or poppin' me with a peashooter."

The word passed up and down the line, and a concerted fire from the 369th surprised the German defenders, who had expected a surrender. The concertina wire was clipped in a dozen places, but at the cost of a dozen more casualties to machine-gun fire and the bouncing grenades.

When Jefferson saw that all was ready, he slung a sack of French grenades over his shoulder. They were the size and shape of heavy green baseballs.

Harris stopped Jefferson as he was starting to climb out of the crater and took him by the arm. "God bless you, brother."

Jefferson smiled. "See you at the top."

The covering fire from the men on either side of the gully had a friendly, reassuring sound to Jefferson's ears. It was almost like having a warm blanket to cover up with. The accurate and constant volleys made the Germans keep their heads down. Jefferson doubted if anyone even saw his creeping ascent.

Once a German soldier stood up behind the sandbags and cocked his arm to lob another grenade. Jefferson held his breath and clenched his teeth, but before the man could throw the explosive, Harris spotted him and picked him off. The grenade exploded right in the lap of the German defenders.

Up and up Jefferson climbed, till the machine gun chattering directly above his head became a constant roaring sound. He paid it no mind and concentrated on inching closer and closer. Swinging the satchel of grenades off his shoulder, he pushed it ahead of him up the slope, conscious of the irony of being shielded by enough explosive force to blow him back to the trench he had started from a mile before.

When he had climbed within reach of his objective, he stuck his hand into the sack of grenades and began twisting the igniting fuses as fast as he could before he even stopped to think. Three were hissing and sputtering, then a fourth and a fifth. Jefferson whirled the satchel around his head with the leather carrying strap. *Just like a sling,* he thought. *Like little David in the Bible.*

The sack sailed up and over the ramparts, landing heavily on the ground right behind the machine-gun nest. Excited exclamations in German erupted from the defenders: *"Was ist das? Vorsicht! Handgranate!"*

Jefferson buried his face in the mud and clung to the slope with both hands as the hillside began to rock with the force of the explosions. The knoll shook so violently that Jefferson wondered if he had caused an avalanche that would sweep him off the incline. Heaps of rubble, sandbags, weapons, and men were flung skyward and rained down around him.

The remaining soldiers of the 369th charged up the embankment with their fiercest cries. They swarmed the top of the hill, their bayonets at the ready. But the fight had gone out of the German defenders, and the survivors surrendered en masse to the Black Rattlers.

✳ ✳ ✳

Flares lit the night sky, illuminating a ghastly scene. Shells exploded all around as soldiers from both sides moved forward, fell back, and inched forward again.

Birch heard the whistle of the shell as it shrieked toward their dugout. "Down!" he yelled the instant the shell burst in front of the trench.

Cheever fell over. A fragment of shrapnel had pierced his skull. Hardboiled Barrett began to weep as another shell screamed toward them.

Birch shoved him hard, pushing him down into the cover of the dugout. Ellis and Max were not behind him when he turned. Had they fallen beside Cheever?

The gas siren began its high-pitched whine of warning.

Mustard gas.

So the artillery attack was more than just gunpowder and fragments of iron. Three loud booms sounded in quick succession. Birch called for Max and Ellis. He dared to peer out from the dugout as he pulled his gas mask on. His two comrades were nowhere to be seen. The earth smoked in a gaping crater where they had been. The body of Cheever was gone, disintegrated by the force of the blast.

Barrett continued to weep. He covered his face with his big scarred hands and wailed. He had no gas mask. He had dropped it in the barrage.

The rats from the lower levels of the dugout began to stream out as mustard gas seeped down and permeated the place. Birch told himself it was no worse than the gas-filled tunnels they had crawled through in training at Fort Dix. But it *was* worse. There had been no rats in the training tunnels. They squealed and tumbled over one another in their mad flight from the fumes.

And Barrett bawled on.

"Where's your mask?" Birch grabbed him by the collar and shook him. A matter of moments and the gas would reach this level.

"I dropped it." Barrett pointed to the opening where the rats poured out. "Down there. Lost! You'll have to get it for me, kid. Please, kid!"

Barrett rolled into a ball and covered his head as another series of explosions shook the earth. The rodents clambered over his body.

"Anybody but you, Barrett," Birch muttered as he crawled to the opening. Kicking the rats from the wooden ladder, he began his descent into the yellow gloom of the gas-filled chamber. Twelve feet below the surface, lanterns still burned. Two dead men lay at the base of the ladder. One grasped the gas mask Barrett had dropped, but he had gotten it too late.

Birch tore the mask from the grip of the dead man and beat the rats away as he fought back up the rungs of the ladder. The yellow vapor trailed him, clung to his clothes, stung the flesh of his neck. His own gas mask felt as though it would suffocate him.

In the dim light of the upper-level dugout, Birch could just make out Barrett covering his head. The first tendrils of the mustard gas reached out for him.

Birch scrambled forward over the writhing rodents. He lifted Barrett's head and slipped the mask over his tear-streaked face. Still Barrett wept, the tears of a man insane with fright.

The earth rumbled, sending a shower of debris down on them. Birch placed his hand against the pocket containing letters and the photograph of Trudy. *Where is Max?* he wondered. *And what's happened to Ellis?* Could it be that the only two left alive were Barrett and Birch? The possibility seemed too bitter to contemplate.

"Get up." Birch kicked the sobbing hulk.

"Don't . . . want . . . to . . . die!" Barrett wailed.

Birch looked at the support timbers holding tons of earth and sandbags in place. One more heavy shelling and they would give way.

"Get up, Barrett." Birch punched him hard. "Look at the roof. We gotta get out or we're done for!"

Barrett managed to lift his eyes. He gasped and insisted he was choking. *Only terror is choking off Barrett's breath,* Birch thought. He tugged the man's sleeve hard, kicking his legs to move them. "The ceiling's gonna go!"

Another shell whistled nearer and nearer. It would hit close. Too close.

"Barrett!" Birch yelled again, then scrambled away, unable to rouse the big man to action.

Birch shot out from the shelter just as the shell burst. Shards of hot metal buzzed all around him. He felt the heat as they tore past him and slammed into the ground. The earth itself revolted against the brutal beating. The soil on top of the dugout quivered like jelly and sank inward with an enormous roar.

There was no use looking back. Barrett was dead, and Birch was alone in the narrow foxhole. Mustard gas moved like a fog across the landscape. The coughing and choked cries of dying men filled the air.

"Max! Where are you? Ellis?" Birch's voice was muffled beneath the mask. His calls went unheeded among the thousands of cries rising from the battlefield. The last battle was nearly over. Shells came fewer and fewer, and still Birch Tucker remained alive. . . .

At last the sky lightened, and the world awoke to the moans of the wounded and the silence of the dead. Birch stood and stumbled back across the desolate field, unmindful of the danger at his back. Someone announced that the war was over. The Armistice had been signed. What did it matter if Ellis and Max had not lived to see it?

Birch stumbled on, peering into the faces of the dead and the wounded, calling out for Max and Ellis as he went.

CHAPTER NINE

Armistice

The wail of distant sirens split the silent night on Orchard Street.

Trudy sat upright in bed and fumbled to find the light switch. Blinking against the sudden brightness, she took the heavy alarm clock from her night table and stared at it as another factory whistle joined the new clamor of church bells near and far.

"Two-seventeen." She said the time aloud, wanting to be certain that she would remember this moment forever. "November eleventh. The war is over."

The calmness of her own voice startled her. After all, the city beyond the thin windowpane was erupting in a passion of joy. It was over. The War to End All Wars was finished! No more casualty lists. No more black bunting over the photographs of young men on the mantel. No more war *forever*!

Yet here she sat, cross-legged in her bed with an alarm clock in her lap. Bells and whistles resounded from open windows all along Orchard Street. Downstairs Trudy could hear the telephone ringing insistently. Two rings, a pause, and two more rings. That meant everyone on the party line was supposed to wake up and answer. Even the telephone company was making a public announcement!

Bubbe Fritz called out from across the hall, "It's over, Trudy. Wake up! Wake up, Trudy! The war is over!" Bubbe threw open Trudy's door while Zeyde, in his nightshirt and no slippers, ran down the hall to pick up the telephone.

"*Ja! Ja! Ja! Mazel tov!* Such a night!"

Wisps of gray hair tumbled out from beneath Bubbe's nightcap. Her deep brown eyes were wide. They seemed to take up most of her plump face. Bubbe had not noticed that she had forgotten her spectacles. Bubbe never took one step from bed without those spectacles, but now she was blindly shouting the news that the war was over to Trudy. Trudy was certain her grandmother could not even see from the doorway to the bed.

"Trudy! You are awake? Trudy! It is over! Over, *Gott sei Dank*! You are a-wake, child?"

"I'm awake, Bubbe." Trudy smiled at last. "Get your spectacles on before you run into something."

The old woman put her hand to her face as if to say, *"So that is what's missing!"* She scurried back to her bedroom to find her sight as the world outside bellowed and cheered and every streetlamp from Orchard Street to Times Square was illuminated with joy.

Now Zeyde ran back to the bedroom. The wreath of his gray hair stuck up as if he had been charged with electricity. He was singing, his voice bellowing above the increasing noise in the street.

Trudy wrapped her quilt around her shoulders and went to the window. From there she could see the residents of Orchard Street hanging out their windows on this cold night. Mrs. Fleischer banged on a soup pot with a wooden spoon. Mr. Henmann was blowing on a trumpet. Up one side of the street and down the other, every kitchen kettle and pan had become a drum and cymbal. Barely three minutes had passed since the first shrill scream of the siren, but the cold, dormant world had awakened with a whoop and had known immediately what had happened.

"Get dressed, Trudy." Zeyde Fritz poked his head through the door. He was tucking his nightshirt into his trousers. His socks did not match. His hair was still uncombed. "You want we should miss the parade?" He whirled around to search for his shoes. *"Ja!* Get dressed!"

But Trudy could not find even a fragment of excitement inside herself as she pulled on her woolen underwear and her bloomers and her warmest sweater and skirt. Her mind was simply quietly pleased that the war was finally over. The killing in France was finished. Cousin Max would be coming home to New York.

She fingered the ribbon she had worn so proudly on his behalf. Yes, she was glad that the war was over for all the young men like Cousin Max.

Trudy leaned against the windowsill and gazed down at the soft glow of the streetlamps on the brick pavement of Orchard Street. Citizens tumbled out of their apartments and into the street. Men and women gushed from the shops where they lived and worked, throwing the doors open to embrace rival shopkeepers and neighbors whom they had not spoken to in years. Joy had broken all barriers tonight, but it had not swept away all sorrow.

Trudy let her eyes skim every window up the block—all lit, all framing smiling faces. All except the apartment above the florist shop where Henrietta and Walter Murphy had lived.

No light. Black crepe still framed the windows. A black wreath was on the door of the florist shop, and the big sign in the window said simply CLOSED.

Trudy wondered if Mr. and Mrs. Murphy were looking out through their dark window at the scene of joy below them. Certainly they could not escape hearing the whistles and bells and the nearer clang of kitchen pots. But they had not turned on their lights. What was the use, after all, for them to turn on the lights of their empty apartment? First their son, Walter, and now their daughter, Henrietta. The lights of their lives had gone out, and not even the joy of this memorable night could push back their darkness.

Had Bubbe and Zeyde Fritz forgotten that Trudy's best friend had slipped away only three days ago?

"Trudy! *Schnell!* Hurry!" Bubbe insisted as the telephone began to ring again. "Come on! The whole world is going to Times Square! Hurry! Hurry!"

From the hallway, Trudy could hear Zeyde's deep, resonant laughter as he picked up the receiver. "No. *Sure!* You think we'll miss this?"

Trudy fixed a smile on her face. It would not do to walk out into this celebration and leave her smile behind. Bubbe asked her to fetch the crate of small American flags. For months the flags had been sold for a nickel apiece in the dry goods store. Tonight, they would be free.

On the corner of Rivington, Trudy spotted Irene Dunlap talking excitedly among a group of girls from the college. The cold air and excitement made Irene's porcelain cheeks rosy. Her blond hair tumbled down in wisps over her forehead, which was unusual for Irene. Usually she was perfectly coiffed and moved with the elegance of a clothing model at Gimbel Brothers department store. As she spoke, her eyes darted toward the Fritz dry goods store. There was no use denying why Irene had gone out of her way was to pass by. She was still in love with Max, in spite of everything. She would have no other, although she could have her pick of the men in her own neighborhood.

Bubbe Fritz did not approve of this because Irene was definitely not Jewish. But tonight, at the sight of her, Bubbe Fritz said in a kind tone, "Well, so Max's little shiksa has come to make sure he is not a casualty in the last hour. *Nu!*"

Zeyde locked up as Trudy hurried toward Irene. Irene brightened at the sight of Trudy's flags and broad smile. Certainly Max was still well if Trudy could smile so broadly.

"True!" Irene hailed her from across the bobbing heads of the mob. She was not the only Irish soul who had crossed over Rivington Street tonight. The place was jammed with plump Irish faces speaking in thick brogue, inviting her to this celebration or that eating establishment for a party. Hordes of children, cutting through the neighborhood, whooped in delight at the sight of their teacher, Miss Dunlap.

Irene pressed against the flow, inching her way toward Trudy. When she finally reached Trudy's side, she grasped her hands and clung tightly to them. "Any word about Max?" She raised her voice above the din of Orchard Street.

What she meant, Trudy knew, was, *Any unhappy news?*

"No," Trudy responded, her eye catching the glare of Bubbe Fritz. She thrust a free flag into Irene's hand, then cocked a defiant eyebrow at Bubbe. "You can truly celebrate tonight, Irene." Then she hugged her like an old friend, even though Max and the secret were the only thing they had in common.

Irene began to weep. She held the flag to her cheek. "Oh, he's coming home! Oh, True, he's coming home!"

Trudy patted her gently and then with a bump and jostle from the side was wrenched away from her and carried off by the current of joyous revelers. Trudy turned to catch one last glimpse of Irene, still happily crying as she was pulled the opposite way by her friends.

"Don't tell me she came all the way here for a flag," Bubbe Fritz remarked dryly as they crammed onto a tram. They were packed like sardines in a can at the store.

"You might as well face it, Bubbe," Trudy replied. "Max is going to marry her when he comes home."

"I don't want to hear such things. He'll get over her." Bubbe lifted her round chin in a pout. "Is this what we came to America for?"

Trudy did not say that she believed this was the best part of America. Everyone crammed onto the same tram together. Everyone cheering with one voice. A girl from the Irish neighborhood falling in love with a tall handsome Jewish boy from Orchard Street. She did not say it because tonight was not a night to argue such things.

Nor did she dare mention that she only hoped there was someone up ahead in her future. She did not care what street he lived on or what his last name was. She wished she had another reason to celebrate the end of the war—someone special coming home to her. Just to her alone. She thought about how life had ended for Henrietta before it had even begun. All Trudy wanted now was to live, to see every day as though it were the beginning of something grand. Like tonight—the beginning of peace forever and ever!

These were all things she had often talked about with Henrietta. She could not mention such weighty matters to Bubbe Fritz, however. Max would understand when he got home.

The giant searchlights perched atop the New York Times Building served as a beacon drawing thousands of people into Times Square.

Trudy was witnessing a miracle, she knew. New York City had never had such a party. All neighborhood boundaries tumbled down tonight. Irish-Catholic mothers from Hell's Kitchen mingled with mothers from Park Avenue. Lower East Side and Upper East Side mixed together like a giant stew. Families of old money cheered alongside immigrant families with no money at all. Dockworkers from Chelsea climbed aboard fire trucks beside debutantes who had spent the night dancing at the Waldorf.

Suddenly there were no Italians. No Jews. No Irish. No Germans. No blacks or whites. Only Americans. One nation together in Times Square. The tiny American flags Trudy passed out to the mobs had multiplied by the thousand, until everyone in New York carried the same little flag as they marched in impromptu parades and banged their makeshift drums and sang songs of glorious victory while the factory whistles shrieked and church bells, large and small, clanged out the long-awaited news. The war was over!

Somewhere in all this commotion Trudy lost her grandparents. One moment she was standing beside Bubbe in Times Square, and the next moment hands were lifting her onto a fire truck, where a young man in a top hat and tails shared a bottle of bourbon with half a dozen stevedores from Hell's Kitchen. A black family from Harlem perched on the ladders between an Italian family and prep-school girls who rocked back and forth in time to whatever music they happened to hear.

Trudy scanned the human sea that stretched up every avenue from the square. The searchlights played on the buildings and scraped the gray underbelly of the early morning sky. She could not find Bubbe and Zeyde. A fireman linked his arm in hers and began to sing, "East Side, West Side" while he waved his little flag.

Sorrow had no place here. There was no room for anything but celebration in such a moment. Trudy raised her flag and banged her ladle against the metal frame of the slowly moving truck.

★ CHAPTER TEN *★*

Slaughtering Day

The morning sun shone bright on the pond in the pasture. Nettie played with her baby dolls on the porch. Each doll had been made out of woven cornhusks, clothed with bits of cloth tied on with string. Nettie named her play-chillen with the same lyrical imagination as Willa-Mae had used naming her six daughters.

Wiggity-Bops was a boy baby. He was wrapped in red flannel from a pair of Jefferson's long-handle underwear. EverLee was a little girl, clothed in a blue-floral rag from a worn-out quilt. Then there were Brother and Sister and the baby named Ezek-yal. Ezek-yal was a girl because Nettie had seen a real baby with the same name. And even though she wasn't sure what kind of name it was, it sounded girlish.

The whole doll family sat together on the willow chair and stared mournfully across the yard and into the barn. From the door of the barn, Nettie could hear the slaughter knife being sharpened on the grindstone.

"Poor things," Nettie said aloud as she looked past the barn to the hog pen. She could just see the red back of the duroc sow lounging in a patch of sunlight. The big head of the Hampshire lay across her. How Nettie hated hog-slaughtering day!

Angel came out on the porch. Inside the house, the clatter of tin plates sounded in the washtub. Angel had the dishrag slung over her shoulder. She leaned against the pole supporting the porch roof and stared toward the pen.

"Poor things," Angel agreed, mentally coming around to Nettie's sympathetic thoughts.

"You think they know?" Nettie pondered.

The grinding knife seemed to grow louder at the question. The hogs still lay happily in the morning sun, wagging their tails in contentment. Winking and blinking sleepily as if they were not living out their last hour on earth.

"Hogs is smart," Angel replied. Nettie heard the shakiness in her voice. "But they don't know what he's doin' in there. For all they know, that knife's for some ol' hen. If they know'd, they'd be bustin' right out and squealin' all the way down to the holler, and Pa would never find 'em."

Nettie imagined herself and Angel running to the gate of the pen, throwing it open, and telling the hogs to head for the hills. It was nice for a moment.

Angel shivered. Not a big shiver, but just enough so Nettie knew she was thinking the same things. "Wouldn't you love to . . . ," Angel began, then stopped. "Pa would whup us for sure."

From behind them, Big Hattie said, "Better them than us." Then her broad, dark face split in a dazzling smile. "'Sides, jest think about bacon in the fryin' pan. Chops for supper. Sausage. Ham in the smokehouse."

"Sure beats possum and sweet taters." Angel rubbed her stomach and licked her lips.

Pa had secret recipes for curing hams and making sausage that were legendary in these parts. There were three things for which he was famous: he could make something out of almost nothing, he knew a good mule, and he cured the best hams in all the South.

But this morning he was in a sour mood because Billy Jones was late bringing back the scalding pot. Without the scalding pot, Hock could not begin butchering the hogs.

A fire burned in the yard, with a pile of oak wood to heat the water in the scalding pot. But Billy, who had promised to bring back the pot at dawn, was not back. The best time for butchering was in the morning, in the cool of the day. That way, if any flies chanced to survive the frost, they would be too drugged by the chill of the morning to dare to land on the carcass of any hog butchered by Hock Canfield. Perfect-tasting meat on the table also had something to do with the way the critter was slaughtered and the exact time of day the deed was done.

Pa would not tell his secrets, but this was a fact everyone knew.

Nettie could hear Pa growling at poor Pink as he sharpened the knives. Pink cranked the wheel while Pa held the blade at the perfect angle. Nobody could sharpen a knife as good as Jefferson used to. That's what Pa claimed, anyway, so Pink was in for a verbal lashing when she turned the wheel too slow, too fast, too unevenly . . . and so on.

Pink was paying the price for that late scalding pot; that was all. Pa was grumbling loudly that it would be a cold day in perdition before anyone ever again was allowed to borrow his scalding pot before such an important event.

Angel and Hattie talked over the gruff voice of their pa. It was best on such a beautiful morning to ignore the buzzing steel and the voice that roared with displeasure like a hive of hornets poked with a stick. Besides, it would give the sweet-tempered hogs a little more time in the sunlight—like the last meal of a man condemned to hang.

Mama joined her daughters on the porch now that the dishes were done and the sausage grinder was set up for the big job. She looked at the sun, a handbreadth above the ridge. Nettie looked, too. If that sun climbed much higher without the scalding pot, Pa could not slaughter the hogs today. And he would be the devil to listen to if his plans were spoiled.

Mama frowned and placed her hands on her broad hips as Pa continued to rail on Pink. Then she sucked her lungs full of air and bellowed a warning: "It ain't Pink's fault you lent that pot to Billy. Now you quit that houndin', Hock Canfield, or you'll have me to reckon with!"

Silence descended upon the barn, except for the rhythmic buzz of the steel against the stone. Mama was good at hushing Pa up. Nobody better than Mama. And she would find something useful for them to do. They had to have a plan, some way to spend the day if slaughtering was delayed.

"Persimmons is ripe down in the south meadow," Mama said. "You know how your pa loves persimmon puddin'. And cookies made with hick'ry nuts." All heads swiveled to look at her. She grinned. "Y'all pick 'em, and I'll fix 'em up."

An enthusiastic chatter rose and then died just as suddenly. There was Billy's rickety wagon wobbling up the road. The scalding pot was in the back.

"I was hopin'—," Hattie began, then stopped short.

At that same moment the buzz of the knife fell silent and Pa stepped out of the barn. Sensing the approach of the wagon before anyone could hear it was one of the uncanny abilities Pa possessed. Pink followed him out of the barn. She looked exhausted from the tongue-lashing she had endured . . . and eager to come to the porch with the rest of the tribe.

Pa strode angrily toward the gate. Billy looked unperturbed in his wagon. He never seemed to take notice when Pa chewed on him. He was smaller than Pa and carried himself like a little black bantam rooster. He climbed from his wagon, patted the broad behind of his mule, and explained in a quiet voice that he was late for a very good reason.

Nettie strained to hear as Pa threw his knife on the ground and gestured to the burning heap of wood, the climbing sun, and the hogs. The hogs slept on, obviously unaware that all this fuss was about them.

Billy picked up the knife and handed it back to Hock, then led his mule and wagon through the gate and toward the barn. His left thumb was hooked in his overalls. He waved and flashed a toothless smile at the girls. "Mornin'," he called, as though Pa were not fuming at his side.

Nettie knew that Pa liked Billy. Once Pa was done being angry, they would share a plug of tobacco and talk about hunting turkeys and quail in the holler.

"Mornin', Billy," Mama said, as friendly as Hock was angry. She shrugged slightly, as if to say, *"Oh, well, you know he don't mean what he's sayin'."*

Billy touched his hand to the brim of his shapeless hat in acknowledgment and addressed Hock. "Shore sorry 'bout this, Hock. I know how you had your heart set on killin' them hogs at the stroke of dawn. But there weren't nothin' I could do 'bout it. Pret near got run down on the way here. Hub nut come off'n the wheel, you see . . . and down come the axle. Well, I woulda toted that scaldin' pot here on my back if I was a man of even half the strength of that boy of yours. Why, if it had been Jefferson with the broke wheel, he'd a carried this here pot three mile on his back. But my back? I been choppin' cotton too long. I ain't got the same back as I use t'." He spit. "I reckon now that the war done ended this morning, y'all gonna be real glad t' have Jefferson back on the place."

Pa stopped dead in his tracks. "What you sayin', man?"

Mama gave a little shriek, making all the girls jump.

Nettie's baby dolls tumbled out of the willow chair.

"What you say, Billy?" Mama cried.

"I say . . . now the war be over . . ."

This morning Doc Warne had chugged off in the automobile to deliver Mrs. Metcalf's baby. Matthew and Mark were up in the north field cutting firewood. Luke was mending the pasture gate where the bull had broken through to get to the heifer yesterday. John had four saddle horses in the corral and was hard at work trimming the feet of a fifth. That left five-year-old Julie at home with Molly. She was under the stairs playing with the dolls her aunts had sent her.

A cardboard box was open on the table. In it were new woolen socks and long-handle underwear, along with a knitted cap and mittens for Ellis in case he got cold in France. Molly supposed that the United States government provided trousers and boots for its soldiers, but a boy could never have too many socks and long-handles. She had also made two fruitcakes. His last letter had informed her that whatever she sent must be well preserved since it might take many weeks to reach him in France. Fruitcake laced with rum seemed the only logical choice in such a situation.

Three flatirons heated on the woodstove. A stack of shirts lay on the kitchen table. A basket of trousers and sheets and handkerchiefs sat at her feet. Molly's ironing board formed a bridge between the table and the kitchen sink. It was positioned so she could see out the window to the barn, to the fields, to the schoolhouse, and to her row of little lambs and silent soldiers. All of her brood were within shouting distance, but this morning it was Ellis she was thinking of.

Molly timed the steady rhythm of her iron on the board to Julie's gentle humming as she sang to her dolls. It was a quiet morning. A peaceful morning.

Then a cloud of dust appeared over the rise in the road. The irregular rattle of an approaching automobile engine blended into the cadence of Julie's song and the thump of Molly's heavy iron. At two hundred yards, Molly supposed that the motor she heard was that of Doc's old four-cylinder Apperson touring car. Fifty yards nearer, and she knew it was someone else.

Unusual. There weren't but a handful of motorcars in Guernsey County, and Molly could tell who was who on the highway from the distinct sound of each engine. Every motorcar had its own voice, after all. This chugging, gasping vehicle did not have the voice of an old friend.

She held the iron above the collar of Doc's shirt and stared at the vehicle as it slowed on the highway and turned up the lane to the big white house. The memory of other unexpected visitors filled her with dread. Was this another telegram? word from France?

She set the iron on the stove top with a clank and watched as John straightened from his work to stare at the car. In the north field, Matthew and Mark laid down their axes and shaded their eyes to look. Luke tested the hinge of the gate once and then climbed up on the top rail to see who was coming.

Julie stopped singing. "Has Missus Metcalf had her baby, Mama?"

Molly knew it was the child's way of asking if Doc was home.

"No. It's not your papa." Molly clasped her hands together to control her trembling as she stared out the window.

"Who then?" Julie asked.

Molly did not reply. She could not find her voice as she glanced at the box on the table and then back to the serious face of John, who wiped his hands and untied the big mare. He swung onto her bare back with ease and nudged her into a slow canter toward the stranger. Why would anyone be driving an automobile out this way? There was nothing out here but Doc Warne's farm, after all. Doc's sons and their wives worked the land. There were no hired hands here.

Still a hundred yards from the house, the automobile slowed to a stop in the center of the gravel road. The driver, dressed in a long over-coat, a cap, and goggles, set the brake but left the engine running. The ve-hicle shuddered impatiently. The horses in the corral milled about nervously at the sound of the motor, but the old mare John rode ap-proached it without concern.

Molly did not recognize the driver. At least not from this side of the hills. But the man waved broadly when John came alongside. He ap-peared to be laughing.

Molly closed her eyes in relief. No one with a telegram to deliver could be laughing, talking, and gesturing with such exuberance. And as he did so, his long coat parted, revealing a celluloid collar and a tie—just like the bank clerks in Camden wore.

The response of Matthew and Mark was also curious. They stopped loading the heap of wood at the edge of the field and tossed their tools into the back of the wagon. Luke dropped hammer and nails into his sack and sauntered toward the barn. John, tall and lanky in his overalls and farrier's chaps, towered over the man in the motorcar. They carried on a lively discussion for a minute. Then John whirled to grin and wave at the kitchen window. Somehow, Molly realized, he knew she'd be watching.

Wondering.

Fearing that it was bad news.

"What? What's he saying, Mama?" Julie had climbed up on a chair beside Molly to study the scene.

Molly grabbed her shawl and dashed out onto the porch. The early morning air was frigid. The steam of John's breath mingled with the ex-haust of the sputtering engine. He was shouting, but Molly could not hear his words. Along the rise leading to the white clapboard church, she spotted Frank Dunn galloping on his red horse toward the building. She looked at the five headstones, then back at the stranger and Matthew, Mark, and Luke, who were running to the house.

At that moment, the distant clanging of a church bell echoed through the valley. It was joined by another and another . . . and finally by the bell of Cumberland Presbyterian on the hill.

Rebecca Moniger appeared over the rise. She stood beside the church for a minute and tilted her head toward the steeple, as if in thankfulness. When she turned toward the house and waved her hat back and forth like a signal, Molly knew.

"It's over," she whispered.

John slapped the old mare and loped to where Molly stood beside Julie. "Mama, it's over! Ellis is coming home! Mama, the war is over!"

Rebecca ran across the pasture, happily calling something. Her words were lost beneath the jubilant ringing of the bells, but her face sang the message clearly: *"It is over!"*

It seemed like a miracle to Birch, one he had not expected. Hours ago he had lost all hope of ever seeing Max and Ellis alive. Then he found Max, looking very alone and dejected, perched on a packing crate outside the field hospital.

"Max!" Birch broke away from the other troops he had marched out with.

Max raised his head slowly, as if waking from a deep sleep. His eyes were glazed, unfocused. It took a minute for them to register that Birch was standing in front of him.

Then, with weary relief, Max stood and stumbled to embrace Birch. "I thought you were dead," he managed to whisper hoarsely.

"I thought the same about you and—where's Ellis?"

Max jerked his head toward the surgical tent. "In there."

"What happened?"

"Shrapnel in the leg. He was bleeding badly. I carried him out." There were large dark stains on Max's uniform, as if he had bathed in blood. "It hit the bone. Shrapnel through the bone just beneath his knee. I don't know. . . ."

Max looked as if he might fall down, so Birch walked with him back to the crate and sat beside him as Max told the story.

Max had carried Ellis out. Off the battlefield. Through shells and machine-gun fire and pools of mustard gas, Max had carried him two miles. It could not be for nothing.

"He'll make it," Birch said, praying he was right.

"They're taking off his leg, Birch." Max was crying like a little boy. "Cutting it off." Head in hands, he sobbed, "How's he gonna play baseball?"

Birch put an arm around Max and let him cry. "He'll make it," Birch said again.

"Did we win?" Max asked at last. "Does it mean anything? Who won, Birch?"

Out on the road, hundreds of German prisoners marched past. "I think *we* did," Birch replied, but he was not certain of it all the same.

The Armistice was a truce, after all—not really the official end of the war. It was simply the cessation of fighting. The war, which had begun with such confidence and high morale, ground to a halt as Ellis Warne fought for his life beneath the chloroform mask and the surgeon's knife. Birch could only think how useless his sacrifice seemed at such an hour. What had been accomplished?

The reality of the question grew even more grim as the days rolled by and the facts became clear. The loss of human life everywhere was on a scale unimagined in all of history.

Max translated the facts and figures for Birch as they appeared in French newspapers over the long weeks that followed. France had been the battleground, the killing field where French generals squandered the lives of their troops with a reckless belief that they could drive back the Germans from their soil. The first year of the war had brought half the families of France to the grave of a husband or a son. After sixteen months of grueling combat, two-thirds of a million French soldiers had died.

All the nation seemed in mourning. Those who had not yet suffered loss considered the figures and concluded that eventually every husband or son in the trenches would be killed or mutilated. The French had believed at first in a "war of attrition." By a succession of massive attacks, they would wear down the enemy.

In May of 1915, an attack had been launched against the Germans in Artois, resulting in a breakthrough of three miles. But the Germans had counterattacked and closed the gap. When the fighting died down in June, the French came to the dreadful realization that they had lost 400,000 men and had gained nothing.

Everywhere the story was the same. The war of attrition had not only worked to hammer away at Germany, it had worked against the French and the British as well.

Only now, when the dead were buried and the maimed were tucked away in hospitals, did the truth of the slaughter become known:

Germany: 2,000,000 men dead.

France: 1,300,000 men dead.

England: 1,000,000 men dead.

U.S.: 115,000 men dead.

A total of 10 million died in the Great War. Another 20 million perished in the flu epidemic. The hearts of all who lived were shaken to the core. The carnage had spared nothing—not families, leaders, governments, or society. The world itself was mutilated, just like the young baseball player from Ohio who had once thought life would be kind to him.

CHAPTER ELEVEN

Avenue of the Suffering

It was as though the fighting had not stopped in France. The casualty lists in the daily news seemed just as long as ever.

News that Ellis had been wounded arrived in a telegram the week after the Armistice was signed. His name did not show up in the newspaper until two weeks after that: *ELLIS R. WARNE . . . Dr. W. Warne . . . Camden . . . WU.*

The *WU* at the end meant that the severity of the wound was undetermined. This was much better than *WS*, Becky explained to Molly, because *WS* meant "wounded seriously." Better than that would have been *WL*, which was the code for "wounded lightly." Best of all would have been if Ellis had never appeared on the casualty list, but Becky was hoping that *WU* really meant *WL*.

All of this was discussed in detail over a cup of tea. Molly did not tell Becky what the telegram had indicated: Ellis had, indeed, been wounded seriously in the leg. Nor did she comment on the opinion Doc had of the quality of medical care being rendered to the wounded boys in Europe. The lists showed only a handful had been killed in action. Nowadays, the initials behind the names were *DW*— "died of wounds." And by far the greatest numbers were *DD*— "died of disease."

Even now, with weeks gone by since the celebration, the whole world seemed to revolve around these casualty lists. Farmers did not check the paper for weather reports or the price of cattle and wheat until they first scanned the casualty lists. There they noted the names of farmers' sons and put the names together with young faces they had known and watched grow up.

This afternoon Rebecca Moniger finished her tea and hurried out the kitchen door on her way to choir practice just as Doc came in the front door. Exhausted, he did not stop to remove his coat and overshoes before he sat down heavily at the table.

"Mrs. Stokes is in a bad way since hearing about Fred. No will to live." He glanced past Molly toward the headstones. "I told her we knew something of broken hearts in this house as well."

Molly helped him off with his coat before pouring him a cup of tea. "She has three other children to raise," she said. "Can she not think of them?"

Doc raised his eyes to meet hers. "You know, Molly. . . ."

Yes. She knew. There was no way around the grief that came when a child was lost. She knew, but she would not give up. "I'll go have a word with her. When will you call again?"

"Tomorrow morning."

"I'll fix a stew and come along with you."

He nodded. "There is no one in all the county who does not have a broken heart." This he said with amazement. "We came here to get away from it—the bad blood in Belfast. Ah, Molly . . ." He did not lift his cup.

"Drink your tea, Doc," she urged. "Will despair make it better? Worse than useless it is, unless you put your grief to work somehow to make things better."

"And isn't that why we came here? to America? To make life better for our children?" He waved a hand toward the window. "They gunned down my own father in the streets of Belfast when I was nine. I was there beside him when he fell. His blood pooled around my shoes. And I grew up hating them. Hating all of them. Hating the men who pulled the trigger, yes, but hating them who nodded their approval just as much. It's no different in Europe now, is it? How many little boys there will grow up without fathers? And what will they do when they are old enough to take up a gun and cry revenge?" He slammed his hand against the table. "What have we solved? Two sons dead and another may not live. And what have we solved in the world, Molly?"

Molly shook her head in sorrow. She had no answer to a question so enormous and imponderable, so she tried only to comfort Doc. She rubbed his broad shoulders and said nothing at all while he talked on and on.

"The world as we knew it is dead," he whispered. "Now President Wilson and the rest will be carving up Europe. The New World Order, he is calling it. But will it be a world without compassion, I ask ye? A world of orphans will grow up with the bitter taste of hatred on their tongues.

And I fear . . . our sons have died for nothing. Ellis suffered for nothing, you see? Because it will only happen again."

✳ ✳ ✳

"Man, we in Paris now," exulted Harris as the 369th disembarked from their train at the Gare de Grenelle. On the left, Jefferson Canfield could see the Seine, where pleasure boats and barges alike were decked out in red, white, and blue bunting. Directly behind the train station, looming incredibly high overhead, was the 984-foot Eiffel Tower.

"Whew," Harris observed, leaning farther and farther back to view the tower. "I never seen nothin' so tall,"

"Careful," Jefferson cautioned. "You fall down, and they'll figger you for drunk."

"You just give me twenty minutes in this friendly town, and they be right. Ever'body's tryin' to hand me a bottle of wine or a bunch of posies."

The uniforms of the regiment had been cleaned and polished until the buttons gleamed in the sunlight and the khaki trousers sported creases. The soldiers wore the once-despised French helmets with jaunty pride.

Forming ranks outside the train station, the men of the 369th prepared to march down the tree-lined street.

"Avenue of the Suffering," translated Jefferson. "Back in them trenches, I mighta said they name this here street for us, but it don't feel thataway today."

A regimental band from the French 4th Army led off, with a rattle of drums and a trumpet fanfare. Then the band broke into "Yankee Doodle," and the procession started off southeast along the boulevard.

The street was lined four and five deep with curious citizens. Jefferson remembered the staring onlookers who had crowded the sidewalks of New York when the regiment had embarked for France. The New York crowds had shown a mixture of amusement and hostility. The comments ranged from laughing jibes about how every "real" soldier was going to have a personal slave to what a disgrace it was to let niggers wear the uniform of the United States. One of Jefferson's friends had thrown words back at the hecklers. "Don't we bleed red, same as you?"

That had been twelve months ago—a year of dragging wearily through the thick, dark mud of the trenches. Friends who had been on the ship from New York were now buried in that mud. The soldier who had dared to respond to the taunting was one of them. The thought made Jefferson angry.

He looked around at the throngs of Frenchmen, his eyes flashing, as if daring them to offer ridicule. But he was wrong. Dead wrong.

The French soldiers in the crowd stood at their stiffest attention as the 369th passed. Male spectators removed their hats in respect. Mothers lifted up their children to get a better look at the famous Negro regiment arriving to be honored for its contribution to the victorious conclusion of the Great War.

A cry broke out from somewhere in the thousands of watchers. Only a few voices at first, then tens, then hundreds, until the entire avenue echoed with the sound: *"Vivat les Serpents Noirs! Vivat les Serpents Noirs!"*

A lump formed in Jefferson's throat. Out of the corner of his mouth he commented to Harris, "These folks really love us. We ain't sideshow freaks. They really think we is heroes."

"You just wait," Harris shot back. "We is gonna be heroes at home, too. We fought the war for democracy, and now we gonna get some for our own selves."

Past the sixth block of houses, the left side of the avenue broadened into the flat, graveled expanse of a parade ground. The regiment drew itself up in companies facing the eight Corinthian columns and quadrangular dome of the Ecole Militaire. Jefferson was in the front rank, closest to the stone steps leading up to the imposing buildings.

Out from the colonnade marched an officer dressed in the imposing uniform of a marshal of France. At the cry of "Attention!" the regiment snapped to order as one man.

"Maréchal Henri Philippe Pétain, hero of Verdun and chief field commander of Allied Forces, will now speak to the valiant soldiers of Regiment 369," a herald announced.

"Soldiers!" the feisty, diminutive Pétain proclaimed. "Comrades-in-arms! We salute you for your role in the glorious victory so lately won."

"Let those to receive special honors take one pace forward!" called the herald. Jefferson and the rest of the front rank stepped forward. From the wings of the parade ground rolled a line of wheelchairs—men too severely wounded to walk to the award ceremony.

Pétain made his way down the rank. The herald was at his elbow, recounting the specific deeds of each man as the marshal of France distributed over one hundred Croix de Guerre and Légion d'Honneur awards. When he came to Jefferson Canfield, the tall, muscular black soldier had to bend down for the shorter white general to place the red ribbon of the Legion of Honor around his neck. The marshal's drooping mustache brushed against Jefferson's face on both cheeks.

Pétain murmured in Jefferson's ear, "You have honored France with your courage. Today we honor you with a token of our thanks. Wear it proudly, soldier of France and America." Flashbulbs popped as a photographer recorded the scene.

On the march back to the train, Harris remarked to Jefferson over the noise of the cheering crowd, "Man, I don't need no wine now. I think I must be drunk already."

Jefferson nodded his agreement. "I feel like I must be dreamin' myself. Harris," he said suddenly, "they gonna respect us at home now. They really gonna."

The wind howled fiercely around the iron girders of the Eiffel Tower. The guidebook warned that climbing the structure was not a good idea unless the weather was clear and calm, but Birch and Max had taken on the challenge all the same. Like every other American in Paris, they felt they could not face the folks back home if they did not climb the tower. The lifts were closed, but still the charge was five francs for the trek to the top. It was 350 steps to the first level and 380 to the second level, containing bars and shops full of Eiffel Tower souvenirs.

Birch was not content to merely trudge to the great illuminated clock. He threw his head back, whooped, and headed up to the third platform at 905 feet. The enormous glass pavilion at the base of the double lantern that crowned the edifice was nearly empty. Breathless and sweating in spite of the freezing wind, Max leaned against the railing and refused to go up the final spiral.

"Come on, Max," Birch chided. "You ain't gonna give out now. All this time you been bragging how you ran up the stairs of the Woolworth Building in New York and beat the elevator. Now you can't even finish the job."

"All right." Max wiped the sweat from his face. "Just give me a minute, will you? You see, we're the only fools to do this on a day when the lifts are closed."

"How come you can climb the Woolworth and you can't make it up here? Just another hundred feet or so. When we get to New York, you're gonna have to show me how you did it."

Max shook his head. "I rode the elevator to the floor below the Woolworth observatory. Then I raced up from there. So lay off, Birch."

"Now you'll really have something to brag about." Birch climbed to the uppermost platform, and Max grudgingly followed. The view was spectacular. To the southwest they could see as far as Chartres, and to the northeast to Villers-Cotterêts, fifty-five miles away.

"It don't look so bad from up here, does it?" Birch tucked his collar up against the biting wind.

Max peered over the railing and scanned the pavement below. "If you don't look too closely," he agreed. Then, with a shrug, he turned his eyes away. "Doesn't do any good to think about it anyway." He brightened. "Let's go to that place Millard was talking about. The one with those girls . . . you know."

Birch scanned the antlike figures milling around the pavement far below. Beggars. Children of the fallen heroes of France. He sighed. Paris in December. Their first real leave in over a year. Here he was in a city he had only heard about in geography class and seen in Sally Miller's stereopticon viewer. But all he wanted was to be home.

Paris in December was a hungry place. There had been no planting in the spring, except the planting of men six feet underground. Countless numbers had been ravaged by war and disease. There had been no harvest for the living. On every corner, hollow-eyed children begged for coins or food from the "reech Yan-kees." Down the crooked lanes, their widowed mothers prostituted themselves for pennies.

"You know what gets to me?" Max said quietly, as though he had heard Birch's thoughts. "France is the country that won the blasted war. And look at them down there." He shook his head. "I wonder what it's like for the kids in Germany. There's a whole generation growing up without fathers, you know?" He leveled his gaze at Birch. "And every one of those little beggars is going to grow up hating us and the French and the English for shooting down their daddies."

"It ain't like they didn't shoot us down, too," Birch snapped back. He had not thought about that, and he didn't want to.

"I am speaking theoretically."

Birch narrowed his eyes. "We ain't gonna get into that again, are we? You just about got us arrested in that café when you were talking about not being so hard on Germany. That man looked mean enough to kill you."

"How was I to know he spoke English?"

"Well, keep it to yourself. Nobody in Paris agrees with either you or President Wilson, and nobody back home is gonna want our country involved in a muddled-up European League of Nations. We get into that mess, and every time some Croat spits in the eye of a Serb, we're gonna be in another war."

Max held up his hand in surrender. He had argued on behalf of the American president enough.

But Birch knew he was right. Everyone in the world wanted his pound of flesh out of Germany. Blood would be squeezed from the proverbial turnip. The orphan sons of German soldiers would simply have to grow up hungry as far as the world was concerned.

Max checked his watch. "One-thirty. Visiting hours are from two until four. We have just enough time to stop and buy a bottle of brandy."

Birch looked indignant. "Ellis don't drink that stuff. You know he's a teetotaler."

"It's not for Ellis." Max headed down the metal steps. "It's for me. You don't think I can go in there without some strong medicine for myself, do you?"

"I swear, Max—" Birch clucked his tongue.

"No, you don't, Birch. And you don't drink either. And you don't go after lewd women. So why am I hanging around you here in Paris?"

"Stimulatin' political discussion, I reckon. And I'm the only one who doesn't think you're a blowhard."

"Then why is it you hang around me? This might be interesting."

"Because you speak five languages and can't say anythin' polite in any of 'em. I feel sorry for you, Max. If I don't stick close, you'll get yourself into a political discussion, and before you know it, you'll be in a heap of trouble."

"A heap?"

"Probably killed. And then when I get back to New York, I'll never get to meet that pretty cousin of yours."

Max grinned back over his shoulder. "You'll meet her over my dead body."

"You're like a mama hen with that girl. And I'm no fox. I just want to meet her."

"She's not your type. I already wrote and warned her that you're smitten. Struck by lightning, more like it." Max grinned.

"Why'd you go and do such a thing?" Birch was wounded.

"She doesn't speak your language."

Birch scratched his head. "Her letters are in English."

"That's what I mean, y'all." Max laughed. " 'A heap!' " he mocked. " 'Let's us-all go on down t' Coney Island fer a heap of fun!' "

Birch frowned. "See what I mean? Five languages, and you can't say anythin' nice. Not even in English. I ought to let you get yourself drunk and beat up by a mob of these Frenchies. Huh! I speak English fine."

"Better than you speak French, anyway."

Birch snarled. "You are an arrogant New Yorker. No argument about it. I've just been wantin' to meet your cousin—"

"You've fallen in love with her picture and her letters. Admit it."

"I ain't—"

"And you're ignoring all these pretty French girls—real live girls to cuddle up to. They don't care what brand of English you speak."

"As long as I got money. No thanks."

Max stopped suddenly on the landing. His face became serious. "Listen, Birch. I'm not going to introduce you to Trudy. Quit asking. She's

Jewish. My grandmother would never forgive me. You're . . . something else."

"What's Irene? She is not—"

"It's trouble. For me. For Irene. Her brothers hate me. My grandmother doesn't approve of her. It would be trouble for Trudy. For you." He thumped Birch on the shoulder. "What if she liked you?"

"We'd be related."

"That's what I'm afraid of." The seriousness of his tone vanished. He grinned broadly. "Believe me, she's not your type."

"And I ain't hers?" Birch felt genuinely irritated.

"You got it. Every day, my grandmother is praying Trudy will meet a nice Jewish boy, see? I'm in enough trouble with her over Irene. Fighting Germans is one thing, but Bubbe Fritz is another." Max turned away, as if he'd just had the last word on the subject.

Birch stared at Max's back and considered letting the New Yorker go on by himself. So what else was new? He had felt that way about Max at least once a day since they had met.

"You coming?" Max called impatiently.

"You're a coward," Birch countered. "Scared of your granny?"

"You're right. And you sulk. Now come on, or we'll be late. We've got to cheer Ellis up."

"Then you'd better stay here, and I'll go alone. You're about as much cheer as a cottonmouth in a swimmin' hole."

"So? You intend to leave Ellis alone with the likes of me?"

Birch replied by clattering down the stairs after Max. "Just speak French to him, will you, Max? That way when you get insultin', he won't take it personal."

CHAPTER TWELVE

The Sea-Change

To Jefferson Canfield and Harris, the city of Paris seemed to be laid out like a series of wagon wheels. Streets fanned out from a circular hub, like spokes overlapping other spokes in a giant puzzle. The little spindle lanes that jutted off those spokes could get a man hopelessly lost.

Harris, with his New York City upbringing, simply shrugged and left the pathfinding to Jefferson. "Man, this sure ain't Harlem." He scratched his head.

Jefferson, who had hunted wild bear and raccoons and possum in the thickly wooded Poteau Mountains of his home state of Arkansas, was undaunted by the confusion of Paris. "Heap of landmarks here, Harris." He jerked his thumb toward the Eiffel Tower. "I know which way is which by that. Whole lot easier than findin' my way home in a snowstorm."

Harris said that he figured Jefferson could find his way around anywhere because he was tall enough to practically see over buildings. Truth was, Jefferson had the uncanny ability to glance at a map, take his bearings, and remember every detail accurately. Small wonder he had led his men to the worst places on the battlefield in the densest smoke and then taken them back out again.

Today, however, Jefferson and Harris were only searching for a small perfume shop. Both men had mothers and sisters at home, and like every other American soldier, they intended to take home their duffel bags stuffed with souvenirs.

Avenue de l'Opera was a wide spoke off the hub of Place de l'Opera on one end and a large square known as Théâtre Français on the other.

Along the avenue's elegant expanse were some of the most fashionable shops in all of Paris. Furs, hats, silk ties, dressmakers, and tailors attracted a wealthy clientele. Displaced aristocrats sneaked in the back entrances of the elegant jewelry stores to sell their diamond-encrusted heirlooms, while the newly rich industrialists entered the front door to buy them.

Into this world strolled Jefferson and Harris. Jefferson wore his Legion of Honor medal around his neck, so they were greeted with admiration by everyone they passed on the avenue. The penniless aristocrats and the new rich alike smiled at them, nodded pleasantly, and sometimes spoke a few words of praise in halting English.

This reception into a wonderland seemed to Jefferson a kind of miracle. All the while, Harris grinned broadly, tipped his hat, and saluted the ladies in their finery. "Man, if we said hello to a woman like that back home, there'd be one less poor boy from Harlem in this old world. They'd hang us from a lamppost."

"Ain't thataway no more, Harris." Jefferson bowed to a smiling matron as they entered the sweet-smelling perfume shop Viville, at No. 24.

Immediately they were greeted with the same attention any duke or baron might have received. Shopgirls put their heads together and glanced at the red-ribboned medal. One girl dabbed a drop of perfume on the wrist of Harris.

"Man, this is livin'," Harris whispered, inhaling the stuff.

Amber bottles lined the shelves behind the counter. Tiny glass vials in the shapes of hearts or butterflies or elephants stood empty and waiting for a choice of fragrance. But there was only one reason Jefferson had come to this place.

"Ma'am." He leaned down low to the old woman dressed in violet, who evidently ran the shop. "I seen a lady . . . *mademoiselle* . . . who had one of them fans y'all been sellin'."

The old woman gazed up at him in confusion. Her soft, wrinkled skin crinkled as she smiled in apology. She spoke a long string of French words too fast for Jefferson to catch the meaning of even one and ended with *"Fansyall?"*

Jefferson knew he had a problem. Here was an occasion when it would have been handy to have one of those lady guides along—the ones known as "universal aunts," who could solve just about any problem and talk French and English equally well. Three groups of soldiers had gone in together to hire one of these ladies, but Jefferson had said he didn't need no old white woman to lead him around like a child.

So here he was. "I seen this lady at the hotel, see? She had a fan . . . you know? A fan for fannin' yourself? My mama gets real hot in church on Sunday mornin'. She fans herself with the hymnal. And I was thinkin' when I seen that fan from y'all's shop that my mama sure would like to have herself one of them for church."

After all this, the old woman shook her head and held up a bottle of perfume for him to smell. Strong stuff. It made his eyes water. Willa-Mae was partial to lemon verbena, anyway. "Smells mighty pretty, ma'am."

He looked at Harris for help, but Harris was talking with a different shopgirl, a young one in a bright green dress. She didn't understand him either, and the only thing she could say was, "You come to my home? meet my papa and mama? eat?" Jeff's medal had that effect on all the French folks, too, but it didn't get any closer to fans for his mama and sisters.

He looked all around the shop. Not a sign of those fans. The one he had liked had been made of painted Chinese silk and was scented with the same perfume the shop owner was waving under his nose. Maybe this place had run out of the things. He looked into the glass case and pondered what to do next. He had his heart set on buying Willa-Mae a fan from Paris, France. Wouldn't she be proud to sit in church on the hottest Sunday of the year then?

He scratched his head and gestured toward a piece of paper and a pencil. As all the shopgirls gathered around, he sketched the fan. And the place came alive with *ooh*s and *ahh*s. Of course they had the *fansyall*.

The old mademoiselle brought out a big box full of fans. All different colors they were, too—red, blue, green, yellow, orange, purple, and pink! Jefferson let out a whoop of joy. "How much you want for them things? I want seven." He held up his fingers.

"*Free*, monsieur," said the old woman, delighted that her fans could bring so much happiness to such a decorated hero. "Sample. You see? *Oui?*" She dabbed a drop of perfume on each fan, then wrapped them individually and tied a ribbon around them. She did the same for Harris, who only needed four, but he took seven—just in case the gals back in Harlem might be interested, he told Jefferson.

After this, Jefferson picked out a crystal elephant bottle and had it filled with the special Viville scent. This, he decided, he would give to his gal, Latisha, because Willa-Mae wouldn't want such a smell in her house. Jefferson knew his mama well enough. When she caught a whiff of something like this perfume, she rolled her eyes and warned Jefferson about "loose women."

He paid a whole lot more for the perfume than he figured he ought—twenty-five American greenbacks. But it was too late to go back on the deal. The free fans were wrapped, and the Viville was already in the elephant.

"Got no money left for eatin'," he said to Harris. So they went to the French shopgirl's house for dinner and met her papa and mama and four little brothers. None of them could speak English either, but they sure were impressed with the medal.

Twenty-four men lay in the long orthopedic ward of Hospital de la Pitié on the Left Bank. This room had once been a maternity ward, the men were informed. It had the largest windows and the best view over the slate rooftops all the way to the Eiffel Tower.

The view was not much consolation to Ellis Warne. He lay on his back and traced the outline of his body beneath the sheets. His right leg was all there. His left stopped abruptly just above the knee. Why, then, could he still feel his toes? Why did he wake up in the middle of the night with a burning itch in the calf of his left leg when it was buried somewhere sixty miles away? Phantom pains, the doctor explained. The severed nerves imagined that everything was still intact and fooled Ellis into dreaming about running down a hill or playing baseball or dashing up the stairs at home.

"Are you—how do you say it—*okay*?" Theo Lindheim, the injured pilot of the German Fokker, asked.

When Dr. Smith had heard how Ellis and two others had saved the life of the German officer, he had moved Lindheim into this ward in the hope that he could help lift Ellis's spirits.

"Thinking." Ellis tore his eyes away from the stump beneath the sheet. "Wondering." He glanced at the box sent from home. "My mama sent me extra socks. You want a pair?"

Lindheim's right leg was fully encased in plaster. His toes stuck out. "Anna will bring me socks today when she visits. And she will bring you real American magazines, she says."

He was a kind fellow, this German pilot. And his wife was pretty and thoughtful as well. Ellis could tell from her clothes that Anna Lindheim was struggling financially, like everyone else in Paris. Still, when she and the little girl came to visit, they had not failed to bring some small gift for Ellis every time. When he protested, she simply said that nothing was too much for the man who had saved her Theo's life.

All of this made Ellis wonder why they had ever fought the Germans. Of course, there were political reasons. But man-to-man, none of it made sense. This disturbing thought caused Ellis to look at the place his toes should have been and wonder again about the impersonal piece of shrapnel that had torn away his leg. What a waste it seemed. How could he write home and tell his family? How could he explain what he himself did not understand?

"You tell Anna what you want, Ellis." Theo's eyes were worried. "There is the black market. She says she finds anything there."

"She can't find what I want." Ellis did not mean to sound so bitter.

Theo nodded, understanding. He whispered a phrase in German and then repeated it in English. "They make a desert and call it peace."

"I am the desert," Ellis said softly. "And I have no peace."

"I know. Some part of the heart dies when we see what we do to one another. War strips away illusion. We see what we are capable of, the pleasure in cruel victory. Before you and Birch and Max came, I lay in the mud and remembered everything I had ever done. My heart always was at war, you know? No peace, and I am telling God this . . . that I have killed other fellows, and I am not sure why. In some way, maybe, I am enjoying this war? I wonder. How dark was my heart that I must be in the dust of death before I cry out to God? Only in Him is peace. The world is a toilet."

"How are we supposed to want to live in it? Take away the illusion and what's left then, Theo?"

"Only myself . . . *yourself* . . . and what sort of man I am after I get up from the mud. For me, I have asked God to clean my heart. The world may stink, but I do not want to smell like it, bitter and filled with hate. If I am not a different man now, then I would have been better to die. You see?"

Ellis nodded. "Life is hard."

"Yes. And that is the truth of it. It always will be. You have lost your leg, and the world is still a toilet. Your loss changes nothing, means nothing, unless it makes you a better man. This is why we suffer. Like a fire, it burns the filth of our souls away."

"You are a wise man, Theo," Ellis replied, gazing at the ceiling. "It is hard to believe we were enemies. You up there, me in the trenches."

"You saved my life. We were not enemies."

"And now you save mine. Push back the darkness. Explain the flames and the changes." He shot a long look at Theo. "I hope our sons do not have to learn the same way."

"They must learn the same lessons for themselves. But I hope in a different way; I hope that the whole world will have . . . what is the word? A *sea-change*."

"Sea-change? I don't understand, Theo."

Theo laughed. "You have not heard of this? It is from Shakespeare. An Englishman." He closed his eyes, as if searching to find the words he had learned in some quiet corner when life had not yet convulsed and died. "Yes. From his play *The Tempest*." Then Theo quoted:

"Full fathom five thy father lies;
Of his bones are coral made;
Those are pearls that were his eyes:
Nothing of him that doth fade
But doth suffer a sea-change
Into something rich and strange."

Theo opened his eyes. "That is all I remember. The bones of a man drowned in the sea are changed, you see, into pearls and coral and something rich and strange. I remember how I was struck by such a thought. Now, at last, I understand it."

He looked out the frosted glass across the rooftops of hungry Paris. "Perhaps the little ones can see the world changed into something rich and strange because their fathers fought and died. . . ."

"A *sea-change.*" Ellis repeated the word as though it held some magic for his own weary heart. "A beautiful thought. Do you think such a thing is possible?"

Theo looked back at him sadly. "I saw the terms of the treaty, and I see only more tempest there. I fear for the hearts of the children who will grow up without fathers to love them. What a stench there will be from the graves if there is no love in their lives . . . if the world is unchanged by all of this suffering."

"Nobody won, did they, Theo?"

"Nobody."

THE
HOMECOMING

part two

A place is nothing,
not even space,
unless at its heart
a figure stands.

AMY LOWELL

CHAPTER THIRTEEN

Coming Home

JUNE 1919

The great troopship *America* had once been a passenger steamer running the route from England, Ireland, and Holland to New York City. This same ship had carried Doc and Molly Warne to the shores of America. Today it carried Ellis home.

Painted battleship gray, she was a weary-looking vessel now. She bore no vestige of her former elegance. Suites had been stripped and lined from floor to ceiling with metal bunks. The painted murals of Greek gods gazed down from the ceiling of the ballroom on gaunt and weary soldiers at long wooden mess tables. Where sleek and elegant ladies of society had lounged on the sundeck, thousands of young men sprawled in restless anticipation of their homecoming.

They talked of families and girls and the life they were returning to. They had fought the War to End All Wars, and they would marry and raise their children in a world where war would never happen again. Their sons would not die in trenches in France like old friends had died. It was over. Forever.

★ ★ ★

The Atlantic was calm this afternoon. The ship was smooth and certain of its heading. New York Harbor lay somewhere just beyond the horizon.

Ellis was steady on his crutches as long as the ship was steady. He made his way through the uniformed throng crowding the promenade deck to join Birch at the rail beneath lifeboat No. 8.

"Seen Max?" Ellis asked as seabirds wheeled above their heads. This was a sure sign that land was near. Could Max miss the first sighting of his beloved New York City?

"He's shaving." Birch shielded his eyes against the sun's glare. "Probably cutting himself to shreds."

"I'll give him my Purple Heart." Ellis fingered the small medal he wore for the first time today. "He can tell Irene he was hit by shrapnel." He laughed. "She'll kiss every little hurt."

The folks back home knew that Ellis had been wounded, but he had not written them everything. Half a leg was something he could not hide forever. After seven months in the hospital, he had learned to get around well enough, even though the artificial leg was poorly made, heavy, and painful to wear.

All the same, he was going home. He had joined his regiment the day they boarded the transport ship in Marseilles. In honor of the occasion, Max had produced three smuggled bottles of champagne from his duffel bag. Since neither Ellis nor Birch was a drinker, Max guzzled the lot himself and promptly threw up over the rail. He had remained sick throughout the seven-day crossing, even though the passage had been smooth and the summer breezes soft and clean. Max blamed his malady on bad champagne and remained in his bunk down in what had been the lounge of the enormous liner.

Only last night, as Ellis sat up in the dark to rub the phantom pains in his leg, he discovered that Max had not stopped with three bottles of champagne but had moved on to brandy. He had been drunk during the whole voyage. As Ellis's wooden leg dangled from the corner of the bunk, Max had confessed that he had never recovered from the fact that he hadn't clobbered the doctor who did this to Ellis. Why had he not spoken up that night the way Ellis had spoken for the German ace pilot?

To this grief, Ellis had replied that it wasn't the same at all. There was no making right what the shrapnel had done, and he knew it. So now one leg was shorter than the other. Now, counting the crutches, Ellis had three and a half legs instead of two. But he was alive, and that was because of Max, wasn't it?

This was a sobering thought, so Max had passed the brandy along to a foursome playing poker in the corridor—for a good price, of course. Then he had bought into the pool of those guessing the exact moment the ship would touch the dock. Except for the hangover, Max's recovery seemed to be complete. If only he could hold his razor steady . . .

In the distance, Ellis spotted a fishing trawler heading out to sea. They were close, very close. He propped his crutches against the railing.

Birch peered over the heads of the troops for Max. "He's got to have the worst hangover—"

"Never saw a man take the loss of a leg harder," Ellis said. He had determined four months ago that he would not let this become a tragedy in his life. Nor would he let others view him as tragic. Not his friends. Not his family back home. He would see them. Embrace them. They would laugh together again over dinner. Mama's roast pork and mashed potatoes and gravy. Something for desert. And then when he got the courage he would say, *"Oh, by the way. My leg . . ."*

"He took it hard," Birch agreed. "It ain't even *his* leg."

At that, Ellis spotted Max's clean-shaven face. Bits of tissue clung to a half-dozen cuts. His hair was still damp, and his complexion was a pale shade of green. His eyes nervously scanned the crowd. Men pounded him on the back, congratulating him that he was up for the last hour of the crossing. He spotted Ellis and Birch and raised his hat in greeting as he turned sideways and maneuvered through the press to join them beneath the shadow of the lifeboat, where it was cool.

Closing his eyes, Max drank in the air. "It will be stifling in the city."

Above them seabirds cawed.

All of a sudden Max's face brightened. "Those fellas roost on the wharf pilings," he remarked and raised his hat again. "Hello, brother New Yorkers!"

✳ ✳ ✳

Three hours before the troopship *America* was due to dock, the whistle of a great steam locomotive sounded its arrival at Grand Central Station.

It was Rebecca Moniger's first trip to New York City. Her eyes widened at the vastness of the terminal as she followed Doc and Molly Warne off the train. Their luggage was collected by a redcap porter to be transferred without inconvenience to the lobby of the Waldorf-Astoria.

Becky looked at the pendant watch she wore around her neck. "Will we be on time, Mother Warne?"

"Three hours? Certainly." Molly put her arm around the girl's shoulders.

Rebecca's pale green cotton dress was damp from the humidity and rumpled from the journey, but Mother Warne assured her she still looked fresh and beautiful. "We'll have time to go to the hotel and check in. You can change if you like."

Becky nodded, turning a complete circle as people surged around them. "But what if the boat is early? He doesn't know we're coming. Suppose he just walks off and disappears in the crowd, and then all this will be for nothing."

Doc paid the porter. "The ship will come in with the tide. They figure such things. Aye." He nodded and hefted two small valises and two hat-boxes. "We'll be there when he steps off." He laughed like a little boy. His broad shoulders and massive six-foot-three-inch frame towered over Molly and Becky. "Follow me, if you please."

Molly fell in line. If one followed Doc, she said, one never became lost. There he was, sticking up head and shoulders above everyone else. "He's been here before," Molly confided to Becky. "Medical conventions and such."

This was a comforting thought. Grand Central Station was a place to get lost in; that was certain. It was a great gallery of polished stone. High glass arcades filtered sunlight down on restaurants, barbershops, bars, haberdashers, bookshops, and gramophone dealers. There were corridors leading every direction, it seemed. Corridors for local suburban passengers and corridors for long-distance passengers. Huge mosaic cupolas towered over their heads. The din of thousands of voices hummed around them, but the smoke and the grime and the thrumming of the trains were left far beneath the shops.

Doc did indeed know exactly where he was going; otherwise they might have wandered around for three hours and missed surprising Ellis. This thought made Becky fear the place more than admire it today. After all, nothing else mattered but being at the end of that ramp when Ellis walked down. She had imagined it for months—through Christmas and Easter. Since the war had ended she had thought of nothing else.

Perhaps it had been the look on her face when Doc told her the date Ellis was arriving that had caused Doc and Molly to whisper quietly together for a moment and then invite her to join them for a week in New York at the Waldorf-Astoria. Becky had seen Philadelphia, but she had heard that even it was a village compared to New York. Coney Island. Madison Avenue. East Side and West Side. She wanted to see it all with Ellis. Perhaps if his leg was well enough they would dance at the Winter Garden. How she loved to dance with Ellis. . . .

Up the sloping ramp they hurried. There was time, plenty of time, but somehow just the thought of seeing Ellis again made them all walk a little faster, talk a little louder. Doc pointed across the vast hall to the exit marked Park Avenue. He looked smugly at Molly as though he had led them through a jungle trail instead of up a ramp. "Well, you see? Taxi's right there, Missus Warne. Unless you'd rather walk."

Molly and Becky answered with one voice. "No!" There would be time enough for walking later when they met Ellis.

A long line of black Ford taxis queued along the curb where the avenue rose to the second story of the building. A heavyset fellow who looked like a palace guard hailed a cab for the trio, bowed in royal fashion, and assisted the ladies into the vehicle. Certainly nothing like Camden's station, Becky mused, although it was a fine station as train terminals go. "But this is just absolutely the palace of all departures, isn't it, Mother Warne?"

Becky talked excitedly all the way to the hotel. By the time they reached the gilded entrance of the Astoria, the cabbie must have known everything about their visit and the surprise. He even volunteered to return at precisely four o'clock to pick them up at the carriage entrance and take them straight to the docks. Well, wasn't that just the finest thing? Their own personal taxi. So it was arranged.

"Don't be late," Becky warned in a friendly way. It would be the most terrible thing if Ellis slipped by them somehow. A disaster.

The driver nodded solemnly and raised his hand in a pledge. They would not be late, he promised, when Ellis came off the ship.

☆ ☆ ☆

"Always I have told Max to marry for love . . . but it is just as easy to fall in love with one of your own kind as it is to fall in love with—" Bubbe Fritz waved a hand in the general direction of the Italian neighborhood and then toward the Chinese neighborhood and finally toward the neighborhood where Irene lived. "So, tonight I have invited every steady customer with an eligible daughter. He'll look. He'll like someone maybe, and all this Irish foolishness will be forgotten." Her eyes implored heaven that it would be so.

"I think you are wrong, Bubbe," Trudy said firmly, turning so Bubbe could button the back of her Gimbel's uniform. It was blue cotton and of the latest fashion for 1919. This was one of the advantages of being an elevator operator at the large department store. Uniforms could be purchased at cost and deducted from one's salary in small installments. Trudy had purchased one for winter and one for summer. The high collar of her summer dress was too hot, however, even if it was pretty enough to wear to tonight's party.

"We will see," Bubbe said, humming softly. "He always admired Zelda Abraham. Such a pretty face."

"She's broad on the beam, Bubbe. You should see her in her gym bloomers. Like a sack of watermelons."

Bubbe clucked her tongue in disapproval. "She's healthy; that's what."

"Big and healthy. A regular cow."

"With money in your pocket you are wise and you are pretty and you sing well, too." Did this not settle the matter? Zelda's father was very rich. "Gym bloomers! Ha!"

Trudy knew it was no use arguing. Bubbe still believed in the old ways. She still thought that Max would come around. She was wrong, but Trudy would not convince her of that. "He will not want to come to his own welcome-home party if you don't include Irene."

"He'll come. He lives here. The party is going to be here. Besides, I am telling him that we are having a quiet little family gathering. Just *family*." Another wave of her hand indicated Orchard Street and all the clan within. "*Nu?*"

"No," Trudy said firmly. If Bubbe had wheels she would be a bus, carrying Max along to the destination she had in mind for him. Big surprise. But if Max had his wish, he'd get off the bus in a different neighborhood. One look at Irene, and he'd decide to travel no farther.

"No?" Bubbe snapped. "So, you think this girl Iris—"

"Irene."

"Iris! *Irish!* Irene! *Whatever!* You think she could ever cook for Max the way he likes? What can a girl like that know about kasheh and blintzes and—"

"It's not her blintzes he's interested in, Bubbe, if you know what I mean."

"Gertrude!" Bubbe was shocked. "Yes! I know what you mean! But how do *you* know what you mean?"

"I'm not so dumb. Man cannot live on blintzes alone, you know."

"What? What is it that you are saying?"

"Something I heard somewhere." Trudy smiled sweetly. "An old Chinese proverb, I think."

Bubbe sighed and swept a wisp of gray hair from her forehead. "This place! The golden medinah we called it in the old country. The sidewalks are supposed to be lined with gold. Instead, they are lined with Fremder."

"Foreigners."

"Yes."

"Like us?"

"If everybody was like us, then no one would be a foreigner." Bubbe sighed. "And I would not have a goyisheh granddaughter telling me to invite Irish-Iris to the party when Max is just coming back today."

"Her name is Irene. And you may invite whomever you wish. I'm just telling you Max would be happier if—"

Bubbe turned away and gathered up the bedding to hang out the window to air. "Max will be happy to see his family. It is enough. We'll talk about the other matter some other time." She sniffed, looking wounded, to let Trudy know she was going too far. "So. You are going to be late to Gimbel's?"

"Bubbe . . ." Trudy felt sorry for her, sorry the matter had been brought up at all. This was the day Bubbe had been planning since the war had ended. Max was coming home, and nothing should ruin even a moment of the day. "He will be so glad to see you." An apologetic kiss on the cheek. "Everything will be wonderful; I know."

Bubbe had not quite forgiven her, but she was trying. "He will miss you at the dock."

"Tell him I had to work. Tell him I love him and I'll see him at six o'clock. He won't notice I'm not there. Not with you around, Bubbe."

The pouting lower lip melted into a smile. Bubbe held up a stumpy finger in warning. "So go to work, already. You'll miss the tramcar, and Gimbel's will dock your wages. And hurry home after work! I'll need you to help with the food."

CHAPTER FOURTEEN

A Brother's Farewell

A swelling tide carried the *America* easily past Sandy Hook Lighthouse and into the estuary. The cloudless summer sky reflected in the water, making the surface shimmer like a pool of silver. Ferryboats, barges, and garbage scows sliced through the water. Muscled tugboats approached to guide the troopship toward her berth in the East River. The harbor itself seemed cluttered and busy, like the streets of the city.

A great cheer arose when the afternoon haze parted and the buildings of Manhattan appeared suddenly like giant stairsteps silhouetted against the glare.

"There she is." Max pointed to the Statue of Liberty.

The ship's horn bellowed along with the three thousand soldiers on the decks. Ellis saluted the statue. "Baby, that's the last time I'll see your face!"

Then the whistle and horn of every little boat in the harbor joined in the celebration of welcome. Max jabbered and pointed at each familiar landmark, but Birch could not hear a word of what he said above the roar. It was plain that Max had forgotten all about the bet he had made on the arrival time. They were an hour early. That did not seem to matter. Max would gladly sacrifice the bet just to step off the ship a few minutes sooner.

On the sundeck above, the company band struck up "The Stars and Stripes Forever." Like a double rainbow, the Brooklyn Bridge and the Manhattan Bridge spanned the river. Max was jabbing Birch and Ellis with his elbows. He looked as though he might jump the rail and swim to shore. Laughing and crying at the same time, he whooped and waved

to the distant orange elevated train as it slid through the canyon of buildings and disappeared. Birch figured Max knew the train well. The sight
affected him like the face of an old friend.

Even as Birch joined in the noisy celebration, he felt a twinge of envy
for Max. The first step off the gangway, Max Meyer would be home
among friends and family. Trudy. Irene. Birch, on the other hand, still
had a long journey ahead of him. And at the end of it, he did not know
what awaited him.

The passing months and a dozen letters from Birch had brought no
reply from his father. It was as though Shiloh, Arkansas, had vanished
when Birch's mother died. Sometimes he looked at her unopened letter—just held it in his hands and stared at the postmark.

Shiloh.

When the loneliness came roaring down on him like a great dark
night, he held the letter and remembered what home had been like.
Then he asked Max if he could borrow Trudy's letters again. Birch knew
when her school had been closed because of the flu epidemic. He traced
her path through the city as she had looked for a job. He rejoiced with
her when she began work as an elevator attendant in Gimbel's Department Store. He read her words and pretended she was writing to him.

"Forget it," Max had warned him good-naturedly. "Not your type,
pal."

When other men pulled out dog-eared photographs of wives and
sweethearts, Birch had made certain Max was not nearby. Then he removed the photograph of Trudy Meyer from the pocket Bible his church
had given him the day he left home. And he pretended, feeling strangely
proud when his fellow soldiers admired her. He did not mention that
there had been a different girl in his life before he went to war, did not
tell them the truth that she had married another man and moved to St.
Louis. Birch let them think that Trudy was his and that there had never
been anyone else.

Somehow the nearness of her home made him uneasy. What if he
saw her on the quay? If his friends recognized her from the picture,
wouldn't they expect something to happen? A kiss maybe? His decep-
tion loomed like the buildings as the tugboats nudged the ship closer to
the dock. Thousands of men and women called up to the soldiers until
every voice was lost in the roar.

Surely Trudy was down there. A second band on the wharf joined the
music on the ship. Handkerchiefs fluttered like little white flags. Families. Waiting. Everyone had been waiting for this moment, and now it
was here.

Tonight there would be a big family dinner in the apartment on Orchard Street. Birch and Ellis were not invited. There were hotels in New York. Vaudeville and theatres on every corner. "Good food and lots to see," Max said cheerfully. "Our place is like a sardine can," he had explained. "In the summer we sleep on the fire escapes."

All the same, Birch thought that Max was the luckiest man in the world today.

✳ ✳ ✳

The ship was early, to Doc Warne's chagrin. Brass bands and fire brigades and welcoming committees from every patriotic organization in New York crammed the streets leading to the wharf. The smokestack of the ship towered over the Cunard Building. Everywhere factory whistles and sirens hooted jubilantly.

"Sorry," said the taxi driver as the vehicle was forced to stop four blocks from their destination. "Looks like a full house today. Can't get you any closer."

Molly cast Doc a stern look. "We're late."

Doc could tell what she was imagining: Ellis halfway to the Victory Arch and Fifth Avenue by now. He considered the crowd that stretched in unbroken continuity between them and Ellis. "Our son was wounded on the front," he explained to the driver. "'Twill be a bit of a problem for him to walk all the way back to the hotel. Can you wait here for us?"

In this way he was telling Molly that even in this mob they would locate Ellis. All that was needed was transport back to the Waldorf. He did not doubt that they would find Ellis, and neither must she doubt it. Ellis was near. That knowledge was electrifying.

Rebecca stared pensively out the window at band uniforms and a sea of straw hats and parasols.

Doc hesitated. How could they ever find Ellis in this throng of people?

"Wounded, you say?" asked the driver. He held up his left hand, revealing three missing fingers. "Had a little scrap myself with one of the kaiser's field guns. Just a little piece of shrapnel. Sure, I'll wait."

He did not ask how long he should wait. Even as a hopeful pedestrian tapped on the glass and asked for a lift to City Hall, he shook his head and informed the fellow that he had a fare already.

"You're a good boy." Molly patted the driver on his shoulder. "An angel."

This seemed to please the cabbie immensely. He laughed loudly. "You didn't tell me. He ain't an officer, is he? Naw. Officers don't have mothers, now do they?"

Molly held tightly to Doc's coattail as he maneuvered through the mob. Becky held on to Molly's hand. "Like market day in Belfast," Doc declared cheerfully. "Without the sheep dung on me boots, but the stench is just as gruesome."

The smell of rotting fish mingled with those of sewage and garbage and sweat. How far this place seemed from home and yet how near.

Ellis was somewhere close by.

The giant loops of rope were secured to the metal cleats on the dock.

Max checked his watch. "I lost the pool. We're an hour early." He opened his mouth to say that chances were his family would not be here to meet him. After all, he had wired them a later arrival time. Then, just as quickly, his words changed into a shout. He saw Irene standing among the thousands on the quay.

Irene was taller than Birch had pictured her. She was slender and beautiful . . . as fair complected as Max was swarthy. She was standing in the front ranks of the crowd. Undoubtedly she had been waiting a long time to have such a good spot. Her pale blue dress made her look like a flower. She carried a wide-brimmed straw hat in her hand.

Birch looked at the faces around her. He had hoped to see Trudy Meyer beside her.

"Irene! Irene!" Max took a penny out of his pocket and tossed it down at her feet.

Birch kept his eyes on Irene. She did not notice the penny. Her eyes scanned the decks in search of Max.

Max tossed another penny.

This time Irene saw it. She looked down and then up along the wall of the ship, her eyes hopeful, excited. Another coin clattered onto the dock. Max shouted until he was hoarse. He flung a handful of change onto the dock. Little boys scrambled to pick it up at Irene's feet.

But Irene still did not see Max. She bent down and asked a child in knickers where the coins were coming from. A small face turned up to the lifeboat. The little hand waved to Max, who now leaned against the rail with seeming nonchalance.

And then Birch knew that Irene had finally seen Max. Tears flooded her eyes and tumbled happily down her flushed cheeks. She put her hand over her heart. Her lips formed his name silently as she waved and held her hand up toward him.

"I'll be seeing you boys," Max said quickly.

Months in the trenches together suddenly held very little importance. After seeing Irene, Birch could understand why.

Max clapped Birch and Ellis on the back. "Good luck to you! You know where I am if you're ever in New York—"

"I'll look for you on a fire escape," Birch said, taking his hand.

"So long, then." All the pallor of days of seasickness was gone. Max cut through the crush of soldiers and made straight for the mooring line.

Irene followed his progress along the quay, stopping when he stopped above the mooring cleat.

"What's he—?" voices called.

Max shouldered his duffel bag and climbed onto the rail. He reached out and grasped the mooring rope, then leaped out onto it a full three stories above the water and the wharf. As the thousands cheered his bravado, he lowered himself down the rope hand over hand. Beneath him, Irene laughed and wept. He tossed down his gear and speeded his progress into her waiting embrace.

Birch and Ellis shook their heads and applauded the passionate kiss that followed. Everyone on the waterfront seemed to enjoy this demonstration of the impatience they all felt. Everyone was grinning, thumping Max on the back, cheering louder as one kiss followed another.

And then Birch saw the elderly couple inching through the crowds. They were the only people not smiling. Their faces, in fact, were fixed in scowls. Birch and Ellis exchanged looks. They had seen the photographs of Max's grandparents. They had heard the tone of disapproval in grandmotherly letters that mentioned the "Irish shiksa" who was forever dropping into the store to talk about Max. Trudy liked Irene, Birch knew. But then Trudy, Max had told him, had not been born and raised on Orchard Street.

When Max and Irene raised their heads, Max's grandparents were there to take over. They seemed not to notice Irene. Each took one of Max's arms. They hugged him and touched his face. The old woman was weeping. For joy? Or for unhappiness that the first one to meet their grandson was this same young woman of whom they did not approve?

Birch could not help but look for the face of Trudy nearby. He patted the pocket Bible where he kept her photograph. He would know her anywhere. Why had she not come to meet Max? He wished he could see her just once, even from a distance.

Max was led away by the elderly couple, Irene trailing behind. Max looked over his shoulder at her, then glanced up toward the lifeboat in a final wave to Birch and Ellis. He did not seem nearly so happy as he had a few moments before. Instead he looked like a man being led off to jail.

"Well," Ellis said enviously. "Lucky mug. What I wouldn't give to see my family. But look at his face."

There was no real reason for Birch and Ellis to crowd toward the gangway. No reason to hurry. Sooner or later they would get off.

"Looks like it's me and you," Ellis said. "Ever seen a vaudeville show?"

"Nearest thing we come to somethin' like that was in Paris." Birch gave a whistle, then broke into song: " 'How ya gonna keep 'em down on the farm, after they've seen Pareeeee?' "

"That good, eh?" Ellis asked as men surged past them toward the gangway.

"If there'd been a pond on that stage, I'd have said those girls were goin' skinny dippin'. Never seen the likes of it."

"I knew I was missing something in that hospital besides . . ."

Ellis's voice trailed off as sunlight splashed through the shadows to illuminate a flash of beautiful red hair. *Just like the color of . . . Becky's . . .*

It was Becky Moniger, sure enough! Perched on top of an enormous wooden crate, she waved her miniature American flag.

Ellis spotted her the instant before Birch asked, "Hey, Ellis! Look at that redheaded gal yonder. Ain't that—?"

Ellis searched again. He peered across the mob below. Could it be? His eyes widened as another petite figure was hefted up onto the crate beside Becky. *Mother!* Unmistakable. Doc was just below them, frowning up at the thousands of soldiers, searching for Ellis among them.

The first rush of excitement was replaced by a sense of dread. Ellis put his hand to his forehead and stared at the crutches. The stump of his leg throbbed and chafed in the heat. More than that, he was not ready to see Doc and his mother yet. And certainly not Becky. *Not here!* He wanted a little time. He had imagined it all in detail. He had mentally written a script for the meeting and planned what he would say to them.

"Ellis? Hey, Ellis?" Birch leaned close. "You okay? You feelin' sick? What's wrong?"

"What are they doing here?" Ellis managed to say. "Why did they come?"

"I reckon to meet you." Birch looked confused. Hadn't Ellis talked about this all the way across the Atlantic?

Ellis turned his back to the dock, scanning the deck as though searching for a place to hide. *Not like this!* "I'm . . . I . . . I'm not ready for them yet. *Next* week. Next—we had plans, you and me, Birch. We got things to do." It was an excuse to cover his raw terror at the thought of being forced to spill the truth before he was ready.

"Don't worry about me." Birch nudged him. "There are a hundred fellows I can hitch along with. Go on ahead."

"This isn't the way I pictured it. *See?*" Ellis touched the crutches. He had hopes of stepping off the train at home without crutches. A few days' practice hobbling around New York would have been the ticket. Hopping on and off tramcars. Climbing stairs. Things he had not done without crutches at the hospital.

Birch scratched his cheek. "You tellin' me they don't know about this? You sayin' you didn't write 'em?" Clearly, this was news. Birch stepped back and looked Ellis full in the face.

Ellis gave a short, nervous jerk of his head. Drops of sweat coursed down his temples. "Right."

"Not a word of it to them?"

"Just that I was wounded." He looked away. "You know, I wanted to tell them myself. See their faces. Show them I'm okay."

"Well, you *are* okay, aren't you?"

"Don't feel okay." Then, "Are they looking?"

"Like hungry hens looking for a beetle in a barnyard."

"Do they see me?" He looked pained.

"You got your back to them, Ellis. How are they gonna see you in the middle of three thousand uniforms? Turn around!"

"No!" Ellis was angry, furious that they had come here without letting him know.

"You gone crazy? That there's your mama and papa. And your gal!" Birch waved and hooted at Becky, who did not know him and could not possibly hear him over the tumult. "Hey, Becky Moniger! He's *right here!*"

"Shut up!" Ellis grabbed for his crutches as though he intended to make a break for it. "I'll see them at home. Just like I had it figured!"

Birch grasped Ellis's left crutch.

"Let me go!"

Birch held on a moment longer. "Never thought you'd be a coward, Ellis." He let go and stepped back to the rail.

Ellis stood still, considering the accusation. He looked down at his boots. Just like every other pair of boots on the ship, they appeared to hold two feet. Why, then, did Ellis feel so naked, as if his stump were plainly visible? He drew a breath. His family knew he had been wounded. Crutches would not be a shock to them.

Ellis turned back to the rail. "Okay. So it's going to be sooner than later."

Birch studied him with steady blue eyes, serious and deep. "I'd give my right leg if those were my folks down there waitin' for me. You better believe I mean it. You're a lucky man, Ellis. Real lucky."

Ellis nodded, understanding Birch's heart. His great, innocent, child-like heart. "Yes. I know." With that, Ellis raised one crutch and put his hat on the tip. He hoisted it up and waved it back and forth. "Becky! Mama! Hey! Hey, Pop! Here I am!" This went on until his voice was hoarse from calling.

At last Becky's head turned in the right direction. She held the flag motionless as she checked to make certain. Then she nudged Molly's arm, and there was a small explosion on the packing crate. They hugged and hollered at one another.

Doc leaped onto the crate and followed the line of Becky's out-stretched arm. His face broke into a wide grin at the sight of the crutch and then Ellis. He raised his hands in a regular Methodist hallelujah.

The wooden crutch did not seem to detract from their joy at spotting him.

✳ ✳ ✳

"You know where to find me if you're ever in Arkansas. Keep in touch." Birch placed Ellis's duffel bag on the ground and extended his hand.

Ellis refused to acknowledge the farewell. "Stick around."

Birch spotted the massive figure of Doc Warne cutting a path through the crowd. "No thanks." He thumped Ellis on the shoulder. "Can't say it's been much fun, but I almost hate to say good-bye."

"Then *don't*!" Ellis looked desperate. "Stick around, why don't you?"

Birch replied with a shake of his head. "Good luck."

From above the hum of thousands of voices came the call, "Ellis! Ellis Warne!" The lilt of the Irish accent was obvious to Birch. It surprised him.

When Ellis turned his head to the voice of his mother, his despera-tion seemed to vanish.

Birch stepped back and merged with the crowd. One glance over his shoulder revealed the tearful faces of Ellis Warne's family as they gath-ered him in their embraces. Sunlight shone on the copper-colored hair of Becky Moniger. She looked much younger than Birch had imagined from the photograph. Prettier, too.

And Molly Warne seemed a fragile counterpoint to the obvious physical prowess of Doc. From her letter, Birch had imagined a strong-looking woman. Broad hipped and big boned, just as his own mother had been. Somehow, he had visualized Ellis's mother with the same voice as his mother. The Southern accent. The good-natured laughter. After all, were he and Ellis not brothers in the trenches? With so much in common, how could they come from such different families?

"Ah, me boy!" Doc's voice boomed out. "God be praised. Ellis. Ellis, me boy!"

Birch stopped and watched enviously behind the cover of the crowd as Ellis was embraced—and kissed—by his father. Yes. Ellis Warne was lucky. Even with one leg, Ellis had everything. Everything . . .

The shadow of loneliness settled heavily on Birch as he turned away. It would be worth everything if his own father would embrace him when he got home. It seemed to Birch that he had been waiting for that his whole life. Samuel Tucker had called Birch a lot of things in his life, but never "me boy!"

Birch touched his fingers to the brim of his hat. "Good-bye, then, Ellis," he muttered. Maybe Ellis was uncertain of his future, but Birch knew at a glance that everything would be fine for the tall, lanky baseball player. Ellis and Becky would probably bring forth an entire baseball team. Nine little sons, eighteen churning legs to run the bases for Ellis. Love was worth more than two legs. Birch did not pity Ellis Warne. He envied him for having the kind of love that carried a man on its shoulders when most everybody else had to crawl.

That thought suddenly transformed into the sickening reality that his own mother was gone. And there would be no kiss from his father when he got home. Birch put his hand to the pocket with Mama's letter. For an instant he thought of finding some quiet place and opening it. Did he not deserve a welcome home like Ellis? a quiet voice? a loving word to help him walk forward when his very soul lacked legs or arms? Mama would have some word for him, something to help him get past this terrible moment of realization that he was coming home to nothing.

He unbuttoned the pocket and touched the corner of the envelope.

"Hey, Birch! Birch Tucker!" Carl Carver yelled to him from a group of men who were also alone today on the quay. "Come on, if you're coming!"

There were a lot of two-legged lonely men around. More like Birch than Ellis. So they would band together, see the sights of New York City alone . . . together. Leave the lucky men like Ellis Warne to their imagined problems. What difference did it make if Ellis had left a small piece of himself back in France? He had a whole family here.

CHAPTER FIFTEEN

Wounded Heart

The same bands and speeches that had already greeted nearly a million returning soldiers reverberated over the noise of the crowd, and Ellis seemed to want to hear them all. While his family watched and wondered, he called out to other uniformed men. He congratulated his comrades. He cheered and wept when "Hail, Columbia" was played. He displayed all the outward signs of joy, yet Molly knew that her son was not joyful. Not entirely.

Ellis looked everywhere but into her eyes. He pretended not to notice that Becky was here. Once his gaze locked with Doc's. Something passed between them. Something that relayed an unspoken message man-to-man that all was not well. That a dark shadow stood at Ellis's shoulder. That he had changed. He was no longer a boy. His face displayed the pain and suffering of manhood thrust upon an unready heart. Doc somehow sensed it. Perhaps he understood it better than Molly.

A quick look at Becky and Molly realized Becky did not understand the change at all. She looked up at Ellis's face. She smiled hopefully, as if urging him to look at her. To notice that she had come all this way just to see him.

Doc clapped his son on the back. "We've got a cab," he explained over the din. "The driver was wounded in France as well."

This news seemed to make Ellis eager to get to the waiting vehicle.

He climbed into the backseat behind the driver. All the way to the hotel the two veterans chatted as though they had known each other in the trenches. Ellis appeared to have more in common with the wounded cabdriver than with his family. It was as if the whistle of artillery shells had dimmed the fond memory of home. Ellis still had not said more than two words to Becky, and that had been only to ask after her folks and then to ask when her brother Howard would be discharged from the service.

Molly glanced at Doc, who was frowning at his son's outstretched leg. Ellis leaned on the back of the cabbie's seat and talked about Marseilles and the French people and the English soldiers. His face was animated as the two shared memories of the war.

Then Ellis looked at Doc. He caught the curious stare in the direction of his stiff and clumsy leg. The smile faded. Ellis grew silent and sullen. He let the driver do all the talking as he stared out the window at the deepening shadows of approaching evening.

"We've brought you presents from everyone," Molly said with strained cheerfulness.

"That's nice," Ellis replied without enthusiasm.

"I've got a whole valise full of things from back home," Becky added hopefully. "You're a hero to them, you know." She reached out and touched the Purple Heart medal.

He drew back as if she had struck him. "If you had waited another week, they could have given the stuff to me in person," he snapped.

Becky's mouth formed a silent *oh*. She looked away quickly at the men and women walking along the crowded sidewalks.

"Ellis!" Molly reprimanded him. "Whatever—?"

Doc placed his big hand on hers and gave a gentle squeeze, warning her to silence. What did he know that she did not? This was so unlike Ellis. Not like him at all! She felt angry at him. Did he not know what it had meant to Becky to come to New York to meet him? They had talked about it and giggled about the surprise like schoolgirls. They had imagined his delight. Envisioned kisses and laughter and bright conversation. If he had nothing to tell them about, then could he not at least ask questions about home? real questions about the place and the people he loved?

Like Becky, Molly grew silent. She smiled, but her eyes were shadowed with questions and unspoken reprimands for this stranger, her son. *How can he treat us this way?*

Doc joined in the conversation with the driver. They spoke of President Wilson's plan for the League of Nations. The restructuring of Europe and the new order of the old world. None of these things meant anything to Molly. She didn't dare meet Becky's gaze, lest they both burst into tears of disappointment. Ellis was not glad to see them, after all. It was more than weariness from a long journey, more than months of war. Something had changed. Something was missing, which the cheerful letters from France had not indicated. *We have made a mistake coming here,*

Molly thought as she watched the eyes of Ellis look everywhere but at her and Becky. She felt frightened.

"The ladies have a hankering to eat supper at Delmonico's," Doc said in a patronizing tone. "Shall we humor them? Or would you rather stay close to the room tonight?" Then he added quickly, "We got you a room of your own. Thought after so many months of company you might enjoy being alone for once."

Molly could tell Doc was trying hard not to look at the leg. She wanted to reach out and touch it, as she had touched a hurt place when Ellis was a child. Could this be the reason Ellis acted so distant?

"Sure, Pop. Dinner. Okay, but . . . just not real late, huh? You know, I'm sort of tired and—"

The driver chimed in. "Name the time and I'll drive you where you wanna go. How long you gonna be in New York? I can show you the whole town. I'll give you a real up-close tour."

Molly and Doc exchanged looks. A week in New York guided by a war veteran? They would never have a conversation with Ellis. He would talk about generals and officers and the mud in the trenches with the familiarity of the fields back home on the farm. Men wounded and maimed seemed to be the main topic of interest to Ellis and the cabbie.

The cabbie held up his hand, once again displaying the missing fingers. "It ain't the same when a fella comes home like this. My gal took one look, and off she went to marry a fella who spent the war in a file room, and here I am. One of the lucky ones, too. Leastwise I got a job."

As he waved his mutilated hand toward the sidewalk, Molly nearly gasped. Suddenly New York seemed filled with beggars. Young men, blind men, they stood beside the entrances of Manhattan's subway stations to beg. Here and there, Molly spotted other examples of the Great War's tragic consequences. A young man no older than Ellis pushed himself with his hands on a wooden pallet with wheels, weaving through the legs of pedestrians.

"That there's Legless Eddie Trahan," offered the cab driver. "Lost 'em in the Argonne. You and me, we're the lucky ones. He was married to a nice girl, too. But she just couldn't take it. It ain't the shrapnel that wounds us—"

Again the hand rose. "Nah. It's the women. They can't take it." He wheeled the vehicle into the covered carriage entrance of the Waldorf just as Legless Eddie scooted around the corner and up to the uniformed doorman of the hotel.

"Here we are," the driver said cheerfully.

Had he noticed the pall of silence that descended on his passengers? Molly wondered.

"You want I should pick you up?" the cabbie asked.

"No, thanks," Ellis said with a cracking voice. "I want to ride . . . the subway. I knew a guy who worked on the subway. Got himself killed in Meuse. I want to ride the subway. See what he was talking about, you know? The real world . . ."

The two clasped hands and exchanged looks of understanding. Doc paid the driver and tipped him extra for his attention, but Molly knew that Doc was relieved to get out of the taxi. She certainly was. As for Becky, she had not said a word for blocks.

Ellis climbed out, steadied himself on his crutches, and hobbled toward Legless Eddie, who carried a bundle of newspapers on the back of his pallet. Eddie sold a paper to the doorman and then to a man in a white linen suit. Then he spotted Ellis in his uniform. His eyes lingered on the crutches and the stiff leg for a long, curious moment. Once again, wordlessly, a look of understanding passed between the two, excluding everyone else.

Ellis took a dollar from his pocket to purchase a three-cent edition of the *New York Times.* "Keep the change," he said under his breath.

"I ain't a beggar," Legless Eddie said.

Then Ellis pulled up the cuff of his trousers a fraction for the crippled man to see . . . *to see what?* The fabric fell back.

Legless Eddie nodded and pocketed the full dollar. "Thanks, brother."

It was over just that fast. They entered the lobby of the hotel, and Becky tried again to speak to Ellis. "That was kind of you, Ellis. Thank God you came home whole."

For the first time he looked at her full in the face. His expression was first one of shock, then withering anger. He did not reply.

Becky stepped back from him in fright and turned away, as if looking for a place to run. Her freckles stood out on her pale skin. "I . . . I'm going for a walk," she said hoarsely.

"Becky?" Molly called after her. "Rebecca?"

"Let her go," Ellis growled. "Let her go *walk!* Let her stretch her legs."

Ever since the troopship carrying the 369th regiment back to the United States had come within sight of the Statue of Liberty, Harris had spoken of nothing but his Harlem home. Jefferson had already decided that he wanted to see the most fashionable black neighborhood in America, but even as the two friends stood on the platform waiting for the train, he pretended to be unconvinced. "I just don' know. I really oughta be headin' on home."

"Man, you got to see it," Harris urged. "You can't leave New York to go on back to Podunk, Arkansas—"

"Pisgah," Jefferson corrected.

"Pisgah, then. Like I say, you can't go without seein' Harlem. Man, why there's more perty gals there and better eatin' and sweeter music than anythin' this side of heaven. I used to think where I come from in South Carolina was special, but that was before I seen New York."

Jefferson surveyed him with a skeptical eye. "Before I left home, my mama told me to keep clear of the big, wicked city. 'Jefferson,' she said, 'New York's worse 'n Babylon. It be Sodom and Gomorrah.'"

Harris looked offended. "Why, man, what she talkin' 'bout? I ain't fixin' to drag you into no back-alley joint. We talkin' high-tone stuff—nothin' but the best for PFC Jefferson Canfield, the man what got the Légion d'Honneur and got kissed by Marshal Pétain besides."

Jefferson self-consciously fingered the red ribbon of the medal hanging around his neck. "I think I oughta at least take this off."

"What for?" objected Harris. "You a for-real hero, and that medal is proof. You wanna dee-prive the perty gals of their chance to see a for-real hero?"

"Ah, lemme be, will you? I feel like I stand out a mile already."

The six orange cars of the elevated train pulled into the station. "Here we go!" whooped Harris. "Hundred and twenty-fifty, and Apollo Theater comin' up."

The train car they entered was not crowded, and this far from uptown, the riders were all white. "Step to the back of the car," growled a fat white man in the uniform of the transit authority police.

Harris immediately bristled and started to shoot back a reply, but Jefferson's big fist closed around his elbow and squeezed it hard. Harris closed his mouth. He gave the patrolman an angry stare, but the two soldiers moved to the rear as instructed, and the train jerked into motion.

As they did so, they found the rear seats occupied with packages. Harris bent down to shift the parcels onto the floor of the car.

"Hey, boy," the guard demanded. "What do you think you're doing?"

"Ain't no place to sit back here," Harris objected. "I'm just movin' these boxes outta the way."

"You just let those packages alone."

"But we paid to ride same as—"

"You better not be taking an uppity tone with me, nigger," warned the guard, "or I'll just have to throw you off."

Again Jefferson gripped his fellow soldier's arm. "Harris," he urged, pointing out through the dingy glass windows, "tell me what I'm lookin' at here. Last time I came through New York it was dark, an' I didn't see nothin'."

A greasy-looking white man with a stubble of beard was sitting across the aisle from a skinny, pimple-faced boy. Each was taking up two seats in the row just ahead of where Jefferson and Harris were now standing. In an overly loud, whining voice, the man remarked, "I told you no good would come of letting those people put on uniforms. Didn't I say that, Cecil? I told you they would put on airs and forget their place, didn't I?"

"Sure did, Uncle."

"Take a waiter or a garbageman that knows where he belongs, and I'll be the first to say that he's a credit to his race. Haven't I always said so, Cecil?"

"You always have, Uncle."

"But you take that same waiter or garbageman and give him a uniform, and the next thing you know, he gets the idea he's a soldier and he forgets his place. Isn't that right, Cecil?"

"Mister," said Harris, puffing up, "you talkin' about us?"

The patrolman bustled importantly to the rear of the car. "What's the trouble here?" he said to the greasy white man. "Are these niggers annoying you?"

"What?" burst out Harris.

Jefferson stepped between Harris and the officer. His huge frame towered over the pudgy patrolman, who retreated a step. "We don't mean to cause no trouble, Officer. My friend here is takin' me to see his home. We is just back from the war."

The patrolman stepped up close and unleashed a blast of garlic-laden breath in Jefferson's face. "Just back from the war, huh?" He scoffed. "Did you do a real good job carrying the honey buckets out to the latrines? Is that what they gave you that shiny piece of tin for?" A forefinger like a short, fat sausage flicked the Légion d'Honneur medallion. "Hey, that feels heavy like a real medal. What is it?"

"It means he's a hero, you—," spouted Harris, practically climbing over Jefferson's back.

"Prob'ly stole it, don't you bet, Uncle?" commented the pimple-faced boy.

"Well, it can't be a real combat award," agreed the greasy man. "They didn't let niggers do any of the fighting. Everyone knows that they would turn and run at the first shot."

"So where did you steal this medal?" demanded the policeman. The officer's chubby palm closed around the decoration. At that moment the train pulled into the next station, and at the same time, Jefferson Canfield grasped the patrolman's wrist in his powerful grip.

The officer gave a sharp intake of breath.

In the softest of voices, Jefferson said, "Will you 'scuse us, sir? I believe I'd like to walk some, so we'll just get off here."

The patrolman nodded slowly, his face pasty white.

"Come on, Harris," Jefferson said. "Tell me some more stories 'bout this here town."

As the two soldiers stepped off the train, Jefferson removed the medal from around his neck. Folding the ribbon carefully around it, he tucked it into his shirt pocket and buttoned the flap shut.

The rattle of jackhammers echoed in the street. Becky stood at the curb and stared bleakly at passing cabs and tramcars. She did not know where to go. Back home? It was a short ride to the train station, but all her luggage was upstairs. She did not want to risk the chance of running into Ellis. He had humiliated her enough.

She was hurt—hurt enough to be angry. This was not the man she had fallen in love with. Ellis Warne had not come home. This was another man who looked like Ellis. She brushed back tears of anger before they had the chance to escape and course down her cheeks. Let him have his army buddies and gruesome memories! After one hour she had decided that she was quite finished with this new Ellis. She would wait a while, gather up her luggage, take a cab back to Grand Central Station, and trade in her old ticket for passage back home this very night.

A taxi pulled to the curb in front of her. "Where youse headed?"

"Ohio."

"Don't go that far, lady." He grinned and eased back into traffic.

"You're leavin' him already, eh?" a man's voice mocked behind her.

Becky turned toward the voice. Pedestrians hurried past, but she saw no one who might have spoken to her.

"Down here," said Legless Eddie from his pallet. His tweed cap was pushed back comically on his tousled hair. He wore a red-checked, short-sleeve shirt, revealing muscular arms. His hands were wrapped by protective rags. Khaki trousers were cut off and sewn shut to contour the stumps of his legs at midthigh. He was grinning cruelly up at her. The same bitter look flashed in his eyes as she had seen on Ellis's face.

Becky met his challenge with anger. Who was he to meddle? "We already bought one of your papers," she snapped.

"Yeah, well, sister, I got some free advice."

"I don't remember asking."

"You dames. All alike, ain't you?" He rolled closer, cocking his head to glare up at her like a petulant child. "Think you can't be happy unless you can dance at the Rainbow Room, huh? A fella gives everything and comes home to the likes of you." He pushed himself backward, then spun around in a wheeled solitary dance of his own. "I left tall and came back short. My old lady wanted a tall man. So I'm out. I dunno about you dames. At least your man has one long leg. Still tall, ain't he?" His eyes narrowed bitterly. "But that ain't enough for youse, eh?"

Becky blinked at him dumbly. "What? What are you saying? Not enough?"

"Gotta have a man with two legs, huh?" Another spin. Eddie's wheels clacked on the cracks of the sidewalk. "You gotta hear two feet walking down the hall."

"What? Two—"

"Yeah, lady." His brown eyes flashed resentment. "Don't tell me about it. My old lady ain't no different. I was sellin' papers when I left for the army. I'm still sellin' papers. Only my wife left me, too." Another spin, and he spat at her feet. "He don't need no Purple Heart medal. God just give him a broken heart." Eddie cursed beneath his breath and, with a deft stroke of his hand, whirled and rattled off to disappear behind a forest of legs.

Becky stared after him. What a wretched little man he was—no wonder his wife left him! Who could live with such bitterness? And what did his situation have to do with Ellis? A leg wound was not an amputation. She was leaving Ellis because his heart had come home mutilated, not his body. Now she was too angry to cry. She had heard that New York was full of busybodies. First the taxi driver, and now this. . . .

In that moment, Becky decided what she would do. Her bags were upstairs, still packed. It had been a terrible mistake to come here. She walked back into the hotel and presented her key to the bell captain. "I am checking out," she proclaimed regally. Then she wrote a note to Doc and Molly. A kind note, but a firm one. Surely they would understand. . . .

Thirty minutes later Becky was back at Grand Central Station with a new ticket in her hand.

CHAPTER SIXTEEN

On the Edge of the World

The quiet family supper Bubbe had described did not materialize. The store and the flat above it were packed with friends and neighbors when Max arrived home. The table was covered with all sorts of food. It was clear to Max that the occasion had taken some planning. Irene was not included in that plan.

Bubbe introduced him as her "war hero." Applause and cheers boomed out.

Max replied that if being a hero meant surviving, then he was a hero.

There was an endless round of questions. What did he intend to do now that he was out? Would he go back to the university? Would he take over the store? Max answered each question a hundred times, it seemed. *Enough!* He did not know exactly what his plans were. But what he did not say was that those plans did not include Orchard Street.

By nine o'clock, Max looked desperately at Trudy. Every window and door in the place was open, yet the noise and heat generated by the pack of bodies were unbearable.

Trudy had not enjoyed more than one embrace and a few words with Max since she got home from work. She was grateful when Max took her hand and led her away from Mrs. Fleischer's Yiddish conversation.

He led her into the bedroom, out the window, and onto the fire escape. A short climb, and they were on the roof. The tar was still soft from the heat of the afternoon sun, but even so, it was much cooler up here. Certainly quieter.

Max leaned his elbows on the ledge, looking toward Irene's neighborhood. His face was tense. Exhausted. "Bubbe had this all planned out, didn't she?"

Trudy joined him to look out at the city lights. "Of course." She put a hand on his arm. "For weeks she's been planning. Baking. Cleaning. You know."

"But Irene couldn't come." He frowned. "I get it. Bubbe didn't mean *family* . . . she meant *this*." He waved a hand over the neighborhood. "Only this. Only *us*. Only Jews."

Trudy wanted to tell him he was taking it too hard. It was just the way of things. "You know what they all call me around here?"

He looked at her questioningly.

"I am a Fremder. Missus Fleischer taught me the word. It means foreign. Listen, if I wasn't your cousin, I would not be invited."

"Lucky you," he said, drawing a deep breath. "All night long they've been asking me what I'm going to do now. Am I going back to school? Yes. Am I going to take over the store?"

"No," Trudy answered for him. Max was also Fremder.

"You're right." Again he glanced toward Irene's street, also a row of redbrick tenements. "I'm getting as far away from this place as I can get," he said defiantly. "They think I want to raise my kids like this?"

He cursed and spat. "I've spent the last year and a half listening to insults because I was born a Jew. And I'll tell you this, Trudy, I'm sick of it. I'll beat them at their own game. Someday I'm going to marry a nice little goy, and if she isn't welcome here, then I won't be either."

He turned his face to where the distant lights of Times Square illuminated the underbelly of the clouds. "There's a life out there for us." He cracked his knuckles. "So, I've been wanting to say that all night." He grinned apologetically.

"I thought so," Trudy said lightly. "I wanted to tell Missus Fleischer that. It would send a shock wave from here to the Bronx if they knew how you felt."

"They'll know soon enough." He looked her in the eyes. "So, how have you managed to survive our tight little world without me?"

"It's been difficult at times," she admitted. "But lovely other times. I don't belong here." Laughter floated out from the window below. "As a matter of fact, I don't know where I belong. But it isn't in this world."

"When you've had a taste of the other—"

"A taste? I'm like ham in a kosher butcher shop. I get along better with the Irish and Italians at school."

Max laughed.

She grinned. Max had always said, *"Nobody gets along with the Italians."*

"Does Bubbe know?" he asked.

Trudy shook her head in amusement. "She would lock me in my room." She leaned in. "I didn't tell her that at home I go to the Lutheran church."

A shocking revelation indeed, she realized. How many sons and daughters of Orchard Street had ever been inside a church?

"Good for you." Max thumped her on the back. "Just keep it to yourself until you're on your way out, eh?"

Trudy nodded, relieved that Max had taken her confession in such a lighthearted fashion. "Well, all this is just to tell you that you and Irene have my blessing."

He did not reply. They stood side by side for a time, as if waiting for his thoughts to come into line and march through his brain in an orderly fashion. At last he turned his attention to Trudy. "What about you?"

"I have a teaching position."

"Congratulations. Where?"

"Home. Fort Smith, Arkansas. At the same school I attended."

He raised an eyebrow. "The edge of the world."

"No." Trudy pointed to the street that divided the Irish from the Jewish neighborhoods. "*That* is the edge of the world. I fell off it a long time ago."

He laughed again. "As they say in this world, *Mazel tov.*" He kissed her lightly on her forehead. "The name of your school?"

"Belle Grove. Every other girl at the university who got a position is teaching at Woodrow Wilson. All in different states. Every new school and a heap of old ones are being named after the president."

"A *heap*?" Max grinned. "I had a friend in the trenches who used that word."

"That is an other-world synonym for *many.*" She shrugged, grateful Mrs. Fleischer was not near to hear her. "My Southern students will understand me. To a child they will." She put on her best teacher's voice, stern and implacable. "Y'all are about to be in *a heap* of trouble!"

Max laughed. "Very convincing. So what else have you learned?"

She smiled. "To keep my mouth shut." She looked past him to the slim figure of a woman waiting in the shadows across the street. "And I *will* keep my mouth shut," she promised. "Irene is waiting."

"You're a champ, True." Max kissed her again and climbed down the metal ladder to the alley. Trudy could hear his footsteps as he walked quickly to meet Irene.

Bubbe's voice called out the window, "Trudy? Trudy? Max? Are you out there?"

Trudy did not reply. A few more calls, and Bubbe went back to tend to her guests. Trudy would wait a minute longer, then slip into the house. If her hands were elbow-deep in the dishwater, no one would expect her to know where Max had sneaked off to. His secret would not be a secret for long. Maybe it wasn't much of a secret, anyway. But Trudy knew this was the last party that could be thrown for Max unless a certain young lady from the other side of the street was also invited.

It was advertised as "the sauciest star and the brightest music play! MITZI! Starring in *Head Over Heels!*"

The George M. Cohan Theater was packed with American soldiers tonight. Birch figured he was the only sober one in the place. How the walls remained standing with such noise was a miracle. The song-and-dance men sang and danced, but Birch could not hear their voices above the hoots and laughter. He could not hear their shoes tapping against the stage. When the dancing girls came out and hopped across the runway, even the orchestra was lost beneath the din.

The place was hot, smelling of sweating men and sour beer. Birch's head pounded with the drumming of boots against the floor. He might have been the only sober man in the place, but he figured every hangover tomorrow morning would not match his headache tonight.

He left the theater unnoticed and unmissed by his comrades. A blast of cool air hit his face as he walked onto the sidewalk. It was raining. He raised his face gratefully to the drops and let the rain wash away the smoke of a dozen cheap saloons.

Forty-second Street glowed in the night like a summer afternoon. The tall buildings remained lit, turning the mist golden. Every sign and marquee glittered with color. The entire alphabet blinked and rolled and tumbled above him. The raindrops seemed to be colored red and green and yellow as they fell through space to reflect rainbows on the wet pavement. The black, shiny surfaces of the taxis looked as though they had been dipped in paint.

To his right, Birch saw a large group of soldiers staggering across the street. They hailed a smaller group to the left. The entire company was out to tear down New York tonight.

"Come on," someone called. "We're goin' to the German district to pound on a few Krauts. Hey, Birch! Birch Tucker! Come on!"

Birch turned away, pretending not to hear. He had pounded enough

Krauts already. He'd had his fill of American doughboys as well. He thought about Ellis. Lucky Ellis. And then he thought about Max. He wondered if they still slept on the fire escapes when it rained on Orchard Street.

With that, he hailed a taxi.

"Where to, bub?"

"Orchard Street," Birch replied. He had surprised himself at his answer. He couldn't just crash in on Max's family, especially not at eleven-thirty at night. What was he doing? "Orchard Street," he said again more firmly.

"Got a number?"

Birch took out the photograph of Trudy. He stared hard at her dark, sensitive eyes. He looked at the address but could not bring himself to tell the driver. "No address. I just want to see Orchard Street."

The driver cast a look at Birch. "In the rain? In the middle of the night? Ain't nothin' open on Orchard Street this time of night. I know a couple of night spots—"

"No thanks." Birch settled back against the seat and let the breeze wash over him. "I've got friends there."

The driver mumbled, "Big place . . . ain't gonna find them without a number. . . ."

* * *

Trudy finished the dishes and slipped onto the fire escape to wait for the first welcome raindrop. Laundry and bedding had been brought in for fear of the storm. Orchard Street was a quiet ship with sails all furled.

Beneath the streetlight on the corner, Trudy could see the shapes of Max and Irene as they talked together. Irene stood with her back to the pole. Max faced her, his hand braced above her head. The perfect posture for a kiss, Trudy mused. As if Max heard her thought, he leaned down and kissed Irene. The world lay in shadow, yet Max kissed her in the glare of the streetlamp. All of Orchard Street would be talking about it tomorrow. Bubbe and Zeyde Fritz would hear about it, and there would be a discussion over dinner tomorrow night. Max would be angry. Bubbe would weep loudly and slam doors. Zeyde would cluck his tongue and blame himself because he had let everything go to pot the moment he kept his store open on Shabbat.

Max kissed Irene again, more hungrily. She smiled up at him and put her hand against his cheek. Then he took her hand and pulled her out of the spotlight and into the shadows of the pickleman's awning. Orchard Street had seen enough.

Trudy had no doubt as to the outcome of the argument. There would be a wedding. Not a Jewish wedding. Maybe not even an Irish wedding. Probably something in City Hall. The government was pretty neutral about such things. As long as Max could pay for a license, who would care what street he lived on?

Lightning suddenly lit the street like a photographic strobe. Irene had her back to the wall of the pickleman's store, her arms twined around Max's neck as he kissed her passionately. The couple did not seem to notice the light. Thunder rumbled through the street. Maybe they thought they were causing it. Trudy envied them. Perhaps there was heartache in their past and ahead, but Trudy envied their love. Max would marry Irene and make it all right.

Trudy sat down on the iron grate and dangled her feet over the edge of the platform. She took off her shoes and pitched them through the dark window of her bedroom. The air began to cool with the breeze that was scented like rain. Trudy gazed at the shadow where Max and Irene were. She knew she was prying, but she rather enjoyed it. She hoped for another lightning flash, a quick photograph of the lovers. This was much more entertaining than the theatre, Trudy thought, wiggling her toes.

"Trudy?" Bubbe called from inside. "Where are you?"

"Out here."

"It's going to rain."

"I hope so." Would Max and Irene notice the rain? Trudy had never been kissed in a way that would make her forget being drenched in a rainstorm. It was just her luck that she had spent four years in New York while the war was on and all the best males had been in Europe. Now that everyone was coming back, she was doomed to return home. In her entire life she had never met a boy back home who made her want to get kissed in a thundershower.

"Come in!" Bubbe poked her head out the window and inhaled deeply. "You'll get wet."

"It's so nice out here, Bubbe," Trudy protested. Then another strobe of lightning illuminated the street. Irene. Max. Did Bubbe see them? A raindrop splashed on her cheek.

"Yes, I see," the old woman said wryly. "So now I know why there is such a storm brewing." She cuffed Trudy gently. "This is not polite. He has been gone a long time. So he needs a few kisses—even if they are Irish kisses. Now come in and quit spying on Max."

This was surprisingly tolerant of Bubbe. Not what Trudy had expected at all. "Yes, Bubbe," she said quietly.

"The world is upside down," said Bubbe. "Who am I that I can keep everybody in their own neighborhoods after such a war?"

Everything was different. That was certain. Trudy felt it tonight as she climbed in and sat beside the open window in the dark. The rain fell heavily on the street, cooling the air.

✬ ✬ ✬

The cab turned from Rivington onto Orchard Street. Rain was falling hard now, sluicing over the cobblestones and making wakes around the tires.

"You sure you want to get out here?" asked the cabbie, extending his arm to touch the rain and then pulling it back quickly.

"Right," said Birch, taking one final look at the back of Trudy Meyer's photo. He tucked it into the lining of his hat and paid the driver.

"But you got no specific address?" The driver sounded worried. "You know, if you want to see the place, the best time is during the day." He waved a hand over the empty street and the dark buildings. "Ain't nobody out in this tonight."

"Thanks," Birch said as if none of that mattered. He tipped his hat and leaped out onto the puddled sidewalk.

"You want I should wait?"

"No thanks," Birch said from beneath the canvas awning of a shop.

With a shrug, the cabbie reset his meter and launched off down the street. Birch took refuge from the rain in the recessed entrance of a shuttered shop. This was nuts, he knew. Every fire escape was empty. The open windows of the upper-story flats were dark. Streetlights looked fuzzy behind the curtain of rain.

Birch told himself that he was only here to see the street where Max lived, to satisfy his curiosity about the place. The truth was, he half hoped to find the lights on above Fritz's Dry Goods store. Maybe some sort of open house had developed. Perhaps strangers had been pulled in off the street and offered sandwiches and cider. *"I just happened to be in the neighborhood. . . ."*

Rain patted the canvas awnings and swished down the gutters where pushcart owners and street vendors haggled with housewives in the daylight hours. Birch looked up at the apartments and imagined all the people inside, people he had come to know through Trudy's letters and Max's lively description. Tonight it seemed an ordinary place. It had fueled his imagination for months, but in the middle of the night, Orchard Street seemed unremarkable.

The halo of a streetlamp reflected on a shopwindow. Birch stopped to examine the gold letters. Hebrew letters, strange little marks that looked like upraised hands and little dancing people. Suddenly Orchard

Street resumed its sense of mystery. Here he was in a transplanted Jerusalem.

He had known all along that Max was Jewish, but this was the first time he'd realized that Max was *different*. Everyone who lived here was different from Birch. He was a foreigner, trespassing in their sleeping world. Max had meant it when he said that Trudy Meyer was not Birch's type.

Birch stepped back and searched the facade for a number. A regular English number. It was cut into the stone face: 75. Birch turned slowly and squinted through the rain to the brownstone building across the street. There in plain English was the name Fritz's Dry Goods. Signs stenciled on paper and hung in the window read Bargains! Bargains! Bargains!

Above the awning the windows of the flat were open. Birch stepped back in the shadow, lest someone peek out and see him gaping.

From Trudy's correspondence, Birch knew that she looked out on the crowded street from the window on the right. That was her bedroom. Lace curtains stirred with the breeze. Was she awake in there, he wondered, listening to the rain on her roof?

Max's words again came back to Birch: *"Not your type, pal."*

He wished he might have heard her voice, met her just once. Her letters were so full of life, like the stories from a book. He would have told her that, if he could have met her. He would have told her how the things she wrote had made them all laugh when life was so bleak in France. He would have said she ought to be a writer because she would make a good one.

"Not my type," he said aloud. A heaviness filled his heart when he realized he would never meet her. And if he had? What difference would it have made? They were from opposite worlds; that was for sure. Max had not been joking, after all.

Birch glanced to the right, to the left, then up at the window before dashing across the street. Ducking beneath the dripping awning of Fritz's store, he pressed his face against the glass pane of the display window. He scanned the dark shapes and shelves and imagined what it was like to work in such a place where people spoke in words written with little dancing letters.

There was the cash register that sometimes smelled like herring. There was the table of fabrics where Bubbe and Mrs. Fleischer stood and gossiped for hours. There were a hundred stories Birch had heard. He regretted the ten thousand that he would never hear. Trudy's letters were the one thing Birch would miss about the army.

She is just upstairs. . . .

A drop of water snaked down the wooden brace of the awning and dripped on his shoulder, like a cold finger tapping him. He looked away from the store and scanned the sky for the glow of lights. A few blocks from here he could find a cab.

He touched the brim of his hat in a silent farewell and splashed back across the street to head for Rivington. Just a few blocks away was a different world, a world where Trudy and Max were considered trespassers.

Grand Central Station was surprisingly quiet this night. Lightning flashed beyond the great glass arcade. Thunder bellowed like the artillery Ellis had written about. Raindrops drummed peacefully against the panes of glass. Alone on a long wooden bench in the vast hall, Rebecca Moniger had never felt so miserable.

She checked her ticket. The midnight express. She would have a few hours of sleep in a Pullman car, and then her sister Violy would be there to meet her. Becky had already wired her and told her she needed to stay a few days in Philadelphia. Since she and Ellis were finished, she might get a job in Philadelphia. After all, what was the point of going home?

Certainly Doc and Molly had gotten her note by now. Becky had half expected to see them come marching into the station after her. But they were probably too busy dealing with Ellis tonight. He had been rude to everyone, hadn't he? She raised her chin defiantly, certain she was making the right decision.

The clack of shoes and boot heels echoed against the polished marble floors of the station, reminding Becky of the words of Legless Eddie. What was it he had accused her of? Needing to hear two feet coming down the hall? What nonsense!

She stood abruptly as the memory filled her with fresh resentment. Gathering her hatbox, she fixed her gaze on the showcase window, where a window dresser was changing the shoes of a male mannequin. He whistled as he removed the molded foot of his subject and slipped the brown-leather shoe onto it.

The PA system bellowed, *"Midnight Express to Philadelphia now boarding at Track 22!"*

That was Becky's train. She did not budge. There was something about the mannequin and the shoe. . . . Becky shook her head, trying to clear her mind of the memory of Legless Eddie's face. What had he been saying to her?

The window dresser evidently mistook her gaze for interest in the shoes. Holding the shoe and the detached foot up to the light, he tied the laces and seemed to admire the merchandise.

He was no longer whistling. He stooped to show Becky the shoe and the foot. *"You like it?"* he mouthed. Then, with a wink at Becky, he replaced the foot. The illusion was complete. Effective.

Becky stared hard at the shoe and then at the rigid pose of the store mannequin. A glimmer of realization sparked in her mind and then faded.

Could it be?

Was there something Legless Eddie knew that she did not yet know? Why had Ellis raised the leg of his trousers ever so slightly?

"Thanks, brother," Eddie had said to him.

"He couldn't keep that a secret," Becky muttered aloud. "He wouldn't . . . *would he?*"

Suddenly Molly was standing there beside her, also looking at the leg of the mannequin. She took Becky's hand as the window dresser removed the second foot and repeated the procedure. "Becky?" Her voice trembled. The truth hung heavily in her tone.

"Why didn't he write us?" Becky said miserably.

"Doc is talking to him at the hotel. He broke down when we got to the room. Doc knew from the first minute he saw him come down the gangway."

"Of course."

"He said he wanted to tell us at home. On his own terms, I suppose. He was not ready for today."

"Should I leave?"

"Oh no, darlin'. His heart would break!"

"I've broken it already." Becky covered her face with her hands. "I told him how glad I was he came home *whole!* Oh, Mother Warne! What a *stupid* thing to say!"

"Not at all." Molly patted her gently. "He did indeed come home whole. His soul has two good legs, does it not? Unless he lets the devil rob him of one of 'em." She shook a fist at the air. "And the Lord will not allow that. Neither shall his mother, I'm thinking. Nor his dad. Nor the woman who loves him!"

Molly reached out and drew Becky into a wordless embrace, and the two women stood hugging each other and weeping.

Finally Becky pulled back and looked into Molly's eyes. "What should I do?" She looked in vain for a handkerchief to blow her nose.

"We can stand here and drip, I suppose." Molly sniffed. "Or we can go back to the hotel and have a proper cry, thanking God that Ellis is with us. Sure, and that's what I'm for." She lifted Becky's chin. "You should give Ellis a chance to see your face all blotched and puffy like this." She managed a smile. "Then you can know if he really wants to marry you!"

CHAPTER SEVENTEEN

Escape from New York

Trudy's carpet valise lay open on the bed. She was taking very little home with her from New York. This one small bag contained all her clothing. A second box was jammed with books and tied securely with twine. The books were much more precious to her than three blouses, three skirts, two pairs of shoes, and underclothes. She looked at the book box and wished she did not have to send it all the way to Arkansas in the freight car. She kept out two volumes to read on the train ride. Tennyson and Dumas would keep her company on the long journey.

The window was wide open, but the heat of Orchard Street was nearly unbearable. Max sat cross-legged and barefooted on the narrow bed. "You can't stay in New York for the summer?"

Trudy gave him a sarcastic smile. "Everyone wants to get out of the city for the summer. There are more New Yorkers in the Catskills right now than the entire population of my home state. Why don't *you* come with *me*?"

"Things to do," he said, looking out the window and across to the tenement building on the opposite side of Orchard Street. "I have planned my escape carefully."

"You make Orchard Street sound like a prison," she chided.

"To me, I guess it is. Tenements. Poverty. I hate it." He smiled. "I intend to become very rich."

"What is it Bubbe says? *Tova toireh mikol sechoireh.* 'The Torah is the best merchandise.'"

"You've been on Orchard Street too long. I'm not talking about that kind of riches."

She laughed. "You're right. I have been on Orchard Street too long. But I do know what makes people happy here is not money."

"That's for sure. Nobody has any."

"Why don't you just marry Irene tomorrow and settle down? Be happy. I expected you to be married by the time I left."

"We're going to wait. I want to have something to offer her besides this." He waved a hand around the tiny cubicle of the room. "Indoor plumbing would be nice."

"I saw the way you kissed her. That did not look like a 'wait' sort of kiss to me."

"You been spyin' on your ol' cousin Max, have you?" he drawled with a Southern twang. "Is that nice?"

Trudy shrugged. She really was worried. There was more going on than a few innocent kisses. "I like Irene." Trudy frowned. "Last fall at the library she came to my table. We talked—"

"Last fall? Before I was home?" His eyes narrowed.

"She said she was worried that you wouldn't want to—"

"I'll make an honest woman of her . . . eventually. But I told her right up front, I'm not getting married until I can walk out of this place and never look back. I've been honest with her. As honest as a man ever is with a woman."

"You know she loves you. She would do anything for you."

"I was counting on that to make my life bearable. It's not like I'm taking advantage of some naive girl without a clue about the facts of life."

"No. You taught her all about that before you left, didn't you? So now you're back and going to pick up right where you left off."

Max glared at her. "I *said* I intend to marry her! Just not before you get on the train tomorrow night. Okay, Cousin? If you will come back in years, you can be a member of the wedding party." His tone had become heated, like the air. "We should drop this."

"Sure." She folded a blouse and placed it in the top of her valise. Tennyson followed and then Dumas. Trudy was angry at Max, but she had not known until now that she was angry. When Irene had told her about what had happened, Trudy had been sickened and sad. Now she was angry. Would the whole dreadful scene be played out again? She had not expected Max to put marriage on a back burner after everything that had happened between him and Irene.

"Well . . ." She closed the valise.

"I do love her," he said miserably. "How much do you know?"

"The doctor in Newark."

"A baby would have ruined her life. She would have had to drop out of school."

"She wanted the child. You didn't even tell her what kind of doctor he was, what he was doing. She said she woke up and it was done." Trudy's indignation was renewed. "A German-speaking doctor."

"She's a teacher now."

"I'm surprised she doesn't hate you, Max. I would. Irene didn't even know about such things."

"She finished school and got a position. That wouldn't have happened if—"

"If she had married you then and had a baby?"

"I was going to a war. No guarantees. You think I would want to die and leave her with that sort of burden?"

"You mean with your child?"

"A kid to raise . . . here . . . alone. I did what I did *for her*. See?"

Trudy glared at him, wishing the subject had not come up. "You're not only selfish, Max, you're a liar. You did everything for Max. For yourself. Just like you're making her wait until you're ready to settle down. And all the while you're climbing in her window and into her bed. Back home we have a name for men like you."

He considered her coolly, his resentment clear in his expression. "What are you going to be when you grow up, Trudy? A marriage broker or a rabbi?"

"A nun in a convent, if you're any sample of the kind of man I might get."

The racket of Orchard Street could not penetrate the silence between the two. Max remained on the bed. Trudy stood in the center of the room with her hands on her hips. How had this happened? She hated it.

"Well, I guess I know why you're not sticking around."

Trudy sank to the bed. "No. I'm not sticking around because . . . I promised Papa. You know that. Oh, Max." She was sorry she knew anything at all.

"You think I haven't thought about it? felt like a bum?" He stared at his hands as though they had blood on them. "You're right. She didn't know anything. I mean nothing . . . about anything. Not how babies got made—"

"Or got rid of."

"I didn't even know about that. A guy at the university told me about this doctor, see?" He ran his fingers through his hair. "Me. The Romeo of Orchard Street, right? And Irene said she thought something was wrong. So I found this doctor in Newark and took her there. He told me she was pregnant, but he could take care of it for a price. Said she wouldn't have to know. She wasn't even sure herself about the baby, see? So I told him to go ahead. If she didn't know, then what did it matter? It was a simple procedure. A few hours later we were in the car, ready to leave. She cried all the way back to the city." He looked pained. "She figured it out. Nobody had to tell her. She just woke up and knew he did something. And then she knew that there had been a baby." He stared out the window. "What a way to grow up."

"So you're both all grown up, is that it? Are you going to do the same thing all over again, Max?"

"I've been away a long time. You don't know what it's like for a man."

"You haven't learned anything."

"We're being careful."

"You haven't grown up at all."

"You can't expect me to be some kind of priest," he snapped. "Celibate. Not after everything—"

"Marry her, then."

"Did she put you up to this? pressuring me like this?"

"You know her better than that."

"Do I? You sound just like her." He mimicked, "'Max, let's get married now. Please, Max, I can't live like this. . . .'" He scowled. "Well, I'm not ready, I tell you. I can't finish school and support a wife and a kid at the same time. I won't do it! I have better things to do with my life. I told her last night I'll send for her—"

"Send?"

A curt nod. "I didn't waste my time in Europe. We were there months waiting for demobilization after the war ended, you know. Time enough to look around. The universities there are—"

"You're leaving?"

"You know the grades I got at Columbia. Oxford University was impressed." He removed a folded letter from his pocket. "I got my acceptance yesterday. A fellowship. Economics and journalism."

"You're leaving Irene here?"

"There's no other way. She understands that. Why can't you? If I am going to make something of my life—don't you see?"

Trudy took the letter from him and scanned its contents. Suddenly it all made sense. But that did not make it right. The fellowship included room, board, and tuition for an unmarried male. A small stipend was also included. "She knows?"

He nodded. "She agrees with me."

"Can she do anything else but agree? You've made up your mind."

"There's risk in this for me, too. What if she meets some guy while I'm gone and—"

"That one won't fly, Max." Trudy passed him his letter. "All the time you were away, even after what you did to her, there's nobody for Irene but you. You know that." She sighed and looked at her valise. "So, when are you leaving?"

"Soon. Next month, in fact. Oxford for graduate school . . ." He gave a slight smile. "Irene is okay about that."

"A month seems like a long time. She'll have you that long, anyway." She was secretly hoping that time could change his mind. Maybe by then he would not want to leave. Anything could happen in a month.

"I don't know what's right anymore." Max's eyes grew sad. "I saw guys get blown to pieces—lives ended, ruined. And I got to thinking that there are worse ways to end your life than dying. Orchard Street . . . the slums. It seems like a living death to me. I've seen what this place can do to people who start out in love. Everything withers and dies here. Irene's mom had seven kids. She was gorgeous once. I saw her picture. She died at forty-seven. Poverty does that. It breaks the spirit a long time before the body dies." He glanced up at Trudy. "I thought about that a lot over there, see? There's got to be something more. The night I got home, I knew . . . even love dies in this place."

"You think money keeps it alive?"

"Maybe. Or maybe it just makes life easier." He wiped beads of perspiration from his forehead.

The conversation had made Trudy suddenly weary. Evidently Max had told her everything he needed her to know. Unlike Irene's confession, his had been full of contradiction and self-justification. Not a confession at all, but an argument with himself.

Now he smiled. Handsome, clever Max. He could do anything he set his mind to, she thought.

"You want to go down for an egg-cream soda?" he asked. "We'll toast love, if you want. And long life."

✳ ✳ ✳

The driver of the hansom cab held the reins loosely in his hands as the horse made yet another circuit around Central Park. The older couple, claiming exhaustion, had been dropped off at the Waldorf an hour ago. The soldier had only just gotten around to putting his arm around the young lady, and that had been at her urging.

"It's a bit chilly, Ellis. Who'd have thought it could be chilly? I left my sweater at the hotel. Do you mind if—?" She snuggled against him, holding his hand in hers, and with the skill of a kitten curling up by the fire, she slipped beneath his arm.

Night after night the driver was witness to all varieties of romance.

Tonight he could tell the young soldier was as stiff as his game leg. He needed help. The red-haired lass at his side was doing her best and was sure to win the game—unless it began to rain first.

"Our last night in New York," she said dreamily. "Will you miss it, Ellis?"

"No." He answered without even a hint of romance in his voice, and there she was, waiting for a kiss. A pretty thing she was, too, her hair done up in tortoiseshell combs, her hazel eyes wide and gazing raptly up at him. The driver could see them reflected in the shiny polished brass of the lamp on his coach.

What was the boy waiting for? Their last night, after all. How long had she been working on him? Here he was, as stiff as a stick.

She looked away, hurt written on her face. The soldier gazed down at her with longing . . . then glanced quickly away before she turned back to him and lifted her mouth to be kissed.

"Well, I will miss it. It has been the most exciting time I have ever had. Think of it. Three Broadway shows, not counting *The Pirates of Penzance.* Fanny Brice . . . I enjoyed her most of all, I think. Of course, it is probably nothing for you after you've seen Paris—"

"I saw Paris only out the window of the hospital ward. No, it's not that. . . . It's just I've been thinking about home . . . and things. You know. Wondering what I'm going to do with myself now."

"Well, you'll just get on with it. And we'll just go ahead—"

"We need to talk, Becky. I mean, really talk about this. Maybe we need . . . you need . . . time to think about what you're getting."

"I have thought. I've thought of nothing else but you. I don't want any more time to think."

"You want to be married to a man who has a yule log for a leg?"

So that was it. The driver frowned and tried to remain unmoving in his perch. The top of the crutches lay against the seat. This girl was not the sort to let a fellow go over such a matter, though. The driver prided himself in knowing human nature. The girl would not let go, but the soldier might well let her go—out of a false sense of nobility.

"Do you think that matters to me?" Her voice was sweet and honest in reply. It did not matter to her that the man she loved had one leg.

"Don't tell me you didn't notice that I couldn't walk to the top of the Statue of Liberty."

"Listen—even if you had two legs, that was not something I plan on doing a second time in my life. Next time we take the lift to the top, provided they have it fixed, or I'm not going up there at all. It half killed your mother, that climb. If that's what's bothering you, you can just forget it. Besides, I know plenty of people back home who have been married for years and years, and they have never even *been* to the Statue of Liberty. That's not part of the marriage vows, as far as I have heard."

The driver smiled. *Very good.*

The soldier appeared a bit stunned, as if considering how she had managed to switch the matter of a missing leg to marriage vows and climbing to the top of the Statue of Liberty.

"There's more to it than that." His voice cracked. "Yesterday Dr. Remington, Pop's friend, said they botched the surgery. Said it looks like a veterinarian did it. And it won't ever be right unless I have another operation. That will mean months . . . months more for recovery until they can fit me with a proper prosthesis and I can walk."

"Well then . . ."

"Three months at least at the hospital. Then home. I won't be starting back at the university for more than a year. So—"

"So then, we'll just have to—"

"Wait. You see."

"No! We'll just have to get married right away!"

"Becky, you don't understand—"

"If we get married right away . . . well, what difference will it make? You know I'll be at your side every minute no matter what happens. If we're already married, then I can take care of you properly, can't I? It's much better this way," she insisted. "You will need a wife to care for you. To love you. There are things a wife can do that even a mother can't."

The driver wondered if either one of them knew how true that statement was. He grinned, scratched his chin, and clucked the horses to a faster gait. If he hurried, they could just make the bridge before the issue was settled. The bridge was the most romantic place in the park for proposals and such. And this was certainly an unusual one.

The soldier's voice grew more thoughtful. "I spent months in a military orthopedic ward. You don't know what you're saying."

"I don't want a whole ward full of men. I want you."

"You've never even seen . . . you don't know. Dr. Remington says—"

"There is your yule log." She rapped on it and gave a giggle. "But this is your leg." She touched his leg right above the knee. "You can feel that, can't you, Ellis?" She smiled up at his chin.

"Rebecca . . ."

"I was wondering if you had lost sensation everywhere else, too." She leaned against him. "You've been so standoffish."

"I didn't want to . . . presume that you would—"

"You've hurt me, Ellis."

"But that is exactly what I did not wish to do!"

She was a bright one, this girl. The driver privately congratulated her.

The bridge was just ahead, and she had her young man where she wanted him.

"Then you should have trusted my love for you. You should have believed in me. When you asked me to marry you, my heart was yours forever. And now you are trying to send me away, trying to pretend that I do not love you, when in truth you do not love me any longer." She bowed her head and sniffled very realistically. The hand remained on his leg.

"Oh, but I do love you! Becky, please . . . I was trying to think of you, of your life with me." He picked up her hand and held her fingertips to his lips. "You must know how I feel about you. Every minute I thought of you! No one else . . ."

The horse slowed automatically as the carriage approached the bridge. There was something magic about this place. Streetlamps reflected in the water. Crickets and frogs joined in a hallelujah chorus as Ellis took Becky in his arms and kissed her properly. For the first time all night she was speechless.

Then he said, "Let's not wait," as if it were his idea. "I don't want to wait, Becky. Tell me you'll marry me as soon as we get home. Say yes, please!"

"Yes," she replied in a dreamy voice. "Please?"

Ellis kissed her again. They did not notice when the carriage made another round of the park. And when at last the hansom cab pulled up to the Waldorf, the driver only charged Ellis for two hours, donating the last half hour to the cause of patriotism.

CHAPTER EIGHTEEN

The Preacher from Pisgah

Max had gotten his old job as a waiter at Luigi's Place three days after his return. Trudy suspected that Irene had timed her visit this afternoon so he would be gone when she slipped up the stairs to Trudy's room.

She carried a small box tied with a blue ribbon. She offered it almost shyly to Trudy.

"Should I open it now, or—"

"Now, I think." Irene remained standing beside the open chest of drawers.

Trudy patted the bed, and Irene sat down beside her to watch as Trudy unwrapped the going-away gift. Inside the box was a whistle, suspended from a black-velvet ribbon. Not just a cheap nickel-plated thing like the ones in the box in the store, but a heavy-plated whistle of the sort used by gym coaches, teachers, and Irish cops on their beats.

"It's a whistle," Irene said.

Trudy resisted the urge to reply to this statement of the obvious. "It's wonderful." She slipped the ribbon around her neck. "I shall use it proudly whenever my little hooligans get out of line on the playground, and then I shall think of you."

"My uncle is a copper," Irene said with a smile. "He got me one when I graduated. I've needed it, too, teaching at the Bowery. Comes in handy when a person needs to break up a brawl."

Trudy laughed at the image of delicate and beautiful Irene tweeting a copper's whistle in the middle of a fight. "Better than taking a broom to them, I imagine."

"Oh, I've done that a time or two as well." She was serious. This was a new side of Irene, quite unexpected. "But usually the whistle works well enough. The little beggars know the sound of a copper's trill and scatter to the four winds when I blow." She frowned. "I don't know what coppers' whistles are like where you will be teaching. Maybe the effect will not be as good."

"I'll write and let you know," Trudy promised. She hugged Irene.

Then, to her surprise, Irene began to cry—very quiet tears, of course, nothing anyone down in the store could hear.

"What? What's wrong?" Surely these tears could not be because Trudy was leaving.

"You're a sweet girl, Trudy," Irene said. "That's all."

"I'm glad everyone doesn't bawl because I'm sweet." She took Irene's hands. "But what is it . . . really?"

Irene looked at the closed door as though she hoped no one was on the other side. "Max didn't like it that I told you. And I'm sorry I did. . . . I didn't mean to make him look small or bad in your eyes."

"I know that." Was this the real purpose of the visit? To talk about Max?

"He was afraid you would think ill of him. I would not have that for anything. And I want you to believe me about that. He is a good man, Max is. Else, why would I love him so?"

Trudy did not let go of her hand. "Max is just Max. I know him."

"He was trying to do what was right. Right for both of us." The tears stopped and Irene drew herself erect. Here was the old familiar pose that Trudy had always admired in Irene. "He says—and I agree—no marriage until he can do right by me." She frowned. "And I wanted you to know—someone should know—I told him that he can't . . . I won't . . . I told him last night that until we are married—"

"Good for you." Trudy exhaled loudly. "No wonder he is so angry."

"For a while I thought we were just going on as it was before. But then he got his letter, and he's leaving. And I thought about what would become of me if anything happened like before. It frightened me, Trudy. I would not want to live if he wanted to take me to another sleazy doctor."

"You've made the right choice. Stick by it. Tell him I said so. And when he gets fresh, just blow your whistle. Call the coppers."

Irene laughed softly. "Oh, Trudy. You would do something like that, wouldn't you?"

Trudy thought for a moment. "I don't know. I've never loved anybody like you love Max. But it seems to me that love, real love, should not hurt like this. Don't let him hurt you, Irene. It's hurting him, too, if you do. Just walk away—run away from him if you have to—but don't let him ever hurt you like that again."

Irene was listening, really listening.

Trudy made a face. "Now Max will really be mad at me for telling you that."

"But you're right." Irene embraced her again. "And I will do my best to be strong."

They talked of other things then, changing the subject easily to teaching and children and the Bowery school where Irene taught. Trudy wrote out her address and tucked it into Irene's pocket. The two women embraced again, and Trudy walked Irene past the cool eyes of Bubbe Fritz and down to the corner of Rivington for the last time.

Grand Central Station was thick with the uniforms of thousands of American soldiers. Within days a dozen troopships had docked at New York Harbor and spilled out their human cargo to whoop it up in the great city, but now the fun was over. Discharge papers in their pockets, every man had the same thought at nearly the same moment: *Catch the first train out of New York bound for home.*

Birch Tucker was one among those thousands who crammed together beneath the roof of Grand Central. He slept sitting upright, wedged between a sailor from Kansas and a marine from Montana.

Most of the previous week, Birch had slept and eaten at the YMCA with several hundred other men who had decided against returning to the nearest army barracks for shelter. Once he had considered returning to Max's place on Orchard Street to beg for a bed on the fire escape. That would have been less crowded, he was certain. All the same, he stuck with the YMCA because the free movies that week included performances by Mary Pickford and Douglas Fairbanks, his favorites.

In the daylight hours he had ridden the subway and the El. He had taken the ferry and climbed into the riveted brain of the Statue of Liberty. He had seen Times Square and Harlem. The folks of Harlem spoke with easy Southern accents and made him homesick. He had left there, gathered up his duffel bag, and come directly to Grand Central Station.

His final impression of New York was that it was just another battlefield. He had shell shock from the constant rattle of jackhammers and the blaring of horns and sirens. His family's farm could easily have fit beneath the dome of the train terminal. Shiloh could have fit within two city blocks. But New York had nothing on Shiloh, Arkansas. Birch wanted only to escape from this enormous place . . . never to return.

There was no direct route to Shiloh, of course. It had taken the ticket agent longer than usual to work out the details, but now Birch slept peacefully with a thick packet of tickets and transfers in his pocket. He was going to see a lot of country on his way back to familiar territory. He would be required to change trains at least a dozen times, but eventually he would get home.

Maybe that knowledge was why he slept with a smile on his face, or maybe he smiled because in his sleep he still believed that Mama and Bobby would be there to meet him when he stepped off the train. In his dreams he heard the rapid ticking of insects in the brush. The cotton was tall in the lower field. The jingle of mule harness blended with the squeak of wagon wheels. The James Fork Creek drifted slowly by, and trout darted from the shelter of the rocks. A hawk cried as its shadow swept across the open ground. Mama called from the back porch as Birch and Bobby climbed the limber birch trees and rode them down to earth again. Clear and loud, the bell of Shiloh Church rang out from over the hill.

Birch raised his head to the sound. Why was it ringing? Was it Sunday? What did it mean?

His head jerked up and the dream vanished. He opened his eyes in confusion for a fraction of a second, then remembered. *New York. Grand Central.*

How many men just like him were having the same sort of dreams? He looked at the clock at the far end of the hall. *Almost 11:30 in the evening.*

How long had he been waiting? sleeping?

He frowned and shook his head clear.

And when did his train leave?

"Final boarding call for Baltimore, Washington, D.C., and—"

Birch jumped to his feet, waking the sailor and the marine. He snatched up his duffel and fumbled for his ticket as he ran for the far corridor. That was his train they were calling!

"Track 29! Baltimore . . . final—"

★ ★ ★

Far down in the bowels of Grand Central Station, the engine of the huge locomotive boomed like a bass drum echoing against the iron rafters of the train shed. It was hot in the crowded second-class car. Trudy released the latch of the window and shoved the pane down so she could hear Bubbe's final instructions.

"And don't speak to strange men!" The old woman shook a stubby finger in warning.

Trudy was surrounded by men. Strange or not, soldiers were

crammed onto the train like sardines in uniform. She was practically the only female on the train. Bubbe was clearly worried by this unforeseen development. "I won't, Bubbe," Trudy assured her grandmother.

Beside Bubbe, Max smiled and winked. "Can she talk to the ones who *aren't* strange, Bubbe?"

She glared at him and cuffed him on the shoulder. "They are all Fremder!"

All foreigners, she was saying. Not a common sight on Orchard Street. That meant they were definitely a threat to Trudy.

Trudy's main concern was that the entire train full of passengers smelled like the barrels of herring that she walked out of her way to avoid. But there was no avoiding several hundred unwashed Philistines all on their way home to somewhere. And she could not hold her breath all the way to Fort Smith.

This might well prove to be the most difficult ordeal of my entire New York adventure, she thought grimly as she tried to fill her nostrils with the scent of locomotive exhaust.

"*Final boarding call! Track 29 . . . Baltimore, Washington, D.C., now departing. All aboard!*"

Bubbe removed a hankie and began to weep profusely. Zeyde Fritz tried to comfort her. His gray hair stuck out from beneath the cap he wore. Trudy fought the emotion she felt. Who could say when—or if— she would see her grandparents again? And Max would be leaving for England. His whole life would be changed when she saw him next.

Bubbe was blubbering loudly, as she did at weddings or funerals. "Tell your mother . . . kiss your mother. . . ." The list of instructions was endless. Including when to eat the corned-beef sandwiches and the potato salad, and in what order the food in the picnic basket must be consumed. There was enough packed to last her all the way to Fort Smith, but it had to be eaten right or she would get sick. Imagine getting sick on a moving train full of goyim. *Oy!*

Trudy nodded and nodded. Then she looked deeply at Max. There was so much she wanted to say to him. She wanted things to work for him and for Irene, for them to find true riches. . . .

The train shuddered. Behind Max a handful of tardy passengers made a mad dash to board. "Wait! Wait! Hold it! Don't leave yet!"

How could the conductor squeeze even one more person on this train?

"We're like a jar of pickles in here," Trudy called, laughing so she wouldn't cry. "Oh, Max!" The drivers hissed and spun against the steel rails, and the train began to move.

"Trudy!" More of Bubbe's tears spilled over. "Be careful!"

Trudy reached out to touch Max's fingers. "Tell Irene—"

"Irene?" Bubbe scowled.

Trudy ignored her grandmother's indignation. "Bless you both, Max. Be . . . good to her!"

"What?" Bubbe was asking. "What is she saying? Irene? The Irish?"

"Good-bye, Bubbe, Zeyde," Trudy said loudly. "I love you both. Thank you! I'll write! Thank you for . . ." But she knew her voice was now lost beneath the thunder of the huge engine, the hiss of steam and churning of wheels against the tracks.

Max raised his hand in acknowledgment. Yes. He had heard Trudy. His heart had heard her wish for his happiness with Irene. He mouthed, "*Love you*" before a cloud of steam rose to conceal the little group from her.

The train moved out from the shelter of the station. The lights of the city gleamed like ten thousand earthbound stars, marking the outline of the place some felt was heaven and others, hell. Cool night air slipped in through the open window, ruffling her hair and cleaning out the heavy stench of sweat.

"Good-bye, New York," Trudy whispered. She was not unhappy to see it slip out of sight behind her.

✯ ✯ ✯

"Sorry, son." The conductor led the way down the swaying corridor of the crowded car. "There's just not another seat on this train except for back there." He waved a hand over the heads of sleeping soldiers crammed into the seats of the second-class car. As the last man to board the train, Birch was plainly out of luck on this leg of the journey. "The last car is supposed to be reserved just for coloreds, but there are a few white men back there, too. Nothing to worry about once you get used to—"

"It's okay," Birch replied gruffly to silence the man. "We were all together in the trenches. I reckon a railcar on the Baltimore and Ohio ain't much worse than that."

Apparently the conductor didn't know much about trenches. To his way of thinking, the coloreds' car was his personal no-man's-land. "I send one of the colored porters in there to collect the tickets. Don't go in there myself. I promise you the minute someone gets off one of the forward cars I'll reseat you, son." He patted Birch on the back.

Birch bristled. "That's mighty white of you," he drawled.

"Why, thanks. I do what I can for our brave boys." Clearly the conductor had not caught the edge of sarcasm in Birch's voice. He yanked open the door and stepped aside for Birch, who ducked beneath the frame and turned sideways to enter the narrow, decrepit third-class car.

Men were sprawled everywhere, sleeping on the wooden benches and the floor, leaning on one another or sitting erect in exhausted misery. Duffel bags were stuffed onto a rack above the seats. Birch swung his bag up toward the dim ledge and found that men had made the luggage rack a bunk as well.

Toward the very back wall of the car, three white soldiers were talking quietly among themselves. Their eyes darted toward Birch as he entered. The aisle was blocked by slumbering soldiers, so Birch sat down in the only available space beside the door. He held his bag on his lap like a child and scanned the car for a place to stash it. Unlike the second-class car, this had only one light—a lantern swinging from a hook above the aisle. In its light, Birch could see the chipped and flaking paint. Graffiti scratched into the wood beneath the window read *J.B. loves K.R. '92.*

The inscription made him smile. This car had probably been old even in 1892 when J.B. had carved his love for K.R. into the windowsill. The Baltimore & Ohio Railroad Company had pulled this old wagon out of retirement, the conductor had explained, to meet the needs of the present transportation shortage. No doubt that meant the thing had been pulled off a rubbish heap somewhere and plunked back onto the track without anything being fixed, except the lantern. Birch could see that the lantern was new. It gleamed in its own light, reflecting in a cracked window that seemed to be stuck halfway down. Moisture had seeped in between the double panes to fog the grimy glass. There would be no sightseeing out windows like these.

He crammed his duffel beneath a nearby seat. The movement made the sleeping giant next to him stir, raise his head, and sink back down into sleep. Birch crossed his arms over his chest to keep them out of the way. Then he, too, let his head fall forward as the rusty wheels clanked over the rails toward Baltimore.

The face of the enormous black man sitting across from Birch was lost beneath the shadow of his military hat brim. Was he sleeping or awake? Birch could not tell. He fumbled in his duffel for the railroad timetable, opened the thin booklet, and squinted at the tiny print in the dim light.

"Eighteen stops 'tween New York an' Washington." The deep, mellow voice floated from the shadow. "You ain't gonna be back here in this car no time 'fore some white man gets off and they come take you on up.

That conductor's scared to come in here with us, though. Porter told me he's scared on account of the race riots." The man laughed.

Birch laughed with him. "Don't look to me like you fellas are ready to riot."

"Naw. We done that in France. A hundred and ninety days straight, we was in them trenches. Them Germans was scared of race riots, too, after we got through with 'em." There was an amused pride in the voice.

Birch thought how unjust it was that a man who had spent nearly two hundred days in the trenches would come home and be treated worse than baggage by the railroad company. So he saluted smartly. "You got me beat. Ninety-two days for me, with time off for good behavior."

Another deep, resonant laugh. "That *proves* you ain't black. So how come they put you back here with us steamer trunks?" He stomped his big boot on the floorboards, letting Birch catch a glimpse through the cracks. Wheels sparked against the tracks. It was a frightening sight.

Birch gulped and looked away. "You guessed right. No room up there."

"Guess they don't know all about Jim Crow, do they?" The big man smiled briefly. "If there wasn't room back here, I bet they wouldn't be takin' me up there with the white folks."

Birch did not respond. The thought may have been expressed with a smile, but it was true, nevertheless. Returning home from the honors of France to the Jim Crow laws of segregation must have been a startling jerk back to reality for the men in the antiquated railcar.

"Where you headed?" Birch asked.

"I'm goin' home. Arkansas. That is, if the floor don't give out 'tween here and there."

"Thought you might be from somewhere round my home. I'm an Arkansas boy, too."

"Well, don't that beat all!" The black man stomped his foot in pleasure at the coincidence. Once again the sparking rails glittered.

"Whereabouts is your home?"

"I'm steppin' off this chicken crate in Fort Smith, and I ain't gettin' on another train ever, no matter which war they want me to fight." The Samson of a man looked as if he could have taken on the kaiser's army single-handed. "Don't live right in Fort Smith. We gots a farm out about a day's walk."

"You don't say?" Birch settled back. "Our place is over in Shiloh. You know Shiloh?"

"See it some from afar off while I was huntin' up in the Poteau

Mountains. Huntin' possum with my pappy. We looked right down over Shiloh, seen the cotton fields and—" he closed his eyes to envision it— "a creek . . ."

"That's the James Fork! Our place backs right up to it, right in the bend there where it comes around." Birch laughed. "Big row of birch trees at the south end of the field."

"That y'all's place?" The man gave a big laugh and another stomp of his boot. "Why I *know* that! Them trees look like a white picket fence down there. Ain't no other trees like 'em nowhere. My pap took a look and says to me, 'Jefferson, some man's done planted them trees so everybody would know where he begins and ends. Somebody might move a boundary stake, but ain't nobody moving them trees without an ax.' So that there is y'all's place!"

"I used to look on down the row and plow straight for one of those trees." Birch was suddenly more eager to be home than he ever thought he would be since Mama died. "It'll be good to see them trees again."

"I reckon." The big man nodded as though he was visualizing the place. "Pretty. But you ain't seen pretty till you seen Mount Pisgah."

"Yeah? You from Pisgah?"

"We got a cabin right at the foot of Mount Pisgah. Canfields been sharecroppin' in the same fields since after the war."

By "the war," Birch knew the big man was talking about the Civil War.

"My granddaddy built the cabin and the barns. We got hogs in the bottom. Hmmm."

"Hogs in the bottom" was a way of saying he had it good down there in Pisgah. Birch knew what he meant. "I think it's about the prettiest country in the world," he agreed.

"Heaven ain't so pretty, I reckon. I told the Lord I wasn't in no hurry to get to heaven and sharecrop His place till I had a chance to get back to my own. And my kin. You see how He pays attention to me? A hundred and ninety days in the trenches, an' I'm still livin'. I figure I owe the Lord a heap of good crops for that."

"Got a wife?"

"Nope. But I got me a big-footed mama who's gonna kick me back to France if I don't marry my gal real quick." His white teeth glinted in the shadow. "Got me a big family of sisters all still livin' at home. You?"

Birch shook his head. "Just me and my pa. I'm hopin' he'll be glad to see me home—at least to help him out choppin' the cotton. Can't say I miss that much, though."

"I cain't wait to feel that dirt between my toes. I missed the plowin' and the plantin' and the pickin', too. Simple things a man can understand. I had enough killin'. Just want that old farm."

"Well then." Birch stuck out his hand. "They call me Birch. Like the trees. Birch Tucker. You got a name?"

"Jefferson Canfield. Sometimes they call me Preacher."

"Preacher?"

"That's what some folks back home call me sometime. Preach and farm, that's what I want."

"The Lord gonna want cotton, corn, or cane?" Birch challenged.

"I reckon He'll be wantin' souls." His head came up slowly. " 'The fields are white unto harvest,' He says. An' I intend to do some pickin'." He nudged the hat brim up with his thumb so Birch could see his features. "I seen you at the front, brother."

"That so?"

"That friend of yourn give me the pigeon."

Birch laughed with pleasure at the small memory. "Glad to see you made it. How's the bird?"

"Died doin' his duty for his country. Saved my life, that bird did. Let him down a dugout, and he come up floppin' from the gas. I reckon y'all saved my life."

"You know, we almost took that bird away with us. Glad it was some use."

"Yep." Jefferson gave a deep nod. "So I reckon I owe you somethin'. You reckon?" He smiled broadly. "Are you saved, brother?"

The question made Birch laugh again, made him feel good all over. Nobody had been much concerned about his soul since he had left home. Certainly he had not heard the question phrased in that Southern down-home manner since he left Shiloh. It was like saying, *"Welcome home, son."*

"I'm saved," Birch replied.

"That's real good. I prayed for y'all when that bird up an' died. Thought you was angels." He laughed, slapping his thick thigh with his hand. "Then when I seen you come on in here, I was thinkin' maybe Jesus put you in here so I could help you get saved. Praise God." The hand raised in joy. "Maybe He's got some other reason."

"You got a church, Preacher?"

"Just the cane field an' the cotton field an' the cornfield. Preach an' plow. Chop an' preach. Ain't nobody gonna walk out on me. Every row is filled." He leaned in close. "The Lord showed me while I was in the trenches—rows of men with chains, men ripe for the pickin'. Don't need more church than that."

"Indeed you don't. You make me homesick for my church in Shiloh. It ain't like those big churches in Europe. Big empty barns. Naw . . . she's little, but she's full up."

"Praise God," said the Preacher. "Well, maybe I just came across you to say thanks. Thanks for the bird that saved my life so I can do His work. Tend them fields."

As the train slowed to stop at Plainfield, the brakes squealed loudly, making any more conversation impossible.

The porter poked his head in the car and motioned to Birch and the three other white soldiers. "Conductor says you come on up now. There's plenty of room in the number 6 car." The black porter grinned at the Preacher. "Y'all ain't rioted yet, now have you? Ain't wrecked up this fancy salon car?"

A roar of laughter replied. "We're havin' a revival. You tell that conductor to come on back here and get hisself saved!"

Birch regretted leaving the good company. If only it hadn't been for the cracked floor and the hard wooden seats, he would have stayed.

"Good luck." He shook the Preacher's hand. His hand seemed to disappear beneath the massive grip.

"Ain't no luck to it. No mistake about it. We'll meet agin, brother," the Preacher remarked with a certainty that made Birch look one last time over his shoulder at the broad face of the big man.

What a small place the world seemed to be on a train. Every soldier on board returning from the same war. But the commonality would end after this journey. Like being born into a new world, each man faced a different future.

Birch raised his hand in farewell. "Sometime I'd like to hear your cotton-field sermons, Preacher."

"Come on back here if things get too stuffy for you up there." He stomped on the floor and guffawed as the door slammed shut.

The roar from the locomotive was deafening in the second passenger car. Trudy decided that when she changed trains in Washington, she would try for something farther back. She was grateful for the window seat, however. The cool night air was refreshing.

The book lay open on Trudy's lap. She kept her hand on it even as she slept. It was a weapon of sorts, designed to fend off unwelcome conversation. After a polite hello, she could pick up her book of poetry and pretend to read if one of the hundreds of soldiers crammed on the train proved to be too forward. She had managed to soothe Bubbe's nerves by explaining this strategy. Already she found that it was a tremendous success. Three times she had drawn Lord Tennyson like a six-gun, raising the thin green volume in front of her face until the talkative soldier across from her either moved or went to sleep.

Then she slept. Voices murmured above her and behind her. The lonely whistle of the train resounded in the night. Bells clanged at each stop as the conductor announced the names of towns like Plainfield, Bound Brook, West Trenton.

Soldiers in brown uniforms got up and others sat down. The train seemed to have stopped and started a hundred times already. Passengers shifted seats and moved baggage around her. They whispered to one another, unwilling to disturb the sleep of the handful of civilians on the train.

"Okay if I sit here?"

"Where you headed?"

"Me? Getting off in Philadelphia. How about you?"

Everyone was coming from the same place. France. But each, it seemed, was headed to someplace different. Trudy kept her face turned toward the window. When she opened her eyes at each stop, every village depot looked alike. Every platform had a family or two waiting for a son or a husband. Again and again the scene was played out as soldiers became just men once again. Like breaking out of a common cocoon, they stepped off the dark green train to be embraced by folks clad in bright fabrics and tweeds and bonnets and caps all unique on this summer night.

Trudy observed each reunion from the window. When some new, brown-clad stranger slipped into the empty seat across from her, she picked up Tennyson to repeat the process all over again. The motion of the train, the shifting of the passengers, the whispered voices all fell into a familiar pattern, a rhythm like the clackity tapping of the wheels against the rails.

In Philadelphia, a third of the passengers left, only to be replaced by an equal number. There were six more whistle-stops between Philadelphia and Baltimore; then the train filled up with sailors, their white uniforms already wrinkled and smudged from waiting in the station for days. They stowed their duffel bags, broke out decks of cards, and commenced to play poker. The loud laughter and whoops of the newcomers were shushed by those who had managed to travel this far from New York.

Wide-awake behind her pretense of sleep, Trudy heard a deep voice say, "You gents mind your language. We got a lady in the car."

After a moment of absolute silence as all heads pivoted to her, the hushed whispers resumed as the B&O pulled from the terminal.

CHAPTER NINETEEN

Passing Through

Farther east another train clanged its bell as it pulled into a whistle-stop station. Ellis poked his head and shoulders out the window and whooped at the crowd standing on the platform.

The remainder of the Warne family and the Moniger family lumped together took up most of the platform at the Camden train depot. More a mob than a choir, they were singing, "I'll Take You Home Again, Kathleen." This song had made Ellis cry every time the fellows had sung it at the barbershop when he was a kid. And it made him cry again—happy tears, mixed with laughter.

He shook his fist, embarrassed by his open display of emotion. "Whose idea was it to sing that?" he asked Doc.

"Mine," Becky replied. "And I only wish my name were Kathleen."

Babies and toddlers were stacked on the shoulders of brothers and cousins and future brothers-in-law. Little nephews pulled the pigtails of squealing girls. Ellis was not sure who was who. They had all grown up so. What he had missed—two years from his life. Babies born. Infants now toddlers, running and jumping and saying "No!" as parents reached to grab them by their collars. It would take Ellis a while to sort them all out. Which child belonged to which brother? Who was part of the Warne clan and who belonged to Becky's family?

There were close to seventy-five family members gathered to meet them, and everybody was talking at once.

The stationmaster looked alarmed. All these for one passenger! What a reception!

All the boys wanted to know how it was in the war. The girls gathered around Becky to ask when the wedding was to take place and what New York had been like. Little hands reached up to touch Ellis's crutches with admiration. Their eyes widened with the observation of his limp across the platform. Here was living proof that there had been a real war. An exciting, *wonderful* war! Maybe Ellis would tell them all about it later.

In front of the station, a dozen automobiles had lined up. It was a regular parade. Despite the late hour, everyone had brought food—after all, it had been two whole years since Ellis had eaten home cooking. And every home in both families had made certain he would be well supplied.

Becky and Ellis rode in the front car with the top down so Ellis could get the full effect of the summer night air, just as he had written. Doc and Molly rode back home with John—a caravan of twelve vehicles in all, packed to the fenders with happy people. Along the way they picked up more stray friends to celebrate. Horns hooted. Cheers were raised. Pastor Hildermeyer came out in the yard in his nightshirt and ran down to ring the bell of the church.

"Ellis is home! Hey, everybody! It really is over. *Ellis Warne is home!*"

The sun was rising over the Capitol dome when the Baltimore & Ohio commuter slid into the station. Even though the day was new, it was already sultry.

Birch mopped his brow as he stepped from the car. His eyes were drawn to the sight of the Preacher and a dozen other black soldiers who yawned and stretched and rubbed their bellies with the same hunger Birch felt.

Birch lifted his hand in greeting. The Preacher responded in kind. The two men would come no closer at the U.S. capital's terminal. Everywhere were signs that warned, WHITES ONLY. There were separate drinking fountains for whites and blacks. Separate bathrooms. One single bench in the waiting area for blacks. The rest of the seating was for white travelers. Jim Crow ruled here.

Everywhere in the station black redcap porters hauled luggage. Black boys shined shoes. In the main lunchroom, black cooks prepared food. But the Preacher and his handful of men were not allowed to eat in that dining room. They ate someplace else. Birch was not certain where, but he wished he could have gone along with them for a plate of "hog hips and cackle berries"—bacon and eggs—if they were lucky enough to get them.

Instead he joined the flow of the white crowd moving toward the restaurant. A number of men broke off to mob the Red Cross canteen that had been set up to serve traveling servicemen. But Birch wanted a whole lot more than coffee and a doughnut this morning. His belly rumbled angrily, reminding him of the fierce appetite he had worked up every morning at home on the farm.

The last meal Birch had eaten in New York was a Coney Island hot dog slathered with everything except the grease from the wheels of the hot-dog cart. Fourteen hours later, his stomach still felt the effects of the assault. He longed for a good hot meal. Bacon, eggs, hash browns, and a stack of toast would do just fine. There was no dining car on the first leg of the journey form New York to Washington, but at Union Station, he was told, the food was served up hot and fast by pretty girls. No doubt about it, the conductor assured him, he'd have plenty of time to make his connection to Cincinnati.

It must have been a long time since the conductor had poked his head into the lunchroom at the terminal in Washington, D.C., Birch thought. He stood at the back of a crowd, which pressed ten deep against the counter. Birch could smell the bacon. He could close his eyes and almost taste it, but it wasn't enough. He spotted the starched caps of the waitresses and figured the "pretty girls" had all aged some since the conductor had last dropped in for something to eat. Haggard-looking, middle-aged women dashed back and forth, shouting orders to the cook, handing over sandwiches, and taking money.

A wall clock hung between the portraits of Lincoln and Washington. The expressions on the faces of both presidents seemed amused by the pure chaos of hungry soldiers and frazzled waitresses. Birch was not amused. He had been imagining good food for six hours or more. His mouth was watering from the aroma of food, but the clock warned him that he would have to be content with sniffing the air. His train was leaving in eleven minutes. Unless he knocked a whole row of men down and climbed over their backs to steal the cook's skillet, he was not going to eat anything this morning. At the rate the line was inching forward, Birch figured he would be two hours late to his train if he did things the normal way.

"Hogs at a trough," he muttered, fighting his way back out of the crush. His stomach growled unhappily, reminding him of the extra mustard he had slopped on the hot dog.

Clear of the mob, he peered down at his timetable, unable to make sense out of it. Feeling miserable, he walked to the drinking fountain and gulped down enough to quiet the rumbling of his belly. He wished now that he had filled his pockets with pretzels like Max had told him to do. *"Pretzels and salami. You gotta take your meals with you on a train these days. A man can live for weeks on pretzels and salami,"* Max had warned.

Ellis had added, "*Sure, and he'll smell enough like garlic that he'll scare vampires. Nobody likes sitting on a train with a guy who smells like Italian food.*"

"*So buy kosher salami.*"

"*Does it smell better?*"

"*No, but it's not Italian.*"

It was too late now. Birch had failed to heed the advice of a man who knew about trains, and now he was paying for it, starving by inches.

He glanced around the enormous lobby. Here and there smart travelers sat with their meals in wicker baskets. Men and women alike munched like contented cows as they gazed vacantly around the terminal. Would any one of them sell him a sandwich? Birch wondered, jiggling the coins in his pocket. He rubbed a hand over the stubble on his face. He glanced down over the endless wrinkles of his baggy uniform. He looked more like a bum than a soldier. In fact, he had been better fed in the trenches than he was now. He frowned, wondering what someone would say if he asked . . . explained . . .

And then, as his gaze swept the room for a likely target, he saw a young woman in a broad-brimmed, white-straw hat. Her chestnut hair was tucked up beneath it, revealing a slender neck. She wore a white blouse with puffed sleeves and a collar like that on a sailor's uniform. She was eating, chewing slowly, folding up the waxed paper neatly and putting it back into her basket. She looked toward the train and then back toward the public restroom.

Birch stared hard at her. He fumbled in his pocket for the photograph of Trudy Meyer. Pulling the picture from his Bible, he held it up as the young woman scooped up her basket and walked toward the door labeled Powder Room. She was pure dynamite. He frowned down at the picture. Nope. The lady could not be Trudy Meyer, but she looked enough like her to be her sister.

Birch stared at her until she vanished behind the door. Now, that was a girl to serve a man a meal! But, too late. She was gone with her basket of food forevermore. Birch slipped the photograph of the real Trudy back into his Bible and scanned the waiting area for another likely looking basket.

The sign above the Red Cross canteen caught his eye: Sandwiches for Our Servicemen. Maybe they offered more than donuts, after all. The crowd around the stand had thinned out. Friendly looking girls in white aprons were handing out sandwiches right and left. There, at the back of the line, stood the Preacher and six other black soldiers from the B&O car.

Preacher spotted Birch and raised his arm to hail him. "I told you we'd meet again," he said.

"The chow line is a likely place." Birch peered around at the heaps of sandwiches. Chicken salad on one tray and fried-egg sandwiches on the other.

"We can't get served nowhere else," Preacher said. As if to emphasize the problem, his belly growled loudly. "I sure am hungry. Ain't eaten since last night in Harlem."

There were four white soldiers to go before Preacher and his men reached the counter. Birch noticed the Red Cross girls glancing at them and whispering among themselves. A moment later the trays were taken from sight.

"Sorry, boys," a blond girl said to the black men. "We just run out of food."

The smiles on the faces of the Preacher and his hungry men vanished. They exchanged knowing looks. But what could be done about it?

Birch stepped from behind the Preacher's broad back. "You mean you got nothin' left?"

Embarrassed by the sudden appearance of a white man and then defiant, the blond put her hands on the counter and addressed Preacher. "Go on now. Get on outta here! You might try downtown. There's a place for darkies to eat downtown."

Birch muttered to Preacher, "Wait over there by that pillar." Then he smoothed his wrinkled shirt and sauntered up to the counter. He waited until Preacher was a few paces away. He looked at the glass panels in the ceiling. At the arches of the doorways and the patterns of the pillars. He glanced over his shoulder to the clock and then whispered, "You really out of sandwiches, miss? I'm mighty hungry."

She watched the retreat of the black soldiers suspiciously. "'Course not," she replied in a conspiratorial voice. "We just don't want to give everything to the Nigras."

"Appears to me you didn't give them anything." Birch laughed as though he was really amused. "You got some of those chicken salad sandwiches left? I got me a train to catch. Hey. You sure are pretty; you know that?" He leaned close to her and then reached down to grasp the tray of sandwiches. "Looks like you got plenty here to give away. And free, too, ain't they?"

She giggled. "Help yourself, soldier."

"That's just what I intend." Lifting the heaping tray he hollered, "Hey, Preacher! This nice gal says we can help ourselves!" He winked at her as she gasped and blustered. "Be right back with your tray." He smiled. Then he yelled again, "Look what they found back there! A whole trayful of sandwiches! Hey, Preacher, come on!"

That morning the Red Cross fed all the soldiers, black and white. Not that the young girls manning the stand were happy about it. They did not even thank Birch when he returned the empty tray.

And he made the train with thirty seconds to spare.

From her window seat in the sixth passenger car, Trudy watched as a handful of tardy passengers made a dash for the train. She was already situated. Across from her sat a banker and his wife from Cincinnati. Their eleven-year-old daughter sat next to Trudy. All of them were reading, which made Trudy look just like a member of the family when she raised her volume of Lord Tennyson.

All around this civilian island sat tired soldiers. Crumpled and unshaven, they all looked alike. Trudy was grateful to be sitting among the banker's family. The lady smelled of lilac water and the gentleman of bay rum. Trudy had just washed and splashed a few drops of La France Violette on her throat and wrists. This perfume was a gift that Max had brought her from France. She had meant to conserve it, but it seemed that each batch of military passengers smelled worse than the last as the trip progressed.

Perhaps that was why the family chose to sit beside her as well. They made a little enclave of sweet aroma, like a perfumer's shop next to a pickled-herring stand. Men swept past her and waved their arms, revealing sweat-stained shirts. Trudy noticed with some satisfaction that, like her, the banker's wife raised her lace handkerchief to her nose at the same instant. Trudy hoped that they were not being unpatriotic, but really, some of these fellows had been traveling for days without a bath.

And here came a prime example. Tall and sandy haired, the soldier took off his hat and ducked beneath the frame of the door. His hair was plastered down with sweat. His face bore a look of relief and amusement as the train lurched forward at the moment he entered the car. He tossed his hat up and caught it on his finger, then adjusted his duffel and, grinning at every other doughboy, moved toward the one remaining seat three rows behind Trudy.

"Made it, I see," someone called. "Did you get anything to eat?"

The soldier patted his bulging pockets. "The Red Cross ladies gave me these right out." Paper poked out of his shirt pockets on both the right and left sides of his chest.

"Hey, Birch, you look like a girl. Better eat those quick."

The whole car rocked with laughter—except for the banker and his wife and daughter. And Trudy, of course, who raised Tennyson the instant the blue-eyed soldier stared openly at her face. *The nerve!*

He inched his way back, ducking his head for the light fixtures. He was looking at Trudy. She could feel his deep blue eyes boring through the book. He walked slower, ignoring the comments from other men. Then, as if Trudy were sitting in his seat, he stopped right beside the banker's daughter and leaned closer to gape at Trudy.

Uncomfortable, she pretended not to notice. Tennyson was in place. She turned the page even though she had not read it, because it was important that she appear to be reading. The banker's wife looked at him curiously, as did the banker and his daughter. Why was he gawking so? Why didn't he take his seat? Why was he trying to see through the brim of Trudy's new straw hat?

He smelled like onions and chicken salad. He cleared his throat loudly.

Trudy ignored him, as if she were deaf. She did not even blink.

He cleared his throat louder. "Pardon me . . . *miss?*"

Trudy did not take her eyes from Tennyson.

"Excuse me, miss? You in the hat there? With the book?"

Trudy dared to look up.

The banker's wife was indignant. Her lower lip shot out and one eyebrow raised.

The soldier smiled curiously at Trudy. "You sure look like somebody I know, miss."

"Well, I am certain I do not know you," Trudy replied sweetly. Her eyes darted back to Tennyson.

"All the same, I wanted to tell you . . . I mean, I ain't seen any girl as pretty as you since before I left."

"Thank . . . you." Trudy's voice cracked. She felt the blush climb her throat and into her cheeks. She did not look at him again, although he lingered above her expectantly for a moment longer.

It was a moment too long. Behind him, the door opened and an elderly man in a white coat and trousers hobbled in, glanced around, and took the last seat in the Pullman.

The soldier gave a nervous laugh and looked at the banker. "Well, guess I'm just passin' through." He nodded to Trudy. "Enjoy your trip."

Trudy thanked him again, then watched him retreat up the aisle in search of another seat in a different car. The air smelled faintly of chicken salad. He was just one among a million traveling this summer morning. Most of them took a second look at Trudy. A few brave boys even managed to speak to her. Like this one, they pretended to know her or recognize her.

A full day passed before the conductor announced the Cincinnati stopover. By that time, Trudy had almost forgotten the crooked smile and the open gaze of the tall, blue-eyed soldier.

CHAPTER TWENTY

War on the Home Front

There were prostitutes waiting in Cincinnati when the troops got off the train. "Time enough," some men said. Birch remained at the station for the three-hour layover.

It was foolishness, Birch knew. Still, he could not resist the urge to speak to the girl who looked like Trudy's picture.

He spotted her standing in front of the newsstand. Front pages of newspapers east and west were tacked up on the awning above the newsboy's head.

The young woman was looking at them as if to read them all. The headlines were phrased differently in each publication, but the message was the same:

"Protesting Germans Sign Peace Treaty!"

It had taken this long for the details to be worked out among the Allies. Germany was dismembered and humiliated, the Austro-Hungarian empire dismantled. New nations were carved out of the wreckage to create Yugoslavia, Czechoslovakia, and Hungary.

The German chancellor had resigned rather than sign the treaty. Those German statesmen who came to the Palace of Versailles were forced to use a separate entrance into the building. They were booed and stoned by the crowds when they left. In Germany, civilians rioted in protest. Off the coast of Scotland, the German admiral Ludwig von Reuter scuttled his fleet rather than surrender. All of this seemed to be of small consideration to the Allied leaders intent on building the New World Order.

Birch stood at the shoulder of the young woman and scanned the headlines and the blizzard of newsprint that covered the event.

"You know," said the newsboy sourly, "these here papers are for sale if you wanna read 'em."

"No thank you," said the girl, adjusting her straw hat. "I couldn't possibly buy them all. Just browsing until departure time."

Birch was not nearly so brazen. He meekly counted out three pennies and bought a copy of the Cincinnati paper.

She looked at him with a smirk. "Why buy the cow when the milk is free?" she questioned, inclining her head to the wall of news.

Was that a hint of a German accent in her voice? Birch wondered.

"Because I would like to read something besides the front page; that's why." He tapped his newspaper. "See, look at this. Continued on page 6, column 3. You ain't gonna get all the milk unless you buy the cow."

"Just the cream. And that's enough."

She seemed not to recognize Birch from his brief intrusion on the train yesterday. "I noticed that your father had a whole newspaper. You could borrow his."

"My father?'

"In the Pullman. Yesterday."

She looked at him blankly. "Yesterday? Was I awake?"

"Sure." He looked at her throat, framed by the V-neck of her clean white blouse. "You blushed."

The reminder made her blush again. She put her hand to her cheek. "Oh. Yes." She quickly turned back to the newspapers.

"I've shaved since then." Birch made no move to leave. "Changed my uniform, too. Shaved with cold water right here in the station. I found a great place if your father would like to—"

"My father is fine, thank you." It was plain to see she resented his familiarity. "Besides, there is a barbershop just over there. You needn't have shaved with cold water."

"Just tryin' to save two bits."

Silence.

He guessed she did not like him much, in spite of the shave and clean shirt. He tried again. "With that two bits I could sure buy a pretty girl a piece of pie."

"Good. I hope you find one."

"You'll do . . . I mean—"

"No, I won't do at all! Please, I am just trying to get home. If I had a nickel for every homesick soldier who wanted to buy me pie—"

"You don't like pie? How do you feel about—?"

She glared him to silence. "Just like a Broadway musical play.

Boy meets girl in the railway station. He buys her apple pie and coffee—"

"Sounds right."

"They talk. The music swells. He sings her a song, and they ride off together on the train to live happily ever after."

He smiled. "If you say so."

"Well, this is not a Broadway musical. It is plain old Cincinnati. Dirty old Cincinnati. And I don't hear music."

"I don't remember offering to sing." He backed up a step.

"Oh," she said in a small surprised voice as though she had not expected to say the things she had said to him. "I did not mean to sound harsh, but—"

"You did a fine job of it, all the same." He tipped his hat and backed up another step. "It's just that you sure do look like this gal I know." He smiled, as someone might smile at an unfriendly dog barking through a rickety fence. "But I can tell you ain't her. No offense intended."

He could tell, indeed, that this was not his Trudy Meyer, whose letters had kept him and half his company entertained as if they were stories out of a dime novel. No matter that she looked like her—except for the hair being all done up. And the face was older. Everybody looked like somebody. But only the real Trudy had a heart that wrote letters to keep a man's mind off dying and killing. He dared one last question: "You don't happen to have a sister?"

"No!"

"Well, then, miss . . . good luck."

She nodded regally. "Same to you."

Birch tucked his paper under his arm and sauntered off to lick his wounds. This gal was one cold-blooded catfish. Thought highly of herself, too. *Broadway musical play!* Pretty, but only skin deep. He wondered if maybe he shouldn't have followed Max's advice and taken interest in one of those French ladies. Maybe it *was* better not to know the same language.

He glanced back at her by the newsstand with her head cocked back so she could see the top row of stories. He sure did not speak *this* woman's language. It seemed a pity. The closer to home he got, the worse he felt. Mama would not be there. Birch would have liked someone soft-voiced and pretty to talk to right about now.

He dared another quick look at her as she walked toward the fountain. She was tall, at least five feet eight inches, he figured. A girl that tall would have trouble finding a tall husband to make a matched team. "She'll probably end up with a short little haberdasher," Birch grumbled under his breath.

Then he remembered that was exactly what Marjorie had done. Married a haberdasher and moved to St. Louis. Marjorie had not been tall enough to suit Birch, however, even though she was pretty.

Birch sprawled out on a bench and fanned himself with his newspaper. This was a use for the news that the sharp-tongued, tight-pursed young woman had not thought about.

She disappeared around a corner, most likely looking for her folks.

"Well, that's the last I'll see of you," he said without regret.

It was just Trudy's luck that the train to St. Louis also carried the soldier who had made her blush twice. She found a safe enclave among civilians in the observation car, but three times she happened to meet the soldier face-to-face in the narrow aisle.

"You followin' me, ma'am?" He smiled.

She blushed. She did not reply, of course. It was too silly to contemplate. She did wish that he would get off at one of the multitude of whistle-stops between Cincinnati and St. Louis. She was always surprised that he was still on the train with her. When he walked by her seat, she looked the other way. When she was forced to pass through the Pullman where he played cards all night with half a dozen other doughboys, she pretended not to see him. She did not want to blush again, and he seemed to have a knack for making her turn pink from her toes up.

The train rolled onto the steel bridge spanning the Mississippi, and Trudy thought that surely this was the last she would see him. There was time enough to change over to the Rock Island Line, the last leg home. She was hurrying through the terminal when the sandy-haired soldier smiled, winked, and waved at her. He was also moving toward the Rock Island locomotive. An enormous black man in uniform walked beside him.

The two were laughing together like old friends, carrying on a lively conversation. Then, even though the Rock Island was half empty, the soldier did a remarkable thing. He climbed the steps of the car reserved for coloreds. By choice. She knew what that meant and liked him for it.

"Gimme a hand with this, Preacher." He swung his duffel up to the black man, and Trudy knew that he was riding back there. Three freight cars separated them from the regular Pullmans. She could wander anywhere else on the train she wanted without fear of bumping into him.

It was vaguely disappointing. The game of hide-and-seek was over. He was no longer interested in teasing her. So she settled in, expecting that he would vanish into the countryside of Missouri somewhere as they moved into the South. Then she would be home. She would write about him, one line in her diary: *He said I was the prettiest girl he had seen since* . . . And she would forget about him, except for the fact that he had made the journey interesting.

So it might have been if the Rock Island train had not stopped to take on water just outside Monet, Missouri.

There was a carnival in full swing just beyond the shadow of the water tower. Bright yellow-and-red-striped tents were scattered among wagons painted with pictures of pygmies and pythons and bearded ladies and giants. Children darted in and out among the tent ropes. Grown-ups strolled among the commotion or sat in the shade eating melons and sipping lemonade.

Trudy could hear the music of fiddle and guitar and banjo and bass above the thumping heartbeat of the train. Was there ever a more welcome sight after hours and hours of cornfields and rocky red earth? The entire left side of the Pullman was instantly crowded with passengers straining like children to see what was outside their little pen.

No doubt some cagey carnival huckster had traveled this same route himself and chosen the most likely place to draw a crowd when the trains stopped for water four times a day.

"Ladies and gents," proclaimed the conductor, as though he were the ringmaster. He held up his railroad watch. "Thirty minutes. Thirty-minute stop. Please be back in your seats at seven-thirty."

There was a cheer from the passengers, as though they had been let out of school. Thirty minutes was just enough time for corn on the cob and a tall glass of iced tea and maybe a jelly apple.

An evening breeze washed over a stand of trees in the west. Trudy raised her face to it. She was genuinely smiling for the first time since she left New York. Inwardly she blessed the clever man who had spotted the water tower and imagined dollar signs sprouting from each Pullman car.

Two hundred other passengers dissolved into the crowd with Trudy. She left Tennyson behind and brought only her handbag and her appetite. Corn first. Then a hot dog, which rivaled anything she had tasted at Nathan's on Coney Island.

Hot dog in one hand and lemonade in the other, she moved toward the music. A dance floor had been built right in the center of the action. Men in overalls danced with women in plain gingham dresses. Their feet thumped against the boards of the dance floor in time to the music. Suddenly Trudy wished she had not been so abrupt with the tall soldier on the train. The music in New York was nothing like this. This was *home* music. It had been a long time since she had danced.

Sipping her drink, she turned to see if there might be a likely partner. Then she spotted her persistent soldier. He was not listening to the music, nor was he smiling.

He stood beside the black soldier, the one he called Preacher. His arms were crossed, his legs spread slightly, his chin raised defiantly as he was challenged by seven men—tough-looking farmers.

"We don't 'low none of you here, I tell ya," said a broad-chested man who spat at the feet of the black soldier as if to emphasize his point.

A second man glared angrily at the half-eaten corn in the big hand of the Preacher. "An' we sure as hell don't feed uppity niggers disgracin' the American uniform. What you wearin' that uniform for? You kill a white man an' steal it off him?"

The Preacher was silent, gazing over the heads of the crowd toward the train. "Let's you and me go on back to the train," he said, nudging his white companion. "Come on. I don' need nothin' here."

"You're goin' nowhere till you take off that uniform," growled another man.

Trudy's soldier did not budge. He stepped forward within inches of the second accuser. "This soldier was a hundred and ninety-one days in the trenches in France. He *ain't* no nigger. You can take that back *now!*"

The man laughed in Preacher's face. "Prob'ly all hunkered down in the mud, wasn't you? Skeert to death, Sambo?" He whistled like the sound of an incoming artillery shell, smiling all the while. Then when the explosion came, he slammed a right fist hard into the belly of Trudy's soldier, who countered with a left and right to the face.

The carnival erupted into chaos. Men surged past Trudy from the dance floor to join in the beating of Trudy's soldier and the enormous black man.

The Preacher hefted a farmer over his head and slammed him down against four others. He fought like a giant bear as men jumped onto his back like a pack of dogs and tore away buttons, sleeves, and finally the entire shirt of his uniform.

"Watch out," the black man called to Trudy's soldier. The warning came too late as a whiskey jug came crashing down over his head.

Trudy cried for help as her soldier crumpled and disappeared. Where were other soldiers who might help? With sickening realization, she saw that several doughboys from the train had joined the mob surging against the Preacher. They pushed and shoved to get a turn at him. Men hung around his neck and clambered on his bare back. Still, he remained standing.

Suddenly shots rang out. The crowd grew silent and backed away from the panting giant. His uniform lay in shreds at his feet. Trudy ran to her soldier, who lay unconscious and bleeding heavily on the ground. Another shot, and the crowd backed farther away as the denim-clad train engineer and his fireman parted the mob. In his gloved hands the engineer held a sawed-off shotgun.

He reloaded and pointed the barrel straight into the belly of the man who had started the brawl. "I keep this scattergun handy in case some critter gets in front of my train. I use it, too. The Rock Island don't like being held up. Don't like trouble. You get it?"

"They started it!" claimed the broad-chested farmer. "Think they're really something! Wearin' a uniform! Uppity nigger and that nigger-lover there. Lookit what they done!" He pointed to where a man sat on the ground moaning and holding his broken arm. "It's the nigger done it!"

The engineer looked sharply to where Trudy cradled the head of her soldier in her lap. She was crying, stroking his cheek, praying he would not die.

"Is this your husband, ma'am?"

Trudy nodded without thinking. "They attacked them . . . they came right up and—"

"I saw it," said the engineer. He gave a stern wave of the weapon. "Now y'all are gonna stay right where you stand while me and my passengers get back on my train. Understand?"

Fearful nods replied.

"That's real good. 'Cause I hate it when somethin' makes me late." He inclined his head toward the big black man. "Gather up the lady's husband and tote him on back to my train for me, will ya?"

The giant scooped up Trudy's soldier in his arms as if he were a baby and came to the engineer's side. He seemed not to notice his own bleeding face. "All right," he said in a low voice, and they backed toward the train. The attackers remained rooted.

The handful of passengers who had joined in the attack now looked at one another and the engineer. "What about us?"

"You got your tickets," snarled the fireman. "But we'll throw you off if'n you try anything else on our line. You got that?"

Nods of agreement. Nine men broke off from the mob and followed meekly and slowly back to the train.

"We'll put your husband in a first-class compartment, ma'am," the conductor said, eyeing the belligerent passengers who had joined against him. He looked at the Preacher. "You get on back to the coloreds' car. And don't be gettin' into no more trouble."

The black man gently placed the limp body of Trudy's soldier in the private compartment. "Lord a'mighty, he's hurt bad," he whispered to Trudy. "Much obliged. Those men would have killed Birch and me."

"Get on to your own place now," the conductor chided, leading him away.

The wound in Birch's head was bleeding profusely. There was blood everywhere. Trudy's skirt was soaked, and blood spilled down over the upholstery.

"Bandages," Trudy ordered, rolling up her sleeves. "Whiskey and ice." Grabbing towels from the rack inside the private compartment, she put them beneath his head.

The conductor frowned at her. "You gonna drink the whiskey?"

"Whiskey to sterilize the wound. Ice for the swelling."

"Good thing he's out cold. You pour whiskey on that cut, and it would knock a man out for sure."

"Well, we don't have to worry about that, do we?" She nudged the burly railroad man from the compartment. "Please be quick about it." Closing the door behind her, she knelt beside the soldier. Who was he? Where did he live? Would they come to his town and pass it by without knowing it?

Trudy had claimed he was her husband simply to get him away from the mob. Now that it was said, she had better find out whom he really belonged to and make sure he got home.

Rumaging through his pockets, she found his packet of tickets and transfers. He was bound for Hartford. That would mean a train change in Fort Smith—impossible with the shape he was in. She turned his head slightly and examined the ugly gash behind his right ear. Shards of pottery from the whiskey jug were imbedded in his scalp. Trudy remembered how Billy Baker had been killed when a horse kicked him in the head in about the same place the soldier had been hit. This was more than just a knock on the head. Her hands trembled as she placed a towel over the wound. Next she removed his wallet and a small pocket Bible from his breast pocket. Surely there would be some identification there.

When the Bible slipped from her hand and thudded to the floor, a photograph fell out. Trudy gasped. She stared back at her own serious face. Picking up the photo, she turned it over. This was the picture she had given to Max the day he left for France! What was it doing in the possession of . . . ?

Suddenly it all made sense. This was the fellow Max had written her about. *The Arkansas boy. With the name of a tree. Birch . . . Birch something.* She opened the wallet. *Birch Tucker. Shiloh, Arkansas!*

Max had warned her that there was a young man from Arkansas who kept her photograph and read the letters she sent after Max finished them. *"And one of these days you'll have to show up on his doorstep. He'll keel over when he sees you. He's been mooning over your photo like a little puppy."*

No wonder he had been so persistent on the train. He said she looked like someone he knew. But he didn't know it was her. Now here he was—keeled over, all right!

"Birch? Do you hear me? It's Trudy. Max's cousin . . ."

No response. A sharp rap on the door and the conductor was back, holding a first-aid kit. "Can't find any whiskey, ma'am." He stepped aside, revealing a portly man with gray side whiskers and a drooping mustache. "But I brought Doctor Cooper of Fort Smith to tend to your husband."

"How-do." The doctor brought his black bag with him. He bent over Birch and peered at the wound. "Whiskey? You think we're in Indian-fightin' days, young woman? You read that remedy in a dime novel?" He made a clucking sound, and his tone turned serious. "What's his name?"

"Birch," she croaked, holding the Bible and the photograph close.

The doctor repeated his name and pulled back the injured man's eyelids.

Birch groaned.

The doctor was silent as he took his pulse. Then, to Trudy, "Where do you live?"

"Fort Smith."

"We'd just as well take him there. If he lives, he'll get better care at home than in a hospital. I won't fool you, young woman. He's got a concussion. A bad one, from the look of it."

Trudy nodded, feeling frightened. She wished she had not claimed he was her husband.

"We'll send a wire ahead from the next stop," the doctor said brusquely. "Have an ambulance and stretcher at the depot." Then again he addressed Trudy as he labored over the wound. "You have family that needs to know you're coming in like this? To get the bed ready?"

"Can't we take him to the hospital?"

"Not with the flu overcrowding the beds. And now there's an outbreak of smallpox locally as well. I shouldn't think you'd want to risk the exposure."

Trudy nodded in agreement and scribbled out a message to send ahead to Fort Smith:

Arriving 2:25. Stop. Bringing home soldier friend of Max. Stop. Injured. Stop. Needs Bed. Stop. Trudy.

Well, if that wasn't a homecoming announcement, there never was one. *No parties or bands, please, Mama. I'm bringing home a soldier wounded on the home front. . . .*

Trudy gazed down at the dog-eared photograph. How long had he carried her likeness? How many letters had he read? She wished now that she would have known. Out of the fifty men who had approached with the line "Don't I know you?" this man really did.

He was pale, his breathing shallow. "Help me get his shirt off," the doctor ordered. "And unbuckle his belt. Come on. Be quick about it, girl. He's in shock. Loosen that—" Then he questioned, "Was he in France?"

"Yes," Trudy replied with absolute certainty. There was much that Max had written her about Birch and the other man, Ellis.

"On the front?"

"Ninety days."

"It would be a shame to lose him after coming through all that," the doctor muttered. "To come home and get hit by a jug of whiskey. 'Twould be a shame."

"He might die?"

"He might live." He elevated Birch's feet and took his pulse. "How long have you been married?"

"I'm not . . . he's not . . . I only said so to get him away."

A preoccupied smile flitted briefly across the doctor's face. "I suspected as much. That was quick thinking. I'll wager they'd have lynched the Nigra. And they might have hanged this brave boy if you hadn't stepped in."

Trudy felt faint. She leaned against the wall of the tiny compartment and stared at the ghostly white body of Birch Tucker. The conductor reappeared with a bottle of whiskey, then took the notes and promised to fire off the wires at the next stop.

"Ah, your snakebite remedy." Dr. Cooper held up the bottle of amber alcohol, pulled out the cork, and took a long swig. "You look like you could use some."

Trudy shook her head. The compartment was reeling. "I feel as if I might be sick."

"Out the window, if you please," he said without sympathy. He let the glass pane down for her and returned to his work.

So much for the carnival hot dogs and corn on the cob and lemonade. She threw up out the window, then slid to the floor in exhaustion. She fixed her eyes on the limp arm of Birch. She wanted to hold his hand. To make him wake up and be well. He was no longer a stranger to her.

"Just be glad you're not married to him," mumbled the doctor. "Little gal as pretty as you is too young to be a widow." After a minute or two he asked, "How long have you known him?"

"He was . . . is . . . a good friend of the family," she replied hoarsely. "On the front with my cousin." She traced the profile of his features with her eyes. A few freckles stood out against his ashen complexion, giving him the appearance of a sleeping child. Sandy-colored hair framed a sensitive face. Straight nose and full lips. Wide-set eyes. Blue, she remembered. Very blue and direct. He was boyishly handsome, and nothing at all the way she had pictured the Birch Tucker of Max's letters.

Somehow she had expected the weathered appearance of a dark-skinned Indian. Tough and leathery and fierce eyed, ready for a fight. That had not been the case with this Birch. Tall and angular, he carried himself with the easy gait of an athlete. When he had looked at her, spoken to her, his eyes laughed and sparkled as though he knew something about her that she did not know.

The fierceness had come later, at the carnival when he faced off against the mob. Then his countenance had changed completely. She had glimpsed the brave and compassionate man Max had written her about.

"He *must* live," she whispered.

Dr. Cooper merely grunted in response and continued plucking out the largest slivers of pottery embedded in Birch's scalp.

✳ ✳ ✳

The conductor tossed Jefferson his crumpled and bloody ticket. "One of those boys back there picked this up outta your ripped clothes. Said I should bring it back here so you'd be sure to get home."

Jefferson rang his thumb over the blood on the ticket. Every stop and every change of trains was now known by his attackers. The ticket had been returned as a warning. They planned to get him somewhere along the line between the Missouri border and home. He mopped his brow and pulled a clean shirt from his duffel bag.

This time he would not make the mistake of wearing his uniform in public. The plain white collarless shirt Mama had sent him would be safe. He pulled it on and looked down at his leggings and army-issue boots, the finest boots he ever owned. He unfastened the leggings and pulled his boots and socks off, dropping them into the duffel. He rolled up the cuffs of his trousers midcalf and left his shirttail untucked. Barefoot and ragged now, he could travel safely through the white man's world. He would speak only when spoken to, and then in a slow and uncertain drawl.

Jefferson would risk no more incidents as he traveled home. He shoved his train ticket deep into his pocket as the train slowed to a crawl and crossed the border into Arkansas. Without explanation, he left the dilapidated car and descended the boarding steps. Just as the train began to pick up speed, he tossed his bag from the train and jumped after it, hiding himself behind an elderberry bush as the other cars slipped by.

He could walk fifty miles before the attackers on the train ever knew he was gone. They might look for him at the next depot, polish their brass knuckles in between watering stops. But the thought of home was too precious to Jefferson to risk yet another battle to get there.

CHAPTER TWENTY-ONE

Changing Positions

It had been a long time since Ellis had played catch with Doc out behind the barn. It felt good to have the ball slam into his glove, to send it back again and hear the satisfying whack as Doc caught it.

"You're still a fair pitcher, Ellis." Doc winked and shook his hand as though the impact had burned him through the leather. "But I've already decided . . . John will be pitcher at this year's tournament."

"I never figured I'd be able to—"

Doc held up his hand. "No arguments now, boy. With that bum leg, you'd be no good on the mound. Couldn't move fast enough."

"Sure, Pop," Ellis agreed. He did not like this discussion. After all, he had given up all hope of ever playing baseball again.

"Glad you agree with the coach." Doc wound up and pitched hard, hurtling the ball home. Ellis caught it easily and flung it back. "So. Now that it's settled, you will take John's place as catcher. 'Tis the only way."

Ellis let his hands fall limp to his side. "What are you dreaming of, Pop? I can't catch." He tossed the ball back without enthusiasm.

"Then what is it you're doin' now?" Doc threw high and wide. Ellis nabbed the ball with the natural response of someone conditioned to never let a ball get by. He stared at his glove with surprise.

"This is different. This isn't a ball game. It's me and you. Behind the barn, like when I was a kid."

Doc was not listening. "When we first came to America, there was a kid named Charlie O'Donnell who had one leg. You were too little to remember him, but you never saw such a catcher like Charlie. Of course, he never tried to hide the fact he was missin' a peg. He just got around. Didn't try to haul a chunk of wood about with him. Here come the ball and *wham!* Up he popped and then sent it on its way."

"Quit dreaming, Pop," Ellis said in a low voice.

Doc ignored his protest. "You'll have to leave that log you got strapped to your hip home on the bedpost."

"And how would I run the bases?"

"All arranged." *Wham!* The baseball slammed into Doc's glove. "Go easy on your old man, Ellis. I told you, you'll not be pitching this year."

Ellis frowned. "I'm not going out in public with half a leg."

"Don't be daft. You can't play catcher with that thing attached. 'Tis true, isn't it? You're much more agile without the prosthesis. The thing is just meant to fill out your trousers. Well, you simply can't play with the leg along."

"Pop, you're not listening."

"Aye, I'm listening. You're arguing with the coach. It's all arranged, boyo. Little Danny Flannigan will run the bases for you. You hit. He runs. The other teams have agreed."

"I don't think I can . . . I mean, it's out of the question. I can't play ball. Everything's different now. I don't know what I can do. . . ."

"Aye. You'll never know until you try." He checked his watch and threw again. Higher and to the right. Once again Ellis instinctively reached out and trapped the ball. Doc grinned. "I know a catcher is not the glory of a pitcher. But you'll do well for us."

"Please, Pop." Ellis felt miserable. "I don't want to—"

"So then." Doc squared his massive shoulders and frowned deeply. "Have you given thought to what medical school you'll be applyin' to?" He changed the subject as smoothly as he hurled the baseball.

"No more thought to that than to playing baseball. You know I have to rethink my whole life now."

Doc poked his finger in his ear and wiggled it as though he could not hear Ellis well. "What's that? Rethink your life? Rethink medical school? Why, Ellis, you're talking as if it was your brains that got amputated rather than just your leg. Your head is still on your shoulders, is it not?"

"Pop," Ellis replied in a weary voice, "how can I be a doctor now?"

"And I'm asking, how can you *not* be? After what has happened, Ellis, why, 'twould be a crime not to make the best use of what the Lord has given you."

"It's not what He's given that concerns me. It's what He's taken away."

"You're talking as if you're a cripple." Doc looked insulted. He tapped his index finger against his temple. "The only thing that can cripple a man is what's up here. Practicing medicine does not require two legs—not unless you plan on anesthetizing your patients with a hard kick to the head." He stood on one foot. "I have yet to use any part of my anatomy below the chest in my profession."

Doc cleared his throat impatiently. "Playing catcher will be a bit difficult, I admit. But medical school?" He snapped his fingers. "There's not been a more promising candidate than you are, Ellis. 'Twould be criminal to let that die. And I'd not forgive you if you killed it."

"I didn't ask for this, Pop," Ellis replied defensively. He had thought it all out and was prepared to give up everything he had ever wanted. Now Doc was telling him he was wrong. He didn't much like it. It was much easier to be resigned to loss, wasn't it?

"Ever since you were a tiny lad you've been following me about, asking about this and that, wanting to know everything I was doing. You mean you've changed the desire of your heart? Just like that?"

"I've been forced to."

"Who forced you? You've got two good hands. Two eyes. Your brain is sharp as ever—except that you're being deceived into thinking you've come home less capable."

"You're saying I'm not?"

"Well, I've made you catcher, haven't I? I admit that much. You'll not be pitching. But there's a wide difference between a baseball game and medical school."

Doc looked at his watch just as Ellis's brothers rounded the barn. They came with ball gloves and bats slung over their shoulders.

Little Danny Flannigan was with them. "Hiya, Ellis! Doc says I get to run bases for you! What do you think of that! Ain't it wonderful?"

Ellis scowled at his father. Why was he insisting that Ellis do the impossible? Why make him an object of pity in front of the whole county?

John sidled up to him and extended his hand. "Sorry, Ellis," he murmured. "Pop says I'll be pitching in your place. I'm not nearly as good as you, but Pop says I'll do." He glanced down at Ellis's leg. "You're not going to try and drag that wooden leg around when you're catcher, are you?"

Doc clapped his hands for attention before Ellis could answer. "We've got a few weeks to practice, boys. We'll have to work hard to get in shape, to get our timing back, but we can do it." He turned his coach's no-argument gaze on Ellis and John. "Ellis, go on in the barn and take that thing off. You and John are just reversing positions. Practice hard. We'll work on batting later." A wide smile. "It'll come back to you as natural as breathing, Ellis. You haven't forgotten a thing. You'll see."

★ ★ ★

From the first day of his trek, Jefferson Canfield stayed off the main roads, traveling the rain-washed lane that followed the course of some nameless creek. South, always south he traveled, stopping sometimes to soak his bare feet in the cool water as the sun arched across the sky.

Wild blackberries hung heavy in a thicket. He ate his fill, grateful now that he had left the train. He hardly remembered why he left. The swollen eye and split lip seemed of little consequence. He wondered why he had not left the crowded train before and set off across country on foot. He felt as though he were home already—the thick feel of the hot air, patches of sunlight broken by long stretches of shade where the woods made a canopy above his head. Insects ticked in the brush. Birds startled and whirred away before him. A black snake slithered across the lane, then lay in the grass and listened as Jefferson passed. The land itself was home, long before he would ever spot his cabin or hear his mama holler out to him.

"This is real good, Jesus," he said aloud. His voice sounded foreign and jarring against the music of the woods, so he did not say anything after that. He simply praised the Lord in his heart and thanked Him with his eyes and senses for what was done.

Jefferson walked until nightfall. A few stars appeared in the sky, and the mosquitoes buzzed all around him. Jefferson rolled down his trouser legs and shirtsleeves and put his socks and boots back on. There were worse critters than mosquitoes out in the night, after all.

Far off on a hill he spotted a light—a feeble, flickering light. A human light that soon grew dim as all the stars brightened to a glistening band across the sky.

There was no moon, but the earth was light enough for Jefferson to see by. The sounds of crickets and bullfrogs erupted. A whip-poor-will called, and an owl answered. The sweet scent of new-mown hay made Jefferson hungry, so he munched on the berries he had picked.

At last he came to an old barn standing in the middle of a field. It had no house beside it, and Jefferson knew it was a barn for keeping the hay. Deciding that the barn belonged to that faraway house on the hill, he climbed through the barbed-wire fence. No dogs barked to tell that he was trespassing, so he moved the rocks that served as props to keep the double doors closed against wild deer that might want to steal a bit of hay. Jefferson did not want to eat it. He only wanted to sleep in it.

With a sigh, he climbed into the loft and lay down. There were no windows in this barn, but through the cracks between the boards and the open barn door the stars still twinkled, and the soft breeze from the creek bottom ventilated his bed.

CHAPTER TWENTY-TWO

The Medicine of Love

At last the roaring in Birch's head was silent. It was quiet now, except for the call of a whip-poor-will somewhere in the darkness. A breeze washed over him and receded, like a gentle wave lapping the shore.

In the haze before his eyes, the image of Trudy hovered just above him. Her hair was loose around her shoulders. Her dark eyes searched his face as his eyes fluttered open.

"*Trudy* . . . ?" His voice sounded far away, dreamlike.

"Yes."

"Am I . . . dead?" He could smell a sweet fragrance. Perfume? Or was it sweet peas on a vine?

"No, Birch." She placed her cool hand on his forehead.

"Dreaming, then." He sighed and tried to remember where he was.

"No. Not dreaming. Not now." Her fingers stroked his face, pulling him back from a dark and deep sleep.

He frowned, trying to remember what he had missed. Maybe Trudy had always been here, and he had dreamed everything else in his life. "Is it you?"

"Yes. It's True."

"But *how*? Am I . . . ? Is this New York?" The memory of Orchard Street in the rain came back to him. There was nothing after that.

"You're at my house." She leaned closer to him. Her hair brushed his cheek as she turned her head. "Mama?" she whispered. "He's awake!"

An older woman with dark, worried eyes appeared behind Trudy.

Her face broke into a sympathetic smile. "There, now. For four days we have been hoping you would wake up. How are you feeling?"

Birch blinked up at her in confusion as he tried to think how he felt. His head was throbbing. "Terrible, ma'am."

"That's just fine." She smiled. "At least you're feeling something." She turned to Trudy. "I'll telephone Doctor Cooper. Leave the light off." Her words contained the thick flavor of a German accent. She padded from the room. The whip-poor-will called again in a song that sounded like home.

"Ain't heard a whip-poor-will since I left," he managed, breathing in the sweet aroma again. He caught the clean scent of the river and new-mown hay. "Smells like home."

Trudy stroked his cheek as though it were a natural gesture. "Almost home. Fort Smith. We brought you here straight from the train. Do you remember anything at all?"

"Nothing," he replied truthfully. "New York. Orchard Street. The rain. Where is Max? . . . *Fort Smith?* How did we get to Fort Smith?"

She laughed, then sighed, as if relieved. "Hold on." She took his hand. "On the train—that is, at the carnival—someone hit you with a jug. Cracked your head. Doctor Cooper was picking pottery out of your skull for an hour. We weren't sure you would ever wake up."

Birch raised a trembling hand to touch the pain in his head. A thick pad of bandages covered his skull behind his right ear. And he could not remember anything about it.

"Is it coming back to you?" She was hopeful.

He looked past her to the tall oak bureau with a doll sitting on top. Moonlight reflected in the mirror, illuminating tiny bunches of roses on the wallpaper. Lace curtains stirred with the gentle breeze. He closed his eyes and remembered gazing up at a window from the sidewalk of Orchard Street. *Longing* . . . Beyond that there was only the darkness and the roaring and a warm rain that had fallen on him, soaking him through to the skin.

He touched his cheek. Smooth and shaven. "Who shaved me?"

"I did."

"Why aren't you in New York?"

"I live in Fort Smith."

"Max . . . the rat . . . didn't tell me."

"Funny. He wrote me about you. 'Arkansas boy,' he said. Named after a tree. Birch." Her tongue caressed his name. " 'A very brave and good-hearted fellow,' Max said."

"He told me . . . you wouldn't like me." Birch slurred sleepily. "Wouldn't introduce me . . ."

"He gave me your address. He said when I was ever out Shiloh way, I should look you up. He insisted that I must . . . *without warning* . . . just appear at your door." She chuckled and shook her head. "Max! And then you and I were on the train together."

"I guess I must've made the train then. But I sure don't . . . can't see it. . . ."

How much did Birch remember? Trudy wondered. "Maybe it's best," she said, more to herself than to him as the image of Preacher and the mob replayed in her mind. "We sent word to your family."

"My pa?"

"In Shiloh." Trudy glanced at the unopened letter on the bureau top with his other things. The return address on the envelope was a woman's name. *Clara.* "I sent the note to Clara Tucker. Is that all right?"

"It's all right." He turned his face to the wall.

"I mailed it four days ago, the day we got home. Doctor Cooper says you won't be going anywhere for a while. You shouldn't be moved. That's what I told them in the letter."

"That's fine, then." Sadness filled his eyes. "He won't be coming for me anyhow, I reckon. Got the fields to tend and all."

There was so much sadness in his voice, it made Trudy want to weep. But she just nodded and listened to the sounds of the night for a while, leaving him to his thoughts.

At last she said, "What a homecoming, eh?"

"I reckon . . ." He searched her face. "But I woke up to you. All the time in France I was dreaming of coming home to somebody. And then I'd look at your picture and—"

She put a finger on his lips. This was too much. Too soon. The yearning in his eyes and voice frightened her. "Hush now. Can you sleep again until Doctor Cooper comes?"

"I don't want to sleep," he whispered, closing his eyes and taking her hand. "Please don't leave, Trudy."

She did not reply, but neither did she pull her hand away from him.

"Trudy?" Sadie Meyer's voice quavered as she called up to her daughter from the landing. "There's someone who'd like a word with you."

Trudy glanced out the window to see a black Model T Ford with a big gold star emblazoned on the door. Fort Smith Sheriff.

"Trudy?"

"Coming, Mama."

Birch opened his eyes as she swept past him. "You coming back?" His voice was childlike, plaintive.

She patted his hand reassuringly and left the dark room. At the foot of the stairs stood a sheriff with his hat in his hand. He glanced up at Trudy and smiled appreciatively at her as she descended the stairs.

"Evening, Miss Meyer," he said in a genuinely friendly way. He was a young man, perhaps a year or two older than Trudy. She recognized him but could not put a name to his face. "I recognized your name on the report," he continued. "So they sent me on over here."

"Oh?" Trudy shook his hand. "Report?"

"About that trouble you was witness to. Up Missouri way." His eyes scanned past her, up the stairs. "You brought one of the fellas home here with you."

"He was badly hurt," Sadie explained. "Would you like a glass of iced tea?"

"No, thank you, ma'am. No time for that." Again his eyes darted to the stairs. "You see . . . seems that Nigra did some real damage—"

"I shouldn't wonder. They attacked him and Birch," Trudy interrupted. "I was standing right there and saw it all. Every bit of it. And it was . . . well, they almost killed Birch."

"Birch." The deputy brightened. "The railroad fellas seemed to think you and this Birch were married. Travelin' together. But ol' Doc Cooper says you just happened along at the right time. Like maybe Birch—" he shot a long look up at the bedroom door—"maybe he was travelin' with the big Nigra."

"Preacher."

"Preacher? His name's Jeff Field." The sheriff grinned. "They know that much. He lives somewhere hereabouts. Leastwise, his ticket was to here. He jumped off the train, though—either that or somebody throwed him off. Although I doubt that, from what I hear about the man. Big fella."

"He's big. But he didn't do anything wrong. I was there."

"So were a whole lot of other folks. They say different. He done a lot of damage all by himself. Broke one fella's arm and fractured the hip of the deputy sheriff's pa. They're plenty mad about it up there."

"He didn't do anything wrong, I tell you." Trudy was pale with indignation.

"Well, that's what we got courts and juries for. To decide. All we know here in Fort Smith is that an extradition order come over lickety-split, and we got to find that Nigra and turn him over."

Trudy could see that her mother's hands were shaking. Trudy clasped her own hands behind her back so the deputy sheriff wouldn't notice she was trembling as well.

"I don't know where he lives." She did not add that she would not have told if she did.

"Sure. Doc Cooper told us you just came along and helped take care of this Birch fella. But if Birch was traveling with the Nigra, he might be able to help us."

Trudy's words came out laced with outrage. "He doesn't remember anything. Nothing at all since he left New York. They—those good law-abiding citizens—cracked a jug of whiskey over his head and would have killed him if it hadn't been for Preacher. And besides, Birch doesn't know where he lives, and he's not well enough to be interrogated by the police, either."

The deputy shrugged and smiled. "I told them down there you was a corker, Miss Meyer." He seemed unaffected by her anger. "I remember you from school . . . take no guff off anybody. . . . Well, I'm just doing my duty. When you got something come down from the top like that—" He shrugged again. "See? It ain't personal."

She swallowed hard and inclined her head in understanding. "Then you've done your duty and may tell them that Birch Tucker does not remember anything. That I only know the circumstances of the confrontation. Mister Tucker and—*Field*, is it?—were defending themselves against the mob. The engineer of the Rock Island will testify to that as well."

He replaced his broad-brimmed hat, smiled politely, and nodded. "That's what I'll tell them you said." He gave a slight bow to Sadie. "Sorry to trouble y'all on such a pleasant evening, ma'am. Thanks for your time."

Trudy hooked the latch on the screen door and closed the heavy oak door, even though it was a hot night. She watched the automobile pull from the curb. "They would have lynched the Negro, Mama. Those people will hang him if they find him and send him back there."

Sadie stood still and silent for a full minute. The shadow of fear was in her eyes. "That would not surprise me, Trudy. . . . Best not to speak of it to Birch. Best not to speak of it at all."

☆ ☆ ☆

"Jeff Field . . . Preacher . . . up Missouri way . . ."

Snatches of conversation drifted up to Birch. He lay quietly, scarcely breathing, as he listened to the words. Images flashed in his mind. A farm at the foot of Mount Pisgah. The cotton-field preacher, Canfield. The name connected with a face, broad shoulders, arms so big the muscles strained at the seams of a uniform. But all other memories eluded him.

The automobile engine sputtered away in the night, and presently Trudy came back, carrying a tray with a bowl of soup on it.

"Ever had matzo-ball soup?" She switched on the bed lamp.

"Heard of it." He blinked against the dim light, which made his head ache.

"From Max, I'll bet." Trudy placed the tray on the night table and fussed with Birch's pillows. "Hungry?"

"No." He wanted to reach up and touch her face.

"Well, you have to eat anyway." She spread a towel over his chest and smiled at him like his mother used to when he was sick.

"Who was here?"

"Nobody."

"Nobody who? Was he looking for me?"

"Not for you. Nothing . . . really." She brushed his question aside so casually that he might have believed her if he had not heard for himself. "You just have to eat and get well. Did Max tell you that the matzo-ball soup is medicine?" She spooned broth into his mouth. It was good.

"Doesn't taste like it. Tastes like chicken soup. Like Ma used to make."

She laughed and put the spoon to his lips again. "It's made with love. The best medicine." The she blushed and stammered, "I-I mean, your mother's soup."

"Sure," he said. "I know what you mean."

"Still haven't heard from your family. But mail is slow."

He could tell she was simply making conversation to cover her nervousness.

"Does this taste as good as your mama's?" she asked.

It did, but he avoided the question, pretending to blow away the steam. Then she blew on it for him, dabbed his mouth with the napkin, and avoided looking into his eyes.

But he kept his gaze locked on her face. The light was soft around her, shining in her hair. He wanted to tell her that since the first time he had seen her picture, she had been the medicine that had nourished him in the muddy trenches of France. It had been her words, her letters, that had fed him. Amused him. Given him something to look forward to.

Those letters had not been meant for him, he knew. The photograph had not really been his own. But there was a power that flowed through his body at her nearness that had nothing to do with matzo-ball soup.

CHAPTER TWENTY-THREE

A Speck of Dust

Morning light streamed through the crevices between the boards, making the old barn a cage of silver bars. Particles of dust swirled up in shafts of light. Jefferson lay on his back and followed their flight with his eyes and wondered about tiny worlds no bigger than a speck of dust, populated with creatures so small that only the great eyes of God could see them.

He smiled. He had not mused on such crazy thoughts since he left home. Life had been too much of a rush and fury to think small thoughts about little dust worlds. It took the smell of clean hay on a cool summer morning to wake his dull brain up again.

Jefferson used to spin such yarns for his sisters whenever crazy thoughts popped into his head. Once he had made up a whole story just for his baby sister, Nettie, about a dust-speck world spinning in the universe of a light shaft. He had told her, "Mebbe the whole world ain't nothin' more than a speck of dust compared to everythin'. . . just whirlin' away in God's shaft of light."

The child had taken to talking kindly to dust specks and hollering up to God, asking if He would please not sneeze in the direction of the world because He would surely kill everybody. Jefferson's mama had walloped him for getting Nettie so worked up. Willa-Mae said everybody would think Little Nettie was a few bricks shy of a full load. Hock and Willa-Mae made Jefferson tell Little Nettie that not a word of any of his stories was truth. There weren't little critters living on specks of dust, the earth was the center of the universe, and heaven was up and hell was down. That was that.

"Shoot," he murmured as he stretched in the hay. "That were a long time ago." Since then, Jefferson had seen a lot of things he never thought he'd see. He had watched men die without God and heard them scream with terror as they faced eternity. He had also heard friends call upon the name of the Lord as their lifeblood ebbed away. He had seen their faces filled with peace. He had heard them joyfully call the names of loved ones gone before and watched the dying men lift their hands as if to be carried away at the moment of death.

All of this had made Jefferson believe that there was a lot more unseen in this old world than what was seen. And maybe heaven and hell were closer than up and down. Some men were windows into the glory of heaven. So close! Others—many others—were like holes in a dam, and the darkness of hell poured through their lives and sucked folks down, drowning their souls in hatred.

Jefferson had witnessed plenty of man-made hell for a lifetime. He wanted to be a window—silver light shining through clean panes, a shaft of light parting the tides of darkness. A hellfighter!

Jefferson Canfield thought these things as he watched the shafts of light and golden flecks of dust. Maybe he would preach about it someday, he thought. He would tell stories about the little things that came into his head, and men would hear and want to know the Lord of Light. It was a happy thought. It made him eager to get home.

He climbed down from the loft and brushed himself off. Only then did he notice that the doors of the barn were closed. The rock props on the outside of the door had been rolled back into place, locking the doors shut.

It would not have been a hard thing for Jefferson to bust through the doors. No trick at all. He had broken down harder walls than this. Instead he put his eyes to the crevice and peered out. Who had locked him in?

A white farmer in bib overalls sat on an upturned bucket about twenty paces from the door. He held a double-barreled shotgun across his knees as he munched on a biscuit. He looked to Jefferson as though he figured to shoot whatever busted through the barn door.

Jefferson stepped to the side of the door, conscious that a blast from the shotgun could easily penetrate the planks. "Howdy out there!"

"Howdy," replied the farmer, shifting his weapon until the barrel aimed dead center of the doors.

"I spent the night sleepin' in your barn, sir."

"I know'd that," the farmer replied without hostility.

"Now you've locked me in."

"I left these here doors propped shut last night. I figger you busted in. Trespassed. That makes you my pris'ner. See?"

"Jus' wanted a place t'sleep," Jefferson called back. "Didn't mean no harm. Beg your pardon."

"You talk like you're colored, boy."

Jefferson put his big hand to his head. He had picked the wrong man's barn to sleep in. "Yessir, I'm colored all right."

"Figgered. What you doin' roamin' all the way out here?"

"Just tryin' to get home from the war, mister." Jefferson leaned his head against the wall. The barn was heating up again. Sweat poured from his forehead. "Didn't mean t'inconvenience you none."

"Don't take kindly to strays on my place."

"Just wantin' to get on back home. It was after dark. The skeeters was mighty bad. Figgered I could cover up with some hay and sleep till mornin'."

The farmer laughed and stood up. "Skeeters was bad all right, but you ain't felt nothin' till you felt buckshot sting, boy." He walked to the stones and kicked them to one side, then opened the door easylike with the barrels of his gun. "Come on out here with your hands up."

Jefferson obeyed. "Howdy," he said again. "Sure sorry I put you out."

The man appraised him as though he were a prize mule. "You're a big'un, ain't ya? I declare, boy, you're mighty big!" He was smiling, but the gun still pointed into Jefferson's middle. "Where you come from?" He scratched his cheek and brushed away a buzzing fly.

"I been at the war."

"Where you get them boots? Mighty fine-lookin' boots for a colored boy."

"They're my boots. Got 'em at the war."

The lower lip protruded from the unshaven face. "Them's the biggest boots I ever seen. You couldn't a stole 'em off nobody livin' who is big enough to fit in them boots."

The farmer was thinking out loud, coming to the right conclusion, and Jefferson was glad.

"No, sir," Jefferson said after a pause. "Only my feets fit these here boots. Army got 'em special for me."

The farmer looked him up and down again. "How tall are you, boy?"

Before he was drafted, Jefferson had not known the answer to that. Now it came easily to him. "Six-feet-five-inches tall without my boots. Last they checked, I weighed two hundred fifty pound. So the army say. But I reckon I lost some weight since then."

The farmer gave a low whistle. "You weigh pert near as much as a full-grown feeder hog." He sucked his teeth. "You hungry, boy?"

Jefferson's stomach growled. "Yessir."

"Well, I reckon you ain't lyin'." The farmer laughed. He lowered the barrel of the weapon. "And I suppose if you took it into your head to kill me, you'd a done it. I got some wood needs splittin'. Come on up to the house. Split the wood, an' I'll have the missus cook you up some vittles."

The postman had just dropped off a bundle of letters when Dr. Cooper descended the stairs. Trudy flipped through them quickly, then pulled one from the stack in dismay.

"That boy has a skull like an iron kettle." Dr. Cooper rolled down his sleeves and mopped his brow. "They could've used him as a battering ram. I got the stitches out—thirty-two of 'em. I told him he can get up and about, but nothing to jostle his brains, and no—" He stopped his chatter and paused at the bottom of the stairs as Trudy looked up from the letter. "What is it, child?"

Trudy held up the envelope. "The letter we sent to his mother . . . returned unopened. See?" She passed it to him. The name *Clara Tucker* had been crossed out with a thick lead pencil. Beside it were the scrawled words *C. Tucker passed away. Return.*

The doctor clucked in sympathy. "Has the boy said anything to you about this?"

"Never a word about his family. Lots about Shiloh. But nothing about—" She raised her eyes as Birch appeared at the banister at the top of the stairs.

"You're discussing the patient?" He was buttoning his shirt.

"Where do you think you're going?" blustered Dr. Cooper.

"You said I could get up."

"Up real easy, I said. You got your boots on."

Birch gave an easy smile. "I figured to go on down to the wagonyard and buy myself a horse."

"A horse?" Dr. Cooper choked. "You're not ridin' any horse for weeks yet. You figuring to undo everything by jostling your head? You don't know how bad hurt you were!"

Birch put a hand to the back of his head. "Feels fine to me." He nodded at Trudy. "My mama used to say fish and company stink in three days. I been here nearly three weeks."

Trudy walked up two steps. "And you're still fresh—in more ways than one. If you kill yourself after all the trouble you've been, Birch Tucker, I'll never forgive you!" Then she looked at the letter. Her voice became quiet. "Birch? That letter I sent to . . . to Clara Tucker? It came back."

He nodded. The smile faded. "I figured it might. My mama, she . . . the flu took her some months ago."

"You didn't tell me." Trudy slipped the letter in the pocket of her apron.

"I didn't want you to have to write another one. It don't make any difference, anyhow. Even if *he* opened it."

"He?"

"My father." Birch ran a hand through his hair. "I need a haircut," he mumbled, before retracing his steps back to the bedroom.

Dr. Cooper scowled up at the closed bedroom door. He lowered his voice. "Never mind what his mama said about fish and company. I want to keep my eye on that boy another week before he travels far. I don't want him stepping out of bed and right into a twelve-hour day chopping cotton. That's likely to happen if he leaves."

Trudy took the letter out again and looked at it. "I recall when he first woke up . . . he said something about *someone*. . . . His father, maybe? That *he* wouldn't come for him."

"Keep him here awhile. I'll stop down at your father's store and tell your folks."

"They won't mind. He's good company—Max's friend and all. We knew him from Max's letters, and—"

The doctor patted her arm. "Yes. And I know a certain young woman who won't mind either."

The color began to creep into her cheeks. Was it so obvious what she was feeling? It was a curse, this blushing. It always gave every thought away. "He is nice . . . Max's friend."

"Oh yes," he chortled. "I almost forgot he was Max's friend."

"And we have an obligation."

"Of course." Another fatherly pat. "Just keep him here awhile, Trudy. There is one telephone out Shiloh way. In Grandma Amos's general store. My second cousin, Winnie Morris, telephoned me from there last Easter. Grandma Amos knows everyone's business. She charges for relaying messages to folks, but it might be worth it to hear a little Tucker family history. If there's bad blood between the father and the son—"

Doc Cooper did not finish the thought, but Trudy nodded in agreement, all the same. He raised a finger in warning. "No horses. Take him out to the Electric Park on the trolley. Walk him through the gardens. That's about as much excitement as he can stand for a while." He did not put on his coat. "They'll have a doozy of a fireworks show out there on the Fourth. It'll do him some good."

✯ ✯ ✯

Farmer Schmidt could not read, so he'd had very little news of the Great War over in France. He sat like a little boy and asked Jefferson a thousand questions about it. Through a half cord of wood split and stacked, he learned as much as Jefferson knew.

Mrs. Schmidt served up breakfast of biscuits and gravy, fried ham, and half a dozen eggs, which Jefferson ate on the back porch. Jefferson could have paid half a dollar for the meal, but he did not mind the work, and the old farmer proved to be good company and a source of unexpected local news as well.

"You're a good fella, and after all that fightin' over there I'd hate to see you come to a bad end so close to home." He gestured to the ridge of mountains twenty miles distant. "You say your farm is on the other side of them hills?"

"That's right. Twenty mile or so."

"Well, go round them blasted hills, even if it takes another week. Don't go up in them hills. It ain't the same 'round here as before." The farmer whispered in a low voice as if he feared being overheard.

Jefferson said, "I hunted coon and possum a hundred times in them mountains, with nothin' to see by 'cept the stars. Used to stand up there and look right down on this here valley, wonderin' who was down here."

The old man hooked a thumb in the strap of his overalls and whispered urgently, "That's what I'm tellin' you. Listen, now! Don't go home thataway. This here's Klan country. Big meetin' up there on that mountain. Ain't safe no more for you folks to go wanderin' up there."

"Well, now." Jefferson mopped up the last of his gravy with his biscuit. "Sounds like it's a mighty lucky thing I slept in y'all's barn, Mister Schmidt."

"You right it is. Anybody else in these parts woulda shot first and then throwed a party. Like an old ghost, the Klan come up out of the grave. My granddad was a Union man; he fought with Mister Lincoln. That were sixty year ago, and folks still look at me and my folks suspicious-like. We ain't never been asked to join up with them bedsheet-flappin' lunatics. And I'm mighty grateful they passed me by with the honor."

Jefferson laughed. "Yessir, I truly am glad I slept in your barn."

"You're laughin', boy, but listen to me now. I ain't tellin' no story here. Don't sleep in nobody's barn. Don't knock on nobody's door. You hightail it on outta this country before dark. They been hangin' colored folks around here, and there ain't *nobody* to stop 'em, neither."

Mrs. Schmidt brought out a paper-wrapped package. "Here's some sandwiches and a jar of cider for later on. Just get on now. And mind what Mister Schmidt is tellin' you."

"Mighty kind, ma'am. I cut that wood so's to fit easy in your firebox."

"You're a good worker." Schmidt clapped him on the back. "Now get, and don't come back here, not unless you're comin' with the Lord of hosts and a flamin' sword of fire. Otherwise, you're gonna get a rope around that bull neck of yourn."

With that warning ringing in his ears, Jefferson put his boots back into his duffel bag and set off down the lane with strict instructions on how to avoid every farmhouse along the way.

CHAPTER TWENTY-FOUR

The Warne Brothers

The Fourth of July dawned with gray and threatening skies. Trudy's mother, Sadie, glared at the thunderheads as if to warn them they had better not ruin the day everyone had been working so hard to make perfect.

The sun was barely up before heaps of red, white, and blue bunting were loaded into the back of the automobile to be trundled off to the Fort Smith Electric Park for the big celebration. Like many other Fort Smith citizens who had emigrated from Germany, Joseph and Sadie Meyer had managed to survive the prejudice the war brought to their doorstep by throwing themselves into the war effort with patriotic zeal. Joseph Meyer had sold more war bonds than any merchant on Garrison Avenue. Sadie had not only donated material for warm clothing for the soldiers at the front, she had also organized the Hebrew Ladies Benevolent Society to sew and pack and mail the items, and now she would not be outdone in the celebration of the victory. Bunting material came from Meyer's Dry Goods store. Her sewing circle matched the output of the Lutheran church Trudy attended, which had a much larger congregation than the small synagogue. This was a fact that Sadie would not let Trudy—or Joseph, who was not the least bit religious—forget.

"When you see the bunting on the bandstand, remember whose hands have put it there," Sadie said regally.

"And remember whose store, if you please," Joseph replied with a good-natured shrug. What did he care if one sewing circle hung more bunting than the next as long as everyone remembered where the fabric came from?

"Just because we are Americans now, we should not forget the old ways."

"Yes, we should." Joseph cranked the engine to a roaring start. "Otherwise, the Lutherans and the Baptists and the Methodists will stay open on Saturdays when I am at the synagogue with you, and suddenly there is no more Meyer's Dry Goods store and no more free material for bunting and nothing for the Hebrew ladies to sew." He smiled. "Give me a little peace, Sadie, will you?"

They rattled off down the street arguing the point for the hundredth time. Trudy stood at the curb beside Birch and watched the pantomimed discussion she knew by heart. When her parents rounded the corner, it was still going on. She knew the matter would not be settled today or ever. She felt strangely uneasy that Birch had witnessed the family "issue."

"Mama is disappointed in me, I think," she confessed to Birch as she breaded the chicken and dropped it into the sizzling skillet an hour later.

Birch sat at a table and peeled potatoes. He had a soft smile on his lips as he looked at her flour-covered hands. He seemed not to hear her.

She wanted to talk to him about it. Surely he had not missed the fact that she was Jewish. Did it matter to him, as it seemed to matter to many people in Fort Smith?

"Mama was hoping I'd meet someone in New York," she said, poking the chicken as it browned.

"Hmmm." He tossed the spiral peel into a bowl and started another potato. "Someone, huh? Anyone in particular? Or just someone from New York?"

"Someone . . . you know, from the old neighborhood. There is not a great bounty of eligible Jewish boys here in Fort Smith, as you can imagine."

She jabbed the chicken harder, wishing she had not said such a thing. It sounded as though she were talking about marriage—which she was, of course. But why was she talking about such a personal thing with Birch Tucker? What must he think about her for bringing up such a topic? "I mean . . . what I mean is . . . as you could see this morning, we still have one foot in that world and one in this world."

"Sort of like tryin' to straddle the Arkansas River at flood time, ain't it?"

"Yes. Mama on one side. Papa on the other. And me, closer to his side than hers. So she's disappointed in me, I think, that I didn't—" She caught herself before she slipped into talking about the real reason her mother had wanted her to go to New York.

"She was hopin' you'd marry somebody from Orchard Street, huh?

Bring him back here to Fort Smith?" He was concentrating very hard on making the peel come off the spud in a single perfect spiral.

Embarrassment crept into Trudy's cheeks. Maybe he would think the color was just from standing over a hot stove. "A pickleman would do. As long as—"

"As long as he's Jewish?"

"Something like that."

"So she sent you stalkin' a husband, huh?" He held up the peel and bounced it like a spring.

"Not in so many words." She was not at all happy with the way she had gotten onto this unpleasant subject. "After all, I got my teaching credentials, and—"

"You could've done that in Fayetteville. Kansas City. St. Louis. You were sent to New York to bag yourself a husband."

"What a thing to say!"

"You said it first. Not me. You were supposed to marry a Jewish pickleman. But now you've brought me home instead." He was grinning in a superior way. "I'll bet she's not real happy about that."

"Nonsense. You don't have anything to do with this." Indignant, she turned the chicken and sprinkled another fistful of flour into the skillet. It hissed loudly when it hit the grease.

"Is that so? Well, well. You could of fooled me. I thought we were discussin' marriage here."

"Whyever would you think such a thing?" This was terrible. Now she sounded as though she were trying to worm something out of him, when that had not been her intention at all. "Really, Birch. We should talk about something else."

"Okay," he said, without the slightest hint of disappointment in his tone—as if it made no difference to him what they talked about.

"Well, what do you want to talk about?"

He was silent for a moment. "You think we'll get rained out today? It would be a shame if all that buntin' got ruined."

Further conversation followed along these same dull lines throughout the rest of the morning. Trudy felt the same vague sense of disappointment that she had felt that day on the train when she realized she would not be seeing Birch ever again—disappointment tinged with uncertainty. Had she only imagined that he had been looking at her with interest, even with affection? Had she misjudged his smiles, the way his fingers had brushed hers when he passed the mashed potatoes at the dinner table? Did she misinterpret the genuine interest Birch had seemed to show when he discussed with her father the perils that Prohibition might bring to the family business?

Trudy had to admit she had hoped Birch's interest in her concerns was more than just friendly. So she was wrong about that. Why, now, did she wish she had been right? It was all very muddled and she could not sort it out.

She glanced up at him as they stood in line to board the trolley. He was so handsome in his uniform. He held the picnic basket on his arm, a sign that he was spoken for, that he was in the company of one Miss Trudy Meyer. Other girls looked at her with envy and whispered to one another as if they knew some secret.

But Birch talked to everyone with the same earnest interest and direct gaze. Trudy now understood that she was nothing special to him after all. The discussion in the kitchen had been academic only. The looks and the smiles and the pleasant words were nothing that he did not give freely to everyone.

Baseball games and the Fourth of July were a long-standing tradition in Guernsey County, Ohio. You couldn't have one without the other. And baseball just would not be the same without the Warne boys on the field.

They had always been unbeatable, these Warne brothers. Of course, there were fewer of them now than in years past, but still there were enough of them to man most of the infield. They were a well-ordered bunch, with Doc Warne as coach. Always before, the Four Gospels had played positions at all four bases. Matthew on first. Mark on second. Luke on third. And John at home plate as catcher.

Before the war, young Ellis had been pitcher—the best pitcher ever seen in Guernsey County. Big-league stuff, he was. And he could knock a ball clean into the next county, the home folks said. His other two brothers, Jack and Tim, the ones who had not come home from France, had also been natural ball players. Along with Doc, they had made a formidable team.

It was a shame what had happened. Everyone said so. Shortstop and center fielder dead. The catcher one-legged. The tragedy had already been thoroughly discussed by everyone at the annual Independence Day picnic and baseball tournament that was held at the Presbyterian church. This year, because of the decimation of the Warne ranks, it was not expected that the Presbyterians would be real competition for the Methodists, the Episcopalians, or especially the Baptists. But these teams could not see that the soul of Ellis Warne still had two legs.

The spectators raised their eyebrows in pity when the one-legged catcher took his position behind the plate. Becky and Molly watched from the stands and listened to the comments of family members of the opposing team from the Baptist church. All comments were whispered, of course, which was supposed to make them somehow more polite.

"Mama! Look at that man! He's only got one—"

"Shhhhh! Shush, Sally honey. It's not polite to notice." At this pause the voice dropped very low. "It's our patriotic duty to let him play, poor crippled thing. How awful. How simply awful. How they expect that poor crippled boy to play baseball, I'll never know. Look there—he's not wearing his peg leg. . . . "

"Is he . . . is he like a pirate, Mama?"

"Shush, Sally. Quit pointing. It's not polite."

"But what happened to his leg, Mama?"

"The kaiser shot it off, Sally. Now watch the game. Here's your brother up to bat. I do hope he's easy on that poor crippled boy."

Becky squirmed in the bleachers. She grimaced and glared at this outpouring of unsought pity. Calling Ellis a cripple, indeed! After all these weeks of practice. The woman didn't have the faintest idea. Becky started to turn around and tell the busybody and her little Sally that Ellis could still outplay the fat-bellied, red-faced Baptist up to bat. . . .

Molly put a soothing hand on Becky's arm. "They'll see soon enough. Let it be." She cracked a sly smile. "Although I would like to bet this month's grocery money on the game."

"Play ball!" shouted Paul Mazurki, the umpire. He was a Catholic and thus free from the temptation to favor one Protestant pitcher over another. To him, they were all semiheathen, so he would judge each ball and strike and stolen base fairly.

When Ellis was crouched in position, it was hard to tell he did not have two good legs under him. John threw the first strike and then the second, and he caught them both without a hitch.

Becky could not help herself. She turned to the mother of the batter. "What do you think of the catcher now?"

"Anyone can catch a ball thrown straight to them." The woman glared beneath her parasol.

"But it seems not everyone can hit one," Becky replied, "no matter how many legs he has."

"Well!"

"Steeee-rike three! You're outta here!"

"Papist umpire," muttered the mother of the batter. Then she grabbed little Sally by the back of her collar and dragged her off to sit someplace with less sun.

"John is pitching rather well today; don't you think so, Mother Warne?" Becky smiled smugly and applauded the boys.

"Considering that he must fill Ellis's shoes," Molly agreed, "he seems remarkably calm."

Becky motioned toward her brother, Howard, who was playing shortstop. Howard, too, had just returned from the war—not a hero, like Ellis, but a survivor of bureaucratic red tape. And, as Howard commented wryly, they didn't hand out Purple Hearts for filling out forms.

A scholar, not a ballplayer, Howard had been drafted to play with the Warne brothers because he was soon to be related by marriage. That was his one qualification.

"There is our weak link, Mother Warne."

"Becky! That's an unkind thing to say about your own brother!"

Becky sighed regretfully. "True, though."

At that moment, Baptist Batter No. 2 hit a hard drive straight toward Howard. Panic filled his ruddy face as the ball zoomed with deadly aim at his nose. "I got it!" he screamed, holding the mitt in front of his face. The ball cooperated nicely, hitting Howard's glove with a force that knocked him backward. When he stopped tumbling, he looked in his hand and beheld a miracle. The ball was where it should have been.

"He's outta there!" the umpire yelled.

"Two up, two down. My, my." Molly shook her head sadly. "I do wish I had put the grocery money on our boys."

"I shall have a new respect for Howard from now on," Becky muttered. "I thought he would duck."

The third batter grinned in a sinister way at Ellis as though he had a secret weapon up his sleeve. He took a few practice swings before stepping to the plate. John and Ellis eyed each other, sending signals that Ellis had tried to teach Becky as they had sat on the porch swing.

"A fastball, I think, Mother Warne."

"No, girl," Molly whispered. "A sinker."

Sure enough, John fired a sinker that homed into the batter's range and dropped at the instant the man split the empty air above it.

"You see?" Molly remarked. "Ellis taught him how. Says he'll make a fine pitcher by and by."

Once more the batter scowled down at Ellis as if Ellis had snatched the pitch right from him. He pawed the ground like a bull and tapped his cleats with the bat.

The windup . . . the pitch . . . the swing!

The Baptist side of the bleachers went wild as the bat cracked with the impact against the ball. They were not cheering a home run, but rather a pop foul that rose sixty feet into the air and arced back behind the plate. An easy catch for a catcher with two legs, but what about this one?

Ellis leaped up, searching the sun for the ball as he wavered. Then,

just as Doc had predicted, it came to him as if he had been born with
only one leg. Three long jumps put him beneath the plummeting ball.
He reached out and nabbed it—easy as pie, thank you.

Silence descended over the Baptists. Ellis tipped his cap to Molly and
Becky and held up the ball for all to see. A cheer arose—from both sides.

"You're outta there!" the umpire roared.

So, Ellis Warne could catch. With his wooden leg hung up on a hook,
he could still outcatch any catcher on the field today. But could he still
hit the ball?

For his turn at bat, Ellis strapped on his wooden leg. He did not even
bother to put a sock on it. There it was, right out in the open for every
Protestant in Guernsey County to see. Wooden. Shaped like a real leg,
only not real. It was a shocking thing, but there it was. He needed it for
balance. He had to have the thing so he could shift his weight from right
to left in the swing.

Every kid and grown man in the stand was bug-eyed as Ellis stepped
to the plate. The ladies pretended not to notice. Little Danny Flannigan
came up beside him and took his mark as though he were running a race.
Everyone knew that Ellis Warne could not run the bases, so in the interest of patriotic spirit on behalf of a wounded war veteran, everyone
agreed that Danny could run for Ellis—if, in fact, Ellis could still really
hit the ball. Which everyone doubted. Otherwise, they might not have
wanted Danny there to run. Nor would they have wanted Ellis to bat.

It was too late for regrets now. Ellis stood ready at the plate, armed
and dangerous. Rather than tap his cleats with the bat, he clunked it hard
against his wooden appendage and grinned. He was ready.

The opposing pitcher was sweating. He had faced Ellis before, and he
had seen the look that said Ellis was determined to kill a cow grazing
somewhere in Pennsylvania with a home-run ball. Here he was again.
The old Ellis. Not Protestant, not Presbyterian, but ballplayer to the core.

Ellis pointed his bat to the plate. "Come on," he snarled. This was the
only time Ellis ever snarled, Molly noted to Becky. Only during baseball
games.

The signals passed between pitcher and catcher. The crowd held its
breath.

The windup!

The pitch!

The crack of contact sent the crowd into a frenzied roar. The ball
sailed up and up—over the head of the second baseman, over the center
fielder, out and away from the diamond, bouncing once on this side of
Mr. Schuler's pasture fence and then over it. The outfielders scrambled to
run for it as Danny Flannigan rounded second base and raced toward

third. The right fielder tripped and tumbled to the ground as the center fielder threw himself over the fence.

"No!" shouted Mr. Schuler. "Get out of the field! My bull is in that field! Get out! Get—"

The center fielder plunged back over the fence without the ball. He also had lost his glove and hat. He lay panting on the ground as Danny headed for home and came in with a slide just for the fun of it.

"Baptists!" Becky Moniger snorted eight innings later. The first game ended 12–3, the Warne boys winning by a landslide. "Look at them—sweating so much you'd think they'd all been immersed." Becky laughed and punched her brother, Howard, playfully in the arm as he guzzled a quart jar of iced tea.

Howard looked as though he had just crawled from a river. "I don't know, Becky," he said wearily. "I'm just the soon-to-be brother-in-law, and these Warne boys scare the bejeebers out of me, too."

"Chin up, Howard," Becky teased. "Only two games to go." She smiled and waved at the row of Methodist players, who were definitely intimidated. "We'll beat them in no time, and then you can rest."

CHAPTER TWENTY-FIVE

What We Were Fighting For

Billy Jones's wagon was filled with children when it pulled up to the gate of the Canfield farm. Billy's wife, Delpha Jean, was dressed in her best Sunday dress and bonnet. She waved her plump arms as Willa-Mae stepped out onto the porch.

"Willa-Mae! Y'all come on into Fort Smith with us. We's goin' to visit Billy's sister. They havin' a barbecue down t'the river. Y'all get dressed an' come on with us now!"

Hock and Willa-Mae and the girls all flocked to the gate to look over Billy and Delpha Jean and the six young'uns, all dressed in their Sunday best despite the heat.

"Cain't go," Hock said flatly. "That old sow's gonna farrow anytime. She's due to have young'uns today or tomorra."

Groans of disappointment rose from the girls. The flock of children in the back urged that at least they should be able to cram Little Nettie into the wagon and take her with them.

Hock shook his head and spit. "It's the Canfield way. If all cain't, then none'll go. But thank y'all just the same."

Willa-Mae furrowed her brow. It didn't seem like Hock ever let the gals go into the big city of Fort Smith. And this was a holiday, too. Still, she did not argue in front of Billy and Delpha Jean. She would argue the matter later on.

"Where y'all gonna camp?" Willa-Mae asked. "Just in case that sow comes early. Then mebbe we'll come on anyhow."

"Oh, I'll be prayin'." Delpha Jean clapped her hands.

Billy waved his hand toward the sun. "That sow best get on with it if she's gonna. If the excitement ain't over by time y'all can get there, we's gonna camp right south of that white folks' 'Lectric Park. You just walk right on down the riverbank and you'll see my old raggedy lean-to—jus' like the one I use when we goes huntin', Hock."

It didn't look likely that the sow would farrow tonight, but Hock thanked his neighbors all the same and sent them on their way. His daughters grumbled and moped for the rest of the afternoon, but some things were more important than watching white folks shoot their fireworks over the river on the Fourth of July. That was a good old sow down in the pen, and Hock would not take a chance on losing her for the sake of the July Fourth freedom celebration.

"Freedom don't mean the same for us folks," he muttered as the girls griped all the way back to the house. "Besides, Willa-Mae, this is the night the devil comes out an' gets right into the hearts of some white folks. I reckon we best stay right close to home, sow or no sow."

☆ ☆ ☆

A tall, smiling, middle-aged man made his way through the crowd of spectators that stood along the third baseline. His cream-colored linen suit was immaculately pressed, and a brand-new Panama hat tilted back from his boyish face at a jaunty angle. As Becky watched, the grinning man stopped to shake hands with two farmers, clapped a third on the back heartily, and stooped to admire a baby sheltered from the sun under a mother's parasol.

"Howard," Becky inquired, "who is that? He surely isn't dressed to play baseball."

"Hmmm?" Howard mumbled, his nose in a book. "What did you say, Beck? I was trying to catch up on my reading before the next game."

"Never mind," she said. "Are you leaving, Mother Warne?" she asked as Molly picked her way down from the stands.

"I just need to deliver a message," Molly replied. "I've been watching the Methodist pitcher warm up. He drops his left shoulder before he throws a curveball. Doc will be wanting our boys to know that, I think."

The two women made their way toward Doc and Ellis, who was still receiving congratulations from a crowd of admiring boys.

"Mother Warne," Becky repeated her question, "who is that man?"

The man in the linen suit had removed his jacket in a concession to informality and was working his way up the baseline toward Doc, still smiling and shaking hands.

"That?" Molly sniffed. "That is the Honorable Judge Hopewell." She leaned so hard on the word *honorable* that it sounded like swearing.

"Congratulations," Hopewell was saying to Doc as Molly and Becky approached. "I see the stories about the prowess of the Warne family have not been exaggerated. It's no wonder you are admired so widely."

Doc started to say thank you, then evidently noticed who the speaker was and stopped. Doc surveyed the newcomer critically, as if examining something unpleasant on the sole of his shoe. "Would you be knowing anything about baseball, then, Judge Hopewell? It's a game played out in the open where everyone can watch to see that the rules are observed."

Hopewell laughed loudly, as if Doc had just made the wittiest comment ever. "And a game of courage and skill, too," he added. "And none more courageous than your son. Terrible shame about his leg. Dreadful, dreadful."

"You are right about his courage," agreed Doc. "Not that it's a subject about which you have firsthand knowledge."

"Now, Dr. Warne," Hopewell admonished, "let's not have any differences. I'm sure we both want the best for all our proud veterans. What a mess this country is in! All these brave boys coming home from the war, finding that their jobs have been taken by bohunks or Polacks. Why, I passed two truckloads of Nigras camped along the highway as I came over to the game. Straight off the plantation, no doubt, with all their little pickaninnies in tow. Why, there ought to be laws against letting them roam so free. . . . As a matter of fact, I expect to soon be in a position to do exactly that."

"Exactly what?"

"Why, make the laws, of course, what with the congressional seat vacancy left by Mills's death. Senator Harding's people have asked me to stand for that position, and I have their complete backing—and that of other real fine Americans."

"How very nice for you," Doc said dryly.

"With that machinery behind me, I certainly cannot lose. But, Doctor Warne," Hopewell said earnestly, "your opinion counts for a lot around this county. It would please me to have your support also."

"Hopewell," Doc said, "if I were ever to find myself on the same side of the fence with you, I'd jump to the other as quick as lightning, even if Farmer Schuler's bull was on the other side."

"Don't be hasty, Doctor Warne," Hopewell concluded. "Think of all the good we can do for this county. My, my, look at the time. Sorry to cut and run," he said abruptly. "I've got to call on other gatherings on this proud American holiday. It's my civic duty, you know."

Becky looked after Hopewell's retreating form. "Who invited him?"

"Nobody had to invite him," Doc said. "His kind just naturally show up. They always do."

"Let it go now, Doc," Molly cautioned. "You'll be getting distracted from the game."

"It's not only that I hate what he says. I hate for people to even see me talking with such as him. What if they believed I agreed with him?" Doc shuddered as if the very thought was like a dose of the vilest medicine.

"Doc," said Umpire Mazurki, "I heard what Hopewell said, and what you replied. I'm glad you have no truck with such as him. No one who knows you will think you agree with him. But you make me think about who we will get to stand up to Hopewell and his machines."

Doc shook his head and shrugged. "Come on, my friend. Isn't it time for you to say 'Play ball'?"

✳ ✳ ✳

It took thirty minutes for the trolley to travel the five miles from downtown Fort Smith to Electric Park. Located on seventy-five wooded acres, the park had been built by the Fort Smith Light and Traction Company to help promote use of the trolleys on weekends and after working hours. While children stood in long lines for the roller coaster or crowded into the swimming pool, the adults played in the theatre, casino, or dance pavilion, or simply strolled along the elegant pathways of the gardens.

Today every lamppost and facade was adorned with bunting. The veterans of the Great War were out in force to mingle with the aged veterans of the Civil War and black-clad widows and mothers of the "glorious dead." Speeches were made by the mayor and the fire captain and the president of the bank. Salutes were fired and tears were plentiful. Then the dance bands tuned up and picnic baskets opened. It was a perfect day, unspoiled by the threat of rain as the earlier clouds had disappeared.

Birch talked about the war with fellow veterans. Trudy talked about Belle Grove School with a group of seasoned teachers.

Birch watched Trudy as she sat in the shade of the gazebo near the dance floor. Other women around her seemed dull by comparison. He did not need to hear what she was saying to enjoy her distant conversation. He memorized the way she moved her hand as she spoke, the tilt of her head as she laughed and the others laughed with her.

Beautiful.

He wished she would look his way. He was sorry now that he had gotten drawn into conversation with the dozen other warriors young and old who sat around the picnic table. They talked about the way things had been before the war and during the war and the way things were now. The conversation swung to the women's right to vote and then to Prohibition. In Arkansas, both issues were enough to raise the hackles on a dead dog.

"Round here, we got us some natural ideas what women are good for. And it ain't goin' to the polls to vote, neither!"

"Almost as bad as lettin' the niggers vote. Now that the war is over, they want a vote," agreed a trembling vet of the Civil War.

"Women pickin' a president! Niggers pickin' a senator! That ain't what I went to fight for."

The subject of Prohibition arose, in between refills of great foaming steins of beer.

"If this thing passes, it's gonna just dry up Fort Smith and blow us off the map."

"I'm tellin' you, boys, if we have to close the saloons in this town, there will be no more business from them thirsty Oklahoma folks. It's gonna hurt us, all right. Shut this place up tight."

"Prohibition. Women's suffrage. The world ain't the same, and that's a fact!"

"Yeah, but like Harve said, it ain't what we went to fight for."

The truth was, no one around the table was sure why they had gone to war. But they had done it and won it, and now they had come home to a whole world busted loose. Women were working at men's jobs and proud of it. And now the whole government was about to go crazy and vote away a man's right to buy a beer in a public place!

Beyond those issues, most of the veterans who sat around that table did not have the vaguest idea that the Austro-Hungarian Empire had been carved up to create four separate nations. Nor did they know that President Wilson was fighting for the life of his League of Nations. Or that the same Congress voting for women's rights and Prohibition was also denying that the United States should have anything further to do with the affairs of Europe. Or that without the backing of the U.S., the League was doomed to failure.

Birch listened to the men, sadly aware that if he had not been with Max Meyer for months on end, witnessing the turmoil in Europe first-hand and talking about the issues, he would have been just as ignorant.

He eyed Trudy across the wide green lawn. She was engaged in some lively debate. Like Max, no doubt, her opinions were better informed and well thought out than the entire rabble sitting at his table. Ignorant, bigoted men, these former soldiers did not have a clue that the war they fought might have to be refought by their sons if the political decisions being made now were bad ones. He would have given anything if he could have gone over to sit among the women just to listen to Trudy.

"What do you think about it, Birch Tucker?" someone asked, penetrating the fog of his inattention.

"What do I think about it?" he asked. "What?"

"About what President Wilson's been sayin' about lettin' the Germans off easier . . . after we licked 'em, he's sayin' they ought not to have to pay for the war. So . . . what do you say?"

Birch and Max had talked about it a dozen times. Birch did have an opinion. "We licked the Germans all right, but they were on French soil when we done it. The French and the English were just as licked as the Germans before we Americans got into it."

This fact was greeted by a chorus of cheers from the proud soldiers. "But, Birch, that don't answer the question—reparations and such. Do we make the Germans pay?"

At this, Birch turned his eyes back to Trudy briefly as he remembered standing with Max, looking out over hungry Paris. "I heard a fella say that war makes the winners vengeful and the losers resentful. Down the line somewhere the losers—or rather the orphan kids of the losers—all grow up hatin' the winners. And they start figurin' how they can get even. Then there's another war. Their kids and our kids. See?"

His comment was answered by boos. "That ain't the question!"

Birch shrugged. "Yes. That *is* the question. We won the war, and now the politicians are plannin' the next one for us."

"There ain't gonna be a next one," someone protested.

"Sit down, Tucker. And shut up!"

Trudy turned her head at the racket and spotted Birch's eyes on her. She paused midsentence, smiled, and looked away. He could tell even from here that she was blushing at his gaze. It made him want to walk right over there, lift her up out of that chair, and kiss her until she hollered for more.

It was a pleasant thought. Much more enjoyable than politics.

He was grinning at that mental image when someone tapped him on the shoulder.

"You Birch Tucker?"

He turned to face a young, pleasant-faced man several inches shorter than he. The fellow wore a white straw boater hat, a white shirt rolled up at the sleeves, and no tie.

"That's me," Birch said, sorry to be interrupted in his reverie.

"How-do." The man gave Birch a quick handshake. "My name is Davey East. I was by to see you a while ago at the Meyer house. You were incapacitated."

"Yeah." Birch raised his hand to touch the back of his head. "I made it through the war okay. Then I came home and somebody broke a jug on my head."

"Yup. I heard about that. You recovered?"

"Mostly."

"Glad to hear it. That's fine news." He paused and also looked at Trudy. "She's quite a gal. Pretty protective over you." He raised an eyebrow. "I had some questions to ask about the Nigra boy who was with you in that fight. Jeff Field is his name. Lives somewhere around here."

"Why are you askin'?"

East flashed a smile. "I'm just a deputy sheriff. They're lookin' for this Nigra. Aim to take him on back up to Missouri when we find him. Guess he done some damage, and they're wantin' to put him on trial over it."

"Why don't they want me on trial? I was fightin' up there, too."

"Well, you're white. And from what I heard, you were well out of the thing before it got ugly."

Images of the fight flashed into Birch's mind. "It was ugly before they ever threw a punch."

"I suppose. Must've been." East was still smiling. "But that ain't for us down here to figure out. They just want to take that Nigra up for a fair trial, and—"

"And you were hopin' I could help you find him?"

A fly hummed around East's face, but the smile remained fixed. Professionally pleasant. "That's about it."

"Then I'm sorry to disappoint you. I don't know where he is."

The smile wavered slightly. "I see. That is bad news. We ain't tracked him down yet. I was hoping to save some work."

"Sorry."

East cast another look toward Trudy, and the smile on his face vanished. It was replaced for a minute by something calculating, cold, perhaps even evil, and Birch saw it.

The man looked back at Birch. "You ain't a Jew, are you?"

The question took Birch completely by surprise. "Why do you ask?"

The smile slid back into place. "Just wonderin' is all." He paused. "I didn't hear anybody at the table ask you what you thought about the Nigras comin' back from the war and gettin' uppity, wantin' to vote like any white man. You got an opinion?" He scratched his head.

Suddenly Birch glimpsed the deputy sheriff's soul. He was a very ugly little man behind the smile. "Those men bleed red same as the rest of us."

"So does my dog, Mr. Tucker."

The hatred was right there, visible—dark and evil for Birch to see.

East tipped his straw hat. "Well, thanks for nothin'. We'll find him, all the same." The same dark look swept toward Trudy. "With the company you keep, I shoulda known you'd be of no help."

Anger coursed through Birch—not at what East said, but at the way he looked at Trudy. Birch could have caught the little man by his shirt, knocked him out with one blow, broken up the party, and gotten arrested to boot. But he did not, nor did he respond to the jibe. Something in him whispered a warning. *Let it go! Let it go!*

Then shots rang out south of the Electric Park—gunfire or firecrackers? At first it was hard to tell. Birch turned his head toward the sound as a dozen men ran to the side of Deputy East. All of them were talking at once.

"It's a bunch of niggers down at the river. Drunk niggers shootin' guns. They killed Vera Allsop's dog down there with their shootin', and Vera's near hysteric about it!"

East removed his tin badge from his shirt pocket and pinned it to the outside so that the late-afternoon sun glinted on it.

"Won't do to go on down there without my gun if they're armed," he said. "I got a couple of rifles in the car, and my revolver." He turned and eyed Birch. Tipping his hat in a businesslike way, he nodded as though to say he was not finished with Birch or the matter of Jeff Field.

✶ ✶ ✶

Everyone in New York who could not afford to be somewhere else was traveling to Coney Island, it seemed to Max. As the city shimmered in the humid summer heat like a vast steam laundry, thousands of sweating citizens traveled by subway to play beside the Atlantic and wait for a cool evening breeze to come along.

Max carried a large woven shopping basket full of all the stuff Irene brought along on their usual Coney Island outings. Bathing suits, towels, a blanket. A small umbrella to keep the sun off her delicate skin. Food to munch on. A book to read. For all of this, they might have been staying a week instead of just the day and the evening.

Usually Irene was as excited as a kid about a trip to Coney Island. But today she was pale and silent. She told Max she felt sick. He would have worried about her catching the flu, but that epidemic was over. He tried to cheer her up, but she would not be cheered. He figured it was because he was leaving tomorrow for England. She sat glumly staring out the window at the dark tunnel, and her expression did not change when the train emerged abruptly into the land of carnival rides and tepid waves and tight-packed bodies on the shore.

"You okay?" he asked her for the sixth time since they'd left.

"Fine," she snapped, and once again he had the feeling that he had committed some unknown crime that had made her sulk.

"You sure? We can go back."

She glared at him. "Go back and do what?"

"Just go back . . . home. If you need to lie down or something."

She ignored his offer and walked ahead of him into the hubbub of the Luna Park sideshows. Every variety of New Yorker wandered through the throng of shows to look at dwarfs and bearded ladies and swimming champions and have photographs snapped with the strongman. High above the carnival, shrieks reverberated from the swooping roller coasters. Organ-grinders cranked their boxes to compete with strolling musicians.

Irene remained detached and uninterested.

It had been two summers since they had been here together. Irene had loved the zany confusion of Coney Island then. Even after Max had taken her for an airplane ride and she had gotten sick, still she had laughed and held his hand and talked about everything.

What has changed? Max wondered.

Beside the ocean they were assaulted by a wave of smells. German sausages, kosher hot dogs, hamburgers, shrimp, oysters, and soft-shelled crab. Suddenly Irene looked terribly ill. Her hand went to her stomach. Her fair skin grew ghostly pale.

She turned to glare at Max, as though he had created the aromas to annoy her. "I'm . . . I don't feel well," she snapped. "Do you even care?" She pushed past him to run for the public changing room.

"Irene?" Max trailed after her miserably, lugging the basket. She bumped into two young girls, who glared briefly at her, then shrugged and resumed their animated conversation.

Max waited for her beside the shooting gallery, where ex-servicemen from the Bronx displayed for their girlfriends the marksmanship that had won the war. Everyone around seemed happy. Every person among the thousands crammed into that narrow strip of sand was smiling about something.

Everyone but Max and Irene. And today was not the first day she had acted this way toward him.

She emerged from the changing room. Her collar was wet, as if she'd been splashing cold water over her face. She still did not raise her eyes to look at him, even though her color was better.

"You okay?" This was question number seven.

"Do I look okay?" Her mouth puckered in a pout.

"You look better."

"No thanks to you."

Max raised his voice enough so that a group of kids glanced at him with surprise. "What did I do? *Look!* I didn't make you get sick, did I? So what am I? Your porter? You just drag me along so I can schlep your basket? It's our last day, for crying out loud!"

She bit her lower lip. Pretty blue eyes filled with tears. "Never mind. Just . . . I want to go home."

"Fine. Why didn't you say so in the first place?"

"I just did!" She broke into a slow jog back toward the subway.

Max walked at a slower pace. He did not want to catch her. He was tired of this . . . *whatever* . . . mood she was in. She had not been the same since he had told her about Oxford. First she had told him how wonderful it was, how happy she was for him. Then this gloom had settled on her. Half the time she said she felt sick. She did not want him to kiss her anymore, did not care if he held her. The passion she had once shared with him was waning. He eyed her as she maneuvered through the crowd. Maybe he didn't care. Things had changed since he had come home.

Max stopped as Irene purchased her ticket and passed through the turnstile. Not once did she look back to see if he was following.

"Fine," he said as she boarded the train. "Go on then." He hefted her basket, then passed it over the rail to a young boy in swim trunks. "Hey, kid, you see that pretty lady there in the light blue dress? Right there—on the train. I'll give you a nickel if you take this to her. She left it behind."

The boy eagerly accepted the task. Max stood with his arms crossed over his chest and watched as the child ran to Irene and gave her the basket. She looked up at Max. Her eyes narrowed angrily. She took the basket and turned away, as though she did not care if Max came with her or not.

The little boy ran back to collect his nickel. "Thanks, mister." He held up the coin. One nickel went a long way on Coney Island. "The lady wanted me to give you a message."

"Yeah? What is it?"

"Drop dead."

The boy skipped off as the subway doors clanged shut and the train slid away.

CHAPTER TWENTY-SIX

Light in the Night

It was nearly nine o'clock before Birch even got around to asking Trudy to dance. By that time Trudy had danced around the pavilion at least once with every short, single young man who had known her at Fort Smith High School. Her toes had been smashed by all of them.

"I was looking for you." Birch cut in on Fred Berger, whose sweating palms left Trudy's hand damp. Birch took her hand. "Feels like you've been washing dishes here instead of dancing."

"Washing dishes might be more fun." She sighed. The band struck up a polka. "Do you mind if we sit this one out? Doctor Cooper will kill me if he sees us hopping all over the pavilion. And besides, this is work."

"I was just going to ask you. You want to walk a bit?"

The night air blew cool against her face. The scent of roses hung sweet in the gardens. Every building sparkled with white lights. Birch led her toward the dark and fragrant woods. "I want to talk to you about somethin'," he explained in a serious tone. "We gotta go someplace quiet."

Their feet crunched on the gravel path as they passed a dozen young lovers sitting on the benches. Trudy tried not to look at them, tried not to envy their embraces or remember the way Max had kissed Irene in the thundershower on Orchard Street. Why did she hope that Birch would take her in his arms like that now?

She could hear the gurgle of a stream, louder than the music from the dance pavilion. "Where are we going?" she asked when it became too dark to see the path well.

"This is far enough." He stopped beside a large oak tree and dusted off a boulder with his hat. "Sit," he commanded.

She was grateful for the dark. Relieved that he could not see the fresh color on her cheeks. "What is it?"

"I have to ask you somethin' important. Really important, Trudy." He paced in front of the boulder.

"What is it, Birch? Stand still, will you? If you're going to pace, then we should have stayed to dance."

"Listen," he said, still pacing. "Somethin' came back to me tonight. Somethin' I have to know . . ."

"Well?"

He put his hand to his head. "When I got hit—"

"When you . . ." She tried not to feel disappointed. Nothing at all romantic about this little walk. Simply a fact-finding mission. "Yes. All right, then. What do you want to know?"

"Everythin'," he said with agony in his voice. "It came to me. Almost like a dream. The big black man. His name is Jeff Canfield. We were on the train together. Then at the . . . a water stop . . . somethin'. A carnival."

"Yes."

"And someone made a remark . . . about him. He told me not to say anythin'. But I did. I think I wanted to fight, hopin' for a chance to knock that fella on his ear. Then . . . it all went wrong. Real wrong. Next thing I knew . . . there you were. Did I dream it, Trudy? Is that the way it was? Because if I . . . if my own—" He faltered and held his fist up, staring at it as though it were an enemy.

"I saw them all around you and your friend," she replied in a soothing voice. "He—your friend—wanted to get back to the train. But—"

"But I just couldn't walk away from it." Birch knew it was all true. "Yeah, I get it. I couldn't just let it go. I had to push a little further when the fuse was lit. Fan the flame. And now. What's goin' to happen to him? The black man? The Preacher, he was called."

"He broke someone's arm. They want to put him in jail."

He sank down beside her. "Ain't gonna war no more," he muttered.

"What? Birch, you can't blame yourself for what happened. You were almost killed."

"Back in France I got another fellow hurt, badly hurt. He didn't even like to fight. Ellis Warne. Did Max write you about him?"

"He lost his leg. The night of the Armistice."

"That's him. And he lost that leg on account of me. Fighting my fight, see?" His voice was so full of regret that Trudy thought he might weep. He had not brought her here to this dark, quiet place to kiss her but to face himself—too hard a thing to do in the light.

"How can you blame yourself for such a thing, Birch? How?" She touched his arm, then took his hand.

"I did it. I wanted a fight. Both times. And there are other fights I wanted. I was never the one hurt . . . until Missouri. Always somebody who didn't deserve it. Ellis. The Preacher. And . . . my mother."

"Your mother?"

He did not reply to the curiosity in her voice. "I can't change any of it now. Can't undo what's been done. But I'll tell you this: I'll not raise my hand in anger again, Trudy. I've seen enough of it. I know what it means. Know what fightin' does. Or what it doesn't do. Nothin' is solved. There is so much damage. Lives ruined—first Ellis, and now they're after the Preacher. And . . . well, I want you to know that, Trudy. I'm done fightin'. You have to know that tonight before I tell you the rest. You've got to know I've got a temper. And then I want you to know . . . that's about all I've got."

She squeezed his hand to let him know she was listening. "Yes, Birch."

"That temper has got folks into trouble. And I've got to try and work somethin' out back home. Then, if I do . . . and if I can come back here with somethin' to offer you . . . I intend to marry you."

She laughed. "Just like that?"

"Just like that. I haven't been able to think about another woman since the first time I heard Max read your letter. The one about Mister Finkel, the pickleman. And the herring. How it made the nickels in the register stink."

"Very inspiring stuff. Just the sort of thing to make a man fall in love. But what if I do not share your feelings, Birch Tucker? What about me? A girl likes to be asked, not told—"

"Doggone it, Trudy!" He took her in his arms and pulled her close. His face was close to hers. His eyes searched her eyes. "Quit playin' with my heart now. We're not strangers on a train from New York anymore. I stood beneath your window on Orchard Street, and I looked up and wanted you. Now you've fed me and washed my wounds, and I don't know what all—"

"My mother and father took care of the rest, thank you." Did he imagine she had bathed him? *The nerve!*

"It doesn't matter. I slept in your bed and thought about you being in it. I watched you move around the room like a shadow, and I wanted to call you back to lie beside me. I loved your heart before I ever met you face-to-face. And now that I've seen the rest, I reckon I'd be a liar if I didn't tell you I want all of you at the same time." He kissed her hard.

She felt suddenly weak. She could hardly breathe. He kissed her again, more fiercely than the first time. She could not fight him; she did not try. Somewhere far away was the sound of cannons booming. No.

Not cannons, thunder! The rain began to fall, rattling the leaves of the oak tree.

"Say it, True," Birch whispered. "Tell me you love me."

"Yes." She raised her face to the rain, impatient to be kissed again.

"Say the words."

"I love you, Birch."

"Then I can face anythin'."

Max had seen enough of the great Independence Day celebration at Coney Island. He had found old friends there among the crowd and had stayed with their group for the day, but his mind had already ridden the train back home.

When he was introduced to a dozen young women from Barnard College at Columbia, he smiled and called the one named Susan "Irene." It would not have been so bad if it had happened only once. But four times? At last Susan had looked at him and said, "Irene isn't here. But I think you should go find her."

The fireworks were exploding overhead as Max boarded the almost empty subway. He saw their color reflect in the grimy windows, but he did not turn to look. The rumbling in the dark tunnel went unnoticed. He slammed his fist on the vacant seat beside him as the train stopped at every empty station between Coney Island and the East Side. No one got on. No one got off. Everyone in the world was on the beach except for Max and Irene. The city was deserted. Only Max and Irene were left in all the world. . . .

He regretted his anger. Why had he not gone with her? His stupid foolish pride had let her go. Childish vengeance had paid the kid a nickel to thrust the basket in her arms. *"Drop dead,"* she had said. Now that the air had cooled and his temper had abated, he already felt as if he might drop dead without her, and tomorrow he would be boarding a ship that would put an ocean between them again.

He was wrong about the city being deserted. Stepping off the train and walking quickly toward the Bowery, he saw that every saloon was open and packed with celebrating Irish patrons. The yeasty aroma of beer filled the hot summer night air.

He stood on the corner opposite Irene's apartment building. It was a redbrick tenement just like every other tenement building on the Lower East Side. Why could she not see that the reason he had to leave was to rescue them both from this life? Her window was dark.

Piano and accordion music competed from two saloons before the raucous laughter of patrons broke out, covering the melodies. Max's head was throbbing as he stared hard at the window, willing Irene to appear.

Leaning against the lamppost, he lost track of time. A large group staggered past him. They were drunk, their voices raised in rowdy song. As the racket grew louder, the curtain at Irene's window parted. She glanced down at the rabble.

Max raised his hand toward her. "Please . . . ," he muttered. "I'm sorry."

She could not hear his words, of course, but she must have heard his longing. She had felt him there waiting for her . . . hoping that she was alone. The curtain fell back, and a moment later Irene put the small potted violet on the window ledge, her signal to Max that she was alone in the house. Her brothers no doubt were down at the corner in Clary's Saloon.

He glanced over his shoulder and walked half a block down the street before crossing over. Doubling back, he slipped into the alley, then jumped and caught the ladder of the fire escape. She was waiting for him when he reached the top. She was crying when she took his hand and guided him into the darkness of the apartment. He could feel her damp cheeks against his face and taste the salt of her tears as he kissed her hungrily.

So she had missed him as much as he missed her. She regretted their argument as much as he did. They did not speak of it or of Max's departure. They did not talk about anything at all tonight.

She only whispered this as he held her: "I love you, Max, and it's too late. . . ."

☆ ☆ ☆

There was something in the night. Something moving across the land. Willa-Mae could sense it more than she could hear it. Hock's snoring and the soft breathing of her daughters were undisturbed, but Willa-Mae lay wide-awake on her back, staring up into the blackness of the cabin rafters.

Far off she heard the bellow of a cow, then another. These were followed by the barking of a dog, joined by two dogs from farther off. The peaceful hum of the night rippled with expectancy. Something coming this way. *A fox maybe? A cougar?*

The cornhusk mattress rustled as she sat up and swung her big legs over the side of the bed. Hock snorted and grumbled in his sleep as the moving of her weight shifted his small body from a comfortable groove.

She did not light the lamp. If the critter was a fox coming this way for the henhouse, then old Boone the hound dog would come out after him at first scent. No need for a light. A light would draw mosquitoes into the house. She could see the fields better by starlight anyway.

The floorboards groaned as she went out onto the porch and took a seat in the willow chair. She inhaled the freshness of the air, the scent of cotton and sweet corn and warm earth cooling in the night. And then that *something . . .*

She raised her eyes to the stars, half expecting to see the Lord of Glory coming like lightning. "What a day that'll be," she murmured. "Oh, Jesus. Hmmm." Then she thought that maybe she had been awakened just so she could sit awhile and pray, so she did that.

There was plenty to pray about. Poor folks and rich folks. White farmers and black. Lord knew they all had troubles. All needed praying for. Willa-Mae could sit and pray all night and not get through the list of praises and troubles alike that needed the Lord's attention.

So she prayed for a while, looking from the stars down to the tree-tops, which moved as if a hand brushed over them. She strained to see the lane as the *something* moved nearer, setting off dogs and chickens and cows like a wave. The something was a man-thing. *Mebbe one. Mebbe more. No fox or thievin' possum would come on down the lane.*

Still, she saw no movement along the starlit track. She was glad she had not lit the lamp. *Maybe trouble is comin', too.* Whatever it was, it had not set old Boone to howling yet. He lay beneath the porch, unmindful of the howls of neighbor dogs. He would tend to the problem when it came within the boundaries he had staked on every fence post and tree around the place. Until then, it was not his business. He would yap when his turn came and keep right on until the trouble went on down the lane. Until then, he would not open his eyes, even though Willa-Mae's weight made the boards creak and pop.

The stars slid slowly across the dark bowl of the sky. Three times Willa-Mae spotted the trail of a shooting star as it streaked earthward. She knew that meant somebody had died somewhere. It made her pray harder, and the hair on her neck prickled when old Boone crept out from under the porch, stretched himself, and turned his nose toward the lane. He sniffed the air.

"Somethin' comin', ol' Boone?"

He did not wag or move. His hound-dog nose searched the shadowed stretch before his eyes could see anything. Then he bayed a warning. Two short yips and a long howl. The hair on his back bristled.

"Stranger comin'." Willa-Mae knew that old Boone never howled like that unless it was a stranger. Such a bark kept the strangers from coming too near the house. Mostly they just stood real still down by the mailbox and hollered up to the house for help.

"Mebbe this one keep right on goin' by. . . ."

Two more loud yips and a long one. Boone growled and pawed at the dust. The stranger was at the gate. Willa-Mae could see slight movement in the dark shadows of the hickory trees that flanked the entrance to the place.

She stood and called to Hock as Boone barked more fiercely. "Somebody comin', Hock." She walked to the edge of the porch.

"Huh?" Hock stumbled out the door and hooked one strap of his overalls. "Who is it, comin' this time of night? Ain't good news that comes in the dark." He cupped his hand around his mouth and shouted over the barks of old Boone, "You just stay where you is!"

A voice bellowed back, "Tell ol' Boone it's jus' me!"

"Sweet mighty Jesus!" Willa-Mae cried. "It's *Jefferson*! Oh, Lord a'mighty, Hock! Praise God! It's Jefferson!"

Willa-Mae lit the lamp. She set it in the yard on an old stump and let the moths and mosquitoes bang into the glass chimney while the Canfields swarmed and hummed around big Jefferson as if he were the flame and the light and the lamp of their joy tonight. Butterflies in their nightgowns fluttered around him. Then they moved inside so Jefferson could eat. Cold buttermilk iced down in the well water was served to him in a tall Mason jar. A whole tin of corn bread was slathered thick with butter and eaten along with a quart of canned peaches and leftover beans and bacon.

Little Nettie sat on one of his knees. There was room left over for a whole flock of play-chillens, and she introduced them to him each in turn. Everyone asked questions all at once. Words bumped into one another. Sentences plowed over other sentences in a jumble of erupting thoughts. Then Jefferson began to laugh and Little Nettie began to laugh. A moment later Willa-Mae and Hock and Pink and Lula joined in, then Angel and Big Hattie, until the whole cabin rocked with their joy. Even ol' Boone joined in, poking his hound-dog head under Jefferson's arm with a dog smile, his tail wagging like a fan.

"Oh, glory be!" Willa-Mae clutched her broad middle.

Their joy was like food and drink. It took a while for them all to laugh their fill. They were all hungry for a good laugh and for Jefferson. And now, at last, he had come home, bringing the laughter with him.

CHAPTER TWENTY-SEVEN

Honor Thy Father

"What you brung me, Jeff?" Little Nettie tapped on his back as he lay sprawled and sleeping in the cabin.

He opened his eyes and studied the familiar patterns of the hand-hewn log wall beside his mattress. For as long as he could remember, he had awakened in the morning looking at the cuts where his granddaddy's ax had cut the tree and hewn it smooth. Each mark was a familiar picture to him. He had sometimes dreamed about the wall when he was far away in the mud-filled trenches. And now, at last, he had opened his eyes to see it again.

"Jeff?" Nettie's voice whined as she stood behind him. She could not see his face, so she couldn't know his eyes were open. He wanted to lie here a moment more and listen to the sounds of home. The giggles of the girls as they washed and hung the laundry in the yard. The *clap-clap-clap* of Hock's hammer against a board. Mama, calling out for Little Nettie . . .

"Where is that chil'? She ain't in there botherin' Jefferson, is she? I told that chil' to leave him be. He ain't hardly slept in days. Glory be! Nettie! Little Nettie! Where is you, gal?"

Jefferson did not move. He said in a growling voice, "Mama gonna whup you, Nettie, if you wakes me. Better get on out, and I'll be out directly."

"You awake?" she whispered.

"No. And don't wake me, neither. Mama'll whup you if you do."

"You talkin' in your sleep?"

"Yup."

"Will you tell me what you brung me?"

"Nope."

"Shoot."

"Get on out before Mama catches you."

She mumbled her way out of the room. "Nobody never slep' so long 'less they was sick. . . ."

Willa-Mae hollered when she spotted Nettie on the porch. "Little Nettie, I'm gonna whup you if you woke your brother!"

"I didn't, Mama."

Jefferson yawned and stretched, rolling over on his back. He tucked his hands beneath his head and filled his eyes with every familiar sight.

How could everything be just the same when he was so different inside? There was Mama and Papa's bed all made up with the red-and-blue-denim patchwork quilt. The rough gray woolen curtain was tied back, revealing the little alcove where their bed just fit. Across the room was the wide bed with the pull-out trundle beneath where the girls slept. The white-pine blanket chest, which also served as a bench, sat at the foot of the bed. The table was on the porch. Jefferson slept on a cornhusk mattress laid out each night against the wall opposite the front door. At his feet were the stones of the fireplace. Above his head was a window, which only in the last few years had glass in it. In the summer Jefferson slept beneath the open window to keep cool. In the winter Mama always tucked him in with his head close to the hearth for warmth. Above him were thick log rafters where each family member had a box for storing clothes. Jefferson counted them, silently reading each name stenciled on the bottom of the boxes.

One thing was different. Widdie's box was gone from the rafters. Mama had written him that they had given Widdie's things away after she died. They had buried her in her favorite quilt—the flower garden, she called it. He could still see it in his mind—blue and light blue flowers, pink and pink-checked flowers, each ringed by small green-fabric diamonds with bright yellow centers. In the winter Widdie used to wrap her fragile flower-stem form in her flower garden and sit right beside the hearth to stay warm. Now the quilt was gone and Widdie was gone, and her box in the rafters was gone, too. All along Jefferson had not quite believed the news—until now. Now that the flower-garden quilt was missing . . .

He glanced at his tightly packed duffel bag. Presents. He had brought something home for Widdie, even though Mama had written him the letter and all. Being so far away he had carried a picture of everything and everyone in his mind. Somehow he had not been able to take Widdie out of the picture.

He closed his eyes and made a different picture of Widdie now. Tall and slender, beautiful Widdie walking through a flower garden. Living flowers brushed her white robes. Flowers grew in pink checks and blue checks with bright yellow centers and edged with green diamonds. They nodded as she passed, reminding her of home.

"I come back, Widdie," he whispered. "I brung you a present. S'pose you won't mind if I give it to Little Nettie. Young'uns like lots of presents."

"I knowd you'd make it, Jefferson. Don't worry none 'bout me." Widdie smiled at him from her garden. *"It shore is perty here, an' Jesus is sooo good, too."*

"That's real good, Widdie," he whispered back. "Won't be long till we all be home with you."

He felt peaceful watching her walk away. After a while ol' Boone barked out in the yard and Jefferson opened his eyes. He didn't mind so much now that the quilt and Widdie's box were gone. He was happy things were so good for Widdie.

Little Nettie was standing on the porch looking in through the wide-open door, her nut-brown face set in an impatient glare. "I declare, Jefferson! I thought you never would open your eyes! You awake now? Or just sleepin' with your eyes wide-open and lookin' awake?"

He sat up and stared real hard at her. "Is that you, Nettie? In the dark last night, I didn't see how big you'd growed while I was gone. Glory be, how you've growed!"

The pout on her face dissolved. She strolled into the house like a French lady out for a walk in her finery. She tilted her head and brushed her fingers along her skirt. "Have I growed? You don't look no different, Jefferson, 'cept you stay in bed all mornin' like some lazy, rich, white man."

"Just had to dream my way back home a bit, I reckon. Had to make all that stuff that happened when I was gone catch up to me so I could be well and truly home, I reckon." He dragged his canvas duffel bag over to him. "Go call Mama and Pappy and the rest. I brung presents."

Nettie clapped her hands and squealed, just like always. It didn't matter that she'd grown a foot since he left. She was still the same Little Nettie.

The chamber off the living room of the Warne home that served as Doc's office, examining room, library, and private retreat was not large to begin with. A sofa that doubled as Doc's exam table reached from corner to corner under the window. It was flanked by a wall of floor-to-ceiling bookshelves and faced another such wall in which the doorway appeared to be an afterthought. The one remaining wall was more than half taken up by Doc's immense mahogany rolltop desk. The desk, like the room, was overstuffed with papers. It had been years since the top had actually been rolled shut.

The only remaining piece of furniture besides a brass coatrack was Doc's low-backed rocking chair. Even with the chair rolled as far against the desk as possible, the tiny space still seemed about to burst from the presence of three substantial members of the community who now occupied the groaning sofa.

Doc regarded the sweating threesome with some amusement. Even though *well-to-do* and *influential* described his visitors, the word that came first to his mind was *substantial*. Their combined weight exceeded seven hundred pounds. That they were squeezed together on the divan was their own fault, though. Molly had offered to seat the unexpected arrivals on the shady end of the porch and bring them lemonade, but they had insisted on a "private meeting."

Doc looked expectantly from the flushed face of his neighbor Jim McBride to the attentive and sharp-eyed countenance of Robert Blaylock, but neither of them spoke. His questioning gaze settled on the craggy features of the oldest member of the threesome, umpire and freight company owner Paul Mazurki.

"Well, Paul," Doc said in a good-natured drawl, "will you be telling me what this committee represents, or should I go to guessing?"

Mazurki's dark eyebrows knit in thought above the deep seams of his cheeks. In his guttural voice, he said, "We want for you to run for Congress."

All three men seemed to speak at once. "I thought we were going to sound him out first," objected Blaylock in his lawyer's tone.

"Now, Doc," urged McBride, "don't be saying no until you've heard what we have to say."

"We think you're the right man for the job," added Mazurki.

When the confused chatter had simmered down, McBride took up the discussion. "You know that Congressman Mills died last week?"

Doc nodded his agreement.

"Well, there's to be a special election to fill his seat for the rest of his term."

"The other side has already announced that Hopewell will be running," noted Blaylock.

"Hopewell?" laughed Doc. "That scoundrel! He's as crooked as a dog's hind leg. No offense to your profession, Bobby, me boy, but they say he always was the best attorney money can buy, and since he made judge, his motto is still good."

"Exactly," agreed Blaylock. "He represents the worst of the big-money interests that want to keep the little man down. He'll be a bad man to speak for farmers and for factory workers."

"Doc," Mazurki said earnestly, "you know how that skunk Hopewell feels about Poles."

"And Catholics," McBride added. "Doc, you're a Protestant and I'm a Catholic, yet we've been fine neighbors all these years. Would you be standing by and seeing the hatreds like in the old country spring up here?"

"I would not, Jim, and well you know it. But why me? What makes you think I could win?"

The three men on the sofa exchanged glances, and Blaylock explained. "You're an educated man, Doc, and well respected in all the countryside around here." He ticked off the first point on his index finger and went on. "Two, you own a farm and your family works the land. Three, you may not be Catholic, but you are Irish, and everyone trusts you to be fair."

"Well, well," Doc said with a bemused look on his broad face. "Is there more?"

"Hopewell is going to work on suspicion and fear by calling immigrant families *foreigners* and *un-American*."

"Like me." Mazurki thumped his broad chest. "Me he will call un-American!"

"But let him try to make such a charge against you," asserted McBride. "You, who have given two sons to America and almost lost a third. If he said such a thing, not even his own dog would vote for him."

✯ ✯ ✯

The horse-and-mule market owned by John B. Williams was located at North Towson and A streets in Fort Smith. It was a thriving business, in spite of the encroaching automobiles and clanging electric trolleys in the town. Men figured nothing could ever take the place of a good horse or mule. After all, mules were pulling the newfangled automobiles out of mudholes up and down the state. Where spoked wheels and hissing engines failed, four strong legs still prevailed.

This was Birch's first outing by himself. He had come to haggle for the best horse and saddle at the best price. The yard was swarming with men, all coming for the same purpose. The trick in horse trading was to discover the reason a certain fine animal was being sold. After all, if it was really so fine, then why sell it or trade it off for an animal of unknown qualities?

Birch knew horses. He knew horses well enough to know there was always a big question mark in any animal unless you raised it from a foal. Even then, the best four-legged friend could surprise a man. Kids watched from the top rail of the fence as men dickered. Every board of the corral was painted with signs advertising everything from two-dollar hats to Poe's Shoe Store.

We Buy—We Sell, the sign read. Birch scanned the animals and wondered, *Why sell?* And *Why buy?*

In the center of one corral, Williams was leading a young-looking horse around in a circle with only a halter and lead rope.

"Look at this fine-tempered animal." He gestured to a potential buyer, a young man with an apprehensive expression. "Watch this!" Williams beckoned to one of the boys on the fence. The child, perhaps nine years old, climbed down and came obediently at the call.

"Yessir, Mister Williams?"

"Can you ride, son?"

"Yessir, Mister Williams!"

"Well, I want you to ride this here horse for the gentleman. Get right on up here." He boosted the kid onto the bare back of the animal. Birch noticed the horse's language by the way he moved his ears. He laid them back briefly and shifted his weight nervously, in spite of the light weight of the child.

"Now, would you look at that," said the horse trader. "See how calm he is? Even a child can ride him . . . bareback."

Well, of course a child could ride him bareback. The kid was hardly any weight at all. The best test came when a saddle was thrown onto the back of a green-broke horse and the cinch pulled tight. Take the halter off and throw a bit in the horse's mouth and then see how he likes it.

"He is a fine-lookin' animal," said the young man, running his hands down the legs of the horse. Again Birch saw the ears nervously moving. The horse trader looked at the kid and winked big. There was a reason why he let those boys hang around the saleyard, all right. They helped him sell what he had bought.

"There's another fella been lookin' at this horse. Said he'd be back this afternoon with the money." Here came the pitch. "I told him it's first come, first serve around here. Best horse on the lot. Came from a widder woman out Charleston way. Family pet. But she had to sell him. I paid her every cent she asked, and all I want is my money outta the deal."

So they shook on it, and the money was paid. Papers were signed in the office while Birch walked around examining the other stock. He waited to see if his assessment was correct.

The horse was tied to the hitching rail. It pulled back hard against the rope. The eyes of the new owner widened slightly.

"All the ruckus. Family pet. New place. You know. It takes 'em a while. . . ."

As the blanket was slid onto the horse's back, the critter trembled. Then came the saddle. Williams had the hired man ease it onto the animal. The horse danced a hoofed jig and gave a fearful shudder beneath the heavy leather. Last came the bit—a D ring snaffle, an easy bit for a horse to take. Up went the head in fierce protest as the hired man fought to unclench the teeth. Finally it was done.

"You might want to ride him in the round pen a bit 'fore you take him out on the street," called the horse trader as he curried another horse and cast around for another prospect. "You know, he was raised by that widder woman out on a farm. Don't think he's been around automobiles much."

And so it went. If there really was a widow woman and she got as much for that horse as the trader claimed, then Williams had been cheated. And since he got every penny out of the deal that he said he put into it, the young buyer was a fool. He was thrown from the horse within the first ten seconds of the contest in the round pen. Then a few brave fellows who liked adventure bet one another that this animal could be ridden down. Three brothers took turns being bucked off until finally the strongest brother stuck on the horse's back and, to great cheers, rode him around the pen several times.

"See?" the horse trader said. "Just like an old dog. The horse probably always been rode bareback—that's all."

The buyer was visibly shaken as he took back the reins of his horse and climbed aboard. One, two, three bucks, and he stayed in the saddle. Then he took control and began to work the animal as the previous rider had done. If the young man survived, perhaps the horse would work out for him. There was hope.

Birch did not want to start from that first rung in the ladder, however. Nor did he want to buy an ex-firehouse horse that would bolt and run at the sound of a ringing bell, or somebody's flashy racehorse with a bowed tendon. All such equine varieties were available in the saleyard. Among the dozens of choices there stood one big bay gelding with black legs and strong black hooves. He looked gaunt and maybe had worms, but his head was noble and his eyes intelligent. His ears perked in a friendly way when Birch slapped his big shoulder and ran his hand down his well-formed legs. He lifted each foot easily when Birch picked them up. He was a well-mannered beast on the ground, at least.

Birch peered into his mouth. The horse had the teeth of a six-year-

old. Young teeth except for the back molars, which had jagged edges pro-
truding from them. So that was the reason for his leanness. It was a simple matter to file the teeth down and make chewing more efficient for an
animal. Birch ran his hands over every inch of the big bay. He was easy.
Unperturbed.

The proprietor spotted Birch's interest and sauntered to the rail.

"Fine-lookin' animal here."

"Needs his teeth floated." Birch clucked his tongue. Up popped the
small, pert ears. "Needs his teeth floated bad."

"That ain't a big deal." The trader cleared his throat. No use trying to
fool Birch. "Belonged to an Indian over at the Choctaw reservation in the
territory."

The man meant Oklahoma, which had been a state for a few years
now. Still, everybody called Oklahoma "the territory" out of habit. "He
got himself drunk. Lost it in a poker game. Fella who won him sold him
to me. Good horse."

Birch looked up at the trader as he examined the right foreleg. "Has
this one ever had a saddle on him?"

The horse trader scratched his head. "Well, you know . . ." He was
amused that Birch had witnessed the last sale. "I reckon a fella could do
'bout anything with this here horse."

"Maybe. He's down now. Put a little weight on him so he's feelin'
good, and he might be a whole different animal."

"You want to give him a try? Throw a saddle on him. You got a saddle?"

"No. If I find me the right horse, I might be in the market. If I find me
the right saddle."

"Just the thing. His own stuff. Injun lost saddle and bridle, too. Nice
rig."

"I ain't buyin' a pig in a poke, mister. I gotta see what he's got," Birch
warned.

"I ain't gonna lie to you. I ain't rode this horse myself. I can't ride 'em
all. I just trade 'em—buy and sell. Take him on out." He glanced down at
Birch's army-issue boots. "You're a vet, ain't you?"

"Just comin' home," Birch said. "Want to bring somethin' fine back
to my pa on the farm."

Williams nodded and spit a stream of tobacco juice. "Then try this'n
here. And if he ain't for you, you can try another. You see, I got a heap of
horses. I ain't out to cheat nobody. You're welcome to try him."

And so Birch did—first in the round pen, where the horse worked in
total harmony with the almost invisible cues Birch gave him. A slight
pressure of leg or shifting of weight was enough to turn him. Now this

was a horse that truly could have been ridden with nothing more than a halter and he would have responded just as easily.

Williams watched Birch work the big gelding from the fence rail. No doubt the price of the animal was ticking upward by the second.

In the noisy rattling world of the streets beyond the saleyard, the bay moved as calmly past a rumbling trolley as he would have down a quiet country road.

How that Oklahoma Indian must be grieving for his four-legged friend right now! How lonely the sober walk back across the river and home would be! Here was an animal who felt the heartbeat of his rider and responded eagerly to his thoughts.

An hour later Birch signed the papers. He paid a premium for the horse. Williams started at two hundred dollars without the saddle. Birch settled on one hundred seventy-five, which included saddle, bridle, new shoes for the horse, and having its teeth floated.

All the while he thought about his pa, who also knew a good horse, who loved a smart trade. Here was a fine big fella to take home to the farm, something in common to talk about—a beginning, if all other words fell short.

✳ ✳ ✳

Earrings made in tiny replicas of the Eiffel Tower dangled from every female earlobe in the Canfield cabin. Even Little Nettie shook her head and let the little Eiffels tap against her neck. She clutched her brand-new French porcelain play-child under her arm. The doll was dressed in a white cotton gown trimmed with stiff lace. Bright blue doll eyes stared out at the profusion of colorful fans and hair ribbons and hand-embroidered silk chemises that Jefferson had brought home for each of his sisters. The earrings Nettie wore had been meant for Widdie, but Jefferson did not tell her that.

"You brung me earbobs just like I was a growed lady." Nettie preened, fingering her right Eiffel Tower.

"Well, you just about is, Little Nettie," Jefferson said, and she drew her gangly little body up primly and batted her eyelashes.

Jefferson smoothed out the map that showed the enormous geometric pattern of the Champ de Mars and the Eiffel Tower. "We got off the train here." He tapped the train station. "It's hard to believe how big that there Eiffel is." He pointed out across the countryside to where the lone peak of Magazine Mountain poked out of the flatlands. "Twice as high as Magazine and standin' straight up in the air like the biggest pine tree you *ever* seen! Got shops and eatin' places way up in the air, like a tree house.

We climbed right up to the top and seen as far as fifty mile. Like all the way to Fort Smith and then that far again."

Every female hand reached up to fondle the tiny great towers hanging from their earlobes. Here was proof that what Jefferson said was true. There really was such a place. Men had built it from iron, and it was taller than a mountain.

Willa-Mae frowned. "Ain't no tower of Babel, is it?"

"No, ma'am," Jefferson assured her. "I went to the top. Them Frenchies got no mountain to climb, I reckon, so they done built this lookout."

That seemed to satisfy Willa-Mae, who tugged her ear thoughtfully. "Huh. That big."

"Wasn't you scared?" Pink asked.

"Naw. It wasn't nothin' at all next to fightin' them German polecats."

Hock had sat patiently observing as the females unwrapped their presents. He sniffed the air as Willa-Mae snapped her red silk fan open, and then his daughters followed suit. The room was filled with the scent of the Viville perfumery. "Smells as sweet in here as a St. Louis house of dis-re-pute," he said.

Willa-Mae gasped and glowered. "Hush up, old man! What you know about sumthin' like how a house full of them loose womens' smells?"

"Oh, I know, all right," Hock defended. "I done walked by just such a place. Smelled them honeyed women an' their fancy perfumes all the way out in the street, too."

"Ain't perfumes from Paris, France, though." Big Hattie also seemed insulted. The fans beat the warm summer air more rapidly, until the place smelled like a flower garden.

"Mighty sweet." Willa-Mae hummed. "Got me the sweetest boy any mama ever had." Then she eyed the colored map of the Champ de Mars. "You let me borrow that map, Jefferson. I'm gonna stitch you a quilt just like that there Chompin' Mares. It make a perty pattern, them gardens and twisty streets. That there Eiffel I'll stitch at the top, an' forevermore you can look down from the top like you done. Say, 'I been there once; ain't no need to go away no more. My mama done stitched me a quilt.'"

"Yes, ma'am." Jefferson thought that was a good idea. Then he looked at Hock, whose arms were crossed. He had the same impatient sulk on his face as Nettie had had earlier. "I got somethin' for you, too, Pa." Jefferson grinned.

Hock scratched his cheek and eyed the duffel suspiciously. "Don't need no fancy doodads."

Jefferson scrounged around inside his bag and pulled out something the size of a thick book, which was wrapped in a pair of red-flannel underwear. "I ain't got you no earbobs, Pa." Jefferson poked the bundle into his father's hesitant hands.

"Well then . . ." Hock unwrapped the flannel and smiled wide as he held up a pair of heavy field glasses. He held them to his eyes and scanned the horizon. "Lord a'mercy!"

"Took 'em off a German colonel," Jefferson explained proudly. "With them things, a man don't have to climb no tower to see afar off."

Hock rushed to the porch as a red-tailed hawk soared over the distant cotton field. "Glory be. I'm ridin' on his wings!"

Jefferson laughed happily at Hock's pleasure at the gift. "I saved the most important thing, Pa." He pulled out a pair of socks that had the tip of a red ribbon hanging from them. "This here's called the Legion o' Honor. I done good, so them Frenchies marched me out on a big field. They saluted and played a big band. Then the gen'ral come and give this here medal to me to say thanks a lot."

Jefferson extended the medal to Hock. It glinted in his hand. "Come on over here and I'll show you how they done it. Gotta stand at attention. Yep."

Hock had a proud smile on his face as he imitated Jefferson's stance.

"That's right. Then they made a big speech 'bout how I done good fightin'. And all the time I'se thinkin' how I be the son of Hock Canfield. How me and you hunted down bears and cougars, and I wasn't afraid when we done that."

He placed the Legion of Honor around Hock's neck and straightened the ribbon. He kissed him on each cheek. "'Twas Hock Canfield taught me how to fight and pray. So I reckon this medal is for you, Pa." He held Hock's bony shoulders in his big hands. "*Honor thy father*, the Good Book says. So this here is the Legion o' Honor. I brung it for you."

CHAPTER TWENTY-EIGHT

The Warning

Doc Cooper leaned against the counter of Meyer's Dry Goods store and sniffed a bar of rose-scented soap while he waited for Trudy and her father to finish with the customers.

Meyer's Dry Goods in Fort Smith was much like the store of Bubbe and Zeyde Fritz in New York, only on a much grander scale. It was the largest dry-goods store on Garrison Avenue. Just across the street from Levinson Furniture Company, it looked out on trolley cars and puffing automobiles and the endless mule-drawn wagons that moved freight up and down the busy avenue. The buildings were of red brick, clean and new looking, without the dark soot of the New York buildings.

Garrison Avenue was crowded with saloons, watering holes for the residents of Oklahoma, which was a "dry" state. Indians from the Choctaw nation traveled to Fort Smith to shop and spend time in the saloons that were forbidden in Oklahoma. Readily available alcohol had as much to do with the prosperity of Fort Smith as the manufacturing companies, some said. If the national Prohibition laws became official, Garrison Avenue would become a gloomy place indeed. Fort Smith would be forced to close its saloon doors. And with the loss of thirsty customers from Oklahoma, no doubt the other businesses in the city would be affected as well.

Trudy's father was discussing this very matter with Miles Smith, who worked for Fort Smith Light and Traction Company as a trolley driver. Meanwhile, Trudy attended his wife, who wanted three yards of cotton gingham to make school dresses for their daughters.

All the while, Dr. Cooper remained patiently rooted at the counter.

Trudy passed him and smelled the distinct aromas of whiskey and tobacco. Here was one local resident who would also miss the saloons of
Garrison Avenue, and business was not the reason for his concern.

"Well then," Dr. Cooper said as Mr. and Mrs. Smith slipped out the
door. He dropped the soap back into the basket beside the register. "I
have some news from Shiloh." He looked over his shoulder to make certain they were alone. Trudy and Papa moved in closer. "It is as we suspected. There is an unhappy history behind Birch Tucker and his father.
Grandma Amos at the general store told me all about it. In detail. It
seems that the boy's father, Samuel Tucker, is a plain old-fashioned
drunk."

Well, if this was not the pot calling the kettle black! Dr. Cooper's
cheeks were ruddy from his afternoon rounds.

Trudy exchanged a look with her father, whose mouth twitched in a
half smile beneath his dark mustache. "Well, well," Papa said.

Detecting a hint of amusement in the fact that one drunk was telling
about another, Dr. Cooper raised his finger to distinguish the difference
between himself and Birch's father. "Samuel Tucker is not just an ordinary drunk, mind you . . . he is a *mean* drunk!"

He shifted the load of tobacco in his cheek and looked for a place to
spit. Papa indicated the spittoon at his feet. Doc Cooper let loose with a
stream of tobacco, hitting the brass bowl with a dead eye. "Years of practice," he mumbled. "As a sober man, there was none kinder than Samuel
Tucker, Grandma Amos says, but sobriety has been a rare occurrence
these last years."

He picked up the soap again. "And here it is as it was given to me: It
seems Sam Tucker was due for an inheritance from his old father. Good
rich bottomland to farm—the best to be had. Instead, Samuel had a falling out with his old man, who did not approve of whiskey for any purpose. So Birch's grandfather died and left the land and a sizable sum of
money for the building of a church. Sam Tucker got nothing. That is part
one." He wiped tobacco juice from his mustache. "The church is built
now, and where tall cotton might have grown for Sam Tucker, there is a
cemetery surrounding the Tucker family plot." He paused as though
there was no more.

"That's all?" Trudy asked, remembering the pain in Birch's eyes at the
mention of his father.

"Not by a long shot." Doc exhaled loudly. "So Grandma Amos tells
me that Birch's father got himself a small farm not far away. Raised his
sons like they were slaves."

"Birch?"

A knowing nod. "And another boy named Bobby, who died of the influenza two weeks before Birch's mama died last fall. But Birch and his father came to a parting of the ways some time before that. Seems our Birch and his mama and brother took a fancy to that little church. Birch got himself baptized down in the creek one Sunday afternoon. His father, drunk enough to get himself in a rage, not only beat Birch, but Birch's mama got hurt when she tried to stop it. That was too much for Birch to see. He thrashed his pa, who pulled a gun . . . and fired it, too. Samuel Tucker warned Birch if he ever came back, he'd end up planted down in the cemetery of that little church he's so fond of."

"Oh, poor Birch." Trudy felt like weeping for him. What did he have to come home to now? His mother gone. His brother dead. Only Samuel Tucker left alive to greet him.

"The boy's mama? Well, she was everything her husband is not, so says Grandma Amos. A good woman. Kept a fine house and raised her boys to be good Christians and God-fearing. Clara married Samuel Tucker before he'd ever had his first drink." Doctor Cooper shook his head sadly. "And there is a drunkard's tale for you. Like something down at the opera house, only true."

Only then did Trudy notice the tall figure framed in the open doorway. It was Birch. His face was pained, white with humiliation. His fists were clenched at his side. He was staring at the doctor's back.

"Discussin' the patient again, I see," Birch said in a low voice, tight with strain.

Dr. Cooper whirled around as though Birch had jumped out and scared him. "What's the good of eavesdropping, boy?"

Trudy started forward, sorry she had heard the story, sorry for her curiosity. "Birch—"

He put up a hand to stop her, then addressed her father. "I have come by to leave you this, Mr. Meyer." He held up an envelope. "It should cover my expenses."

"But you mustn't—"

"No. It's only fair. And . . . you've been paid, Doc Cooper. I see you already spent it here on the avenue."

"Well, my boy . . . I simply called Shiloh to notify your relations. . . ." The doctor began to cough nervously. "You see."

"Yes, I see. And most likely my pa will be waitin' for me at the end of the lane with a scattergun." A sad smile. "Is this what you were wantin' to know, Trudy?"

She shook her head. "It doesn't matter to me."

"It *should* matter," Birch said sharply.

"Please, Birch, don't go. You don't need to go back there! Papa says—"

Joseph Meyer took over from his daughter. "You are welcome here,

Birch. We are a growing company. Here is a good place for you to stay and work—"

Birch put a hand to his head as though the wound ached. "I'm . . . a farmer. Only I got no farm. I gotta talk to my pa. He'll need the help." He looked away. "Anyway, I bought me a horse. I left with nothin'. At least I can come home with a good horse. And if he kills me—"

Trudy rushed to him, throwing her arms around him. "Don't go, Birch! You once asked me not to leave, and I stayed all night beside you. *Please* don't leave me! Not like this! Wait a while. You can write him a letter."

"I wrote him a hundred in my head. And the ones I mailed I never got an answer to." Birch kissed her cheek. "I won't forget what you said to me, what I promised you. But I got nothin' to offer you. No future. Not even a small plot for a garden." He lifted her chin. "What sort of man would I be if I made you my wife now? I've got to go home. He needs me now that Bobby and Mama are gone. Maybe things will be different. Just . . . I have to go home. See?"

Trudy was crying, frightened for him. She wished she had not asked to know the whole story. "Of course."

"I didn't want you to worry. I wish you didn't know it all. I ain't gonna fight him. I made my promise, and I aim to keep it." He raised his hand for her to see. "I ain't ever gonna fight another man. I told you that, and now you know why. Fightin' don't do no good, does it? So I'm goin' home and tell him that. Tell him I'm sorry for everythin'. Sorry about his life bein' so broken to pieces." His clear eyes reflected hope. "If he can hear that I love him, Trudy, then maybe I can help him. It ain't him; it's the whiskey. I remember what he was before. It ain't *him!*" Beads of sweat formed on his brow. "My mama said that. She believed it. That's why she stayed. She would want me to do this."

Willa-Mae saw that there was one more fan wrapped and ribboned in the duffel . . . one more unopened box of earbobs and another little package besides.

"I reckon you should be gettin' on over to Latisha Williams' place before too long, Jefferson," she said, as he finished his noon meal of corn bread and beans. "That gal has spent all her days moonin' for you." She imitated the sorrowful voice: "'When is Jefferson comin' home? Heard any word 'bout Jefferson?' She asked me every week at church. Pestered Big Hattie every week at Baptist Trainin' Union. You best get on over there and end that gal's misery. Set the date you gonna get hitched."

Jefferson cast a soulful look at the rumpled uniform in his duffel.

"Yes'm. Except . . . I was figurin' on wearing my uniform when I went to see Latisha."

"No need to dress up. As far as that gal is concerned, you already put the big kettle into the little pot. She thinks you can do anythin'."

"All the same," Jefferson said, "I ain't gonna wear that ol' soldier suit no more, 'cept maybe at my wedding. I'd kinda like to let her see me in it once."

"Well then, go on down to the creek and wash yourself. I'll scrub your suit and wrench it and hang it to dry. Won't take more'n an hour to dry in this heat." She raised a finger. "But that gal wouldn't care none if you showed up in your jippies."

"Her pa might have somethin' to say about that." Jefferson laughed.

"I'll iron your suit up. Ain't gonna do much good. You'll sweat it all limp before you get there."

$$\star \; \star \; \star$$

Willa-Mae was right about that. Jefferson was soaking with perspiration by the time he walked the four miles to the Williams farm. He topped the rise and gazed down over the cotton field ripening in the sun. It looked as if Latisha's folks would have a good crop this year to split with The Man they sharecropped for. The little white house beyond the field was shaded by a ring of enormous hickory trees. The place seemed to be asleep. Even the dog drowsed in the shade at the side of the porch. It was a familiar picture, like the one Jefferson had carried in his mind when he had been away.

Suddenly the screen door banged open. Latisha's mother stepped onto the porch and hollered for her daughter. "La-tishaaaaa! Tish? La-tishaaaaa! You off readin' them books? I got work for you, gal!"

Tish appeared in the shadow of the tall double doors of the barn. She seemed small by comparison to the barn, but she was a big gal. That's what Jefferson liked first about her. She was five feet ten inches and strong. Jefferson figured she matched him just right. She was lean and muscled and could work as hard as any man. But she also liked books. She had learned to read down at the little schoolhouse and borrowed the books from Mr. Howard, who owned the land the Williams family sharecropped. Someday, Latisha had told Jefferson, she would have kids and send them to college. She was a strong-souled woman, and Jefferson liked that about her more than anything.

"La-tisha!" Mrs. Williams sounded angry.

"Yes, Mama." Latisha made no move yet to come out of the cool shadows of the barn.

"You put that book away, gal! Your pappy gonna wallop you if'n you don't get—"

"HOWDY, GAL!" Jefferson boomed across the cotton field. "I DONE COME HOME!"

The dog stood up from beside the porch.

"Praise the Lord!" Tisha's mama said.

Latisha stepped from the barn, shaded her eyes against the glare, and gave out a laugh. Then she waved and left her mama to stroll unhurriedly through the fields, meeting Jefferson halfway. Her mahogany skin glowed. Her white teeth glinted in a smile as she wrapped her arms around his neck and kissed him hello just as if he had seen her only yesterday.

"Howdy, Jefferson," she said. "I just about give up on you. You didn't write for a while. I figgered you found some other gal to marry."

"Just you, Tish." He touched her face. "I brung you some presents back from the war."

She took his hand in hers. The insects buzzed around them. "Mighty glad to see you, Jeff." Her voice was quiet. "Mama'll have some tea for you on the porch."

✯ ✯ ✯

It was another four-mile walk from the Williams farm to the home of the Boss-man, Mr. Howard. He owned most of the land around Mount Pisgah just as his great-granddaddy had owned it before the War between the States. Back then Mr. Howard's great-granddaddy had also owned the men who worked the land. Jefferson's great-granddaddy had belonged to the Howard plantation. He had worked the same land and planted the same crops that Hock planted now.

The original Mr. Howard took pride in the fact that he was good to his darkies. When emancipation came, he had told them they were free to go if they wanted. Some had left the place, while others stayed. Their children had stayed, too, and now their grandchildren, to sharecrop the land.

So it was that Jefferson made the long walk to the big white house where The Man sat reading the newspaper on the front porch.

Jefferson stayed outside the gate and called up to Mr. Howard. "Howdy there, sir. It's me. Jeff Canfield. I come home from the war."

Mr. Howard shook his paper, finished a line, then peered over the top of his glasses. "Well now," he said, not unpleasantly, "good to see you back, boy." Mr. Howard always seemed to show a liking to Jefferson.

Jefferson had overheard The Man telling someone once that he ad-

mired his strength and size and ability to work like two men put together. He'd said that Jefferson Canfield was pure evidence to Mr.
Howard that Great-granddaddy Howard had a good eye for the slaves he
bought. Good workers and strong, they had passed along those fine
qualities to their progeny.

"Yessir, Mister Howard. Good to be back." Jefferson hoped that Mr.
Howard would comment about the campaign medals on his uniform,
but the man simply looked him over and nodded.

"You're all in one piece, I see," said The Man.

"We done a heap of fightin'. Fierce it was. But now I'm home again
and ready to work."

"That's real good." The Man rested back in his chair. "Your pappy
tells me we're gonna have a real good crop of cotton this year. Y'all are
back just in time to pick."

Jefferson touched the gate, wanting to open it. Wanting to stride right
on up to the porch and tell The Man what he had been thinking while he
was gone. But he remained outside because that was proper unless he
was invited in.

"Yessir. And it's work I'm wantin' to talk to you about."

The Man raised his hand slightly. "Well now, Jefferson boy, you know
I split the profits right down the middle with your pappy. I don't give
him no trouble about it, and he does right by me. I expect you'll just keep
right on with the tradition."

"That's what I been wantin' to talk about." Jefferson held his soldier
hat in his big hands and smiled hopefully. "You know I aim to marry
Latisha Williams."

"Oh?" Mr. Howard seemed pleased.

Jefferson had figured The Man would be. After all, Latisha was also
big and strong. And he knew The Man hoped for another generation of
hardy sharecroppers on the Howard land. Howard knew Latisha. She
had been educated right here at the plantation school. She could read
well enough that when the flu took the former teacher, Latisha continued working with the children, teaching them their letters. Latisha was
sixteen years old, plenty old enough to marry.

"Latisha's a good'n, boy," Mr. Howard said.

"Glad you approve, Mister Howard." Jefferson bit his lip and glanced
at the ground. "Because you know me and Latisha can work. We been
thinkin' . . . or I been thinkin' about it. We'd like to sharecrop for you.
Stay close to home. Our families is here. Tisha's folks and mine."

"A right good idea, Jefferson," said Mr. Howard sipping his tall glass
of iced tea.

Jefferson studied the white pickets of the gate. He wished he could come closer. Talk to The Man from the yard. The stable hand was listening to every word. The servants could hear Jefferson's business. But he stayed outside. "Well then, what I was thinkin' all this time . . . I was thinkin' about that land right next to my pappy's land."

"The woods?"

"Yessir. It's all growed up now in scrub oak and persimmons and such, but my pappy say that his pa told him that used to be good land. Some of the best on the old plantation."

"Not in my lifetime," said The Man. "But yes, I reckon back then it was all good."

"I'd like t'clear that land. There's an old cabin back in them woods. Me an' Latisha could fix it up real good. Build us a barn and some pens."

"That's been woods for as long as I remember. I used to hunt down in them woods. Slept many a night in that old cabin." He frowned as though he could not let those woods of his memory be cleared away. "Don't know, boy. Now that the war is ended. They say cotton prices gonna go right on down."

"We can grow most anythin' on that land, Mr. Howard. Besides, half of somethin' for you would be more than those woods is givin' you now."

The Man scratched his throat and nudged his Panama hat back on his head. "I reckon that's so." His lower lip protruded and his eyes narrowed. "You'd need a team of mules to pull the stumps and a plow . . . and tools and such. I gotta think about my investment here. I'm gonna have to put a heap in till I get somethin' out."

"I been studyin' on that, too." Jefferson had hoped The Man would not figure in the costs of mules and tools, but Howard was a businessman. "Me an' Latisha can get by with only one third of the crops until we pay for them mules and such. That way, you be comin' out ahead in mebbe just a year instead of three."

The Man nodded and took another long drink of his tea. By the expression on Mr. Howard's face, Jefferson could tell that the offer seemed more promising now. "And if I can't do it?"

Jefferson frowned. "Hadn't thought you couldn't. Thought maybe you *wouldn't* . . ."

"How long you figure it'll take to clear that forty?"

"We got cotton to pick soon. But if I got me a good stout team of mules, I can plant me ten clear acres come plantin' time. And then maybe a crop of beans. I can clear it and plant . . . clear and plant. Won't be no time."

The Man rose and stretched. He wiped sweat from his brow. "Gonna be a hot one today, ain't it, boy?"

"Yessir."

He stepped to the door. "You keep one-third and I take two?"

"Yessir. Until the mules is—"

"You know I treat my people right."

"Yessir."

"Well then. I'll draw up the contract. You can sign it, and I'll have Folz pick you out a team. Don't go neglectin' the work on your pappy's place, though. Got a crop to bring in this year, too."

"Yessir. I can work both places. Even by moonlight."

The Man turned toward the door. "And, Jefferson . . . that uniform you're wearin'?"

Jefferson drew himself up proudly. "Yessir!"

"It ain't a good idea for you to be wearin' it out in public in these parts." The Boss-man looked away and across the countryside. "You know how some of the folks are around here. I'd hate to see you in some kind of ruckus over it. Understand?"

The smile faded. Jefferson nodded silently. He ducked his head. "Yessir, Mister Howard. If you says—"

"That's good, boy." The Man disappeared into his big house.

✶ ✶ ✶

Even before Jefferson came within earshot of Billy Jones's old wagon parked at the gate, he could tell something was wrong.

Billy's wife was hugging on Willa-Mae and crying. The children were wailing and all gathered around Hock, who had a look on his face as if some great disaster had happened.

Pink and Big Hattie spotted him on the rise. They pointed and ran toward him. They were also crying. "Jefferson! Jefferson! Something terrible . . . they . . . poor Billy . . . they done took him!"

Jefferson jogged down to where Delpha Jean Jones was crying and calling for the Lord to have mercy. It sounded like death to Jefferson. He had heard such grief before, but only when someone had died.

"Talk slow," Jefferson urged her. "Who took Billy? And where they take him to, Miss Delpha Jean?"

Hock shook his head and wrapped his spindly arms around Billy's children. He clucked his tongue. "Poor babies."

Jefferson saw the tears in his father's eyes. "What happened?" he asked again. "Can't help if we don't know what happened, Delpha Jean."

"We was . . . down to the river. The chillens set off a string of crackers—"

"Weren't no guns!" claimed the middle boy. "Just crackers, Jefferson! They say we gots guns!"

"Who?"

"The white men. They come down like a swarm of hornets." Delpha Jean buried her face in her hands as if to shut out the sight. "They say we done killed some ol' dog! But we got no guns! Just firecrackers is all. Then the sheriff man, he say Frank gotta come on to jail and get locked up. But Billy—" she raised her face to heaven—"I told Billy not to argue with the man, but Billy said, 'Why you lock him up? We don't do nothin'.' Then the man smacked Billy hard. Billy looked him in the eye and said, 'The Lord rebuke thee.' "

Once again the sobs filled the air as the memory came fresh to the minds of Billy Jones's family.

Delpha Jean went on. "And then the sheriff said he don't forget no uppity niggers. He took Frank on to jail, and we got on the road. Darkness come, and then the mens come and block the road. . . ."

Willa-Mae bit her lip and looked hard into Jefferson's face. "It was the Klan," she finished for her friend. "Fifty of 'em."

"They took Billy!" Delpha Jean wailed. "Called him uppity nigger and said they'd teach him a lesson like other uppity niggers in these parts! They sent us on away. Billy! Oh, my man!"

The children began to cry again. Hock and Jefferson exchanged looks of dread. Hock glanced at Jefferson's uniform. "Go and get outta them clothes, Jefferson. We best be goin'. We gotta find our ol' Billy out in them woods."

✻ ✻ ✻

It was dusk when Jefferson and Hock came to the place in the road where fifty members of the Ku Klux Klan had blocked the path of the Jones wagon. The road was scarred with the hoofprints of their horses. The path they had taken into the woods was an easy one to follow.

Jefferson had brought the dog with them for tracking, but he was not needed. The men who had kidnapped Billy did not attempt to conceal their trail.

The hot afternoon air cooled some as the sun dipped below the lip of the earth. Night critters made sounds just as though nothing had happened in their home, as though what had transpired the night before was a natural part of these woods.

"They crossed the creek here." Hock pointed to the chewed bank that slid down into the waters. "And look here." He stooped to find the tracks of a shoeless man in the mud. He touched the print he knew belonged to Billy Jones, then peered up at the steep bank on the opposite side of the creek. What was over there, just out of sight? Hock was trembling. He did not need to see in order to know.

"You wait here, Pa," Jefferson said in a low voice.

Hock began to weep. "You know what we'll find, don't you, Son?"

"Wait here. I been to a war, Pa. I seen my friends die at my right hand and my left hand, and still I kept livin'. No matter what we find over yonder, Pa, we gonna keep livin'! Now stay here." He traced the track where Billy had stumbled and been dragged up the bank. It was plain to see for anyone who had eyes. "Go on back to the road. I'll go on."

Hock remained kneeling beside Billy's footprint. He shook his head and wept quietly. "Go on, then. I'm just gonna wait here."

Jefferson stood slowly, then stepped into the stream. His heart was beating as it had in France when the order had come to attack over the top of the trenches. "Help me, Lord. Oh, Lord God . . . help." Ascending the far bank, he stood at the top and looked through the trees to where the dark shadow of Billy Jones hung suspended from a branch of a tall hickory. Just beyond him was a clearing where the charred remains of a burned cross stood, barely visible in the waning light.

"Go get the wagon," Jefferson managed to say when he got back. "I'll bring Billy on and meet you at the road."

CHAPTER TWENTY-NINE

In Need of a Father

The swing on the front porch rocked with a familiar creaking, as much a part of summer around the Warne home as the smell of the hay drying in the fields or the sight of the cardinals darting in and out of the buckeye tree that stood beside the house.

Doc's arm rested on the back of the swing around Molly's shoulders. He cleared his throat as if about to speak. Instead he looked up at the tree, then out across the farm into the deepening blue of evening. At last his gaze traveled down to the rich dark auburn of Molly's hair. He gave a great sigh that seemed to hold more sentiment than just contentment.

"What is it, Doc?" Molly asked. "Did you think I'd not be noticing that you have something on your mind?"

Doc sighed. "Have I told you lately how much I love our home, Molly? Isn't our life together something grand?"

"Indeed." She reached up and patted his large, strong hand with her tiny one.

"You have no thought that I could ever wish for more, do you now?" Doc asked. "For myself, I mean. We may still be ambitious for our children's success and happiness, but I feel no lack for me."

Grasping Doc's hand firmly, Molly looked into his eyes. In the same voice that she used to give instructions to the children, she said, "You must do it, you know."

"What? Do what?" he replied, startled.

"You must run for congressman, just as Jim McBride and the others are wanting you to do. Didn't you know," she went on, "that I could guess what the great secret was that brought those three out here and left you in such a stew after? To my way of thinking, it took them a week longer than was needful to come asking, seeing as how you are the only right choice."

"But it will mean time spent away from home campaigning and giving up my practice if I should win. . . ."

"*When* you win," she said firmly.

"Then I'll have to live in Washington part of the year, and for what? I have no longing beyond what I can see and touch right here."

"Now you listen to me, Doc Warne. Do you remember what you said about coming to America? How you'd not bring up children in a country where a little boy such as yourself could see his father murdered for being the wrong religion?"

Doc tried to indicate his agreement, but Molly was not finished yet. "Will you stand by and let a man be elected who feeds such hatred for his own ends? Listen to this—" Molly picked up a copy of the Marion *Daily Star* and read from the editorial page:

> "*The recent despicable outbreak of lawlessness in Chicago can be nothing less than the work of 'Red' agitators trying to stir up the Negro population. These foreign provocateurs are attempting to disrupt the normally calm relations between whites and coloreds by their inflammatory rhetoric and wild promises of equality. They may masquerade as law-abiding citizens, but be warned: Behind the innocent-sounding label of Catholic or Jew hides a godless Communist.*

"Would you be knowing who wrote that letter, Doc?"

Doc admitted that he had already read the letter and knew the author to be Hopewell. "But, Molly," he added, "where does it say that *I* must be the one to stand up to him?"

Molly stood up abruptly from the porch swing and put her hands on her hips. "Doctor Warne," she said forcefully, "I hope it is only me that you are arguing with so and not your own conscience, for I will forgive your weakness, but your own heart would not. Just you look there." She stood ramrod straight and stretched out her hand in the direction of the family cemetery. "'To make the world safe for democracy,' they said. Was that a lie, William? I'll not have my sons die for a lie. And Ellis . . . did he give his leg for a lie? For shame, Doc! You must run, and what is more, you must win!"

Doc rose and stood beside her. He wrapped his arms around her in an embrace strong and tender. "Ah, Molly, what can a man not accomplish when he has the backing of a woman such as you? All right, then, I'll tell the committee tomorrow that my answer is yes."

* * *

It was said that there were two classes of New Yorkers: those who could afford a trip to Europe and those who had paid their last penny to get out of Europe.

Max's family belonged to that second category, so it was small wonder that Bubbe Fritz wrung her hands and wept for two days before Max boarded the great liner at Cunard's Pier No. 86.

It seemed to Max that half of Orchard Street had come along to see him off. Picklemen and pushcart vendors, steady customers and proud Yiddish mamas all pushed onto the elegant ocean liner along with a dozen old classmates of Max's from Columbia.

There was only one face Max wanted to see tonight, but Irene had not come to see him off. They had said their farewells last night. She would not come to the pier, she told him, because she was certain she would cry in front of his family. She did not want to make a fool of herself.

The ship was scheduled to sail at midnight. The custom had been revived since the war that farewells were made after the theatre and before supper. The corridors and enormous halls and drawing rooms of the ship were packed with the elegantly dressed friends of those New Yorkers who could afford to go to Europe. Visitors seemed deaf to the warning bells. The windlasses were already hauling up the hawsers as the orchestra blared. White-uniformed page boys hustled by Max and his weeping committee of leave-takers. Baskets of flowers and last-minute gifts were being delivered to staterooms and first-class cabins.

Max was far below all this. His room was a tiny cubbyhole several decks down. All the same, Bubbe had packed him an enormous food basket, and there was a large bouquet of flowers from Murphy's florist shop on the floor.

"You will be a good boy?" Bubbe pinched his cheek. "You will write your Bubbe and Zeyde, *nu?*"

"Every week," Max promised. His eyes looked past his grandparents as a tall, elegantly dressed blond strolled by in the corridor. How he wished Irene had come to see him off. He would not have minded her tears half so much as he missed seeing her one last time.

"You should let us know what you need." Zeyde ran his hand through his wreath of gray hair. "Things are bad over there, you know," he said, his tone almost accusing. "That is why we came here in the first place."

Max knew his grandfather was unhappy about this return to Europe. How many times had he said it? "You can get something over there that we do not have here? Just tell me where it is."

The siren bellowed, signaling that the gangway was about to swing up. There was a flurry of last embraces. More tears, and then Orchard Street filed out past elegant ladies in evening clothes and gentlemen in black ties and tails.

Max was alone in his cabin when the ship trembled and moved away from the pier. He had hoped to feel some sensation of excitement at his departure, but he did not.

He clasped his hands and stared at the floor. Looking at the narrow shelf of his bunk, he thought of sleeping there alone without Irene beside him.

They were well under way when the white-uniformed steward rapped on the door of his cabin. He held out a white envelope on a silver tray. Max recognized his name written in Irene's handwriting. Tipping the steward, he closed the door and switched on the lamp above his bed to read what she had written.

My darling Max,

By now you are on your way. The distance of an ocean may put our love in perspective—for both of us, I hope. I have often thought about how desperately you long to escape the drudgery of Orchard Street. I have looked in the mirror and remembered that once I carried your child. That baby somehow was a symbol of everything you want to get away from. All summer I have been afraid of what could happen, yet I am too weak to refuse to give you what you want.

Oh, Max, how dearly I am paying for that weakness now! I am once again carrying your child. Afraid to tell you face-to-face, I let you go without knowing. And as you leave, I know that I will not see you again. Even as you sail from New York, I am on a train going away as well. I will have this baby, although I know you would not let me if you were here. I take a part of you with me to love for the rest of my life.

Farewell,
Irene

Even in the darkness of night, Birch recognized the sounds and smells as unmistakably those of home. To the south, the Poteau Mountains were silhouetted against the starlit sky like the great hunched back of a sleeping bear. Birch's home lay just at the base of those mountains. He recognized the light of every farmhouse and could call each place by name. He knew the number of children, their ages, the color of their hair and eyes, their family histories. They could do the same with him.

There were no secrets in Shiloh. Everyone knew Samuel Tucker's fondness for whiskey. All of the families here grieved for what had happened to the Tucker family. All of them had prayed about the tragedy during services at Shiloh Church.

The preacher and the deacons had come to call on Birch's father unannounced one afternoon and had simply been ignored. Samuel Tucker had butchered two hogs in silence while they spoke of forgiveness and charity, and when they were finished and he was finished, he had wiped his bloody hands on his apron and said, "This ain't between you and me. It's between me and my pa. In the name of God, he whipped me. In the name of God, he gave away my inheritance to build that church. I intend one day to be buried there. That's my right. But neither me nor my children will ever set foot inside that building. I don't intend to give the old man that pleasure, even if he's dead. I'm bound for hell, just to spite him, so don't waste your time prayin' for me."

Then he had sent the visitors away with a load of fresh pork chops for their trouble. Sam Tucker was a stubborn man. Stubborn and bitter. When Birch and Bobby had followed their mother to the little church, it was a sort of betrayal. The embers of hatred Samuel felt against his father had been fanned into a flame by his own wife and children. Everyone who lived along the road to Shiloh knew it. The twisted truth of it could not have been more obvious.

Tonight Birch could have stopped at any of a dozen farmhouses and been welcome. Nobody who knew the tale would have blamed him if he spent the night with his cousin J.D. and then went on home in the light of day, when Samuel was more likely to be sober.

But Birch had set out to go all the way home. He would sleep in his own bed tonight or out on the road. Or maybe his father would kill him when he set foot on the front porch, as he had threatened. Birch had looked death square in the face a thousand times since he left home. He wasn't afraid. He was done with fighting. His pa was alone now, with no family left but Birch. Maybe they could talk. Maybe work it out . . .

The half-moon slid up behind him, dimming the stars and illuminating fields of cotton. An owl hooted from the stand of trees in the holler, and a dog barked in the yard of the Morris place as he passed by. That bark was answered by a half dozen others across the valley.

Birch turned his face to where he knew his dog would be. The last Mama had written, ol' Shuggie was still on the job, guarding the henhouse, protecting the yard. Birch pulled up his big bay horse and waited for a moment in the center of the road. He smiled as the familiar warbling howl resounded from the southwest. There would be at least one friend to greet him when he turned up the lane. He could picture Shuggie's coarse brown coat standing straight up as the dog bellowed his deep-throated warning. Then Pa would come out on the porch, lean against the post, and raise his head to sniff the night air for the nameless threat Shuggie was warning him about.

"It's only me, Pa," Birch whispered into the breeze. "Get your shotgun. Your son has come home."

The lamps were all out at the house of Cousin J.D. Three dogs were chained to the old hickory tree out front. They sprang to their feet and strained at the end of the tethers as Birch rode quietly past the house.

J.D. always kept too many dogs, Birch mused. *Mean ones, too.*

Across the wide field, Birch glimpsed a spot of moonlight reflected in the windows of Shiloh Church. He swallowed hard, knowing that his mother and brother now slept beside the church building. He fought the urge to tie the horse to the iron ring embedded in the oak tree in the churchyard. *It's too late to pay a call,* he told himself. Too late and too lonely tonight. He had business to tend to with the living.

He averted his eyes from the forest of white stones illuminated by the moonlight. He did not want to see the new ones in the Tucker family plot. There would be time enough for that. Clucking the horse into a trot, he ascended the last hill before home. Shuggie's trembling howl became more fierce. The dog would not be chained. No need for that. He would not dash out onto the public road to chase an intruder, but neither would he let Birch's horse place one hoof on the graveled lane of home without a challenge.

Still fifty yards from home, Birch rose in his stirrups and gave a low whistle. He did not call out the name of his dog, but the whistle had once been all that was needed. Would Shuggie remember after two years?

Another whistle. The howling dropped to a whine and then the frantic barking of the joyful dog as he scrambled at a dead run to greet Birch in the lane.

The bay horse pranced nervously as Shuggie danced and hopped around his legs.

"Yep, it's me, Shuggie," Birch replied with a laugh. He stepped from his mount and braced for the inevitable lunge as the big dog leaped into his arms. "Just like always. That's a good boy. Yep, it's me, ol' feller. I'm home."

Shuggie replied with a torrent of sloppy licks. Then Birch put him down and proceeded to the house on foot.

Like J.D.'s place, his father's house was dark. The wide porch that circled the house was shadowed. On hot summer nights they had often slept on the porch—the Shiloh version of an Orchard Street fire escape. Birch stood still and searched the shadows for some sign of life. Was Sam Tucker home? Had he gone out drinking like old times? or maybe to a cockfight? Had Birch come home to an empty house? He could not find voice enough to call out. He looked at the dark windows and longed for a lamp to come on. He ached to see Mama lean out and call down to him, *"Why, Birch! Is that you? Praise the Lord! Oh, praise the Lord!"*

Shuggie darted toward the steps, then back to Birch, urging him to come along. *"Why are you hanging back?"* Shuggie seemed to ask. *"What's wrong?"*

Everything was wrong. Mama gone, Bobby gone. Birch looked at the empty swing hanging from the tree. Only Pa and Shuggie were left . . . not even one candle in the window.

From the corner of his eye Birch caught a movement on the porch. A darker shade flitting through the shadows. Silence. The dogs quit their barking. Crickets chirped. Fireflies moved drunkenly among the elderberry bushes. Far off, the gentle rushing of the James Fork Creek sounded.

And then a low voice, the groaning of the rocking chair on the porch . . .

"So you finally come back."

Birch jumped involuntarily when his father spoke. It took him a moment to find his voice. "It's me, Pa."

"Figgered it was."

Birch remained rooted in the yard. The horse stood behind him nibbling the grass, pulling up stalks from between the stones of the walk and then chewing languidly while Birch stared into the darkness.

"Your mama and Bobby is dead." The voice was emotionless, as though Sam Tucker had only reported on the price of cotton or the weather last week.

"I know that, Pa. Maybelle wrote. And Doc Brown."

"Then what you come back here for?" The tone was hard, suspicious.

Birch could tell his father had been drinking. "I came back to see you, Pa." Birch's heart pounded, the blood in his ears drowning out the sound of the James Fork. He wished his father would step out into the moonlight.

A bitter laugh. "You figurin' I'll die, too?"

"No, Pa—"

"You figurin' to take over this here farm from me?"

"That ain't why I come back. . . ."

"Well, I'll outlive you, you whelp pup. You needn't a'bothered, 'cause I'm here to stay."

"Pa, please—" Birch took one step.

"Hold it, boy. You forget I sleep with a gun at my side?"

Birch froze in his tracks. Shuggie sat between him and the porch, looking unhappily from one to another. "I came back to tell you, Pa, I ain't gonna fight you anymore. I came back because I'm sorry for what happened. Sorry. And I wanted to tell you so. I've been tryin' to write you and tell you."

Silence descended again—thick, almost palpable. Birch could feel his father's eyes study him from the cloak of night. "Sorry are you, Birch, boy? What you tellin' your old man?" He was mocking. "You tellin' me you're all done with that Bible-thumpin' life? Gonna throw your Good Book into the James Fork? Ain't goin' down to that church sittin' right smack in the middle of my land?"

Birch was trembling. "I won't go to Shiloh Church anymore, Pa. Not if you don't want me to."

"Is that so? Done with Je-sus, are you?"

"No, sir. I ain't done with Jesus. But I won't go down to Shiloh Church anymore if you say so."

The rocking stopped, and boots sounded hollowly on the planks of the porch. Shuggie stood and wagged his tail hopefully. Sam Tucker appeared in the moonlight just beyond the shadow of the eaves. He held a shotgun in one hand and a half-empty bottle in the other. His powerful arms were bare. He wore an undershirt and trousers, his suspenders hanging down to the sides. His face was still concealed in the shadow of his hat brim. He smelled sour from the drink.

"C'mere." He motioned with the bottle.

Birch stepped forward and tied his horse to the rail. Shuggie whined happily.

"Yessir." Birch stood at the bottom of the rough-hewn stone steps. He was close enough that his father could have touched him. If he wanted to.

"So my boy's come home. Out of the goodness of his heart, to tell me he done me wrong. Ain't gonna be a Judas no more, huh?" He held out the bottle. "Let's us drink on it. Down with Bible thumpers."

Birch winced and did not raise his hand to take his father's offering. "No, thank you, sir."

"No, thank you?" Sam Tucker slugged back a big drink. "No, thank you, sir. I don't touch none of that *sinful* stuff, sir!"

The fury was growing. Mindless and fierce, the fire was there, burning. It would make little difference what Birch said. What gesture he made.

"You won't even have a drink with me. Too good for your own father!" Sam cursed. "But you ain't too good to stay in the house of them fancy Jews!" He thrust the bottle at Birch, spilling whiskey on himself and on the ground. "Ol' Gramma Amos hears from that Fort Smith Doc you maybe even gonna marry yourself a Jew-gal! Is that so, Birch? You been beddin' down with a Jew-gal? You grown fond of them Christ-killers? Kill your Jesus? You maybe thinkin' you're gonna bring her here?"

It was hopeless. Birch simply gazed up at the faceless shadow that had once been his father. There was no point in talking. No point in staying when he was like this. "No, sir. I won't bring Trudy here."

Sam Tucker's laugh rang out, wild. He leaned against the post and howled at the moon. Then suddenly he fell silent and menacing. He cursed with a low growl. "Does that mean you aim to give her up?" His gold tooth glinted in the moonlight. "Like you're gonna give up Shiloh Church and Jesus and your Holy Roller ways?"

"No, sir." Birch glanced at his horse. He needed to leave.

"Figgerin' on leavin' your ol' pa so soon?" Again he thrust the bottle at Birch. "You should have a drink, Birch, my boy. Have a drink to seal your bargain."

"No, sir. We got no bargain."

"And you ain't gonna fight me no more neither, I suppose."

"No, sir, I ain't."

"We'll see!" At that, Sam Tucker raised the bottle and brought it down with a crash on Birch's head, only inches from the wound that had taken so long to heal. Birch staggered back, raising his hands to protect himself against the blows that followed.

"Don't you raise your fists to me!" Sam Tucker pounded Birch again and again. Birch fell dazed to the ground at his father's feet. Sam kicked him hard, and then Shuggie plunged in to protect Birch. Growling and barking, he latched onto Sam's leg.

For just an instant Sam's rage was shifted from his son to the animal. He cocked one hammer of his shotgun and pulled the trigger. The roar of the gun illuminated his wild face for an instant as Shuggie was blown back to tumble across the yard.

Birch lay still on the ground. He moaned and beat his fist on the ground, damp with his father's whiskey.

Sam Tucker stood panting above him, sobered for a second. Then he cursed the dog and swung the barrel of the shotgun until it was pressed hard against Birch's neck. "Get up," menaced Sam. "You see . . . you see what you made me do! You ain't changed! Every time you're around somethin' . . ."

Sam's voice was choked by a sob. "You!" The second hammer was cocked back. "Get up! You self-righteous . . . just like my ol' man! You *get!* Get on back to your Jew-whore! And don't come back here no more!" Another sob. "You think I won't kill you? I thought more of that hound out there than I think of you! *Git! Git! Git!*" He punctuated each command with a jab of the barrel.

Birch staggered to his feet. The stars whirled above him. The ground tilted crazily as he groped for the reins of his horse and managed to pull himself onto the saddle.

He could still hear his father's mindless shrieks as he rode back down the lane. The horse leaped into a gallop as the boom of a shotgun sounded behind them. First once, and then, after a pause to reload, a second blast and a third, as though Sam Tucker were shooting at ghosts.

No lamp was lit inside Shiloh Church, yet the starlight reflecting on the old rippled glass of the windowpanes was a beacon, calling Birch to stop. He reined up and gingerly felt for the cut on the side of his head. It was swelling into a good-sized knot, but the bleeding had stopped. "I reckon I'll live," he muttered.

Birch slid to the ground and tied his horse to the hitching ring in the old oak. There were two doors in the front of the church: one for entering and the other for coming out a new person. He tried the latch on the door for going in. It was locked tight, so he climbed the stone steps to the door for leaving and turned the knob. It creaked and caught and the door groaned inward.

The small sanctuary was hot and still from baking all day in the sun with the windows closed. Even so, the scent of hymnals and wilted flowers and air left behind from ten thousand prayers and songs and sermons seemed like home to Birch.

He stood in the darkness and traced the shadows of the pulpit and the pews and the dusty pump organ, where every Sunday night old Mrs. Ray pumped and played the wheezing thing.

There, in the third pew, was where Mama and Bobby and he had sat. The place where he had found himself and found his faith. Tonight he felt utterly lost and surrounded by a cloud of doubt.

He went to the window and looked out over the graveyard. It was full of people he knew. Old men and women and children he had grown up with. And then there was the Tucker family plot. Two new obelisks pointed heavenward from the small iron-fenced encosure. One for Clara Tucker. The other for Bobby. There they were . . . the only family he had dreamed of coming home to. The emptiness they left behind seemed almost too much to bear tonight.

Birch sank to his knees with a half-choked sob. "So it's true."

In that moment he wished he were among that silent congregation gathered beneath the soil of Shiloh. For an instant he looked up to pray, and then he saw the rafters and remembered the strong thick rope tied to the saddle outside. Would it make any difference if he quit now? Why had he come back? Why had he not died at the front, when there had been so many men with reasons to live who never came home? Where was his future now? What did he have to offer Trudy?

"Nothin'," he whispered aloud. "You've been foolin' yourself, Birch—thinking you could marry a gal like her, come home, raise kids with her, and farm. All dreams. Useless."

Birch raised his head to look through the gloom where the dark shadow of the cross hung on the wall behind the pulpit. "I need a word, Lord. Some word of comfort to my soul."

Outside, a breeze stirred the brittle leaves of the oak trees. Birch waited, holding his breath, hoping for some voice to speak to him. But there was nothing but the wind and the trees. No voice. No answer here in this place where he once thought he had found every answer to the longing of his heart.

He stood slowly and put his hand on the pocket Bible where Mama's letter waited, still unopened, to speak to his heart in just such a moment of despair. There would be no better time to hear her words. She would have something gentle to say to him. Some word of hope to offer him. An image of heaven beyond the hell of his loneliness.

Birch took out the envelope and staggered to the third pew from the front, where she had held his hand and prayed for him the last Sunday before he left. He stretched out on his back and placed the envelope over his heart as he gazed up into the darkness.

Closing his eyes, he could almost hear her speak:

"I told the Lord the day you was born, you're His child, Birch. The Lord is your Pa wherever you go. I loved you when you wasn't nothin' but a squalling, useless little runt. I loved you and changed your diapers and nursed you when you was hungry. I loved you before you ever plowed a furrow or split one stick of firewood. Hear me now, boy . . . when you're all alone over there, feelin' scared and like your heart's gonna break, you remember the Lord loves you even more than I ever could. And He's right there with you. He'll feed your heart when you're hungry, clean you up when you need to be changed. He'll tuck you in when you're cold inside. You just lay yourself in the Lord's arms like a baby,

Birch. You don't need to be strong all the time. Let Him love you. He ain't hard on His children."

The voice seemed clear. Had he heard it with his ears or only with his heart? There was no need to open the letter. He could not find the strength to open his eyes, let alone light a candle.

"I'm in need of holdin', Jesus," he whispered. "In need of a Father tonight." And then, with a sigh, he fell asleep.

* * *

Jefferson cut Billy Jones down from the hickory tree. He carried him and laid his frail body in the back of the buckboard. He took him home and brought him in to his widow and children. He built the coffin out of planks that had been meant for a new chicken coop. For all of this, Delpha Jean Jones asked that Jefferson be allowed to preach the sermon for Billy's funeral. The old preacher nodded his white head and said he reckoned it was only fittin'.

So Billy Jones was buried down in the cemetery for colored folks. No granite markers stood here, no stone angels pointing skyward. Billy's name was printed on a whitewashed plank and set up at the head of the grave marking the place where he was laid to rest. Jefferson read from Psalm 103 in the Good Book, about how the Lord pities His own like a father pities his children. It was generally agreed that in this life that was the only pity a man could count on. An ocean of salty tears fell that morning. A flood of grief washed over that place, and Billy Jones began his sea-change, giving back to the land the nourishment he had taken from it in his life.

Jefferson Canfield said, "Amen" and lifted his head to look out over the cotton fields and the stands of corn.

Folks glanced at one another, for they could see the Holy Ghost had come upon Jefferson, as had happened before.

Jefferson raised his hands, and his voice rang out across the fields. "The Lord says this: The life of a man is jus' like one little cotton boll. He grows up, an' sometimes the ol' devil boll weevil eats him up inside before he has a chance to bloom. Other men make good cotton. But it's always the same, says the Lord. Ever'body, young an' old, is gonna get picked by the angel of death. An' that world we're growin' in don't pay no mind when we're gone. The wind comes an' blows over the field, an' the proud, tall cotton ain't there no more."

Murmured "Amens" echoed his words, but Jefferson was not finished yet.

"Oh, Lord!" he said so loud that the white men in a passing wagon turned to look at the group on the knoll. "Have mercy on them men that killed our Billy. Them men don't see what's comin' at the end of their lives! They don't see that no fancy headstone's gonna keep Judgment Day from comin'. Have mercy on them Lord . . . for Your justice will be terrible when it comes upon them!"

No one said "Amen," but they all believed they had heard the word of the Lord boom from the lips of the young preacher.

LOVE
AND WAR

part three

Boll weevil in de cotton,
cutworm in de corn.
Devil in de white man,
war's goin' on.

CHAPTER THIRTY

Whistle-Stop

The special train expected to arrive at the tiny station in Camden, Ohio, was three hours overdue, but that fact had not decreased the size of the crowd waiting expectantly on both sides of the tracks. Temporary grandstands, hurriedly erected, had already been filled to capacity since early morning. No one had been tempted to give up his place, even though it was now midafternoon.

The assembly had a carnival atmosphere, with vendors loudly hawking paper bags of roasted peanuts and Nehi sodas. Their singsong chant competed with the cry of the souvenir sellers offering commemorative red, white, and blue striped ribbons painted with the likeness of President Woodrow Wilson and tiny American flags to wave.

The platform of the depot was occupied with all the local dignitaries who could wangle an invitation to sit in such an exalted location. Mayor Thompson, sweating profusely in his suit coat and stiff collar, still clutched the notes of his welcoming speech, even though the ink had long since smeared and the paper crumpled. He of all the crowd sincerely hoped the ordeal would be over soon.

For the rest, the anticipation of a whistle-stop visit from the president of the United States had transformed the late-summer day into a real occasion. Stores were shuttered, the bank was closed, and the surrounding countryside had emptied its population into Camden as if it were already the week of the county fair.

Children yelled and played tag, not at all clear what all the fuss was about, but enjoying the excitement. Doc Warne called his grandson Howie up onto the platform to where Doc sat two chairs away from

Mayor Thompson. Doc handed Howie a handful of pennies. With a wink he said, "Now you know what to do, don't you, Howie?" Howie gave a solemn nod and scampered off.

Several small boys, including another of Doc's grandchildren, were using the roof of the train station as a lookout post. There had already been three false alarms, so the crowd was not quite as quick to react as it had been earlier when Patrick shouted, "Train! Train's coming!" But this time it was not a mistake. The Presidential Special, carrying Wilson on a cross-country tour to secure the support of the people for the League of Nations, was chugging into view.

Soon the dark blue flags bearing the president's seal of office could be seen waving above the cowcatcher. The combined instruments of the volunteer fire department band broke into the Princeton fight song, in honor of the college professor now called the "schoolmaster president."

Instead of stopping even with the platform, the special train pulled all the way through the station until the rear of the last car was at the edge of the grandstand. There was a final convulsive blast of steam from the locomotive, and then all was still with anticipation. An honor guard of uniformed veterans of the Great War filed out to line the track. Among them was Ellis Warne. He was using his crutches, but he looked happy and proud. Doc looked down at his son from the group of dignitaries and smiled.

The band struck up "Hail to the Chief," and the door onto the rear landing opened. The gaunt, aristocratic-looking man who had been president for six years and led the country through the Great War emerged, blinking into the sunlight.

Mayor Thompson did a credible job welcoming the president to Camden, praising his accomplishments, and reflecting on what a great honor this was for the town, the county, and the state, but Wilson fidgeted through the honeyed words. It crossed Doc's mind that the president was not the cause of the train running behind schedule. He appeared to be a man on a mission—or perhaps *crusade* was a more apt word.

When Thompson had gushed a last gush, Wilson wasted no time soaring into his theme. "My friends," he said in a hoarse but resolute-sounding voice, "I stand before you today as I have stood and will stand before thousands of your countrymen. I bring to you and to this great nation a message of the gravest importance that is indeed for the entire world."

The crowd waited politely for a coughing spell to pass.

"By the grace of almighty God, we have won the late war that cost so many families so dearly, such as I see represented here before me." He paused and gestured toward Ellis and the others of the honor guard.

"And I am sure that you all carry the memories of others who have made the ultimate sacrifice in the name of freedom and democracy.

"But winning the war is not enough. Now we must also win the peace! We stand on the threshold of an opportunity to remake the world nearer to our hearts' desire, with lasting peace and a means of settling disputes between nations without violence or sacrifice or loss. I am speaking of the proposed League of Nations. The stage is set, the destiny disclosed. We cannot turn back. We can only go forward with lifted eyes and freshened spirit to follow the vision. America shall, in truth, show the way. The light streams upon the path ahead, and nowhere else."

President Wilson paused to receive a round of applause. He continued. "So is there a shadow that darkens the path? Only in the minds of small, contemptible men. Pygmy minds. Selfish, narrow minds that never get anywhere, but run around in circles and think they are going somewhere."

Doc knew that Wilson was speaking of the Senate Foreign Affairs Committee and of Senator Henry Cabot Lodge, in particular. Lodge was outspoken in his opposition to the United States' participation in the League of Nations, and he and his isolationist colleagues had held up senatorial approval of the League.

"You must help me stem this tide of ignorance and fear and unwillingness to step out boldly. Say to your senators, 'America must lead! From the pain and sorrow of the late war must come the birth of a new world order.'

"You must speak with your voices and with your letters and, most important of all, with your votes. You have an opportunity to send this urgent message to Washington in the most valuable form: in the person of a congressman who understands both sacrifice and leadership. I urge you to support the candidacy of Doctor William Warne as your next representative!"

There was a stunned silence and then a burst of thunderous applause. William Warne meant Doc. Doc Warne, who took out tonsils and set broken arms and delivered babies. The president of the United States was speaking of *their* Doc—had asked for him by name!

There were some concluding remarks, but the crowd only half heard. By the time Wilson had thanked them for coming and bid them farewell, a line was already forming beside the platform to shake Doc's hand. They kept him busy for an hour after the train had pulled out of Camden.

Finally the last farmer had wished Doc well, and he stood alone except for little Howie. Doc bent down and asked. "Well, Howie, did you get them all picked up?"

"Yes, sir," said Howie, "all except for one that Susie Mercer picked up and kept. She said finders keepers, and—"

"Never mind," Doc said. "We won't begrudge her one. Let me see them."

Howie began to empty the pockets of his overalls. Twenty-nine copper pennies, smashed into flattened ovals by the passage of the special train, filled Howie's hands. "I think . . . I'll be taking this one," Doc said, picking one at random. "Now you share the rest with your brother and cousins. Someday you can show it to your grandchildren and tell them you got it when you were just their age, on the day you heard President Wilson speak."

"And, Grampa," Howie added, his eyes shining as brightly as the pennies, "the day the president asked for *you* by name."

"Aye, lad," agreed Doc, tucking the token into his watch pocket. "That he did."

★ ★ ★

Each morning Trudy timed her household chores so she would be finished when the mail came. Beds were made, breakfast dishes washed and put away, and the parlor dusted. Trudy took the broom from the closet and began the slow, careful sweeping of the front walk just as the postman turned the corner onto Seventh Street.

By the time the Johnsons' Airedale terrier began his frantic barking across the street, Trudy had worked her way to the bottom step. The postman, his hand full of letters, stepped onto the brick sidewalk and hailed her as cheerfully as usual. "Y'all got a heap of mail today, Miss Trudy."

She dared not hope for the letter she had been waiting for, *praying* for! Taking the mail from the postman, she bade him good morning and disciplined herself not to tear through the stack in search of a postmark from Shiloh.

"Anything interesting, dear?" Sadie Meyer asked from the kitchen as the screen door banged shut.

Trudy propped the broom in the corner. Only then did she let herself flip through the stack of mail. "One from Max!" she told her mother, setting her cousin's letter on the side table in the foyer. The rest of the envelopes were addressed to Trudy's mother or bills addressed to her father. The phone rang three rings and a pause, then three rings again. That was the Meyer signal on the party line.

"Answer that, Trudy!" Sadie called. "My hands are all in silver polish!"

Only halfway through the sorting, Trudy reluctantly picked up the receiver and leaned in to speak loudly into the old wall phone. "Meyer residence."

"Hello. This is Miss Brown at Belle Grove School. Miss Trudy Meyer, please?"

Trudy tried to juggle the earpiece and scan the postmarks at the same time. "Trudy here."

"Trudy?" Someone picked up the party line and the clarity of the connection diminished. "Trudy Meyer?"

"Yes!" Trudy said exultantly. It was not that she wanted to speak to the secretary of Belle Grove, but here in her hands lay the precious letter she had been looking for. "Yes, this is Trudy!" Was the excitement so evident in her voice?

"Well then," Miss Brown shouted into her end of the line, "the principal is requesting a meeting with you. . . ."

"Wonderful! *Wonderful*, Miss Brown!"

"I suppose," the woman replied dryly. "He says it is urgent, Miss Meyer."

Well, that was a new one. Old Miss Brown had never called her anything but Trudy. It must have been a mark of respect offered to the newest Belle Grove teacher.

"Just whenever . . . anytime is fine. Tomorrow? In the morning before it gets too hot?" Trudy clung tenaciously to Birch's note and dropped the other letters onto the floor until the irritation of the telephone interruption was over. Then she clattered up the stairs and closed the door to ward off her mother's questions about where Birch was and when he was coming back and . . .

She slit the envelope with her penknife and removed the letter as she took a seat beside the window. It was a short note, one page on a child's notebook paper. Trudy bit her lip as she tried to read his signature through the back of the paper. Had he written that he loved her?

She unfolded the paper and scanned the three lines, then gasped and read them aloud. Could this be?

"Dear Trudy,
Nothing worked out the way I thought. I have nothing to offer you in spite of all I have felt about you. It is better if you forget me and go on with your life.

Birch Tucker"

"Trudy . . ." Sadie's impatient voice penetrated the fog of Trudy's pain and anger as she stared at the note. "You left the mail on the floor!"

Trudy read the note again. She turned it over, not comprehending that there was nothing else to it. How could he be so cold? How could he have said the things he said? kissed her as he had? And now *this*! She felt dizzy and sick. Groping for the bed, she lay down, unable to answer Sadie.

"Trudy! Where are you? Trudy!"

"Here, Mama," she managed after a moment.

"Well, *get down here*!"

"Not feeling . . . I feel sick, Mama!" she called, hoping that she would not cry. No man was worth crying over. Especially not one who was such a dreadful liar! A man who could toy with a girl's affections and then . . . *this*! She shoved the note under her pillow as Sadie entered.

"What's wrong?" Sadie asked.

"Oh . . . you know, Mama."

"Ah, that time again already?'

"I think so." Trudy closed her eyes against the burning tears that threatened to spill over. Her voice quavered. She did not want Sadie to see her like this. To guess what was really wrong.

"So soon? Hmmm. Should I get you an aspirin?" Sadie pulled the shade. Merciful darkness.

"No. Just need a little nap is all."

"Headache?"

"Hmmm. A little. Please, Mama." Trudy felt as though she would break if she had to answer any more questions.

"All right then. . . . You dropped the mail on the floor, you know."

"Sorry, Mama."

"All except for the letter from Max. From England." Sadie's voice was thick with curiosity. "He wants to know if you have heard anything from someone named Irene." She held out the letter.

"You read it?" Trudy sat bolt upright, snatching the envelope from her mother's hand.

"I saw the return address. I did not think it was private. After all, Max is family—"

"Mama!" Trudy snapped. "Max's letter?"

Sadie handed it to her reluctantly. "Max says this Irene person has just disappeared from New York. Wrote him a letter and vanished. He says he has spent every cent of his stipend for the month sending wires from England trying to track her down. Her brothers don't know where she is or why she left, but Max is very concerned that he find her because as soon as he can he will marry her and—"

"Mother!" Trudy shouted Sadie to silence. "This was a *private* letter!"

"Well, *have* you heard from this Irene person?"

"No."

"Who is she?"

"Please . . . a teacher. A friend from Columbia."

"More than a friend to Max, from the sound of it." Sadie remained rooted in the doorway. She pried for the information that was implied but not spelled out in Max's letter. "She is a good girl, this Irene person? Or trying to trap your cousin?"

"Mother!"

"Mind your tone."

"Please." Trudy held back the anger she felt. "Please . . . *shut* . . . my door."

"When you write Max, tell him there are plenty of other fish in the sea, Trudy. You young people think that you can never get over a broken heart. Tell him this Irene person is someone to forget about!"

Trudy glared at Sadie, who had evidently said all she cared to say. Trudy knew she would repeat it again later, but for now the motherly wisdom would be put on the shelf. "My door, please?"

Sadie sighed. "Sure," she replied, and the door clicked shut, leaving Trudy alone in the dark, stuffy room.

Trudy read through Max's letter. He sounded desperate, heartbroken, and helpless. All of his funds were gone. He could not afford a steamer ticket back to New York. The Academic Foundation had paid for his passage to England, and now he was stuck there.

She has left New York without explanation to her brothers, who are frantic to find her. Perhaps you are the only one who can guess what this means. I am desperate to reach her. To make things right this time—to marry her. Perhaps she has written you. Please tell her for me . . .

"Oh, Max," Trudy whispered. Suddenly her own broken heart seemed of small consequence compared to this. She could get over Birch. Maybe her mother was right about that. But Irene and Max—no doubt their tragic affair would soon concern a third little person. Trudy was certain of why Irene had run away. "*Never let him hurt you again. . . .*"

How had everything gotten so muddled? Trudy closed her eyes so she would not weep for Irene or for herself. She had made a promise that she would never be so silly as to cry over any man, so she bit her lip and furrowed her brow and fought the urge to give in to self-pity. She had wept once when Birch left her. What a foolish thing that seemed now. She would never be so foolish again.

CHAPTER THIRTY-ONE

The Battle Begins

Smoke from Doc's curved-stem briar pipe spiraled upward around his ruddy face. He was seated in his office chair again, but this time the meeting had been liberated from the confines of his tiny office, and the committee was spread around the living room of the Warne home, as if to take full advantage of the additional space.

McBride sat on a window seat, while Mazurki had a couch all to himself. Molly had seen to it that all the iced-tea glasses were filled. She had intended to leave the men to their deliberations, but Doc had asked her to remain. She was perched on the piano stool in the corner of the room. Open on the piano's music rack was the sheet music to "Over There."

Blaylock was the only one who did not appear to be relaxed. The attorney was up and pacing about the room.

"All right then, Bobby," Doc said as the lawyer completed one more circuit, "when do we begin getting serious about this campaign?"

"The farming community is already with you," Blaylock began, "but that isn't enough. Hopewell has the backing of Senator Harding and Harding's newspaper. Hopewell will be able to keep hammering the city folk with his own brand of fear—fear of the Reds, fear of foreigners, fear of trouble with the coloreds—and he'll wrap all these in the worries of lost jobs and shrinking paychecks."

"Then how we gonna fight back?" rumbled Mazurki.

A loud crash interrupted before anyone could give Paul an answer. At the rear of the home, the screen door that led into Molly's kitchen banged open against the side of the house not once but twice. Pounding feet on the hardwood floor mingled with shouts of "Mama! Mama!"

and "Gramma!" The noise and commotion made Molly think that at least four hundred children were riding a herd of buffalo through her kitchen.

The swinging door from the kitchen into the living room flew open and little Julie burst in, closely followed by Howie and Tim. Molly took one look and decided that Julie had been wrestling wildcats instead of riding buffalo. Julie's auburn curls, which had been neatly piled on her head when she left for school, were hanging down all around. The right side corkscrewed down to the collar of her blouse, as if someone had tried to pull that particular curl clear off.

"She called you an Injun, Papa, a dirty red Injun," Julie reported loudly to Doc. Half the buttons were ripped off Julie's blouse, and its tattered tail bore the marks of having been used to wipe her bloody nose.

"Not red *Injun!*" Tim, who was a whole year older, corrected with authority. "She called Grampa a dirty Red!"

"Who did?" asked Doc. "Julie, Love, have you been fighting?"

Julie looked indignant. Weren't her battle scars proof enough that she had been defending the family honor? She rounded sharply on Tim, who backed up quickly. "It's the same thing," she insisted. "And, Papa, she said you were a lousy Mick, too. You aren't a Mick, are you, Papa? She said I was one, too! We're not Micks, are we, Papa?"

Doc looked around at his friends as if to say, *"Somebody help me make sense of this."*

Molly sorted it out. In a firm voice she instructed Julie to go immediately and wash her face and change her clothes. As soon as Julie was out of the room, Molly turned to Howie, who had not yet spoken, and asked him to explain.

"It was Amy Wallace who done it . . . *did* it," he amended. "Julie was talking to Susie Mercer about how Grampa was gonna get elected, when all at once Amy says, real loud, 'Your daddy is just a dirty Red. My mommy says so.' And then they went to fighting."

"Well, all right," Doc said, "I think we get the picture now. You and Timmy best run along home now. And don't you be fighting, understand?"

"Wait a small moment," Mazurki requested. His eyes were dancing as he looked at the boys over a nose that bore the evidence of many a fight of his own. "You did not say who won this battle."

Howie and Tim looked at each other in careful consideration. "Julie did," Tim announced.

Howie agreed. "Both of them tore each other up somethin' fierce, but when Miz Morrison broke it up, Amy was crying, but Julie was still mad!"

When the boys had departed, Molly went off to see about Julie, and Doc and the other men tried to resume their interrupted discussion. "What were we about?" Doc inquired. "Ah, Paul. You were asking how we'd be fighting back against Hopewell. 'Tis a timely question, that. It seems the war has already begun!"

The earth of the strip mine had been carved away tier by tier, leaving an ugly gash across the cheek of Franklin County, Arkansas.

Many of the heroes of the Argonne and Meuse and Belleau Wood returned to their homes to find that during their two-year absence, the old familiar land had been turned over to other sharecroppers. In the eyes of the law, the landlords of the South were innocent of any crime when they sent the heroes away. What else was to be done? With farm prices dropping through the basement, could absent tenant farmers expect the owners to let their farmland lie fallow?

The strip mines were filled with bitter, displaced men who had spent their lives harvesting white cotton. Now they labored twelve- and fourteen-hour days in the black grime of coal dust. Their bitterness blossomed into hatred—for the landlords, for the government, for foreign workers and black sharecroppers who would work for less of a share than any white man. The first wind in the late summer of 1919 carried with it the searing heat of human rage. The deep pit of the Franklin County coal mine nurtured discontent and hatred among the men who found work there.

Birch Tucker considered himself lucky to find work at all. To get the job, he traded the fine bay horse to the mine foreman for a team of shaggy mules and hitched them each morning to a coal wagon at the bottom of the pit. It was Birch's job to drive the heavy wagon halfway up the steep switchbacks of the strip mine. At a level landing, he traded the full wagon for an empty one, which he drove back down to the floor of the pit.

Birch envied the driver of the upper level. At least that man could reach the top and see something more of the world than coal and gouged earth for fourteen hours at a stretch. There was no hint of breeze. No shade in which to stand, even for a moment. The sun beat down with merciless harshness, like the curses of foreman Ned Oliver, who was from someplace else. Oliver did not like the men who worked for him. He hated the steaming heat of the Arkansas coal pit, and he took it out on the laborers.

"Coal ain't like cotton, you lazy crackers!" he would cry at the end of lunch break. "It don't just fall out of the boll and holler, 'Pick me!' Get your backs into it!" Birch might have been able to tolerate the verbal lash upon his own back, but Oliver also laid a whip to the back of the bay horse. Birch regretted trading off the big bay to the foreman in exchange for the strip-mine mules. Day after day Birch watched and listened as Ned cursed and spurred the gelding up the crumbling slope until the animal was lathered and heaving. Something stirred deep inside Birch when the foreman jerked the reins hard in that sensitive mouth and slammed his spurs deep into the sides of the beast.

This morning the sun was barely over the lip of the crater, and already the bay was wide-eyed with obedient terror as the foreman whipped him to a gallop past the loaded coal wagon.

A dozen yards above Birch on the switchback the horse stumbled, sending the foreman into a torrent of rage. The leather quirt slammed against the bay's shoulders and rump, leaving welts on top of welts in the damp hide. Birch stiffened and then clucked his mules on, even though the foreman battled the dancing gelding and blocked the trail.

"Whoa up your mules there!" commanded the foreman. "Can't you see—" The lash punctuated his words. He cursed the bay and spun him around. Eyes wild and mouth open against the hard pull of the bit, the bay reared slightly. The whip pummeled his head, landing with audible thuds between his ears. Birch clucked his team on, as if to run over the foreman in his struggle. Now the foreman turned his whip on the face of the mules.

"Lay off it!" Birch rose, pulling the team to a halt.

The foreman jerked his mount around and kicked him hard until he pranced and squeezed in between the wagon and the wall of the pit. He cursed Birch and raised his whip as though he would bring it down across his face. "You lousy white-trash dirt farmer! Trade me this mad dog you call a horse! I been fightin' him up and down this hill for two weeks while you smirk behind your hand!" The whip crashed down on the bay again. The horse lunged forward only to be brought back by a brutal jerk of the reins.

"You want these mules back?" Birch challenged.

"Without them mules you got no job," menaced the foreman.

"Take your mules, mister. I want my horse."

At that the foreman leaped onto the wagon and slapped the bay hard on the rump, sending him on a frantic run to the bottom of the pit. He snatched the lines from Birch and then shoved him off the wagon. "Get outta my mine!" he yelled, slapping the weary mules with the same force as he had pounded the big bay.

Birch stood on the slope and looked up after the wagon. The bay had reached the floor of the pit. He stood trembling beside an empty wagon. His bridle was broken where he had stepped on the reins. One ear was out of the headstall, and he chomped on the dislodged bit.

Grimy faces turned upward to look at Birch as he trudged down three switchbacks to the floor of the mine.

"You fired, Tucker?" asked one.

"What's it look like?" Birch reached out to touch the stripes on the neck of the horse. The animal backed away from him.

"What you gonna do now, Tucker?" A wheelbarrow of coal slid into the wagon.

"I dunno." Birch took a step toward the bay and turned his hand palm up. "I reckon I'd better try and make it up to this horse." The animal was head shy from two weeks of beatings. "I doubt he ever had a lash put to him before this." He cast an angry look to where the foreman stood at the switching level beside the wagon.

"Welcome to the real world," said another man to the horse.

Once out of the pit, Birch let the horse break into an easy trot. Even though Birch spoke softly to him all the time, it took several miles before the animal's ears quit flicking nervously backward and forward at the sound of a man's voice.

When they came to a wooded area with a creek, Birch reined in the bay and turned him aside to graze on a patch of grass. The horse nickered with gratitude as obvious as a spoken thank you. "I know how you feel," Birch said to the horse. "Ain't had nobody treat me nice in a while, either."

As he pulled the saddle from the mount's back, he discovered a small leather saddlebag tied on behind the high cantle. "What's this?" he said aloud. "That ain't mine. What did we make off with? I wonder."

Out of the pouch tumbled a folded white bedsheet with a hole cut out of the center and a hooded mask. "Thunderation," said Birch, "why couldn't it be somethin' to eat?" He stuffed the robe and mask back into the bag. Punching it once for good measure, he put the makeshift pillow under his head and tried to sleep away his growing hunger.

Returning to Belle Grove School to teach was like coming home for Trudy. This morning as she climbed the steps of the large redbrick Gothic structure, she could remember being a student here, and how she had dreamed of being a teacher. Today she carried her lesson plans in the leather portfolio her mother and father had given her for graduation from Columbia. Looking up at the tall bell tower above the entrance, she felt that this day was one of the proudest of her life. She at least had her pride and accomplishments left, even though Birch was gone from her life.

The office of Professor Bolt, acting principal of the school, was just off the main entrance. Trudy waited behind the counter as Miss Brown finished typing a letter and glanced up at her.

"Oh . . . hello, Trudy," the woman said in a distracted way. "Here to see the principal, are you?"

"Morning, Miss Brown. Can you imagine? Me coming back to teach? Wonderful, isn't it?"

Miss Brown did not reply. Maybe it was the heat. Only nine in the morning, and it was already a scorcher. The woman rapped on the principal's door. "She's here."

"Well, send her in."

Trudy could hear his desk chair groan. Hear him sigh. There seemed to be a cloud hovering over them both. Just the heat, certainly. Trudy would not let their gloomy voices break the enthusiasm she felt. Summer sunlight streamed through the tall arched windows that were thrown open for ventilation. A small electric fan sat on the principal's desk, but still perspiration streamed down his face and dripped on his high collar.

Barely smiling at her, he looked up and then down quickly. "Please do sit down, Miss Meyer."

"It seems strange to hear you call me Miss Meyer after all those years I was just plain Trudy sitting in your classroom. And now here you are the principal, and I'm going to be teaching in your old classroom, I hear."

He did not respond, except to raise his hand slightly to stop her. Something was wrong. Bad news of some sort, perhaps. Someone ill in his family?

"Trudy." He glanced up at the frosted-glass door of his office, which stood slightly ajar. "Miss Brown," he called to the secretary, "would you close the door, please?"

Typing stopped and the door closed quietly. Only then did Professor Bolt look Trudy full in the face. His pinched features were grim. Large pale blue eyes blinked at her through his thick spectacles.

"Are you . . . feeling unwell, Professor?" He looked ill, Trudy thought. "It is so warm this morning," she tried.

No reply.

"I mean—"

He inhaled slowly and mopped his brow. "Trudy . . ." He paused, examining the open file in front of him. "Trudy, I always thought you were a bright girl, a good student. I told your mother and father you would go far." The words were kind, but the tone was flat, without enthusiasm.

Did he want a response? "And you were my favorite—"

He stopped her with a shake of his head. "Please, let me finish."

She nodded. A sense of doom descended on her. This was not the usual meeting of a principal with a new teacher, a returning pupil come home to teach.

"As you know, Belle Grove School has a long and honorable history. It began right here in a brick house in 1870 under the direction of Professor Lemon and three teachers. In only two years the school had two hundred forty students and six teachers employed. Since then the children, grandchildren, and great-grandchildren of those first students have attended here. And this is what we have become. A proud and distinguished school. A place you were proud to be part of." Here he paused. "There has never been a scandal within these walls." He frowned and his lower lip protruded. He corrected himself. "Well, anyway, scandal was always dealt with promptly so as not to affect the morals of our students."

"*Scandal?* One does not bring up such a word unless there is a point to it." Trudy sat very straight with her head high. Somehow she was at the center of some scandal or potential scandal at Belle Grove. She wanted him to get on with it. Whatever it was, there would be no defense against it. Some decision had been made before she had ever been called to this meeting.

"Yes. I am getting to it." He glanced nervously at his hands and then seemed to gather courage. "Scandal. The very hint of it is unacceptable in the life of a young woman who will be affecting the minds of young people. Do you understand?"

"Yes."

"Good. I want . . . that is, the school board wants you to understand that. Because there has been a hint of scandal surrounding you and a young man. It is said that you were traveling with a soldier on a train from New York to Fort Smith."

"A friend of my cousin's—"

"You were involved in an ugly incident at a rail stop in Missouri. A brawl, in fact, in which a Negro and this traveling companion of yours—"

"Birch was not my companion. We shared the same train; that's all. Both of us were traveling home to Fort Smith."

"This traveling companion of yours was injured in some way, and you had him carried to your private compartment. And then the railway officials were told he was your husband. As a matter of fact, Doctor Cooper believed him to be your husband—"

"I only said that because—"

An impatient wave of the hand cut her off. "Do not make this difficult for me. This is an unpleasant duty at best." He mopped the perspiration from his neck and took a sip of water to calm himself. "This traveling companion of yours was taken to your home . . . your parents' abode . . . to recover . . . to be nursed by you."

"He was a friend of the family—"

"What does it matter? The word is *scandal*, Trudy! Do you hear me? It is all around town that this fellow and you . . . well, it is said . . . and then at the Electric Park on the night of the Fourth, several children were hiding in the bushes. They say they saw you and this soldier fellow together, locked in an embrace."

"He kissed me. Where there no other kisses in the Electric Park that evening?"

"That does not matter." Professor Bolt was firm. "Trudy . . . Miss Meyer . . . the board has instructed me to inform you—"

She stood abruptly. "Professor, please. Nothing more needs to be said. I . . . was thinking all along that perhaps it would not be a good idea for me to teach here, so close to home and all. I think I will look elsewhere for employment." She stopped, fearful that if she said even one more word, she might weep. The truth of the situation was totally irrelevant. Nor did it matter that Birch Tucker had now ridden out of her life. That what she had hoped was love meant nothing to him. The damage was done. The word *scandal* had been whispered.

"My dear." Professor Bolt looked more miserable than relieved. "My dear . . ."

"I'm all right, Professor. You know what stuff I am made of."

"I am sorry for this. I argued on your behalf."

"No need for that. Gossip, you know. It can draw blood like a knife, and then there's no putting the blood back."

"Listen . . ." He frowned and glanced past her at the door. He lowered his voice almost to a whisper, and again the typing fell silent. Miss Brown was no doubt straining to hear each word. "I know of a small school. The teacher passed away six months ago. There's been no one qualified to step in. It's just twenty miles outside Fort Smith. A house comes with the position. I shall write you a letter of recommendation. The place is beyond the gossips of our fair town. You may teach there, perhaps. Would you like that?"

Trudy nodded. Anything. Only she did not want him to speak so kindly to her right now or she would certainly weep, and then Miss Brown would tell everyone about her tears. "Thank you." She raised her eyes. "You really are a kind man. I always thought so."

"Let's not speak of my character just now, Trudy. Duty has done you a great injustice, I fear. And I am part of it." He glared at the frosted-glass pane. "Be cheerful when you leave, will you? Bid Miss Brown a good day."

Professor Bolt opened the door for her. With his gaze on her, she followed his advice, cheerfully saying good-bye.

"Well!" she heard Miss Brown hiss. "She certainly took it well."

"She has other offers," the professor replied.

Then the doors of Belle Grove School closed behind Trudy, shutting off the rest of what he said to save some shred of her pride.

Trudy held her head erect as she walked quickly down North Sixth Street. She looked straight ahead, suddenly feeling as if complete strangers were staring at her . . . *whispering.* Two boys trundled their red wagon past her on the sidewalk. Their laughter would not have affected her yesterday, but this morning it felt to Trudy as though every word and look and thought was somehow directed at her. *The Scandal . . .*

She did not turn when a man's voice called out to her. "Miss Meyer? Trudy Meyer?" Deputy East cut across the street to walk uninvited at her side.

"Good morning." Trudy looked away from him. Certainly East was among those who knew—or thought he knew—every detail of the shocking affair.

"Somethin' wrong?" He was prying, hoping for a response.

"I need to get home . . . work to do."

"Your mama told me I could find you at Belle Grove School." He was smiling, evidently enjoying what he knew must have happened at the school this morning. Could he make Trudy talk about it? "You had some sort of meetin' . . . before school begins?"

Trudy felt a flash of anger at the injustice of her dismissal, and now . . . this prying little weasel! Certainly everyone in Fort Smith had known before Trudy what the meeting was for.

"Actually, I had to tell the principal that I will be taking another position. Belle Grove is too close to home for my liking. Too many prying eyes and wagging tongues."

East expelled a brittle laugh. "Is that so? You ain't goin' back to our old stompin' grounds, eh? I figured you'd want to be there since you done so good as a student and all. Made the rest of us look like pure idiots, you did, with all that brainpower." Another laugh. He was walking fast to keep up with her. "Must be them German brains inside that head of yours. Always did admire them German brains."

Trudy stopped midstride and swiveled to face him. He was smiling, smug in the knowledge that his words were like little needles, pricking her to anger. "German brains, Deputy East?"

"That's what y'all are, ain't you? *German?*"

"Don't be insulting," she replied. Then, "What exactly do you want? You didn't track me down and follow me all the way down Sixth Street just for the pleasure of hearing me admit that I am Jewish and educated at Columbia University in New York City, did you? I know that such a confession is tantamount to saying I am an anarchist in these parts, but is this what you are paid for, East?"

His eyes glinted hard behind the smile. "I don't know *what the—*" He stopped suddenly and shrugged. "Pardon me . . . I don't know what you're talkin' about.".

"Yes you do. And I don't pardon you. I am a lady, and you will mind your language, or I will write a letter to your superiors about it."

"You ain't no lady, Miss Meyer. I don't figure nobody at the station would think so, either." The smile was replaced by open hostility, controlled disdain. "Now then. We're just lookin' for that boyfriend y'all kept at your house. We want to ask him a few more questions."

Trudy shook her head and walked on. A small Ford coupe filled with teenagers rumbled by. Three girls pointed openly at her. "There she is . . . that Jew-gal . . . teacher from—"

"Miss Meyer?" East did not follow. "You know where that fella is?"

"Last I heard he was in Shiloh," she replied. "Go ask him anything you want. It doesn't concern me a bit."

The dreaded flush was on her cheeks. She had no reason to be ashamed, yet she suddenly *felt* ashamed. Did Mama know what people were saying?

"You ain't gonna walk away so easy," East called after her, but he did not stop her. He did not follow when she boarded the streetcar to ride to the store.

Another police officer stood in front of Meyer's Dry Goods when she stepped from the trolley. Papa was standing in front with him. The plate glass of the display window was broken inward, and jagged shards protruded from the frame. Joseph Meyer looked pained when he saw her. The knowledge of trouble flickered in his eyes. Did the smashed window have something to do with her? with Birch?

"All of them threw stones at once. Stood in the back of the truck and screamed and just—" Joseph gestured to the plate glass littering the sidewalk.

"Did they say anythin' specific? Something . . . so's you might know *why* they done it?"

"No," Joseph replied as Trudy joined him.

He was not telling the truth. Trudy could see it on his face. The men in the truck had indeed shouted something, but her father would not repeat those words in front of her.

"Probably just drunk," said the officer. "You know, probably Oklahoma Injuns spendin' their government money. Can't say I'm gonna miss them comin' in here causin' trouble like this." He closed his notebook.

Joseph put his arm around Trudy. "They were not Indians," he said in a quiet voice. "The truck was driven by a big man. . . . I have seen him here before. I know this. Not Indian."

"Well, if you spot 'em again, give us a call. There's not a thing we can do about somethin' like this unless you got positive ID and we can catch 'em at it."

"Papa?" Trudy saw that his face was very pale. He would not look at her. His eyes scanned every passing wagon and automobile. She followed his gaze. Everyone was looking back at them—at the policeman, the window, and at *Trudy*! Some expressions were openly hostile, some amused. Some were ashamed and sorry.

"Go inside, Trudy," Joseph instructed her. "Go help your mother clean up the broken glass."

She nodded and stepped away from him.

He lowered his voice to a whisper. "They were not Indians. *Something else* . . . and there *was* something they shouted." He waited until he heard the bell over the door ring for opening and closing before he finished explaining what had been shouted as the stones crashed through the glass.

CHAPTER THIRTY-TWO

Overalls and White Linen

Jefferson signed his name to the tenant-farming contract that old Mr. Howard had drawn up. Then he went back outside the gate to finish their conversation. That was the custom.

"Well, boy," Mr. Howard said to Jefferson from his porch, "hear you preached a good funeral for little Billy Jones."

"'Spect I did, Mr. Howard," Jefferson returned with a nod. "That's one I'd rather not preached."

"Life has unexpected turns. Too bad this came along right before pickin' time. This is gonna be a good year, I reckon. Billy was tellin' the foreman just last month he thinks we're gonna get a half bale more than usual out of his field."

Jefferson was grateful The Man had brought that up. It made it easier to say what was on his mind. "Some folks been thinkin' on that. Billy and Delpha Jean worked hard on that place. Always brought you profit."

"That he did. Good worker, Billy."

"Well, we was thinkin'—"

"It's dangerous to be thinkin' too much on such a hot day."

"Well, we been thinkin' in the cool of evenin' and the dead of night, too. Frettin' over Delpha Jean and them young'uns."

The Man seemed surprised. "Don't you fret none. I intend to let 'em stay on until after pickin' time. Giving Delpha Jean what would have been Billy's share, too. Then she can go on up North, Chicago way, where her sister is livin'."

Old Mr. Howard recited this plan as though it were something Delpha Jean wanted. Jefferson knew it was not. She did not want to raise her young'uns in Chicago. Hadn't her sister just written that there was no work to be had, and the Klan was stronger there than in the South?

"Delpha Jean is a good picker." Jefferson tried to think how he might phrase her wish to stay on so Mr. Howard would not take offense. "She can pick over four hundred pounds a day. I seen her do it. Outpick a man."

"But there are other men who can come along and take her place. Not that we won't miss her and little Billy, but I've found the next tenant already. My only nephew. He needs a place to put some roots—family obligations and such. So if you were thinkin' maybe you could take over Billy's place, I gotta tell you it's spoken for."

"No, sir. I wasn't thinkin' that at all. I was just tryin' to figger out how Delpha Jean could stay on the farm. They had family there, same place, sharecroppin' for fifty years."

The Man lowered his head and looked at Jefferson over the rim of his glasses. "Then I reckon it's time things change some around here."

The tone of his voice was soft and gentle, like it usually was, but there was something else behind those words that made Jefferson regret coming to talk about the Jones farm.

Jefferson smiled and jumped onto another topic. "Well, I wanted to tell you, Mister Howard, things are goin' good down at the woods. Good mules. Hard workers . . ."

"I like to hear such news, Jefferson. You are a good worker. As long as you do your work, we're always gonna get along, you and me."

Mr. Howard sat back and fanned himself harder. There were tea stains on the front of his white linen coat, and Jefferson thought to himself that even a rich man like Mr. Howard would look better if he dressed in overalls. But Mr. Howard wanted to look different than just ordinary folks. He couldn't wear plain denim, which would not show the stains of what he ate for breakfast. He had to wear white linen—just like his pappy had done, and his grandpappy before him.

"Well, sir, Mister Howard, I'd best be gettin' on back, then."

The Man inclined his head like a king from his veranda, then turned his attention back to the ledgers piled on the table beside his chair.

✳ ✳ ✳

Chicago seemed a long way from Mount Pisgah. A different world. A frightening, hellish place.

Delpha Jean Jones had brought the news clipping her sister had sent to her from Chicago. The children had all gone off fishing down at the creek. Only Willa-Mae, Delpha Jean, and Latisha remained at the Canfield house to clean the dishes from the big supper.

The three sat together on the porch, and Delpha Jean passed Latisha the letter and the clipping to read. Latisha always helped Delpha Jean with writing letters and reading the ones that on rare occasions came back to her. This was the kind of letter that Latisha never liked to read aloud, as though the utterance of bad news could somehow call trouble down upon them all.

"This come from the paper. Tells all what's goin' on up there."

"Well then, read it," Delpha Jean urged. "I been waitin' all day to know what it say."

"Bad news. Like what happened here," said Latisha. She cleared her throat and read aloud:

"The riots began at a public beach in Chicago when Negro bathers who believed that a young Negro boy had been stoned and drowned by whites began the stoning of white bathers. Rioting has continued with uncontrolled violence for five days. Rumors of atrocities circulate through Chicago. The members of both races crave vengeance. White gunmen in automobiles speed through Negro neighborhoods shooting indiscriminately, and Negro snipers fire back. Roaming mobs shoot, beat, and stab their victims. The understaffed police force cannot stop the waves of violence that have spread to the north and west sides of the Loop, Chicago's downtown business district. The toll thus far in human life has been—"

Latisha stopped and looked up into the faces of Willa-Mae and Delpha Jean.

"—well over five hundred Chicagoans have been injured. Twenty-three Negroes and fifteen whites have died thus far."

Willa-Mae shook her head and glanced skyward. "Lord, the world's gone wrong." She sighed and put her arm around Delpha Jean, who began to weep.

"Oh, Lord! I don't want to take my babies up to Chicago! It's bad here—they kill my Billy. But if we go up to Chicago, maybe they kill my babies, too, just 'cause we's black! *Why?* Why this goin' on, Willa-Mae?"

"Don't rightly know," Willa-Mae said grimly. She and her girls could just as easily have been thrown off the land if Hock had died instead of Billy. And where could she go? Where was one place better than another?

"What am I gonna do? How can I take my babies to some place with a *bigger mean* than we got right here? I know how to fight here! I just look down and say, 'Yes'm . . . yessir . . . no'm . . . no, sir'! I think to myself, *I can do this. I live a humble life. Don't make no waves!* But they killed my Billy anyway! Left my babies without no daddy and *no* place to live. Now what will become of us?"

Willa-Mae silently pondered the despair of her friend. There seemed to be no answer. "Mister Howard says he gotta clear your land so's his nephew can come here to live. He told Jefferson his nephew got no place to go. Don't think the Old Mister means to do evil to y'all, Depha Jean. Reckon he just thinkin' 'bout carin' for his own family. Figgers you'll go away, and your sister will take care of y'all in Chicago."

Latisha raised her chin indignantly. "Might be the way things is, but it don't make it right. Feels like dyin' to me. The men take what they want from us, then cast us off. Don't feel right."

Willa-Mae agreed. "No, it ain't. And we gonna pray on the matter. We gonna pray us up a storm and see what the Lord's got in mind for you, Delpha Jean. You heard what Jeff done preached. The Lord loves you and those young'uns like a father loves his chillens."

"Like Billy loved his chillens." Delpha Jean dabbed her tears and lifted her face to the heavens. "Oh, Lord, we all in need of a Father now that Billy's gone!"

"Go on now, shoo!" Becky Moniger urged the black-speckled hen. "It's such a pretty day; get on outside and enjoy it."

The speckled hen was almost a family pet. It was always the last to leave the chicken coop when someone had to go inside to clean the roost.

Cleaning the chicken manure out of the pen was pail-and-shovel work, but Becky did not mind. Since the roost was cleaned every week, it was never too big a chore, and Becky connected the sharp, acrid odor of the coop with planting roses in her mother's flower garden.

On the other side of the wall from the coop was a row of stalls for the dairy cows. The planks that formed the wall were not thick, nor did they fit tightly together, so Becky could overhear her father talking with old Bedford Evans without meaning to eavesdrop. Of course, since Mr. Evans was hard of hearing, he tended to talk loud anyway.

"Got your heifer ready to load, John?" he shouted at Becky's father.

"Right here, Bedford, and a fine young animal she is, too," John Moniger replied.

"This one right here, eh? You won't be sorry, John. My Samson has the best bloodlines of any bull in the county."

Becky could hear the shuffling of the heifer's feet as John Moniger circled the pen and slipped a lead rope over the sweet-faced Guernsey's neck.

"Say, John, I seen your Becky in town the other day with that Warne boy that has only one leg. Is it true that they're gettin' hitched?"

"That is the fact of the matter, Bedford. They surely will make a handsome couple, if I do say so meself."

Becky smiled to hear herself and Ellis described by her father. Even though she felt a twinge of guilt, she could not help moving closer to the wall and peeking through a crack. Her short, stocky, bearded father was beaming with obvious pride at the mental picture of his daughter and soon-to-be son-in-law.

"What are you gonna do to stop it?" Evans asked.

Becky could not believe she had heard correctly.

Her father also appeared confused by the question. "What are ye sayin', man?"

"Can't you hear good, John? Got a touch of that trouble my own self. A charge of powder went off right—"

"No!" Her father was shouting, too. "Why shouldn't they be married?"

"Can't believe you don't know, John. The whole county is talkin' about how Doc Warne is a Red Bolshevik. Why, he wants to invite a whole mess of foreigners to come take over our land. Niggers, too. Bring 'em in by the truckload, I hear tell!"

Becky saw her father's five-foot-four-inch frame stiffen at the ignorant words. "How do ye come to be listenin' to such foul gossip, Bedford?"

Bedford Evans seemed not to hear the question, because he continued his railing against Doc. "Don't hold with Reds, nor foreigners what can't talk good English. No sir! And I bet that son ain't any better. Prob'ly filled his head with strange notions over there in U-Rope. Losin' his leg an' all, wouldn't be surprised if he was some kinda anarchist fella— what? What you doin', John?"

Becky gasped and clapped her hands in a mixture of indignation and delight. Her father had snatched the lead rope out of Evans's hands and shut the heifer up in the pen. "Get out!" he ordered. "Best get off me place, Bedford Evans, whilst I still have some of me self-control remainin'!"

"What?" the other man demanded again. "Whatever is wrong with you, John?"

"Bedford," said Becky's father, shoving Evans toward the door of the barn and picking up a pitchfork for emphasis, "I've already told ye. I have no further use for your bull!"

✷ ✷ ✷

The first crop from Jefferson's forty acres was to be cords of fine-split firewood, which Jefferson intended to take to Fort Smith to sell.

Tree by tree, oak and pine came crashing down to be hewn and cut to twenty-four-inch lengths for the fireboxes of the city folks. Pine, which was a soft wood and quick to burn, was kept separate from the rock-hard, long-burning oak.

Hock and Jefferson had a lot of wood loaded into the back of Hock's wagon by the time the sun marked high noon. Latisha appeared at the edge of the clearing. She was wearing a loose white shift and a wide-brimmed straw hat that concealed her features in shadow. She stayed in the cool shade of a tall pine tree and cupped her hand to call, "Y'all come on now! I brung vittles!"

Jefferson pitched the last stick of wood into the wagon and wiped his brow. Hock unhitched the team and let them browse in the tall grass around the wagon as the men made their way to the blanket Latisha spread out for them beneath the pine.

It had been this way: work all morning from before sunup at the Can-field farm, then move down to the woods and start in clearing. Stop for lunch and go on until there was no light to see by.

Soon the cotton would be ready for picking, and Jefferson would have to give up clearing his land. With the cotton bolls splitting open almost audibly across the fence from where he worked, he did not want to waste even a minute to walk up to the house to eat. And so every day Latisha brought the noon meal to Jefferson and his father. Today she brought news as well as fried catfish and corn bread and cool water.

"Miz Young down at old Mister Howard's house says we gonna get a new schoolteacher," she said quietly to Jefferson as Hock napped on the blanket.

Jefferson cleaned the catfish right off the bone and reached for more. "That ought to make you right happy, Tisha. You ain't gonna have to teach them young'uns letters all by yourself no more."

"I don't mind. I suppose I can help her some. . . ." There was something more she wanted to say to him on the matter. Something else besides just that a teacher was coming.

"What is it, gal?" he asked, searching her face. "Somethin' troublin' you?"

"Just . . . I was thinkin' . . . after we get hitched—"

"Yes? I was thinkin' 'bout that, too." He smiled and reached for her hand.

Hock just lay there with his hat over his face . . . like an old log asleep.

Jefferson pulled Tisha down and kissed her. "Soon as I get this field cleared an' get me some cash money, then we can set to work on that ol' cabin yonder."

"Well, I was wonderin', Jeff . . . when that teacher comes?"

"Yeah? What is it? Just ask me."

"After we's hitched." She lowered her eyes shyly. "Miz Young say this schoolteacher is a real educated woman. Some big school. Ain't like the last one who weren't much smarter than me."

"That's why you was put to work on the young'uns," Jefferson said proudly. "You're smart, Tisha. That's one thing I like about you. Ever'body says so."

"You gonna make me quit school when we get hitched, Jeff? Make me just stay home and . . ." She paused. "I like school a lot."

He lifted her chin. "I reckon you can go as long as you like, then. I ain't gonna stop you. 'Cept when you start havin' young'uns, I reckon you'll need to stay around close. You can teach them."

Latisha sighed with relief. "Thanks. Mama told me no man would want his woman goin' to school after they's hitched. But I said you was different than other men." She kissed his big hand and calloused palm. "I'll be glad when that cabin is fixed." She closed her eyes as he stroked her cheek.

"After the cotton is baled, I reckon. You and me . . . the Lord smilin' down on us, Tish. I feel Him smilin' all the day. You go on to that school and learn all you can so you and me can have a bushel of smart chillens."

A woodpecker hammered the tree above them, reminding Jefferson that time was short. If the field was to be cleared and the cabin fixed, there was little time for talk. He roused Hock, who grumbled about a day so good for fishing going to waste, and they set back to work on the thick trunk of a felled oak in the sunlight.

CHAPTER THIRTY-THREE

Barefoot Schoolmarm

Dust from the road billowed from the jarring wheels of Joseph Meyer's delivery truck. Trudy sat silently beside her father. Neither had spoken a word since leaving Fort Smith. It had all been said already. Joseph and Sadie had consented to Trudy's acceptance of this teaching position only because there was nothing else open to her.

The dismissal from Belle Grove School only two weeks before opening term had left any other desirable positions already filled. Joseph had resigned himself to the fact that Trudy would never be hired to teach in Fort Smith after this, and gossip had a way of spreading from one place to another. No doubt the better schools in Fayetteville or Little Rock would also be closed to her, despite the high recommendations from Columbia. Perhaps next year she could apply to good schools in Tulsa or Oklahoma City, where folks had never heard of Birch Tucker or the train ride from New York.

In the meantime, at least there was someplace in the wide world so desperate for a qualified schoolteacher that they did not ask questions or call relatives in Fort Smith to check up on young Miss Trudy Meyer. And the little school was not so far away. Trudy could get home to visit occasionally.

To the right and left of the rutted highway, cotton fields rolled away into the distance. The cotton bolls were just beginning to crack open, showing the soft white cotton.

Trudy looked at the fields and wondered about the sharecroppers who farmed them and the children she would teach. "The letter said that the school closes in October so the children can stay home and pick cotton," she said to her father.

"Even the little ones?" Joseph seemed surprised, but he knew these farms used every hand, young and old, to bring in the harvest. He had seen the tiny seven-year-olds stooped and dragging cotton sacks along beside their elders.

"*Everyone,* the letter said, except babies and tots."

"Well then, can you come home awhile?"

Trudy cocked an eyebrow at her father. "I am *invited* to help tend the tiny children for their working mothers."

"Invited?"

"At my regular pay, the letter says. And Mister Howard says he will provide me with two 'darkie gals,' as he calls them, to help me."

"Sounds like more than an invitation to me." Joseph looked disturbed all over again.

"Part of the duties." Trudy shrugged. "Along with sweeping the schoolhouse and cleaning the grate of the stove before school."

"Primitive," Joseph snapped. "We sent you to Columbia for this?"

"Maybe I will write a novel, Papa," she soothed. "I do not know *anyone* else in my class who will have such an experience!"

"You were educated to *teach,* not have experiences," he said gloomily. "Your mother and I wanted you to have a way to provide for yourself with some dignity. What else is there for a woman but to teach? And now *this*—gossips and liars, *bigots,* have reduced you to such a post as *this*! Teaching sharecropper children their *ABC*s when you might be educating young scholars and—"

"Papa," she interrupted, "it's all right. These children need their *ABC*s as much as the children of bigots need history lessons. I can teach either, equally as well." She was confident she would manage the challenge.

"But forty students in one classroom, Trudy! And only one teacher . . . *you*! It is madness." He was angry again. Trudy did not want to go over the same argument she had been hearing for the last two weeks. "How will you manage them all?"

"I will do more than manage," she said firmly. "I will educate them." She studied his set jaw and grim face. "I am your child, after all, am I not?"

"We should have stayed in the North. I could have done as well in Indiana or Illinois—without these rock-throwing lunatics."

Trudy did not reply for a moment as they jostled along. Heat waves shimmered up from the distant green mountains, making them appear closer than they were. Her father had marveled at the beauty of this land when he had first seen it.

"You love this place, Papa. And things are just as bad right now in the north. The race riots in Chicago. The Klan is strongest there. Two hundred thousand strong in Illinois and Ohio."

"My mother and father left the old country to escape such madness."

"And the madmen came here too." She glanced at her hands, remembering the shouts of the teenagers in the passing car, the baiting remarks of Deputy East, the rocks hurled through the window of the store. "I don't think there is any place better than another for us."

"If only your mother wouldn't *insist* on going to synagogue! Maybe—"

"Let it go." Trudy put a hand on his arm. "We cannot fix what is wrong in men's hearts. Besides, it isn't everyone. Your friends, your customers, don't even think about where we come from. The window . . . it was a fluke. They are angry because they think I'm not telling everything I know about Birch's trouble in Missouri."

Joseph appraised his daughter. "No, they are angry because they know that even if you *could* help them, you *would not!* That is the issue. Can we deny it? We have known injustice. *These* people—the ones who attacked Birch and his friend—they *are* injustice! You think they can't *feel* you looking through their hypocrisy? They hate that you see through them. They hide behind religion. Righteous words, Trudy. They say righteous words but live something so evil and dark."

"Then I'm glad to be on the other side," Trudy said firmly. "I'm glad they think I'm different enough to be driven out." Another bump lifted her from her seat. "And what a drive, eh, Papa?"

Thankfully, there was nothing breakable in the boxes in the back of the truck. Trudy's mother had packed bedding and a good supply of household items from the store. A mop and broom and buckets were accompanied by soap for laundry and soap for washing dishes and rose-scented soap for Trudy to bathe with. The plates were of blue-enameled tin. Coffeepot and pots and pans were still packed in the original store boxes.

Apart from a few dresses and personal items, the main cargo in the truck was books. Crates and crates of them. Trudy had taken every classic from the shelves in the parlor. History books and volumes of poetry were packed together with the twenty-volume set of Dumas novels and the *Leatherstocking Tales* of Cooper. There was nothing more that Trudy would need to survive the isolation of the tiny plantation school. She could console herself with books if the hours became unbearably lonely. She could read and forget . . . and there was much she wanted to forget.

✳ ✳ ✳

In his white-linen suit, string tie, and broad-brimmed straw hat, old Mr. Bundy Howard looked every inch the Southern plantation owner. His white hair and drooping mustache reminded Trudy of photographs of Mark Twain. But Twain had been from an earlier era, she reminded herself as she stepped onto the old gentleman's porch. He rose from his rocking chair and doffed his hat. Still clutching the straw fan, he indicated two chairs for Trudy and Joseph to sit on. He called to the portly black house servant to bring two more glasses of lemonade double-quick.

"Well now." Mr. Howard appraised Trudy with an appreciative eye. "Smart and educated and lovely as well. I regret my nephew Scott left yesterday. He'd like to meet you!" He winked at Joseph. "I congratulate you, sir. It's uncommon for a man to pack both brains and beauty into his offspring. In a woman it can be a frightenin' combination." He fanned himself, evidently enjoying his monologue as his tired, thirsty visitors smiled politely and made small talk about the weather and the vast fields of cotton surrounding Mount Pisgah. Such pleasantries were merely starting points for Mr. Howard to tell the history of the Howard plantation and, finally, the school where Trudy was to teach.

"We've had the school for our Nigras as long as I remember . . . on back into my daddy's lifetime and clean into the days before the war. It was always a philosophy that our people learn to read—at least enough so they could read their Bibles, which they do right eagerly. There is much in the Good Book that speaks to the mind of a slave. The tenets of obedience and trustworthiness and such . . . it made it easier to manage 'em, havin' the Good Book as moral overseer, you might say."

At that instant the black house servant came out with cookies and lemonade on a tray. Trudy studied the woman's face to see if she was taking in Mr. Howard's lecture but couldn't see even a hint of change in her expression. But that didn't change the fact that the old man's philosophy was offensive to Trudy.

"So that's why we built that school. Don't want the Nigras to learn more than is good for 'em, though, Miss Meyer. Well, you'll see what I'm sayin' is true when you work with 'em every day. We don't have trouble down here with our Nigras like the Yankees and their riots in the North."

Trudy thanked the black woman quietly for the lemonade and tried to catch her eye. But the woman acknowledged Trudy with only a nod. Mr. Howard talked around the black woman as if she were simply a post holding up the roof of his porch or an old faithful dog lying at his feet.

"How many children are in the school?" Trudy asked. "I was told forty."

"Sometimes more and sometimes less. We're none too strict on the young'uns comin' all the time. Some have work to do. It's strictly volunteer. It's dropped off quite a bit since the former schoolmistress passed on from the flu last winter. Odd stuff, that influenza. It just came on people all over the county—sneaked up and took 'em. I just drank my fill of black draught tea, kept my bowels cleaned out so no sickness could settle in. . . ." He looked momentarily confused. "What were we talkin' about? Before?"

"Attendance is not mandatory," Trudy offered.

Her father sat nervously fidgeting in his chair. The afternoon sun was creeping across the sky, and he still had to drive all the way back to Fort Smith.

"No," Mr. Howard said, "except for the teacher." He laughed. "You have to be there, or you don't get paid." He removed a copy of the same duty list Trudy had received in the mail last week. "You got this?" He waved it in front of her. "Now, when you were hired, old Doug Bolt—"

"The professor?"

"That's right. Little Dougie Bolt. He grew up here, son of the overseer. He was schooled in the white children's school over across the creek there." He searched for his spectacles and balanced them on his prominent beak of a nose. "Yes . . . I was sayin' . . . when Pro-fessor Bolt sent the recommendation from Belle Grove, he didn't mention that you were a Jew-gal. As you can see, we have this requirement for all our schoolteachers that they attend church regular. Folks would think you were odd if you didn't go to Sunday service. I don't give two hoots what you believe as long as you keep it to yourself, Miss Meyer, but those are the rules and we all abide by them."

Trudy could see her father visibly stiffen in his chair as the old man proceeded through the list of regulations that no doubt had been carried over since the days when the sharecroppers on the land had been slaves. To all of this Trudy simply smiled and nodded, finally asking, "Since there is a white children's school and a school for black children, is there also a white church and a black church?"

"Oh yes!" The old man laughed. "They have their own ways, these Nigras." He chuckled as he sipped his lemonade, as if to say, *"The idea!"*

Trudy looked at the list once again. "Why have you had such a time finding someone to take this position?"

From the corner of her vision she caught sight of Joseph's face and his hand tugging on his lower lip to hold back a smile at such a question.

"I can't rightly say. Young Latisha Williams has been helpin' with the young'uns. She's a smart one, that gal. But as far as a *proper*-educated teacher . . . well, I suppose a lot of gals take up teachin' as a way to go out and find them some widower farmer to get hitched to. Since this is an all-Nigra school, the prospects aren't likely, if that's what you came for."

Trudy leveled a serious gaze. "There's always church."

At this, Joseph doubled over coughing, as if trying desperately to conceal a laugh.

"You all right there, Meyer?" asked Mr. Howard. "Suck that lemon in wrong?"

"Pulp," Joseph managed, standing up and wiping his eyes. "And now . . . I'm sure you'll treat my daughter just fine, Mister Howard. Which way to the school? I have to unload and drive back before too long, or I'll be caught by nightfall."

Thus ended Trudy's job interview at the Howard Plantation. Old Man Howard was the sole member of the school board, and apparently Trudy had passed muster and was hired on.

A spindly arm pointed down the road. "Over the rise, and then turn after two miles at the white building, which is the church," Mr. Howard explained. "Not the first church, the one on the right, but the second church, on the left. The one with the steeple. The school is a half mile past that in a grove of trees. The teacher's residence is right next to the school. You can't miss it."

"Trudy, you'll have to watch your sarcasm," Joseph warned as they climbed into the truck and trundled away.

"I intend to avoid conversation with the ol' massah as much as possible. And when we must speak, I will take copious notes and enter every word down to use in a novel someday. He really is a relic from another era, you know. At Columbia they would put him on display in a cultural anthropology class and label him *Antebellum Bigot*."

"He's not so rare a species as you may think," Joseph said, suddenly serious. "His sort seem to be everywhere. And he's mild compared to—"

"It doesn't matter. I won't change him, but the kids in my school are mine to teach, aren't they?"

"Stick with the three Rs and you won't get into trouble," he warned.

"You mean Racism, Reactionism, and Repression?" She was smiling.

Joseph was not. "It is not too late. You can go back with me, work in the store until—"

"This will look great on my *résumé*. Another *r* word for new teachers who are tainted by scandal." She nudged him. "I'm all right. Really."

There was no missing the road to the schoolhouse. First one church appeared and then another. Wagons and workers and broad-backed mules moved far to the right as the rattling Meyer delivery truck passed by to make its delivery of the new schoolteacher.

Even as Trudy stared openly out the window of the truck at bronzed, sweating faces and tattered overalls on gaunt bodies, no one looked back at her at all. The people continued in their conversations or let her pass by with a studied indifference of the sort Trudy had seen on the face of the house servant. Trudy meant no more to their lives than the passing shadow of a cloud over the cotton fields.

One teacher had died last winter, and another one had finally come to take her place. When Trudy left, as she surely would, someone else would come eventually. But these farmers, hoes slung over shoulders, toes poking out from shoes, would still be here when Trudy was gone. If the schoolhouse burned down, it made little difference. There was the cotton and the land, and at the big white house there was The Man rocking on his veranda. Some things never changed. What was yesterday, it seemed, would always be.

So Trudy came like a small cloud, hoping to cool the sweat of their labor, if only for a while.

Joseph Meyer slowed and turned onto a deeply rutted lane that wound off into the light-dappled canopy of a wood. Grass grew in the center of the road, and Joseph praised Henry Ford for building the chassis of his little black beast to clear a high center. The slow pace became a careful crawl as the lane shrank into a faint wagon track. It had been a long while since any wheeled vehicle had passed this way.

He grimaced as a creek appeared at one side of the road and wandered across it to the other. He stopped and exchanged a look with Trudy. "It's still not too late. I can drive this thing backward all the way to Fort Smith. You can work in the store until—"

Trudy patted his arm and shook her head. "No." Kicking off her shoes, she climbed out of the vehicle and hiked her skirt to wade into the creek. The cold water felt luxurious. She laughed and waved as she reached the center of the stream, which rose only to midcalf. "Come on! It's okay, Papa!"

He shook his head, and the Ford lunged forward into the rocky bottom and on across. Trudy did not get back into the truck with him but walked just ahead, blazing the way. Trees reared up above her head. Sunlight caught the leaves as they shimmered light and dark green against the bright blue sky. The track curved sharply to the right, and then the white-frame building of the schoolhouse appeared, looking more like a church than the church.

It was an old building, perhaps as old as the plantation itself. The main structure was built on square-hewn logs. The front was whitewashed plank lumber shaped into a primitive imitation of an antebellum mansion. Instead of Greek columns, four perfectly matched round logs supported the roof of the porch. The door was tall and flanked by windows that were as high and narrow as the door. The little glass panes, wavy with age, were shining clean, reflecting the green of trees and sky and light, and finally the fractured reflection of the truck, which seemed an image completely out of place in such a setting.

"Beautiful," Trudy said, and she meant it. Clean and scrubbed, her building was a place that someone took great pride in. She could see the tracks of rakes all around the dirt. But there were no human footprints, as though someone had walked on tiptoe and scraped away all traces of human existence. Even the ground was perfect.

Joseph switched off the truck, and blissful silence hung in the oaks for a moment before the twittering of birds and the hushed bubbling of the creek filled the vacuum. Trudy turned to look at her father, who, for the first time all day, had a peaceful look on his face. "Well, now," he said in surprise. "Well, well . . ."

"Well?" Trudy pointed to the covered well at the side of the building. One of her duties was to bring in a bucket of wash water every day from the well. Was it deep? She hurried to its stone lip and looked down into the cool tunnel of mossy darkness. Perhaps she would not even mind this duty after all.

From there she peered through the window of the building. A large black potbelly stove was in the center of the room. There were no desks, only long wooden benches worn smooth from generations of children sitting on them. There was a slate blackboard. Above it was a picture of George Washington smiling his Mona Lisa smile from the clouds. Beside him was a map of the United States, minus a number of states that were marked as "territories." Oh well. Trudy would set the geography of Mount Pisgah right.

"Oh, Papa!" she said joyfully. "It's wonderful! And it's mine!"

He embraced her and also peered into her classroom. "You will do fine, Trudy," he said in pleasant resignation. "I'll tell your mother. You have been dropped into an enchanted forest. Bavaria without Bavarians." He laughed. "They leave no footprints, you see." So he had noticed, too. He pointed up a curving path to a small log building perched on a tree-studded knoll. "And there is your lodge, I assume?"

"We may as well start carrying stuff. There's no way to drive closer than this." She was not concerned, although the boxes of books might be a problem. "Let's have a look first." Grabbing her carpet valise full of clothes, she dashed up the path to the cabin. It, too, had wrinkled glass windows and a door that had worn the threshold smooth from a hundred years of openings and closings.

She turned the latch—there was no lock—and the door groaned back to a room that smelled sweet, like a smokehouse. A small iron bed sat against the far wall. It was made up neatly with a blue-and-red flower-garden quilt. There was a table in front of an open stone fireplace, where all cooking and heating must be done. The only lighting appeared to be a kerosene lamp on the table. Tin plates and cups were stacked neatly on a narrow shelf beside the fireplace. Split wood was on the hearth.

"It appears you are expected," Joseph said quietly.

Jefferson was eating his evening meal at Latisha's place, so he would miss the most interesting parts of the story the first time it was told. It would be repeated many times, but the first telling was always the best.

"Oh, she's perty, Mama!" Big Hattie passed the bowl of grits to Little Nettie, who then took up the conversation about the new teacher.

"She's tall as Hattie, 'cept built more like a willow tree than an old oak."

Big Hattie nudged her sister hard, uncertain as to whether the comment was an insult. No matter. The teacher was the thing. "Her hair all piled up on her head. The color of ol' Mister Howard's chestnut carriage horse. Eyes brown like that horse, too, I reckon. An' she had on a yeller dress."

Nettie giggled. "An' when that man stopped the truck at the creek, an' he wasn't gonna go no farther, she done took off her shoes an' *whups!* There she go. Pulls up her skirt—"

"Mighty white legs she had, too. Long, like for runnin'.'"

Nettie banged Hattie. "You hush! I'm tellin'!" She proceeded as the whole family leaned in close to hear the details of the trip from the Old Mister's house to the school. "So, there she go, wadin' right on in the Petty Jane. *'Come on,'* she hollered, *'it's okay, Papa!'* "

"An' what you think? That man jus' rattly-bang right on over," Hattie said. "But she didn't get back in. No sirree. She left them fancy shoes in the truck an' walked on down the lane like she some old field hand in bare feets. Then she tell her pa she like it . . . dirt between her toes."

"An' they went to peekin' in the windows an' sayin' what a *perty* place we fixed for her, Mama. An' tellin' how someone raked all around an' don't leave no tracks."

At this remark, Pink drew herself up proudly. "I told you, Mama. I can make even the dirt look good if nobody walks on it."

"You done good, Pink." Willa-Mae nodded. "She like the cabin?" she asked Hattie.

"We just hear little bit of that. But they was *oooh*s an' *ahh*s 'bout near ever'thing, I reckon." She laughed. "An' she made her pa unload crates an' *crates* into the school 'cause there weren't no room for a *library* up at the cabin, she say!"

"Library!" Angel exclaimed. "Books, you reckon? Wish I'd been there, too."

Willa-Mae consoled her. "You was needed to look after Aunt Lou's young'uns. There's plenty of time to get your eyefuls of this new teacher."

Pink also looked disappointed. "But we ain't gonna have a chance to see her bare feets no more, I reckon. Nor watch her peer into winders."

Lula, who was the oldest, sat smugly in her place. She had not been privileged to watch the coming of the teacher from behind the bushes, but she also had news. "Well, Miz Young done served up lemonade to her down to Mister Howard's, an' she tell me *ever'thing* they say to The Man."

Heads swiveled in amazement and curiosity at such news. Then Lula began the recitation in exact detail until all the family, including Hock, were laughing near to bust.

"'There's always church,' she said after that. Then her pa doubled up coughin' and chokin' and laughin' behind his hand, and ol' Mister Howard, he don't know nothin' what they's laughin' 'bout! So Mister Howard said, 'You swaller that lemon down wrong?' 'Pulp! Pulp!' said the gal's pappy; then he nearly grabbed her up by the scruff an' hauled her into the truck before she said somethin' more than she oughta say an' the Ol' Mister figgered out she's pullin' his leg!"

"Well now," Hock said when he got his wind back from the laugh. "Sounds like she's a smart'un! You young'uns gonna have to watch yerselves. If she don't take no guff off the Old Mister, then she be wise to y'all the minute you open your mouth."

Throughout all that evening, news of the arrival and the doings down at The Man's house was passed from house to house until every dinner dish in Pisgah was flavored with humor and seasoned with respect for the new white teacher who hiked through the Petty Jane Creek barefoot and brought her library safely through the passage.

CHAPTER THIRTY-FOUR

Saturday School

Trudy opened her eyes well before the alarm clock was set to wake her. The woods surrounding the cabin were alive with a thousand sounds— all chirping, clicking, bubbling, and rushing into the dawn.

It was cool this morning, as though the world had forgotten that it was supposed to be summer. She pulled the soft quilt around her chin and lay still in the blue predawn light to listen. No human sounds marred the perfection of this primeval symphony—no jarring voices or streetcar bells or rattling engines.

Trudy closed her eyes and inhaled the pungent aromas of the woods. How long had it been since she had really smelled a pine tree? It made her feel hungry. She eyed the neat stack of home-canned fruits and vegetables beside a pan of corn bread that someone had left for her. For the first time, the regret she had felt over losing her place at Belle Grove did not weigh upon her. It was as though the woods and the sounds and the smells offered her a badly needed gift: the gift of serenity.

She sat up in bed and hugged her knees. The ticking of the big windup clock seemed intrusive. Trudy decided she did not need the thing. She could wake each morning to the clock of the woods around her. She would take the clock down to the school and use it to teach the little ones how to tell time, although that skill seemed of little importance here in Mount Pisgah.

What day is it? What month? What year? What century? The only answer that mattered was the first. "It is Saturday," Trudy said aloud. This was important to know. No school on Saturday. She would have the entire weekend to unpack and stack the books down at the school. Her own meager belongings would not take more than an hour to organize here at the cabin, but the classroom was another matter! So much to do . . .

She washed in the cool water of the wash bucket on the back porch. Dressing in a denim work shirt and crisp new bib overalls, she left her shoes off and carried corn bread and a jar of peaches with her to the schoolhouse.

The door of the school was open. *It must have blown open in the night,* she thought. She would have to be careful of that. A good stiff wind and a heavy rain could do damage to the library if the door accidentally blew open. She took the steps two at a time and entered her domain.

As forty heads pivoted toward her, Trudy gave a little cry. Every inch of every bench was crammed rump to rump with pupils. Their dark eyes widened in astonishment to see the schoolteacher dressed in new blue bibs and a work shirt like any old field hand would wear. The overalls were rolled up midcalf on those long white legs, and at the very bottom was a wondrous sight—bare feet!

A few giggles erupted, quickly silenced by the stern and threatening look of a tall, slender young woman. "Hush now, y'all," said the young woman as she rose and smiled timidly at Trudy. "Howdy, ma'am," she said, noticeably averting her eyes from Trudy's feet. "My name's Latisha Williams. This here's your class."

"But . . . but . . . but . . . it's *Saturday!*" Trudy croaked, clutching her corn bread to her and fumbling with the peaches until every child gasped. Would the peaches hit the floor?

"Yes'm," Latisha said. "It's Saturday." Her eyes flicked down from face to neck to buckled straps to rolled cuffs and then to those legs and toes. The smile faltered.

Trudy could tell what the young woman was thinking: *Is this the way the teacher dresses?*

"We ain't pickin' cotton, ma'am," Latisha blurted out, and the whole class roared with laughter. Latisha whirled on them. "Hush up!"

The class fell instantly silent, except for a giggle or two from the very young.

"You mean we have class on *Saturday?*" Trudy knew her voice was an octave higher than usual. She knew she looked as though her eyebrows might just go up over the top of her head. Her hair was only halfway piled up, just to get it out of the way. She smoothed it and looked down at her own feet in horror.

"Yes'm. We gots school ever' day 'cept the Lord's Day."

Trudy stared at the young woman, barely comprehending this disaster. "Well then," she said, trying to hide the peaches behind her back, "not *this* Saturday. I . . . as you can see . . . *Latisha*, is it?"

"Yes'm."

"I was not prepared . . . I . . . books . . . and my . . . some work to do." She lowered her voice to a whisper. "Monday, we will . . ."

Latisha's face fell in disappointment. And that's when Trudy noticed. Latisha was dressed in what was most likely her best Sunday dress. Every female head in the place sprouted hair ribbons.

"If you says so, ma'am," Latisha murmured. "But we come ready to learn. Been a long time since we had us a real teacher."

The air buzzed with a chorus of "Uh-huh. That's right . . . been a long time. . . ."

"Well then . . ." Trudy scanned the eager faces of her pupils. "If you can wait awhile, I shall go up to my house and—"

"Oh, we can wait." Latisha beamed. "Been waitin' *so* long, I reckon nobody gonna mind waitin' a little more."

Trudy backed from the room and mastered her urge to run up the path. Instead she carried herself with the dignity expected from a new schoolteacher.

✲ ✲ ✲

That first Sunday, Trudy made her required visit to old Mr. Howard's church. She was introduced and asked to stand. She was thoroughly looked over and spoken to in short, probing questions afterward.

"Whyever did you come to teach at such a place?" was the most common question.

"I am writing a novel," Trudy replied. Although this was not entirely true, she intended to write a novel someday. In the meantime, the statement somehow explained everything. Still, even as she met the smiling faces of dozens in the church, she saw hands raise to cover whispers and heads tilt in to hear. Twice she heard the words *"Jew-gal"* murmured.

So this was to be the worst she had to endure. Six days a week she could joyfully teach her children from the stack of ancient McGuffey's readers. She could read to them from *Uncle Tom's Cabin* after lunch and watch their eyes widen at the story.

Only Sunday would be difficult for her. Only the day of rest would be work. The other six days she would rest in the adoration of her pupils.

And so her Sunday chore was completed. Her shoulders ached as she walked back toward home. Far down the road was the church where her students attended. Trudy could hear the music of the Mount Pisgah congregation still raised in song:

"Roll, Jor-dan roll! Roll Jor-dan roll!

I want to go to heav-en when I die

to hear ol' Jor-dan roll!"

Trudy slowed as she passed the ragged little building. Paint flaked from the weathered boards. The roof sagged a bit. But through the windows Trudy could see them—bright ebony and hair ribbons, hands raised and bodies swaying in song. And Trudy wished she could go inside to rest awhile.

The bandstand in the park at Greysville was the perfect place for a political rally. Doc Warne could stand on the platform while the crowd sprawled comfortably on the grass, and everyone could see and hear him just fine. The cleared space in which the gazebo stood was ringed by trees, tall maples, and elms in full leaf. The audience naturally shifted around to the side that was shaded from the afternoon sun, and Doc, facing them, had taken off his coat and rolled up his sleeves as he prepared to speak.

Greysville was only fifty miles from Camden, and it was in the same congressional district as Doc's hometown. But if the area around Camden was mostly given to farming, Greysville was more concerned with manufacturing. The war had been good for the economy of Greysville, especially since the local armory had landed a fat government contract for machining rifle parts.

Now that the war was over, a lot of people were nervous about their jobs ending. Adding to the tension was the fact that returning veterans were looking for work, too—more job hunters than ever for fewer positions than before.

This was the atmosphere that surrounded Doc on his campaign. He needed to gather support from the townspeople or he could not hope to win.

"There are those who will tell you times are going to be tough," he began, "and it may be that many things that have changed are not done changing yet. But the shortest way through tough changes is forward, not backward. None of us would want the war to still be going on, would we?"

A murmur of agreement rippled through the crowd. "If you want to speak of tough times," Doc urged, "try asking one of our brave boys. Ask my son." Doc did not mention that Ellis had lost a leg, but most of the listeners had already heard of it, anyway. "Ask him if he wants his children to have to fight in another terrible war because we who have the duty to build the peace turned aside from doing what is right."

Doc paused to let his message sink in. "*And what is right?* you may be thinking. Right is for America to take the lead. Victory without revenge is what we must insist on, and settling disputes without bloodshed. But we cannot make our voice heard if we do not belong to the League of Nations. If we build a wall around this country to keep out what other countries would sell to us or to keep out families that would come here to live."

"To keep out the Red anarchists!" a voice from the back of the crowd called harshly. "Keep them all out, I say! Do we want revolution here like they have in Russia?"

"We are not speaking of anarchists," Doc said firmly. "We are speaking of families who want to come and live and raise their children in the greatest country in the world. They want to work hard and build a life for themselves here, and they will be building up America as they do."

"Tearing it down, you mean!" another voice countered, this time from the opposite side of the crowd. "Coming here with their litters of whelps and taking bread out of the mouths of our own children. And that phony League of Nations! League of Foreign Entanglements is what it really is! Listen to what this Commie says, and you can bet that your children will be fighting in all the future wars in Europe! Well, I say never again! Take that, you no-good Commie!" A rotten tomato soared over the heads of the crowd to smack into a post of the gazebo near Doc's head.

From three different places in the crowd, a hail of rotten vegetables arced toward Doc, spattering him with a smelly, gooey mess. Doc's well-wishers in the crowd chased the hecklers away, but he never regained the crowd's attention sufficiently to go on with the speech.

☆ ☆ ☆

"I don't like it one little bit, I'm telling you," Molly complained to Doc as she scrubbed at his shirt, trying to get the tomato stains to come out. "Those hooligans should be arrested for this. Them and that skunk Hopewell who sent them."

"Now, Molly," Doc cautioned, "'twas nothing to get so riled up about. Just some hotheads who probably lost their jobs. They are mad at the whole world, not just me."

"That may be your story, Doctor Warne, but the truth is they brought a bushel basket of garbage to throw at *you*." She threw the shirt back into the sudsy water in disgust. "Or were you thinking that they were carrying it to the rubbish pile when they just happened upon your speech?" Her voice was charged with sarcasm.

"I'll not have you fret over a juvenile prank," Doc said. "Besides, the people who saw it happen now also know what sort of shenanigans the other side will resort to."

"Now you admit that they did belong to the other side! Oh, Doc, what if they had been throwing bricks instead of tomatoes?"

"I'm certain it won't happen again. Why, the public won't stand for strong-arm tactics, even if they don't happen to agree with my politics."

A sputtering, popping Model T drew their attention. Doc recognized the driver as Robert Blaylock, even though he was wrapped up in a canvas driving coat and a cloth cap. The automobile pulled into the Warne yard and shuddered to a halt.

When Doc met Blaylock at the door, the attorney was waving a newspaper. "Have you seen this?" he practically shouted. "No, of course not. I just saw it myself. Look at what this says."

Blaylock unfolded the newspaper and spread it out on the dining table. It was that morning's edition of the Marion *Daily Star*. "NEAR RIOT IN GREYSVILLE," the headline read. Just below that in only slightly smaller type it said, "Inflammatory speech by congressional candidate Warne causes civil commotion."

"Don't bother reading it all," Blaylock said. "It's full of vicious lies and slander and innuendo. The editorial page even goes so far as to say that the people of Ohio won't stand for Red Agitators uttering Socialist sentiments. Doc, they make it sound like you . . . like you . . ." The attorney stammered into silence.

"I know, Bobby, I know," Doc concluded with a rueful look at Molly. "And were they able to get in the part about me throwing tomatoes at myself?"

Mount Pisgah General Store was owned outright by Mr. Howard, Trudy was told. A stubby little bald man named Mr. Moss was the store manager.

Mrs. Moss was the part-time postmistress. Her domain was located in the back-left corner of the store behind a dark oak partition with iron bars in front of the opening. "Miz Moss," as she was called by even her closest friends, was the source of all stamps, all money orders, and all gossip around Mount Pisgah. Everyone, including Trudy, had to ask her for the mail, which was put up in little pigeonholes behind the wispy-haired Miz Moss. She knew every letter coming in and every letter going out.

Miz Moss could report accurately that the new teacher received one letter each week from her mother in Fort Smith, and that a letter had been forwarded here to Mount Pisgah all the way from England. *"Don't that beat all. . . ."* There had also been one letter from New York, the return address scrawled in a spidery hand by someone old, no doubt. It was a curious thing to all concerned—which included everyone—why such a bright and attractive young woman as Miz Trudy Meyer had not one letter from a beau. No young gentlemen writing or calling. Here she was, all hidden away back there teaching the Nigras! Her, with all that highfalutin education. Even if she was a Jew-gal, it seemed curious that she had not done better for herself.

Miz Moss and Miz Digby discussed it thoroughly. When the schoolmarm came in for her one letter, they held their tongues, except to wish her a pleasant day and ask how the Nigra pickaninnies were getting along. Then she bought a few supplies, like always, and drank an orange soda, like always, and left.

The two women looked at each other and asked again what secrets there could be in the life of this schoolmarm. After all, nobody came out to Mount Pisgah unless they had to.

"I've got me a second cousin livin' in Fort Smith," said Miz Digby.

"Is that so?"

"I'll just drop her a line. What you say the name of the teacher's family is? A store is it they own? On Garrison Avenue? Why, Millicent will know just where that is." Miz Digby stared hard out the door as the schoolmarm cut across the road. "Maybe it's nothin', but I got me a feelin'. . . ."

CHAPTER THIRTY-FIVE

The Invisible Empire

"Becky," Julie asked coyly, "do you think I look the least little bit like Mary Pickford?"

Becky smiled over her shoulder to where the little girl rode facing backward on the small parcel rack of the buggy. "Perhaps just a little bit . . . but much, much prettier," Becky said to Ellis's five-year-old sister.

Ellis flicked the reins, and the gray horse moved out from the rail and down Main Street away from the Camden Cinema. They had just seen the film *Rebecca of Sunnybrook Farm*. Julie had seen it four times already, but Ellis had never seen it before, since it had come to town the first time after he had already left for the army.

"Of course," Julie said seriously to Becky, "you should get to *be* Rebecca, because you've got the same name as her. Ellis," she asked her brother, "don't you wish that you could hear the people talk in moving picture shows?"

Ellis gave the matter some thought. "No," he said, "that would ruin them. If we could hear them speak, they wouldn't have to be as good at acting as they are now."

Ellis and Becky had asked to take Julie with them into town to see the show since Doc and Molly were fifty miles away at a political rally.

"I shall be an actress when I grow up," said Julie, her hand on her brow in her best fainting-heroine style.

"Last week you wanted to be a nurse and work with Pop delivering babies," Ellis teased.

"Papa is going to be a famous congers-man," Julie replied. "He won't need a nurse for that."

The road to home rambled past St. Francis Catholic Church, located about halfway between the Warne property and Camden. From the top of a rise, Ellis could see the steeple of the church standing out of a little hollow in the hills. "That's funny," he said. "Look at how bright the steeple looks tonight—like it has a light shining on it."

Julie stood and turned around, leaning over the shoulders of her brother and future sister-in-law. "Where?" she demanded.

"Just there, honey." Becky pointed out. "Looks like a fire to me, Ellis. Do you suppose there could be trouble?"

"No," said Ellis, "it's probably just a campfire." But he urged the horse into a faster trot just the same.

"Do you s'pose the Catholic folks are havin' a wiener roast?" Julie wondered.

"I doubt it," Ellis said, "but we'll know in a couple of minutes." A breath of breeze carried the faint sounds of singing to them. The music rose and fell, muffled and indistinct.

The glow from the firelight grew stronger and stronger until it was clear that the fire was, in fact, located right in front of the church. At last the roof of the church and the upper part of the wall could also be seen over the trees. The light suddenly grew more intense, as if someone had tossed on a log to make it blaze. Shadows flitted on the wall of the building—strange swirling shapes, vague outlines with spiked points.

"What in the world is that?" Becky asked.

"I know what it is," said Ellis grimly. "It's a Klan rally."

After one more turn of the road, the lane led directly to the church, and the buggy was pointed right toward it. In front of the door of the building was a flaming bonfire, and at its center sprouted the hissing, crackling torchlight of a burning cross eight feet tall.

A circle of figures stood around the flames. Those nearest the cross were robed in white from head to toe. Their faces were masked, and they wore tall pointed hoods. Behind the circle of masked figures was another ring, this one made up of women. They also wore white robes, but their faces were uncovered. They were singing "The Son of God Goes Forth to War."

As the buggy approached the scene, one of the masked figures raised his arms over his head. The rest of the group grew silent. "God," the hooded man said in a loud voice, "cleanse this country, we beseech You. Don't let the evils of Roman idolatry have a place here any longer."

A murmured chorus of "Amens" agreed.

"Clear out from among those races You have cursed—papist heathen, Christ-killing Jews, and especially those with the mark of Cain, the Nigras. By the illuminating glory of this flaming symbol, we swear—"

Ellis knew the sound of the buggy's wheels could be heard approaching, crunching on the gravel. Several in the group turned around to look. Ellis kept the nervous horse in a steady trot, keeping him controlled in spite of his urge to whip him into a gallop.

They went past the edge of the clearing. On the wall of the church, several of the pointed shadows leaned together in whispered consultation. No one spoke aloud or moved toward the buggy. Ellis looked straight ahead, and Becky hugged Julie tightly.

Around the feet of the women several children were playing in the grass. One of them was wearing a tiny replica of her mother's robe and had on a copy of a tall pointed hat like her father's.

Julie gasped and pointed at the little girl, whose face sneered and gloated beneath the hat. "It's Amy Wallace!" Julie said. "She's one of the ghostly people!"

Ellis and Becky spent the rest of the drive back toward the Warne farm looking over their shoulders and peering into the darkness ahead at every suspicious bush or gnarled tree. The flickering shadows of the "ghostly people" and their hideous bonfire faded from sight as the buggy climbed out of the hollow and crossed the next low divide. But their singing floated after the trio in mocking pursuit: "His bloodred banner streams afar," it challenged. "Who follows in His train?"

Becky believed that she would never again be able to hear that hymn without shuddering.

By the time they arrived at Becky's home, just up the road a ways from the Warne place, Julie had fallen asleep. The little girl had drifted off with her arms wrapped around Becky's neck.

Ellis glanced over at her. "You could lay her down in the back if you want to."

"It's all right," Becky said softly. "I don't mind. Poor thing, she trembled for a long time. I pray she will only dream of happy things—growing up to be Mary Pickford and such—and not that awful wickedness back there."

As the buggy pulled up in front of her house, she asked, "Do you want to come in for a while, Ellis? I'm sure Papa and Mama won't mind if we put Julie on the couch while I fix us a cup of tea."

Ellis considered a minute, thinking about ending the evening on a more pleasant note, then shook his head. "I'd really like to, Becky, but what with my mother and father away tonight . . . well, you know, I just feel like I should check on things."

Ellis bade Becky good night and watched her until she entered her house. Guiding the horse with one hand on the reins, he used the other to hold Julie beside him on the seat. He whistled softly to himself as he drove through the dark, telling himself that there was nothing to be frightened of and no reason to be uneasy. Just the same, he was grateful when the fence line around the home place showed up just ahead. He was glad also that he had thought to leave a lamp burning in the front room. It shone through the window like a beacon, revealing Julie's kitten sitting on the back of the sofa.

When he had rounded the side of the house and was on the gravel drive leading to the barn, he saw it. Like a baleful eye glaring at him out of the dark, a glowing orange light winked from the middle of a dark form that lurked out in the yard under the gloom of a buckeye tree. He pulled on the reins with such an abrupt jerk on the bit that the horse reared slightly and backed up. "Whoa, easy," Ellis murmured.

He stared into the dark, trying to make out what it was. It seemed to be suspended in midair—a wraith in the night. A breeze stirred, and the thing swung with the gust, raising an ominous creaking sound as new rope rubbed against old bark.

"No!" Ellis eased Julie onto the seat, jumped from the wagon, and charged into the darkness. "No," he breathed again. "Please, God, don't let it be!"

Ellis stopped just short of touching it. He reached out a shaking hand, unable to make himself take the last step forward. The wind gusted again, and the thing revolved until its face peered down at Ellis from the end of the hangman's noose.

It was a dummy, a scarecrow. Its canvas skin had been painted with a cross-eyed gaze and a dopey smile. The glow was coming from its chest. Whoever had hung it had tried to set it on fire, but its straw stuffing was wet and so it only smoldered.

On the ground nearby, carefully pinned in place by a pile of rocks, was a crudely lettered sign. It warned: REDS AND NIGGER-LOVERS, GET OUT!

CHAPTER THIRTY-SIX

Water Is Water

The Sunday duty.

Trudy's head turned to the music of Mount Pisgah Church as she walked by. Inside, her bright students sat wedged on long hard benches and sang harmony of the sort Trudy imagined was only sung in heaven. *Such music!* It made the rasping voices inside old Mr. Howard's church sound like the rattling of dry bones. Trudy sighed with envy at the thought of spending Sunday morning inside the shabby little church among her children . . . her *young'uns!*

She was early to the prim little white clapboard church. Old Mr. Howard was smoking a cigar under the spreading branches of a hickory tree among a group of men. Folz, the overseer, stood between him and another young man, who was fashionably dressed in a white boater, suit, and tie. *No farmer, this one,* Trudy thought. He had a swarthy complexion and the physique of a runner. A gold watch chain looped across his vest. Trudy could make out the shape of a fraternity key dangling from it.

She knew her eyes had lingered on him too long when he smiled at her and touched his fingers to the brim of his boater in a salute. She responded with a smile.

Then she watched as the overseer's lips formed the words *Jew-gal,* as if warning the young man. Abruptly she turned away. The muscles across her shoulders were already tense, and the morning had only begun.

"Miss Meyer—" The hoarse voice of old Mr. Howard beckoned her back. She turned and he crooked a finger at her. "I want you to meet my nephew, Scott."

"Pleased to meet you." Scott's dark eyes swept over Trudy in approval. "Uncle, why didn't you tell me there were such beautiful women in these parts? I would have come down sooner."

"We had to import the little lady, Scott, boy." The Man winked at Trudy and chuckled. "If I'd known she'd draw you on down here, I'd have got her here sooner."

Folz had a cold look on his lean face. He did not approve of flattering talk to the likes of Trudy; that was obvious. Each Sunday he refrained from anything but the most perfunctory of greetings. "Miss Meyer. How them little pickaninnies comin' along? Give you any trouble? Thievin' little—"

"Well now, Folz, you're too hard about the Nigras," Mr. Howard soothed. "Miz Meyer has a fondness for the little things. Teaches down to the Nigra school." He nudged his nephew, who had not taken his eyes away from Trudy. "She's teaching them to read the Good Book."

At this, Folz snorted as though he knew the truth of what Trudy was teaching. "Sight more she's teachin' than readin' from the Good Book. Puttin' all sorts of other books in them little nigger hands, as I hear it. Brought her whole library, from what I hear. And a phonograph—"

The old man's nephew stepped deliberately in front of Folz, cutting him off. He toyed with the fraternity key on his watch chain. "Good for you." He met Trudy's eyes, his expression indicating that he shared her weariness at the ignorant spoutings of Folz. "Literature and music at Mount Pisgah. Culture and beauty, too."

"I told you." The Old Mister clapped Scott on the back. "We've got more here to offer than you think, boy."

Trudy let her breath out slowly. Could Scott see that she was grateful? The church bell rang. "It was good—," she began.

"Please—" Scott extended his arm—"would you join me?"

Trudy felt Folz's glare as they left him standing there beneath the tree. Later, as the service ended and Scott drove her home in his buggy, she could see the necks of every man and woman in the churchyard pivot in unison to watch them go.

Scott tapped the horse with the whip, urging her into a trot. "Pretty tense back there," he said, nudging his boater back on his head. "I don't know if I'll ever get used to it."

Trudy raised her eyebrows in astonishment and laughed. "*You*? What would your uncle say if he knew?"

"He's a sly old codger. He knows, all right. He told me that nobody cares what I believe—or don't believe—as long as I keep it to myself and attend church every Sunday."

"So I am not the only hypocrite," she replied.

"I'd say the whole place is filled with the hypocrisy of custom." Scott's eyes sparkled with amusement. "But it's good if I intend to be here awhile that there is someone else—someone as pretty as you—who is honest."

"If I were honest, I wouldn't be there each week."

"Well, then, *smart*. Because you are there, even if you don't want to be." He slowed the horse to a walk. "There's no need to hurry unless you have social plans this afternoon. Tell me where you're from."

"You mean you haven't heard that already?"

He shrugged. "Ah, Mount Pisgah! One giant ear for gossip, this place." He winked at her as though nothing he had heard made any difference. "Shall I tell you about myself first, then? After that you can help me sort out the fact from the fantasy that has been dreamed up about the young, single schoolmarm."

A graduate of the university in Fayetteville, Scott Howard was more businessman than farmer, he claimed. The only nephew of his childless uncle, Scott was being groomed to take over the land when the old man was gone. And he had great plans for the place, too.

"But I'm boring you," he said as they passed Mount Pisgah Church and Trudy turned her face to the music.

"'I come to the gar-den a-lone. . . .'"

"No. It's just . . . I love coming by and listening to them sing. . . . Sometimes I want to go in, that's all."

Scott laughed and clucked the mare to a trot. "I have better things in mind." He held her in his gaze. "Will you show me your library?"

Trudy did not invite Scott to her cabin, but she opened the schoolhouse and showed him the rows of books she had brought to keep her company.

"So these are the subversive novels old Folz is so worried about putting in the hands of the darkies." He held up a copy of *Uncle Tom's Cabin*. "A man like him has never heard of emancipation, I suppose."

Trudy plopped down on the end of a bench and looked at the handsome face of her visitor. "I wish I had been able to talk to you the first day." She sighed. "I have felt so alone."

Bright hair ribbons and turbans, floral-print dresses made from flour sacks, faded black Sunday suits with frayed cuffs and too-short sleeves made up the Sabbath finery worn by the worshippers at Mount Pisgah Church.

Jefferson stood in his uniform behind the old pulpit donated by the first Master Howard seventy-five years before. He grasped its sides, worn smooth by the ebony hands of dozens of preachers—some freemen and others slaves. Looking over the close-packed congregation, Jefferson smiled easily. It was just as he remembered it, after all. Like a flower garden, his people were, all waiting to be watered by the Word of their true heavenly Master. And there on the front bench, fluttering like the wings of butterflies, seven brightly colored fans cooled the faces of his sisters and his mama and his gal.

"This ain't heaven—" he looked at Willa-Mae, who nodded and fanned more fervently—"but it's home, and home's the next thing to heaven, ain't it?"

A chorus of "Uh-huh, Amen" and "Praise be, you home" filled the little sanctuary. The fans bobbed up and down with heads. It was, indeed, so good to be among the folks!

"Yes!" Jefferson raised his big hands heavenward in gratitude. "Thank You, Jesus!" There was much rejoicing and laughter here. After all, big Jeff had left a mighty big empty hole when he went away to fight in the war. Nobody quite ever could handle the pulpit the way Jefferson did. Folks still talked about the Sunday night he got to preaching so hard that he lifted the heavy mahogany pulpit right off the floor and up over his head as if he were Samson pulling down the heathen temples. He never noticed how heavy it was, he said later. He just got filled with the Holy Ghost. He could have picked up the whole church if the sermon had called for such a demonstration!

So now he was back.

"Tell us what the Lord told you over there, Jeff!"

"What you see out there in the big world, Jefferson?"

"Preach to us, Jeff!"

"Was the Lord in that war, Jeff?"

Once more, big hands caressed the sides of the pulpit. Jefferson's broad smile faded as he recalled the Great War—the dying, the suffering. And then he rustled the pages of the Good Book, and the room fell silent. The Canfield women folded their fans flat and waited expectantly.

"Yes," he said after a time, "the Lord was there. He's every place where men are suffering and dying. I seen Him beside a German officer. Seen Him by a poor black soldier like me. Heard a fella cry out to Him after I shot that fella my own self. I sat down in the mud beside that man as he was dying. I held his hand and cried for mercy on his soul . . . and on my own for the killin'. . . ."

He raised his head and surveyed the somber faces of his friends and family. "The Lord was on both sides of that line, where men was dyin' and where men was killin'. He's fightin' old Lucifer for men's souls. Sometimes He wins and sometimes He don't. I suppose the unseen battle is just as bloody as the one I seen."

A dozen "Amens" answered him.

"How'd you get that there medal, Jefferson?" called one of the young men, jerking a thumb at the Legion of Honor medal Hock Canfield wore around his neck.

"I stayed put and fought when everybody else was runnin'," Jeff replied simply.

"You a hero, then?"

Jefferson shook his head slowly. This was the very subject he planned to preach upon. "There was a time—a real short time—when I thought I might be a hero. Ain't nothin' so fine for a man as black as I am as wearin' that medal and walking down a street in Paris, France. French folks take one look at that medal and they don't know what color skin I got. They say, 'Come on home to supper.' They say, 'Have you got a place to sleep tonight?' They say, 'You wonderful American gentleman. *Vive l'Américain!*' Which means, *Hurray.*"

This revelation was met by looks of wonder from the congregation. "You mean white folks say such things to you?"

"That's right. Right on the street. Stop me and say such things until I got to thinkin' that maybe things would be different when I came on back home. That maybe white folks here would think I'm all right. Like them. That I could ride on the same train, like in France. Eat in a café, like in France. All this time I was thinkin', *Jefferson, you gonna* be *somebody when you get back.*"

He smiled sadly and searched the faces of the congregation, who met his gaze with knowing eyes. Everyone knew that nothing had changed. Nothing at all. Black was black and white was white, just like always. Not like France.

"Well now," Jefferson continued, "I was feelin' mighty proud. . . . Then we came home." He turned another page of the Good Book and traced the words. "So here I am. Just Jefferson. And this is what I learn from the Lord about heroes and such: It ain't what I do in this world what makes me worth somethin'. It's what the Lord's already done that makes me worth somethin'."

He began to read:

"The Lord executeth righteousness and judgment for all that are oppressed. . . . The Lord is merciful and gracious, slow to anger, and

plenteous in mercy. . . . He hath not dealt with us after our sins; nor rewarded us according to our iniquities. For as the heaven is high above the earth, so great is His mercy toward them that fear Him. As far as the east is from the west, so far hath He removed our transgressions from us."

Jefferson paused and looked up. He tapped the page with his fingers. "As far as east is from west. That's mighty far, sisters and brothers. A man can't walk that far. An eagle can't fly that far. No fish is gonna swim an ocean that wide! God put our sin that far from us! Jesus took it all away when He died for me. Now, don't that make me worth somethin'? Ain't that what makes Jefferson Canfield stand as tall as any white man who could spit in my face and say I'm nothin'?"

The little sanctuary rang with voices responding in understanding. Hands raised in praise, and the fans snapped open with excitement at the revelation.

"I don't need no medal to tell me I'm somethin'. Don't need nobody to ask me home to supper. Don't need to ride in a first-class coach. Jesus already told me: 'Jefferson, you're worth My life. Jefferson, you're worth My sufferin'. Jefferson, the Son of God Almighty loves you. Your life and your soul are worth eternity! You're worth *everythin'*, and don't matter what any man say to you. You hang your hat on *this* peg. . . . '"

Once more he read from Psalm 103:

"Like as a father pitieth his children, so the Lord pitieth them that fear Him."

Jefferson threw back his head in a laugh of purest joy. "You hear that? The Lord loves me like I'm His own baby! His own child! I've seen when babes get born—they ain't worth nothin' if you figure them by how much cotton they can pick! They can't pick cotton, can't hoe weeds, can't ride a mule! Babies ain't nothin' but squallin', messy, hungry little things! But, oh my, how they is *loved*! Not because of what they can do, but just *because*."

He shook his head. "I don't need to fight no great wars. Don't need to be white or rich. I just need to know . . . Jesus loves me! Lay in His arms and let Him love you. Be His baby, and He'll teach you how to walk, how to talk, how to run and laugh and sing! But first you gotta feel His love. Know that you ain't *done* enough for Him to love you."

A stillness settled in as mothers and fathers looked at their children.

Jefferson could sense that they understood what he was saying. He gave a satisfied nod. "As far as the Lord sees, Jeff Canfield is worth as much as President Woodrow Wilson! Now, ain't that somethin'?"

That night Trudy stood on the porch of her cabin and gazed at the stars that winked through the tree branches. Closing her eyes, she tried to think of Scott Howard. But instead she found herself thinking only of Birch—his arms around her in the gardens of the Electric Park, his lips against hers.

"You're an idiot, Trudy," she muttered aloud, taking a deep breath of the humid night air. She had a handsome, intelligent man like Scott Howard looking her way. Possibly he represented the only man in the entire little self-contained world of Mount Pisgah whom she could talk to. Yet he left her cold inside, longing for another man.

She went inside, undressed, and settled into bed. Listening to the sounds of the night, she felt more lonely than ever. *I will have to forget Birch*, she resolved. And then she forced herself to think about Scott . . . about his hands, strong but uncalloused—a gentleman's hands. She knew he wanted to kiss her, but she had not let him.

Maybe next time, she mused. *If there is a next time.*

✼ ✼ ✼

"But it's not her fault," Becky flared at Ellis as he skimmed the letter for the fourth time.

"Of course it's her fault! What kind of a best friend is she, anyway, if she lets her father say she cannot be in our wedding—not even attend! And you've already bought the material for her dress, too!"

Becky glared at him. The anger she had felt at the letter from Miranda Smith in Greysville was now entirely directed at Ellis. "It's *politics*! You think Miranda cares one bit about whether Hopewell or your father gets elected? No! Look! Look at the way the ink has run on the paper! She was crying when she wrote it! Weeping! My poor Miranda!"

"Crying all right," Ellis said dryly. Then he began to read. "'If only old Doctor Warne had not taken it in his smudge *to* smudge *against our dear Judge* smudge . . . '" He flipped the paper at her. "I would not *have* Miranda in *my* wedding!"

"*Our* wedding. And if her father relents, then I say she *shall* be my maid of honor."

"Over my dead body."

"*You!* This whole dreadful political . . . *thing!* A girl's best friend suffers over the politics of a girl's future in-laws and—"

"You're talking like you don't agree with Pop."

"I agree. But I wish it would stay out of my wedding plans."

"Then maybe a girl ought to get herself a different best friend." Ellis threw a rock at Mrs. Moniger's prize speckled hen strutting in the yard. And he hit it, too. It squawked and flew up with a cackle as feathers scattered. Then the chicken fell over, flopping, and died.

This was the final straw. First Becky's bridesmaid . . . and now her mother's pet chicken lay dead in the yard! She gasped and jumped up from the hay bale. "Get out, you brute!" She hit Ellis hard on the arm. "You've killed Mother's chicken! Poor thing. Look what you—"

Ellis blinked at the dead lump of feathers. "I didn't mean to. I was just . . . you know . . . pitching."

"That *hen* was not home plate!" Becky said indignantly.

John Moniger stepped out from the kitchen door and peered at his daughter, then at Ellis, then at the chicken. "What is it?"

"Ellis killed the speckled hen! Threw a rock and . . . *KILLED HER DEAD!*"

John shielded his eyes against the glare of the sun. "Well, pluck her and clean her and throw her in the stewpot, Becky." With a shrug the little man went back into the house.

Becky stamped her foot. "Don't men know *anything*?" She whirled around. "I *will not* marry a man who would murder a defenseless chicken out of a bad temper!"

"Then you'll never get married." Ellis rose, swayed a bit, and limped to retrieve the dead hen. "Pluck *this*, Becky Moniger, for you will not be plucking me of my manhood or my right to say what is only true!" He shoved the thing into her hands.

For an instant it looked as though she might hit him with the hen, but she didn't. She lifted her chin haughtily and glared at him. "If that is the way you want it, I shall write poor Miranda and tell her the wedding is *off*! Then she will feel better because she's not going to miss a thing!"

"Fine." Ellis walked to the buggy. He did not look back at Becky as he clucked the mare into a brisk trot.

✷ ✷ ✷

Trudy walked home from the general store slowly. Her mother would have accused her of dawdling, and perhaps she was. She went to the store only once a week after school and then to church on Sunday. Other than that, she was firmly rooted in the tiny world of her woods and her cabin and her school. She loved the peace and quiet each day when school ended, but an edge of loneliness sometimes crept into her solitude.

She longed for conversation about something other than cotton prices or the quality of Preacher Hammond's sermon each week.

"He just didn't move my heart today for some reason. . . ."
"The singing was rather poor today. . . ."

As for school, she had discovered what old Mr. Howard had meant when he said that attendance was not mandatory. After the first week of classes, attendance had dropped off by a third, and it seemed that a different group of children was absent each day—except for the Canfield sisters and Latisha Williams, who came early and stayed late every day.

Latisha was reading every book she could get her hands on—checking out a volume and then returning it completely read through two days later. She had a ravenous hunger for knowledge, yet Trudy knew that when the young woman married, chances were that her education would end. Latisha was only sixteen. By the time she was twenty, she would probably have children of her own to tend.

No doubt the same future was in store for the Canfield sisters. Early marriage and childbearing seemed to be the natural way of life here in Mount Pisgah, and not just for the black population. It was also true among the whites. Only last week at the church Trudy had seen the newborn infant of a fifteen-year-old white girl. The school, it seemed, was merely a holding pen for the youngsters of these parts. Trudy had hoped to make it a depot where they might catch some larger dream and ride it as far as they could go.

But she had to start small. Regular attendance was the issue. Trudy knew she was an object of curiosity—perhaps even suspicion—among the parents of her students. How could she get to know them? make them trust her enough to help?

A wagon carrying the six Jones children creaked by. Three boys and three girls jumped up and down at the sight of their teacher walking on the road. Perhaps it seemed strange to them to see her outside the classroom. Teachers were not supposed to have mail to pick up or places to go besides school, were they?

"How-do, Miz True," they said in unison.

"Good afternoon, children," Trudy replied. "I have missed you in class."

They grinned, glad to be missed. "We all miss you, too, Miz True," said little Polly shyly.

The big, broad-rumped woman driving did not even look at Trudy. She simply guided her mule on. Her dark eyes looked straight ahead, as though she were thinking very serious things.

It was an impulse, but Trudy raised her hand and called out, "Missus Jones!"

The faces of the children expressed amazement that their teacher would flag down their mama on the road like that.

Mrs. Jones pulled up the mule and waited patiently for Trudy to catch up. The woman did not raise her eyes to look at Trudy's face. "Yes'm," she said quietly.

"Missus Jones, you have such bright youngsters. I enjoy them in class."

"Thank you, ma'am." The woman studied the reins in her hands, still not daring to look at Trudy.

"I was wondering—" Trudy plunged forward with her question, not quite knowing why—"could I come call on you? Perhaps we can chat. About schooling and such."

"Yes'm," agreed Mrs. Jones. Her face was set like flint, without any expression one way or the other, as though she would agree to anything just so Trudy would let her get on her way.

"Well then." Trudy stepped back. "Will you send word when it would be convenient?"

"You say when, ma'am. Don't make no nevermind to me."

"All right. May I ask Latisha Williams to come with me? To show me the way?"

There was some flicker of relief. "Yes'm. Latisha knows the way to my door right easy."

As Mrs. Jones clucked her mule on, Trudy wondered if she had only wanted to go calling because no one had ever come to her little cabin. *Just to have some company.* She fingered the letter from her mother. She would carry it home and read it without enthusiasm. She had been hoping to hear again from Birch.

✹ ✹ ✹

"Nothing but a lovers' spat," Doc told Ellis as the boy grieved on the porch before supper.

"Tell that to the chicken," Ellis said miserably, cradling his head in his hands.

"You'll just have to replace it," Doc instructed him. "One chicken is pretty much like another."

"Not this chicken. Black with spots. Looked like one of those ladies' hats we saw at the Waldorf in New York. Only it cackled and had legs."

"A moving target," Doc mused.

"I'm not the pitcher I used to be, Pop. I only meant to stir up the dust under it. Then *wham!* If it had been a batter, the ump would have sent her to first base."

Doc clucked his tongue, a very henlike noise. "And you're out of the game."

The telephone jangled. Molly called out to Ellis. "Ellis? It's Missus Moniger. She says Becky is on a crying jag and wants to know if you'd come over for supper."

"What are they having?" Doc called jauntily.

A moment passed as Molly asked, then replied, "Speckled hen and dumplings."

✶ ✶ ✶

"Teacher'll be here soon!" Pink and Little Nettie checked each other's hair while Big Hattie smoothed the quilt on the big bed and Lula placed a tin cup beside the water dipper so the white teacher would have her own cup to drink from.

Latisha Williams was with the teacher, acting as guide to the surrounding farmhouses of every student at Mount Pisgah. Today Miz True was coming to the Canfield farm. It was the closest to the school. Maybe that was why it was last on the list. Miz True and Latisha had begun their visits five miles out and each day after school had worked their way around the perimeter of the community, moving closer in until at last they were coming here.

As if it were Christmas, Willa-Mae had made a cobbler for the occasion. The Canfield girls had more time than the other children to think how they could make the teacher's social call into something spectacular. That peach cobbler would certainly do it. Hock and Jeff were down carving up a pine tree so it would fit into some fancy stove in Fort Smith, but no stove anywhere could make cobbler like Willa-Mae's! She warned her girls that this was for the teacher to have as much as she wanted. As for the girls, they were to take only tiny portions for themselves and make sure there was enough for Jeff and Hock when they came in tonight.

Nettie had named her new French baby doll Teacher and placed her up on a pillow to instruct all the other play-chillens, who were propped on the mattress in an obedient row. She intended to show Miz True this little classroom when she came.

"Here she comes!" Angel announced.

Willa-Mae moved back the curtain just enough to see but not be seen. "Uh-huh. She ain't dressed like no field hand today. I'm kinda disappointed—I wanted to see them great big feet y'all been tellin' me about."

Miz True was dressed in a plain gray skirt and a white blouse with puffed sleeves, like the clothes the French doll was wearing. Sunlight on her hair reflected red highlights in the deep chestnut color. She was of a darker complexion than most of the white women around these parts. They dreaded the sun and always wore bonnets to keep from tanning.

"Well, she's bareheaded, anyhow," Willa-Mae remarked. "Ain't fittin' for her to be out in the sun without no hat. Folks gonna think she been pickin' cotton, even if she don't wear them bib overalls she got."

"She's perty though, ain't she, Mama?" Lula said. "Like a paper doll outta Sears and Roebuck."

Willa-Mae adjusted her blue-checked turban and smoothed her apron. She glanced around her home and felt some twinge of nervousness. Never had a white teacher at Mount Pisgah School *ever* visited the homes of students! Willa-Mae was glad they had not been the first, because then she truly would have been nervous. Word had come back that Miz True was just about a perfect guest.

She had sat on a stump in Miz Young's yard and admired all the patterns of the quilts hanging on the line. Miz True just looked right past Miz Young's underdrawers and talked about how she had never seen such beautiful quilts, saying they ought to be displayed in a museum. Then she had gone on about museums and what they were and how there really ought to be a room just for quilts from Mount Pisgah.

She had made quite a stir. Some folks thought she was overnice. But Willa-Mae liked the teacher already, because above everything, she was good with all the young'uns. Miz True went to old Mr. Howard's church regularly. Willa-Mae had seen her every Sunday morning coming and going past their own little church. Once while Jeff was preaching, the teacher had stopped and stood out by the edge of the cotton field and pretended she was looking over the crop instead of listening to the sermon. Kind of a lost and lonely looking little thing she had seemed.

Now here she was coming straight up the lane! Talking and talking to Latisha like they were old friends. *My, they sure are talking!*

Clapping her hands, Willa-Mae called all her girls to attention. They stood in a stairstep row starting with Lula, then Angel, Hattie, Pink, and Nettie. Willa-Mae tugged braids and set hair ribbons straight.

"Mama, how come you have *so many* gal-babies?" Little Nettie asked in a small voice.

"So's I'd have so many perty things to fuss with," Willa-Mae replied.

Then the line fell silent as the voices and laughter drifted into the cabin. Nobody much had ever heard a teacher laugh before, except maybe *at* some child, but never *with*. Here she was laughing at something Latisha was saying. And she was asking what old Boone's name was when he wagged up to meet her.

"Boone, is it? After Daniel Boone?"

Latisha laughed. "I reckon, Miz True, could be. Jeff says he got named for chasin' a bear cub clean down into Boonesville and settin' the whole town upside down when the mama bear come after her young'un. Folks near up an' died at the sight. Jeff tol' me he just wanted to remember that day because he never seen so many white folks *sooo* white!"

The line of Canfields all giggled because that was the truth of the story—and there was a whole lot more to it, too, but the details were for Jeff to tell.

Now here she came, right up into the yard, this teacher. All smiles, even though it was hot. Latisha dipped water out of the common drinking gourd and took a sip. Then Miz True did the same, *drinking right after her!*

"Glory be!" Willa-Mae whispered from the doorway. She stared at the special cup set on the table just so the teacher could have her own cup. Willa-Mae had never seen *any* white person to ever drink out of the common gourd. "Sweet Jesus, Lord Almighty," she wheezed. "I hope she don't do that in front of Mister Howard. The Old Mister'll send her right on back to New York City!"

Necks craned from the astonished rank. "She can't help it," Lula defended. "She thinks water is water and cups is cups. Mebbe they don't teach her about white folks drinkin' and us—"

"Hush!" Willa-Mae commanded. "Here they come!"

Even as Miz True came into the house and admired the play-chillens and the girls and the quilts, Willa-Mae was thinking how she sure hoped her daughters didn't get any free-and-easy ideas from the way this one white woman treated them all. After all, if any other white folks saw even such a small thing as a shared drinking gourd, Miz True would be sent away. And there would be trouble here for the black folks of Mount Pisgah over it.

Miz True ate the cobbler and chatted about schoolbooks and things that were pleasant enough. All the while, Willa-Mae was speaking in polite tones and saying, "Yes'm" and "No'm" and thinking that this teacher needed to learn a thing or two before she got herself into a world of hurt.

It was plain to see that something was bothering Latisha. Her eyes were red rimmed, and her hands trembled slightly as she placed the copy of the Upton Sinclair novel on Trudy's desk. She stood beside it a moment, with her fingers lingering on the cover of the book as though she did not want to give it up.

"What is it, Latisha?"

The young woman bit her lip. "I just didn't know white men treat other white men so bad as this in the North, Miz True. I thought they only done it . . . did it . . . here, to us folks." She frowned. "Is this here book the way it is up North?"

"The way things were when the book was written thirteen years ago. But a book like this can change things. People see great injustices and then they do something about it, you see."

Latisha raised her eyes and looked out the window, as though she could see some injustice out there and longed to write about it. "Yes'm. Sounds to me like it's worse up Chicago way where this book happened."

"I suppose it may be."

"Delpha Jean Jones got to take her young'uns on up to Chicago. Soon as the cotton is picked, they got to get out."

Trudy started and glanced outside to where three of the Jones girls— Delsy, Sue, and Polly—played on a swing. They had not mentioned that this would be their last week at Mount Pisgah School. Cotton harvest would begin soon, and school would be closed during that time. When it reopened, the Jones children would not be here.

"Get out? Leave their farm? But why? Is someone making them leave?"

Latisha tapped her finger on the book again. "Yes'm. They hafta go. I'm gonna tell Miz Delpha Jean about this book—tell her not to let them young'uns go to work in the Chicago meatpackin' place, I reckon." She sighed and walked slowly outside, as though it were too much effort to talk about it further.

* * *

Trudy had just lathered her hair when Scott called from the pathway leading to her cabin.

"Scott!" she said with frustration. He had ridden up unannounced after school was out and the young'uns had gone home. She rinsed the soap in the bucket and told him to stay outside. He seemed not to hear her.

Opening the door, he stuck his head in and laughed at her wet head and bare feet. He was dressed in denim work clothes and boots. "I think we ought to name you after the baseball player Shoeless Joe."

"Joe is my father's name," she said dryly. "Scott, really! Can't you come back later?"

"Why? When you are so vulnerable right now?" He stepped inside the cabin and tossed his hat onto the table. "I never met a woman with her head in a bucket who wasn't—"

"Scott, people will talk, you coming in like this." Trudy felt uneasy as he stood over her. She reached for a towel.

Scott took her wrist in his hand. "No. I like you like this." He stooped to kiss her neck.

She jerked away from him. "I don't like *you* like this," she replied angrily.

He shrugged and tossed her the towel, which she wrapped as a turban around her hair. Hands on her hips, she faced him. "Let's go outside."

"When winter comes, are you going to make me court you outside in the cold?" He looked repentant, embarrassed.

"Is that what you're doing? Courting?" Instantly she forgave him for barging in. They sat together on the step.

"I was hoping."

"That's very flattering, Scott. But I don't think I . . . I'm not ready. And you? You're here because I'm someone with books—"

"And a gramophone. And you smell nice."

"Didn't you have all those things in the women of Fayetteville? I hear they're the most beautiful girls in the world."

"Probably true," he mused. "But . . . they're not you."

Trudy bit her lip and remembered someone else's arms around her. "I'm not ready for this, Scott."

"That other fella, eh?"

She turned to gaze at him with a question in her eyes. "Maybe."

"The soldier boy." He seemed amused, as though he knew much that he was not telling her.

"Every girl had a soldier boy in the war." She tried to put him off.

"But not everyone traveled with one, called him her husband." He raised his chin and appraised her, laughing. "Miz Digby has a second cousin in Fort Smith, it seems."

Trudy covered her feet with her skirt, suddenly aware that Scott was imagining things about her that put a fire in his eyes when he looked at her.

"So you have heard the fantasy." She felt her cheeks grow warm. "None of it is true, Scott. Nothing happened. Nothing except in the excited minds of a bunch of old women who wagged their tongues and talked me out of my position at another school. That's why I'm here."

"It wouldn't matter to me anyway." Scott leaned close to her and put his arm around her waist. "Tell me you haven't thought about me."

"Please . . . don't. Don't move so fast, Scott. I need time to think." She pulled away from his desire.

"So is there someone else?"

"No. Not now. But . . ." She sighed and swept her hand toward the little schoolhouse. "I am coming to care about these people. About this position. I would not want to lose it."

He cocked an eyebrow at her. "This is Pisgah School, not Belle Grove.
You think the darkies are going to care about your morals? And as long
as you keep your secrets to yourself—"

"They would care. And *I* would care. I don't want to do anything that
could make them think badly of me."

Scott laughed at her concerns. "You do have funny ideas, and I think I
may set my mind to changing them for you." He stood abruptly. "Until
then, Miz True, may I call with my buggy to pick you up for church on
Sunday?" His eyes flashed. "You see, I can play the game when I must."

"You must," Trudy said. "And yes, you may call for me."

"Doc, I tell ye the election is good as won," John Moniger said emphati-
cally. His bushy beard waved up and down on his chest in time to the
nodding of his head.

"I'm thinking it's a mite premature to be counting our chickens,
John," cautioned Doc. "They say Hopewell is holding a big rally in the
north part of the district tonight. He still packs in the folks."

Moniger snorted. He poked Doc in the chest, which was about level
with his own shaggy mustache. "Now you listen to me, Doc Warne.
Don't you give that snake Hopewell any credit at all. The only folks who
come to see him are those too dumb to think for themselves or hopin' to
profit by the promises his kind fling out."

"It's true, Pop," said Ellis, agreeing with his future father-in-law.
"Lately, even people who thought they wanted Hopewell have been
stopping me to tell me they were wrong, and they are going to vote for
you. Seems Hopewell has pushed anger and hatred too far, and folks are
getting wise to him."

"Perhaps you're right," Doc said, looking thoughtful. "I thank you
both for the encouragement. The next week or so will tell the tale, I'm
thinking. One more set of speeches in the big cities, and then I'm
through campaigning."

"And we are all through talking politics tonight until after supper,"
declared Molly, bustling through the living room. "Let's get to table, if
you please. Julie!" she called up the stairs. "Suppertime, child."

"Coming, Mama." Julie's voice floated down the stairs. "I'm just putting kitty to bed, but he's being naughty and doesn't want to stay!"

CHAPTER THIRTY-SEVEN

Cold Feet

In the clapboard house down the road from Camden, Ohio, Ellis awoke to the insistent clanging of his alarm clock. He slammed down his fist on the thing and snuffed out the noise as his four young nephews groaned and turned over again.

Terror stabbed Ellis's heart as he rose from among the cramped bed and swung his legs onto the cold floor. His hands were trembling, just as he remembered them doing in the trenches across the wide Atlantic.

The day he had longed for—the day he had dreaded—had finally dawned. He looked out the window to where summer raindrops clung to the leaves on the buckeye tree in the yard.

"What have I done?" he muttered as the aroma of wheat cakes and bacon penetrated his senses. He inhaled deeply, trying to shake the sense of dread. "What have I done?" he moaned again.

His mother was preparing those wheat cakes just for him as a special treat, because of the significance of this day.

Ellis dropped his head into his big, calloused hands. There was no getting out of this now. He knew his mother would beat his selfish, despicable hide if he backed out now. Everything was done. The clothes. The parties. The invitations. The church. The preacher . . . *Rebecca!* And now the breakfast. The last breakfast in his father's house as a single man.

Ellis lifted his eyes heavenward. *Have mercy.* He prayed for lightning to strike the house. He did not wish for the house to burn down, of course, but how could there be a wedding today if the groom's house was struck by lightning? Surely such a disaster would put the wedding on hold. The guests and the pastor would understand that a son could not leave his family in such a case and run off to get married and then travel to Niagara Falls with gaping holes in the roof and everything in disarray.

"What's wrong with you, Ellis?" His nephew Patrick sat up and scratched his flaming red hair.

Ellis had forgotten about Patrick and all the others who were sleeping all over the house. There were beds made on nearly every square inch of the floor. Cousins. Nephews. Nieces. Family by the bushel. The whole house was filled to capacity, like rolled socks stuffed into a too-full drawer.

There was no room for a lightning bolt to slip through without killing some member of the Warne family. It was hopeless. Ellis rolled his eyes and revoked his prayer for divine interference. He would have to go through with this. He would have to marry Rebecca Moniger, and there was no getting out of it.

The wedding had been billed, booked, and sold out. Everyone had come from far and near to watch this momentous occasion—Ellis, the first homegrown American, was marrying another American. Was this not an occasion for all the world to celebrate? Would this pair not make more little Americans, of whom Molly could brag, "Sure, 'tis a fact, Ellis and Rebecca have babes who are *second-generation* citizens, mind you!"

Ellis thumped his chest and breathed in hard.

Alarmed, little Patrick roused the rest of the tribe. "Hey, wake up! Ellis looks sick."

Ted, Jim, and Howie stared at the gasping Ellis from their pillows. "You all right, Ellis?" asked Jim with a frown.

Ellis managed to shake his head both ways. Yes and then no and then yes again.

"Call Gramma," Ted said sleepily. "Ellis is chickening out."

The air exploded from Ellis's lungs with a loud *oof* of protest, but he sucked in another breath too quickly to reply. His hands were like ice. His lungs seemed starved for air. He could not fill them deep enough or fast enough, and he could not speak.

The discussion resumed. "He's not sick, I tell you."

"Naw . . ."

"But look at him . . ."

"Not sick. Just petrified."

"Don't you remember? Same thing happened to Uncle John on his wedding day. White and sick-looking like that. He puked!"

"Yeah, I remember. Then Gramma took a broom to him. Told him to straighten up because the house was full. And Doc said he should not disgrace the family and should marry Arleta even if he didn't want to."

A small reedy voice piped up. It was little Howie, the result of the union between John and Arleta. "You're a liar!" Howie proclaimed and flung himself upon Ted like a tiny puppy upon the neck of a mastiff. "A lousy dirty . . . liar!"

Ellis winced. Evidently Howie did not like the revelation that his father had puked at the prospect of wedding his mother.

In the scuffle one of Ellis's crutches was knocked over, hitting Jim on the head.

Instantly the room was divided into a miniature version of the Civil War. Brother against brother. Cousin against cousin. Bed on the north wall against bed on the south. Pillows and fists.

As Ellis gasped for breath and struggled to control the terror that had gripped his very soul, the door flew open. Bleary eyes and tumbled-down hair and rumpled nightshirts of relatives crowded through the opening to yank this boy up by the scruff of his shirt and that boy by his ear and the next by his hair.

The scene could not have been any more explosive if God Almighty Himself had indeed sent a lightning bolt through the house.

"What's this?"

"What are you doin' now?"

"He said you threw up when you married Mother!"

"Naw! I said—"

"Then he said—"

"What I was sayin'—"

"And that you didn't want to marry Mother!"

"Naw! I was sayin' Ellis looks sick like—"

Suddenly the tumult grew still. Peace came to the troubled waters. An ominous silence descended, except for the wheezing breath of Ellis Warne, who sat chalky white against the wall among torn feather pillows and bedding.

All eyes turned upon the bridegroom in pity, in memory, and then in amusement.

John, who had indeed gotten the shakes on his wedding day, towered over his brother. "Fear of marriage," he said with authority. "Runs in the family." He looked to his sister-in-law Cecile. She nodded and shrugged.

Then through the crowd of barefooted spectators came the only one fully dressed . . . Mother Warne. There was fire in her eyes and a stack of wheat cakes in her hand. No one was downstairs eating them, evidently. They were all upstairs, staring at her American-born son.

"Well?" she said.

No one replied.

"I *see*." She looked scornfully at Ellis, who was still trying to breathe and talk. "So I have raised myself another coward, have I?"

Ellis nodded miserably. Nervous laughter tittered across the room.

"Get *out!*" Molly declared as she surveyed the wreckage. There was a mad scramble for the door. Cousins, nephews, brothers, a few nieces who had managed to cram in—all of them tried now to go out the small opening of the doorframe at the same moment. They surged past Doc, who stood in the hall behind the mob with his arms folded defiantly across his chest. All sizes and shapes of family members escaped within seconds before Doc strode in and slammed the door behind him.

Mother and father were now alone with their child. Doc looked unusually grim as he stared at the trembling heap that was his son. "Well, Molly?" he growled.

"What shall we do?" she asked. "The guests are all invited. The church decorated. The hall and the preacher hired. The train tickets to Niagara Falls bought, and his suitcase packed."

"We could send him on the train to Niagara Falls alone," suggested Doc in a helpful manner.

Ellis looked up hopefully. Would they help him escape this trap he had set for himself? "Pop—," he managed.

Molly interrupted. "Rebecca would be heartbroken. Although what she wants with such a lump as this . . ." She shook her head.

"Aye . . . *Rebecca.*" Doc put his chin in his hand and gazed thoughtfully at the alarm clock that was still ticking where it had fallen in the donnybrook. "We've still got a few hours. We can't disappoint Rebecca. Such a lovely little thing."

Ellis swiped sweat from his brow. He had almost forgotten about Rebecca in all this. "Mother—" He managed to get out two syllables.

Molly raised her hand to silence him. She turned to Doc. "A few hours, Doc. That's time enough. We'll just put a bag over his head and leave him here alone awhile. If he's still gibbering and sweating, then you and Matthew and John can dip him in the trough and dress him for the wedding. His other brothers can hold him right through the service. By the time he comes around, Rebecca will be knowing how to fix him."

Solemn nods from Doc.

There is no escape! Ellis gulped. "Please . . . no bag . . ." He motioned to his head. "I . . . I'll be all right. Just . . . a little . . . time . . . alone . . ."

Doc nodded. "I understand."

Molly said regretfully, in a voice she might use if she overcooked a meat loaf, "We should have let him sleep alone last night, Doc."

"True, true." He patted his son's head. "We've all lived through it, Ellis. You'll be pleased to have done it by tomorrow morning."

Then he opened the door to reveal at least a dozen sets of ears pressed against the thin wood. They scattered and ran for cover as Doc boomed his annoyance into the midst of them.

Molly followed, scolding that her wheat cakes were certainly ruined forever, but that those who caused this calamity could eat them all the same or go hungry.

The door clicked behind her. And Ellis Riley Warne was left alone for his last few hours of bacherlorhood.

✳ ✳ ✳

The last of the sweet-faced Guernsey milk cows stood in the stanchion, her udder full to the point of being painful. She rolled her eyes in relief and bellowed as John Moniger adjusted his milking stool and, like a concert musician, began to squirt a melody into the tin bucket.

Rebecca scratched the velvet nose of the beast and studied her father by the soft light of the lantern. Today her father would be giving her to another man, yet here he was, milking the cows just like always. His small and wiry frame bent easily to milk the little Guernsey. Rebecca wanted to remember him like this, going on about his business as if there were nothing unusual about the day.

She was the youngest of eleven children and the last of the Moniger girls to wed. Her mother had spent the past week weeping at odd moments over this loss of her baby girl. Rebecca preferred the matter-of-fact attitude of her father, so she followed him from chore to chore, as though she were a five-year-old child learning all she could from him.

There was strength in the warm, earthy scents of the barnyard and in the sight of John Moniger about his business.

There was peace in the memory that a man who had spent his youth in violence and rage was now milking a cow in Ohio on the wedding day of his eleventh child.

Rebecca had a thousand questions she wanted to ask her father. She felt as if she were leaving him forever and would never have the chance to ask him anything again. Of course, this was not true. But after today, she would belong to Ellis, and things would certainly be different.

She leaned against the stanchion and pulled her jacket close around her, as if the thought had chilled her.

The ring of foamy milk against the tin pail took on a new rhythm as her father shifted his humming to a livelier tune. He squinted up at Rebecca and raised an eyebrow curiously. "Sure, and you never did like milkin', Rebecca," he said, his Irish brogue gentle and refined by years in America. "Yet you've followed me out here as if you've never seen where milk originates." He smiled from behind his long, gray beard. "Well?"

"I . . ." She faltered and stared at the stream of milk and then at her

father's forehead pressed against the side of the cow in a sort of affection-
ate embrace. He was a good man—always had been for as long as she
had known him. He had mellowed since the old days, she'd heard. She
could ask him anything. If only she could find the proper phrase.

"Well . . . what was it like . . . for you and Mother?"

He raised his head off the cow and gave a silent laugh that made his
small frame shake. "Not a blessed thing like this, I'll tell ye! Much easier."

Rebecca shifted her weight uneasily. She cleared her throat and nodded as if she understood. And maybe she did understand. After all, the
last few weeks had been terrible: fittings for the dress, invitations, arrangements to be made, irritation, moments of terror. The big argument
with Ellis over . . . well . . . who could remember?

"Your mother and me had none of this to contend with." The *ting,
ting, ting* of the milk streaming into the pail slowed a bit. "No preachers
or priests. No weddin' dress or guests. No bawlin' women or grievin' father." The shoulders sagged a bit. "You know, I was a hunted man. A price
on me head. I was on one side of the troubles, and your mother's family
was altogether on the other. Catholic. Protestant. Makes no difference
now, of course—not here. Ah, but *there* it mattered what a man was."

The head again rested on the warm hide of the Guernsey as he talked
and milked. "But your mother, there she was. A beauty that spanned the
gulf of politics and religion. Seventeen, she was, like you, Rebecca—and
you're just as much the beauty as she was."

Rebecca knew this story, but she let him talk on. There was something at the end of his much-recited tale that she had never asked him.
This morning she would do so.

He continued without pause. "So, me comrades had a longboat
waitin' on the beach for us. We could see their torches burnin' as we rode
old Coal across the moor. Both of us, your mother and me, knew that we
could see our home and families nevermore from that night forward. . . .
She wrapped her arms tight around me back lest she fall and be picked
up by the riders comin' fast behind."

His eyes clouded with the memory of that fearful night, as if he were
living it still. Then he finished milking and fell silent for a moment as he
patted the cow and moved the pail. "You know the rest, girl. We fled
across the Channel to France, and there we were wed. After that we came
here, where it matters little if a man kneels in church or stands erect. And
we brought you eleven up with that in mind. You're better men and
women for it, too, I'd say."

He hefted the pail and the stool and stretched himself to his full five
feet, four inches of height. "So that was me weddin' day." He grinned.
"Like I was sayin'—a much easier ordeal than your own, I'm thinkin'."

Becky did not move from her place when he reached to release the cow from the stanchion, as if she were holding the creature hostage until her real question was answered. "But . . ."

He looked at her with puzzled amusement. "Poor Gertie has given all she's got, Becky. Shall we leave her tied up until after your weddin', then?"

"What I meant was—" Becky had so much she wanted to ask, needed to know. But how could she speak of such things to her father?

"Aye?"

"I meant . . . what happened *after*?" she whispered.

"After what?" He glanced over his shoulder as her voice became mysterious.

"The . . . wedding."

He looked at her as if he could not believe she had missed that part of the story he had been telling for years. "We came here. To Ohio . . ."

Becky blushed and then gulped. "No, Father. I mean, I need to know . . . *something*. About . . . *men*." She said the rest in a rush. "I don't know, you see. Not about what happens after the wedding and the supper, and I need to know, but—"

The face of John Moniger reflected his surprise. "Has your mother not had a word with you on the matter?"

"I asked, and she burst into tears."

He drew himself up and sniffed uncomfortably. "And your sister Violy?"

Rebecca nodded slowly. "She said that on a girl's wedding night . . . that . . . a girl would have to do things she didn't want to do, but that she should go ahead and do them anyway."

At this, John Moniger placed the pail of warm milk on the barn floor. He scratched his beard and sat down on his milking stool. He waited until Rebecca's red cheeks returned to a more normal color.

"I suppose that's more than your mother knew on our weddin' night, but I'll not send you into this as ignorant as that." He stared at his clasped hands for a minute before he gestured toward the calving pen. "Sure, Becky, you know more'n you think you know. You know what happens when we put the bull among the heifers."

Rebecca blinked at her father, not quite fathoming what he was saying. "Yes."

"Well then." He waited.

"Yes. Calves."

"Well then—" He waved his hand. The discussion was over.

"Is that all?" Rebecca asked, incredulous that her mother's tears and her sister's ominous warning could be related to something so simple as that.

Milk pail in hand, John Moniger led the way back to the house. "I explained it just that way to your mother on our weddin' night. And here you are. . . ."

The church was packed as Molly and Doc took their places in the front pew of the groom's side. Becky's mama was tearfully happy.

Ellis and his brothers filed in the side door and stood at the front. Ellis limped a bit, but today he did not use either cane or crutch. It had all been rehearsed. No kneeling down and getting up. No climbing the steps to the altar. The sacrament would be brought to him and made easy. All he had to do was stand up and say the words. His brother John was at his elbow in case he looked faint, as Warne men often did at their own weddings.

Ellis turned and faced the congregation. He spotted Molly and smiled, then limped toward her and bent to kiss her cheek. "She is so like you, Mama," he whispered. Then he was back in place again, hands clasped in front of him as he looked toward the back of the church. The rain started to fall, pattering against the roof of the old church as the music began. The row of bridesmaids from little to big paraded down the aisle with a dignity and poise no one would have believed possible. At last the sound of everyone rising filled the church. Molly looked at Becky, pink-cheeked beneath her veil, her childlike face framed by red hair wreathed with blue flowers from the fields around Camden.

Molly looked out the window to the place where five matching bouquets of blue flowers lay at the base of five granite markers. Three babies. Two soldiers. And she thanked the Lord for the one who had come home—for Ellis, who was blushing as he took the arm of his bride and turned to face the preacher.

It had been a lovely wedding. Everyone said so. The day had been cooled by the rain, flowers had not wilted, the bride and groom appeared calm. Mostly calm, anyway. Ellis had forgotten his lines almost the minute the preacher had said them, but Becky helped him out. Anyway, the final "I do" had been said. The bargain was signed and sealed and the newlyweds put on the train for Niagara Falls.

Finally, the house was quiet and empty. Grandchildren, nephews, and nieces had all been packed away home. Little Julie was off visiting her cousins. Doc and Molly slept late and made love to the rumble of a distant thunderstorm.

"So, this is what it will be like when they're all grown and wed," Doc said without any regret at all. "You know, I knew there was something more I was looking forward to in my life with you, Molly dear."

It was nearly ten in the morning when the telegram came from Ellis. Molly was still in her housedress, her hair all tumbled down around her shoulders.

Doc answered the door and opened the telegram with a roar of laughter. "It seems that Ellis is finding out something about connubial bliss." He passed the yellow slip of paper to Molly, who also laughed and quietly blessed Becky, who was the perfect match for Ellis.

POP YOU WERE RIGHT STOP CAN'T FIGURE WHY WE WAITED ALL SUMMER TO TIE THE KNOT STOP WOW ELLIS

At noon the telephone rang. Molly answered it just as Doc came in from the back porch. Her face had gone instantly ashen.

"What is it?" Doc asked, assuming some medical emergency would call him away.

"Why are you—?" Molly's voice was shaking with anger.

"Molly?" Doc took the phone from her. "Doc Warne here."

The voice on the other end of the line was dark and sinister as the threat was restated. "If you know what's good for you and your family, Doctor Warne, you'll get out of the race." Then the phone clicked dead.

The operator could not tell which exchange the call had come through. After half an hour of trying to trace the source of the threat, Doc sat quietly beside Molly, who was still trembling.

"'Your *family*,' he said! He mentioned Julie and Ellis and . . ." Molly buried her face in her hands.

"A crackpot," Doc said angrily. "I'll rip the phone from the wall before we'll endure any more such threats." The rage of old memories was in his eyes. "I'll ring the operator. No more calls to come through to the house unless she has the numbers."

* * *

The face of the postmistress held a definite smirk as Trudy asked for her mail and was handed one letter from Sadie.

"Well, how you makin' out down there to the schoolhouse, Miz True?" Miz Moss asked as Miz Digby and Miz Morgan stepped back and pretended not to be listening.

"Beautifully. Really bright students," Trudy replied, but she knew the question was about something other than class.

"You got yourself a new student, I reckon." Miz Moss glanced at the other two ladies. "Been seein' young Mr. Scott ridin' off down your way quite frequent."

So that was it. "Really? You must tell him I said to stop by sometime." Trudy pocketed her letter. "Good day, ladies," she said, turning to purchase what she needed for the picnic she and Scott had planned for after church on Sunday.

Trudy found that the gossip did not even bother her today. She had been thinking a lot about Scott, bending her thoughts toward him and all the good things she knew about him. Her nights had been less lonely with the thought that she would see him again. Her days had become spiced with anticipation. Perhaps their common interest in books and music was a place where she could begin to build something more with the handsome young man.

Besides, all the gossips of Mount Pisgah seemed to be enjoying themselves as well.

CHAPTER THIRTY-EIGHT

Burning Dreams

Great heaps of oak wood were piled like haystacks in the field. Stumps dotted the clearing like the stubble on an unshaved face. The whack of ax against wood and the crack of splitting limbs rang in the air twelve and fourteen and sixteen hours each day. The rhythm did not slow from the first hour to the last, stopping only when Latisha came to the clearing with her basket.

"Like money in the bank," Jefferson told her, drinking water from the gourd dipper and then splashing another dipperful over his glistening torso. "I figure to sell some in Fort Smith this year. Sell enough to split with The Man an' have enough so's you an' me can get hitched after the cotton is picked. Them rich white folks gonna use this wood all winter long an' say, 'Ain't never had wood fit so perfect in the firebox an' stack up so pretty in the woodshed.' They'll be lookin' for me to come on back with more, I reckon. Five dollars a cord, gal. We gonna be rich folks by the time I clear this whole forty."

Latisha walked beside one of the three great piles of wood. "Big as a barn, Jeff. Even splittin' with The Man, you practic'ly rich already! We'll be married in no time!"

She turned to see the tall buckskin horse of Folz, the overseer of the plantation. Next to him on a shorter bay horse was a young man. The second man was dressed in denim work clothes, but they looked new, and his tall riding boots shined as if they'd never been scuffed.

Both men were leaning over their saddles listening, eyeing the wood as though they, too, could see the wealth in it.

"Howdy, Mr. Folz," Latisha said, wishing the tall, lean man had not overheard their happiness. Happiness was a thing to steal, after all.

"Howdy there." Folz's pale blue eyes narrowed, hiding the color of them as he squinted. "Reckon you two ain't met Mister Howard's nephew, The Young Mister Scott. He's fixin' to farm the Jones place." He indicated the other rider, who nodded agreeably and stepped down from his horse. It seemed to Jefferson that this newcomer did not look needy or desperate for a place to live.

"You got The Man a heap of wood here, Jeff," Folz continued. "I told Mister Howard how you been workin' to get the land cleared. He's mighty glad you been so thoughtful about cutting the trees into firewood."

"Yessir, Mr. Folz," Jefferson replied, but he did not like the way Folz let the word *thoughtful* linger on his tone. "Nothin' thoughtful about it. Just common sense."

"How many cord you figger we got here?" Folz asked. "You been at it awhile, ain't you, boy?"

"Yessir. Since the day we buried ol' Billy Jones. I come down here fit to bust an' break an oak with my bare hands."

"And I reckon you could do it, too, big as you are. But how many trees you busted up down here?"

"Got fifty cords, I reckon. Maybe more."

Folz whistled through his teeth and raised his eyebrows. "You hear that, Mister Scott?"

The younger man was bent down, running a handful of dirt through his fingers. He looked up and nodded. "Mighty rich soil, this. Been lyin' fallow a long time."

Folz smiled at Jefferson. "Fifty cords is right nice. Mister Howard'll be glad to hear what you done for him."

Latisha stepped forward. She shaded her eyes to look up at Folz, who was framed by a ring of sunlight at his back. "Jeff's cuttin' this wood so's we can get hitched, Mr. Folz. He split it with The Man, just like the agreement says."

Folz gave an indignant snort at her words. "What are you talkin' bout, gal? There's nothin' in the tenant agreement about this here wood. Them trees weren't planted by nobody, 'cept mebbe God. Ain't no part of the agreement. Jefferson is just clearin' this land for The Man, so Jefferson can farm the land. But the wood belongs to The Man. Every stick of it. Ain't that so, Mister Scott?"

The owner's nephew climbed back up on his shiny English saddle and pushed a neatly brushed Stetson up on his forehead. "That would be my opinion."

Jefferson simply stared up at Folz's grinning face. The overseer's cheeks were hollow from where his back teeth were missing. Folz's yellow-toothed smile made his face seem like that of a skeleton.

Latisha stepped back, knowing there was no use arguing. All the work that Jefferson had done had come to nothing just that quickly. To argue about the matter would be dangerous. Folz could tell old Mr. Howard that Jefferson was an ungrateful troublemaker, a thief who planned to steal the wood from the forty acres.

"But Mister Folz," Jefferson tried, "I had intend to sell this wood an' sharecrop the profit with Mister Howard. You see, sir? It don't do no good to cut down a tree an' don't make use of it."

"That is so, Jefferson. But these trees ain't yours. You didn't plant 'em. They ain't nobody's but the Old Mister's. You got no claim to what you ain't growed."

"But I done the work—"

"Y'all are just clearin' the land like you was told to." The overseer rose in the saddle. His voice had an edge to it, a warning.

"But—" Jefferson held his tongue. He caught Latisha's eyes, and she shook her head. Could he risk losing the use of the land because of the wood he had cleared from it so far? "Lord knows I done what I done," he muttered.

Folz and the young Mr. Scott wheeled their horses around and rode out of sight at an easy canter.

Jefferson gazed after the two men, then looked at Latisha with weary eyes. "We shoulda burned it. Heaped it up and burned it like brush. Then they wouldn't have paid it no mind, Tish." He picked up the ax and hurled it at the largest pile of wood. It struck with a whack, sending the fragments of a log flying.

"They don't take kindly that you thought of it on your own. White men don't like black folks thinkin' an' doin', Jeff. They'd rather see it all go to waste before they let a nigger make anythin' good come of it."

"Fifty cords of wood. Five dollar a cord. That's enough that you an' me coulda got married right away." The big man looked beat. He sat down on a stump. "That's all I been thinkin' whilst I been down here workin'. Been thinkin' 'bout you an' me."

He raised his head and gestured through the trees toward the dilapidated little cabin. "Been thinkin' I could put a new roof on before the rain come." He turned to face her. "All night I dream 'bout you, Tisha. I think 'bout what it be like when I make you mine." He picked up a twig and broke it in two. "That's what this wood meant to me! It don't mean nothin' but money to the old Mister Howard an' this here Scott an' Folz. Don't mean they can quit achin' inside for a woman."

He moaned and rested his head in his hands. "I ache for you, Tish. Can't help it. I pray an' work, an' all the time I'm burnin' for you like my soul's afire."

She did not come close to him, as if she sensed that at this moment his fire could burn them both. "The Lord put such fire in a man for a woman, Jeff. Ain't no sin in it. Like you was readin' in the Good Book, Jacob loved Rachel an' worked seven years for her."

"I reckon he's a stronger man than I am. Reckon he didn't look up an' see that gal comin' across a field an' think the things I been thinkin' 'bout you."

Latisha smiled at his misery. "I been thinkin' about you, too, Jefferson—thinkin' how I don't want to wait no more, neither. Let's get hitched right away. I don't want to wait. Don't want my whole life waitin' on some heap of wood or whether old Mister Howard gonna let you keep what's your own. We don't belong to Mister Howard. You say we belong to the Lord, an' He's gonna tend to His own flock. Appears to me He's tellin' our hearts we better not wait, else we're likely to do somethin' we need to repent of later."

Jefferson looked up sharply at her and then at the cabin and back to her. "Get on home, Latisha," he warned. "Go on before I ask you . . ." He paused. "An' don't come down here alone no more, gal. It ain't smart."

He rose but did not move from beside the stump. "Get goin'. An' send my pa down here right quick. Tell him I said to bring a coal from the fire." There was already fire in his eyes. "We're gonna clear this land before I go to pickin' cotton for The Man. Tell him to hurry, Tisha. Then you stay clear, gal."

✷ ✷ ✷

The buckskin horse was lathered when Folz jerked it to such a sudden stop that it was set back on its haunches. He jumped from the saddle and was already running toward the pile of burning logs before young Mr. Scott also rode up to the scene.

The blazing fire was causing a tall column of smoke that Jefferson knew Folz had to have spotted from miles away.

"What y'all doin' here?" Folz demanded of Hock and Jefferson.

"Whoo-ee," said Hock. "It be almighty hot for this kind of work today. But if'n we gonna get this here field cleared *an'* pick cotton, we can't spend no more time in foolishness. Ain't that right, Jeff?"

"Shore 'nuff, Mister Folz," Jefferson agreed. "Can't be spendin' time cuttin' stove wood when that cotton's fixin' to drop out'n the bolls. No sirree."

"But this wood belongs to Mister Howard. You can't just burn it up thisaway!" Folz swore at them.

"See, Pappy," Jefferson said to Hock, "I told you we oughta haul these trees into the field yonder an' leave 'em heaped up."

"Wait a minute," Folz demanded. "That ain't right, neither."

Jefferson looked confused. "What you say, Mr. Folz? We can't burn it an' we can't haul it outta the way? What we supposed to do with it?"

Mr. Scott called from the back of the bay horse, "Come along, Folz. I think a little discussion with my uncle can resolve matters." Then to Hock and Jefferson he added, "Just see that you don't burn any more till we send word on how to split it up."

"No, sir," Jefferson agreed. "It's way too hot for this kind of work anyway."

✷ ✷ ✷

Little Nettie was brokenhearted. She had seen the same thing Angel and Pink saw, and she took the French porcelain doll away from the classroom of play-chillens and shoved it under the bed. "You ain't no good, Teacher," she told the doll, giving it a nudge out of sight with her toe.

"We seen that Mister Scott there with Teacher, Mama," Angel said. "Miz True ain't no different than all the rest of them, I reckon."

Pink just sat on the blanket chest and shook her head. "She was with that man. Lettin' him kiss her, too."

"I ain't goin' back to school," Little Nettie wailed. "I ain't goin' nowhere that teacher is!"

Willa-Mae continued ironing Jeff's Sunday shirt. "Mebbe Miz True don't know what this young Mister Scott is up to."

"She was right there in the buggy with him." Angel seemed indignant that her mother could defend anything so vile. "An' he looks out over the whole country an' says, 'This all gonna be mine. . . . It can be ours if'n you'll have me.'"

"He means he's takin' Billy Jones's place an' stealin' all of Jeff's wood an' maybe take our fields away from us, an' he gonna give it all to Miz True as some kinda weddin' present?" Hattie blurted out. "She been talkin' like we got a future, Mama, talkin' about us goin' off to college. Why, that's like old Mister Howard talkin' to Billy's kids about how great Chicago is gonna be where the Klan's so big an' they shoot colored folks down in the streets. She just talkin' 'bout college to us so we'll go away from our homes, an' her an' that Mister Scott can take all we got to live for."

Willa-Mae frowned. "Miz True say she gonna marry the young gentleman?"

"No." Hattie said the word thoughtfully. "But she sure let him kiss her! Let him kiss her so's her cheeks get all pink an' she say he shouldn't go so fast because she ain't ready."

"What ain't she ready for?" Nettie asked, looking sadly at the play-chillen on the bed who now had no teacher.

Willa-Mae thumped the flatiron onto the sleeve of Jefferson's shirt. "That means she's still not sure about this polecat. He ain't drug her to the altar yet."

"All the same, Mama," Angel said, "she looked like she was enjoyin' them kisses."

"Young, perty gal." Willa-Mae shrugged. "She's lonesome. Got no company of her own kind. It ain't surprisin' she liked it."

Angel's eyes narrowed. "Like kissin' a cottonmouth snake, if anyone ask me."

Willa-Mae chided her daughter. "Nobody asked you, I reckon. But y'all go prowlin' around snoopin', you gonna see an' hear things you ain't gonna like. You hear me now?"

"Well, I ain't goin' to school no more, Mama," Nettie declared.

Willa-Mae flared up like a hen with feathers all puffed out. "You mind the way you talk to me, Nettie! You sass me, an' I'll take a switch to your backside quicker'n you can figure who done it! You hear me, gal?" She swept her eyes over each of her girls in warning.

"Yes'm," Nettie replied, her lower lip quivering.

Willa-Mae turned to the whole group. "There ain't gonna be no more snoopin'! Y'all hear me now? That gal don't have the sense to know which gourd she ought to drink from. How's she gonna know that The Young Mister ain't nothin' but a thievin' snake come down here to run us out one family at a time?" The iron clanked down hard on the stove. "Leave it be!" She shook her finger. "An' y'all are going to school just like always!"

The chorus replied obediently, "Yes'm," and that was the end of the discussion.

All the same, the teacher play-child stayed out of sight under the bed.

☆ ☆ ☆

"They're good and married now, I guess," Molly said to Doc as the newly-weds stepped off the train.

"They've got the look about them, don't they?" Doc agreed.

Indeed, there was something older, deeper, about Ellis and Becky that made Doc and Molly stand back for a minute and marvel at the miracle of oneness that had changed children into adults in the matter of a little time away from home.

Ellis tipped the one porter at the Camden station, then glanced down at Becky—looked at her as if he held her to himself in that glance. He didn't seem overly eager to search the platform for parents and family. Becky was his family now, and that was as it should be.

Neither did Becky seem hungry to see anyone but Ellis. It was as though the return home was just another stop. As though everything dear and familiar to her had suddenly paled in the total knowing and being known of marriage.

It took a moment before the handbill pasted on the round column of the train depot evidently caught her eye. Then she nudged Ellis and tugged him over to the recently placed poster.

VOTE DOC WARNE
THE PEOPLE'S MAN IN CONGRESS!

Ellis smiled, and only then did he look around to find Doc and Molly.

There were embraces, but the hugs of reunion were no longer the hugs of children for parents. Equality had moved into place, and although the conversation was of things seen and done, wonderful unspoken secrets lay beneath every word on the way back to the farm.

Doc picked up the threads and reported the progress of the campaign. But about threats and warnings he said nothing at all.

✶ ✶ ✶

Birch's horse was Oklahoma born and raised, and the big bay gelding wanted only to cross the Arkansas River and get home again. The weeks in the strip mines had been enough to convince the animal that he had seen hell. Heaven was over on the other side of the Arkansas River. Birch did not doubt that if he laid the reins down and went to sleep in the saddle, he would eventually be carried straight to the middle of an Indian reservation in Oklahoma.

Birch tied the horse to a picket line each night as he bedded down under the stars. "Sometimes you just can't go home again, big feller," he said to the horse that he had never named. "I know that Indian of yours must have cared for you. But if I let you go back, he'd just lose you in another poker game. Then I'd be afoot, and you could end up back in a strip mine."

The gelding nickered low at the wisdom of Birch, a sound like a shudder of fear at such a thought.

The two had become fast friends. Both hearts were homesick and yearning for familiar pastures, but neither was able to return to what it loved best. They had wandered from farm to farm, trading work for food for a day or two and pressing on to someplace else. Heading north, they came to a sign pointing to Fort Smith. The horse turned his head as if to go that way, and then from there, perhaps, to Oklahoma.

Birch reined up the big bay in the center of the road and gazed down the fork toward Fort Smith. He thought of Trudy as he had done a hundred times each day since he left her. No doubt she was teaching at that fine school in Fort Smith. By now, no doubt, Birch was nothing but a memory to her. Maybe she had even come to despise him for the way he had left, for the fact that he could not keep his promise to her. No, it just would not do for him to appear on her front step like some hungry stray cat.

Max had been right all along, hadn't he? Trudy was not Birch's type. This was a polite way of saying she was way out of his league. It was one thing to talk about love, quite another to love a man without a home or family or future.

Still, heat waves shimmered from far down the road to Fort Smith, drawing him, calling him back. The big gelding sensed the slightest movement of Birch's leg and leaped forward down that highway at a gallop. Birch let him rip, then reined him in to an easy lope that ate up the miles.

By midafternoon Birch was once again on Garrison Avenue. Joseph Meyer's store was in plain sight three blocks up, but Birch did not continue up the broad street. He could not let her see him like this—a week's growth of beard on his cheeks, his tattered clothes and once-new army hat stained with sweat. For an hour he stood beside the hitching rail and gazed hopefully at the front of the store. He wanted to see her face, watch her move from a distance . . . and remember.

For his meeting with old Mr. Howard, Jefferson dressed in his Sunday suit. Willa-Mae had washed and ironed his shirt and pressed his trousers. His coat sleeves were too short, and his trouser cuffs came to the tops of his ankles. He wore his army boots, but he left his army hat at home and went to the old man's house bareheaded.

The Old Mister sat up on his porch along with the young Mr. Scott, who stood behind him. Mr. Scott had a funny smile on his face, like the look of a man who had been beaten at poker but had to keep smiling just the same. He looked at Jefferson with that hard smile as Jefferson came to the gate. The old man seemed nervous. His fan lay on the table. There was no iced tea within his reach. Miz Young, the house servant, was not here today. This meeting was private.

"Good afternoon, Mister Canfield," said The Young Mister.

"How-do," Jefferson replied, standing at his usual place outside the gate.

The Old Mister nodded. The muscles in his right cheek twitched. His eyes blinked rapidly behind his spectacles. "Well, Jeff?"

"Yessir." Jefferson had not asked for this meeting. Word had been sent to him to come.

"I suppose you're wonderin' why I sent for you?"

"It crossed my mind."

The Young Mister said, "Come on up here. Sit down."

Jefferson frowned at the gate. Did this young man know of the custom he was breaking, a custom as old as the days of slavery? Jefferson glanced at The Old Mister to make certain it was all right.

The old man tapped his hand on the arm of the chair impatiently. "Well, what are you waitin' for? You heard Mister Scott. Come on!"

"Yessir." Jeff pushed back the gate and climbed the steps slowly. He towered over the two white men on the veranda, but he could not bring himself to sit down. What if he had heard wrong? What if The Young Mister had not meant to ask Jeff to sit? Men had been lynched for less-impertinent acts than sitting uninvited on the porch of a white man.

"Well, *sit down*, Jefferson!" the old man growled.

Jefferson sat in a wicker chair that squeaked beneath his weight. It was not a chair built for a big man. Jefferson did not know what to do with his hands, so he clasped them in his lap as if he were praying and looked at his boots so he would not glance toward the plume of smoke that still rose from the woodpile.

The Old Mister sniffed. "I still smell the scent of burning oak, Jefferson."

"Yessir."

The Young Mister laughed—a short, sharp laugh. "Boy, you sure outsmarted us, didn't you?"

Jefferson frowned. He had indeed, but he would never say so. "Don't rightly know what you mean."

Another laugh. "Yes, you do." The Young Mister stepped around his uncle's chair and leaned against the railing. The smoke rose at his back, as though it were the smoke from his own anger. But his face did not appear angry. Only his eyes. "You don't have to play that dumb-nigger act

with me, Mister Canfield. You knew full well what you were doing, setting a torch to that wood. Uncut and unsplit, wasn't it? Not more than
five cords compared to the fifty you cleared and cut."

The Old Mister slapped his palm on the chair as if he were killing a
fly. "You made a fool out of Folz, Jeff. You know he don't cotton to that.
That man's got a long memory." *Whack!* He banged the chair. "Y'all
know I take care of my own. The Howards always took care of their people. You could have come straight to me instead of settin' fire to that pile
while Folz was still close. Well, you've surely lit a *fire,* boy."

Mr. Scott turned and glanced at the plume. "How long you figure that
wood will burn?"

"Oak burns long," Jefferson said quietly. "Another couple of days."

"Folz is gonna burn a lot longer," the old man snapped. "Now, what's
this all about?"

Jefferson thought to himself that the old man was right. Unless Folz
got his soul right with the Lord, he would indeed burn a long time, but
that was not a thing to say out loud either. Jefferson stuck with the details. "I been clearin' that land like you told me, Mister Howard, thinkin'
I could turn it into profit for the both of us. Thinkin' I could marry
Latisha after I sold that wood in Fort Smith an' split with you. That's all."

"Well, I ain't gonna split that wood with you," hissed the old man.

"No, sir. I been told that."

"But I'll pay you a dollar a cord for loadin' it an' takin' it on into Fort
Smith to sell." The old man leaned forward expectantly. "That's fair."

Jefferson swallowed hard. It was not fair, but it was something. It was
better than seeing his labor go up in smoke. "Yessir. I can do that for
you."

Silence. They had won *something,* but not everything. Was there not a
small victory for Jefferson in that? Did he sense their hatred of his small
victory?

"You're a smart man, Jefferson," said The Young Mister. "Just mind
that you're not too smart—both you and that gal of yours. Best let things
simmer down. Better to just get along."

"Yessir," Jefferson said. He left them on the veranda and went home
feeling real good inside.

CHAPTER THIRTY-NINE

The Weaning House

Trudy's class size had shrunk by more than half, and now the children who sat before her did not look up and smile into her face as they had before. The Canfield girls were present in body, but their spirits and minds were somewhere else. When Trudy attempted to draw them back to the present, they flashed her dark and sullen looks.

Latisha also seemed preoccupied. She worked with Little Nettie from the speller and scarcely answered when Trudy called her over to show her the flier she had received for her from the Tuskegee Normal and Industrial Institute.

"Well, ma'am," Latisha said—not *Miz True*, but *ma'am*, like she might address Miz Moss at the post office or Miz Digby. "I ain't interested in the Tuskeegee Institute, I reckon. Me an' my man are gettin' hitched soon, an' then I'm through with schoolin'. Schoolin' don't make a gal into a lady nohow."

The day wore on with whispers behind hands and silence at the recess. When Trudy blew her nickel-plated copper's whistle, no shrieks of laughter replied. The students simply lined up in orderly fashion outside the door and glared up at her.

There could be no mistake. Something dreadful had happened, shattering the safe little world Trudy had built around herself here at the school.

The hands of the big alarm clock dragged toward three o'clock amid the heaviness of some unspoken disapproval. At last Trudy called Little

Nettie to the side and asked her, "How is your play-teacher getting on with the play-chillen school?"

Nettie raised her nose. "She don't like the play-chillens no more," Nettie said with a haughty look.

Trudy touched Nettie's slim arm. It felt stiff and unresponsive, where before the child would have eagerly hugged her. "But whatever has happened?" Trudy asked, hardly able to bear the unexplained anger of her students.

"That teacher . . . she's goin' around with a mean man. She likes the mean man a whole lot more'n she ever liked the play-chillens. She lets the mean man kiss her, jus' like kissin' a cottonmouth snake! And he's gonna take all the play-chillen's land. He gonna send Billy's chillens to work in them Chee-cago slaughterhouses. He's stealin' away big Jeff's wood so him an' Latisha can't get hitched!"

Trudy blinked at her in disbelief. "The play-teacher . . . her beau is doin' all that?"

"Yes'm," Little Nettie declared. "An' I reckon a heap more, too. That's only jus' the little bit my play-chillen told me about. I reckon if I was bigger, I'd know more."

Trudy stared past her. Could Scott have done such things? Not Scott! He was educated and sensitive. Surely he cared about the tenant farmers of Mount Pisgah as much as Trudy loved their children. Some misunderstanding. There must be some mistake. A rumor, perhaps. Trudy knew all about rumors.

"Thank you, Nettie," she said. "I'm sure that play-teacher loves her students. I am sure of it—you'll see. There is some mistake, I think." She glanced up to see the cool stare of Latisha, mocking her hope that there was some misunderstanding. Latisha's brown eyes seemed to say, *"You don't know much."*

Shindler's store was the closest thing Camden had to an emporium. Ellis and Becky might pore over the Sears catalogue, but it was to Shindler's they went when it was time to buy. This particular trip was to pick out material for new dining-room curtains.

They had the use of a 1906 Sears runabout, and Ellis and Becky had polished the green enamel paint to a high gloss, and rubbed neat's-foot oil on the leather upholstery until it gleamed in the sun. The silver-gray carriage horse was only a little bigger than a pony, but he pulled the one-seated buggy with ease and even seemed to enjoy getting into harness. It took only a flick of the reins to set him to trotting, and Ellis and Becky laughed in the breeze of the ten-mile-an-hour clip that carried them into town.

Ellis turned the buggy onto Main Street, but the horse would have managed just fine without his guidance. In fact, it pulled directly to Shindler's and stopped. Ellis prided himself on his ability to hop out of the buggy, despite his wooden leg, and get around to Becky's side of the runabout to help her down. This time was no exception, and she was smiling warmly into his eyes as she set one foot on the step.

"Well, well," said a sneering voice from across the street. "Will you look there, Stewart? Don't it seem like she ought to be helpin' him?"

Ellis looked across the street to where two rough-looking men leaned against the wall of the barbershop. They stared back insolently. One was dark-haired and had scruffy whiskers covering a jowled face. The other man was thinner and taller. A cigarette hung from his lower lip almost as if he had forgotten it was there.

Both men stepped off the board sidewalk and sauntered over toward the buggy, flanking Ellis.

"Do you men want something?" Ellis said.

"Yeah, we want somethin'," the heavy man said as he held the horse by its headstall. "We want jobs. We want all the hunkies and the niggers to go back where they come from, and we want your old man to quit his spewin' about races livin' in peace."

"Okay," Ellis said coldly, "I got your message. Now, run along and tell whoever sent you that you did your duty."

"You high-and-mighty Mick," retorted the heavy man. "Where do you get off talkin' like that to me? You think you're better than me 'cause you come back from the war without no leg? Well, I was in the war, too."

"Becky," Ellis said quietly, "go into Shindler's. Now."

Becky stepped back into the buggy and sat down, moving toward the other side.

"I don't think he really understands the message, Stewart. Let's explain it to him."

The thinner man threw down his cigarette butt and lashed out with his foot at Ellis's wooden leg, knocking him to the ground. "Lie there and think about what we said," he ordered.

"Whatever you say," Ellis said, appearing to be compliant.

"See, Mac, he ain't so tough," Stewart observed, right before Ellis swung the lower half of his body as hard as he could and his stout wooden limb connected with Stewart's flesh-and-blood knee. With a howl of pain, the skinny man doubled up in the dirt, clutching his leg.

As Mac started to the aid of his friend, Becky grabbed the reins and flipped them sharply across the horse's back. The frightened animal lurched forward, and the buggy crashed into the heavy man, thrusting him under the runabout and knocking the wind out of him.

Shindler and several of his customers had come out of the store to see what the ruckus was about. "Ellis! Miss Becky! You want I should get the police?"

"Yes, Mr. Shindler, get them right now!"

But the two thugs were not waiting around for the police. Mac crawled out from under the buggy and helped a groaning Stewart to his feet. He shook his fist at Ellis. "This isn't the last you've seen of us," he threatened. "You tell your old man. You're all gonna be real sorry!" Mac clutched his ribs as he and Stewart lurched across the street, into an alley, and out of sight.

Trudy never stepped off the streetcar in front of Meyer's Dry Goods store. Birch waited and watched until Joseph Meyer pulled down the shade and locked up at five-thirty. The patrons in front of the saloon where he had stood all afternoon came and went without paying any attention to Birch. He was nothing more than just another vagabond, one of the hundreds of drifters passing through Fort Smith.

Birch had spotted men who looked like mirror images of himself. They walked up the street on their way to the rail yards, with scruffy beards, worn-out army boots, and tattered clothes. The boxcars of a thousand trains carried such human cargo in all directions. Compass points and places on a map did not matter anymore. An entire generation of young men had been plucked from the farms and thrown together into the sack of war, to be shaken until east and west were all the same. Now they were dumped out into the world again and many—too many, like Birch—could not find their way back home.

As Joseph Meyer boarded the trolley that would take him home, Birch sank to the curb. *Just to see her face! Only for one moment! Or to hear her speak . . .* He lifted his gaze to the telephone wires humming above his head.

Why had he not thought of it before? He stood and looked up and down Garrison Avenue for someplace where he could call.

"Is there a telephone in there?" Birch asked a stout-looking businessman just entering the saloon.

"Every place has got a telephone," the man admonished. "You been out in the sticks awhile?"

"Guess I have," Birch said, wishing he had thought of the telephone

weeks before. He pushed past the man and laid a nickel on the counter
of the bar. As the honky-tonk piano blared, Birch rang the operator and
asked to be connected to the residence of Joseph Meyer.

Three rings and a pause. Three rings and a pause. Then Sadie Meyer
picked up the telephone and Birch heard echoes of home in his heart.

"Missus Sadie, this is Birch. Birch Tucker!" he shouted joyfully above
the piano music blaring behind him.

"Birch! *Well!*"

Silence. Stony and unpleasant.

"You still there, Missus Sadie?"

"I am where I have always been."

"That's . . . real good . . . and Trudy? How is Trudy?"

"Very well, thank you."

"May I speak to her?"

"No, you may not."

Now Birch supposed he had been right. Trudy had come to despise
him. He couldn't much blame her. "Missus Sadie, I was meanin' to call,
but see, I just didn't think of it."

"I am sure Trudy is not interested in speaking with you."

He felt sick and desperate. "I just . . . *please* . . . just for a minute."

"She is not here." Sadie was adamant. "And I should think after all
the trouble and heartache you have caused my daughter, you would not
have the nerve to telephone and expect that you would be greeted by
cheerful, happy voices!"

In the background Birch could hear a door slam. "Who is it, Sadie?"
asked Joseph's voice.

"It is that Birch creature, asking to speak to Trudy," she explained.
Her voice became muffled, as if she'd put her hand over the receiver.
Then she came back on the line. "Well, Birch. Are you in Fort Smith?"

"Yes, ma'am."

"Don't come by. Trudy will not see you. She is quite settled in. *Quite*
over you! The nerve!"

"Yes, ma'am . . . I just wanted to—" Birch swallowed hard—"I was
hopin' to tell her I'm sorry it didn't work out."

"I shall give her the message." A long pause. "Good-bye, then." The
line went dead.

Birch replaced the receiver and groped his way to a bar stool, where
he sat down heavily.

"What'll it be?" asked the bartender.

Birch shook his head slowly. "Nothin'," he replied quietly. "Nothin' else, I reckon."

A voice to his right said, "That's where you got it wrong, Birch Tucker."

Birch raised his eyes to the smiling face of Deputy East. "Fancy meetin' you here."

"Just what I was thinkin' about you, Tucker. What's your business in Fort Smith?"

"Just passin' through."

East looked him up and down with a measuring glance. "You lost some weight since last we met. Hard times?"

"You could say so."

"Then you'll be leavin' Fort Smith right away?'

"I reckon I will."

East nodded. He pulled a handbill from his pocket and unfolded it. "Lookit what I got from up Missouri way." On the paper was a rough sketch of an enormous black man hurling a much smaller white man to the ground:

WANTED: TALL NEGRO, POWERFULLY BUILT. GOES BY NAME JEFF FIELD. WANTED FOR ASSAULT AND BATTERY. REWARD $200 . . .

There were details in the fine print that Birch skimmed before East put away the notice. "It might help you out to turn him in, if you know where we can find him."

"You just don't give up on it, do you, East?"

"'Fraid not."

"Why does this little matter make a hill-of-beans difference to you?"

"Just doin' my job." East sat down beside Birch.

"Well, you'll have to do it on somebody else. I told you once and then again. I don't know a thing about it."

East shrugged. "No matter. I'm just tryin' to do it the easy way. We've sent this notice out all over these parts. We'll find the buck nigger and bring him in, too. And then I got somethin' comin'."

"What? A promotion? A medal from the state of Missouri? The hand of a princess?" Birch shook his head in disgust. "Don't give me your speech about justice and duty again. In the first place, I don't believe in such things anymore. In the second place, it just doesn't sit well comin' out of a mouth like yours."

At that, smile still intact, East motioned, and two strong-armed men in work clothes stepped to flank him. "You don't know about power, little man," East threatened. "Jail? That's nothin' to fear. There's no power there. But what I got will make you tremble when you see it in action."

Birch looked from him to the two goons beside him. They were wearing identical smirks. "You don't say."

"You and that Jew-gal of yours. You know why she ain't here in Fort Smith no more?"

Birch stiffened. "What are you talkin' about?"

"We run her out. *We*. And we aim to run that Jew-father of hers out of business. Nigger-lovin'—" He swore and stared at his men. "Watch your back, Tucker," he warned. "We're just gettin' started down here. We need us a few good examples, and we're gonna clean this country out. You just might live to see it if you mind yourself."

Birch clenched his fists as East poked a finger hard into his shoulder. He understood everything now. It was not only the law in Missouri that sought Jefferson Canfield. It was the Klan.

✳ ✳ ✳

Three times Birch tried to talk with Sadie and Joseph Meyer by telephone. Each time they recognized his voice and the line went dead.

There was nothing he could do for them. No doubt they already were feeling the sting of a boycott against their business. Had they guessed that the reason for the boycott had nothing at all to do with whatever gossip had been spread about Trudy? Did they know that a decline in business and the loss of Trudy's position had everything to do with the Klan's desire to "purify the land"?

At least their lives were not in any danger. Not yet, anyway. But Jefferson Canfield was another matter entirely. Birch was certain that if Deputy East ever found Jefferson, he would not make it alive to face the courts of Missouri over the assault charge. East was hoping for a lynching, planning on making Jefferson Canfield an example to every other black family in the area.

True, East's information was incomplete. Jeff Field was not the same as Jefferson Canfield. But it was only a matter of time before some member of the Klan put the proper name together with Jefferson's enormous physique. A few more questions would show that he had been on that train from New York. If that happened, not even the federal marshal could stop what East and his kind had planned for Jefferson. Birch knew he must at least warn him. *"Heaven ain't so pretty,"* he remembered the Preacher saying to him about Mount Pisgah. Jefferson had not imagined that an ancient hell was encroaching on his paradise.

Birch did not look back at the lights of Fort Smith as he rode out to-

night. He listened for hoofbeats at his back, but the land seemed decep-
tively quiet and peaceful.

"*Watch your back,*" East had warned. But somehow Birch sensed that
all the darkness and danger lay ahead of him.

✳ ✳ ✳

Birch spotted the lights of two dozen lanterns gleaming among a colony
of tents and lean-tos clustered in a hollow beside a stream. The smell of
open campfires and fried catfish turned his head and made his mouth
water. He had earned two bits cutting fence rails. Maybe it was enough to
buy him a meal. With the shift in his weight, the horse believed that this
was the place Birch had meant to go all along. The big bay perked up his
ears at the nickering horses.

Nearer the lights, Birch could see a tall, lean man standing near a
campfire. His narrow shoulders moved up and down. He was harangu-
ing a group of men seated around the fire.

"Thinks he put somethin' over on me, does he? We'll teach that uppity buck nigger to mind his manners. Haulin' wood to Fort Smith is he?
We'll show him what a fire really looks like, from right up close, won't
we, boys?" The man nudged a burning log with the toe of his boot.

"Hello the camp," Birch called. The ragged men looked up from the
yellow light of their fire. Their expressions were dead looking, as though
their hearts had been eaten away, leaving only empty shells to be
warmed by the blaze.

The speaker spun around and confronted Birch with an angry look.
"This here's private. You got no business here 'less'n you come for the
meetin'.'"

"Not me." Birch shook his head. "Just smelled your catfish and was
hopin' maybe I could buy me a meal." He backed the horse a step as
other men rose to look menacingly toward the edge of the clearing.

"I'd advise you to go catch your own catfish, mister," the tall man
suggested with a grating voice. "We got other matters stewin', and strangers ain't welcome."

Birch did not reply. He scanned the group. Some of the men wore bib
overalls and a few wore suit coats. They were not all homeless men . . .
not all hungry.

"Get now!" warned the leader again. "Before we get annoyed."

"Right." Birch wheeled the bay around, letting the animal find his
own way back to the road.

That night Birch rode on past the flickering lights of farmhouses. He did not stop to make his bed until he was well out of the territory of the meeting that was taking place in the hollow.

✳ ✳ ✳

Tomorrow was the Lord's Day. Normally that would have pleased Jefferson, but there was so much to do!

The bonfire in Jefferson's field still burned into the night. There was light enough so that Jefferson worked on, tossing sticks of firewood into the back of the freight wagon. He had sent Hock up to the house three hours before. Jefferson did not feel the same weariness he had felt only this morning before the meeting with The Old Mister. There was time enough, if he left for Fort Smith after church tomorrow, to sell the first cords and return for the next load before the cotton harvest began. Although his profit was only a fraction of what he had originally planned on, it would be enough—enough to see him and Latisha through the winter months until they could plow and plant and bring in their own crop next year.

He sang loud as he worked: " 'Roll, Jordan, roll! I wants to go to heaven when I die, to hear ol' Jordan roll!' "

The light of a single lantern moved through the woods beyond the clearing. It stopped to illuminate the little cabin, then continued to where Jefferson worked.

The voice of Latisha called from beneath the big pine tree at the rim of the field. "Jefferson? I brung you vittles."

He pitched one more log onto the wagon and looked up to where she stood bathed in the golden light of the lantern. His breath caught in his throat when he saw her standing there. She was dressed in white, with a red shawl draped over her head and around her shoulders.

"What you doin' out so late, Tisha?"

"Smelled the smoke from the fire when I was in bed. Then the wind carried your singin' to my ears. Couldn't lay there while you was down here workin' so hard, Jeff."

"Does your mama know you come?"

She took a step toward him and stopped. "Mebbe she do." She held up the basket. "Got chicken here. Corn bread. And strong coffee."

"That's fine, Tisha. But you mind what I said an' don't come no closer to me with it." He gestured toward the wagon and the fire. "You see, my pappy ain't here."

"I see." She smiled shyly and took another few steps across the clearing.

"Hold now, gal. Stop right there. Put the basket down on that stump yonder, then get back home afore your mama wakes up an' sees you gone."

"Jeff?" She put the basket and the lantern down, then walked out of the halo of light until she was only a soft voice in the darkness. "I was *thinkin'* of you . . . wishin' . . ."

He swallowed hard and stepped back, grasping the back wheel of the wagon, wanting to tie himself to it until she was gone. "Go on back, Tish," he pleaded. "I got work to do before I can do right by you."

"I don't want to wait, Jeff."

He gripped the wheel harder. "Gal, I didn't know you could be so cruel. How am I gonna work if you talk so?" He turned away. "Get on out of here, Tish. It ain't the time. Not yet!"

He could hear her footsteps coming nearer, her skirt brushing the stumps of oaks and the grass. "I ain't goin' back, Jeff," she said, close enough that he could have taken her in his arms with only a few strides.

"Don't do this."

"I ain't goin' back to bed unless you make me a *promise*."

"What you want?" Both of his hands gripped the spokes. "Lord Jesus, I'm being mighty tempted."

"You gotta promise me if I go back tonight . . . like Ruth done with Boaz when she came to him on that threshin' floor?"

"I know that story, Tisha. She pert-near drove old Boaz crazy, too, I'm thinkin'."

"Mebbe she meant to." There was a smile in her voice. Suddenly she was behind him, wrapping her arms around him. *"Spread the corner of your garment over me, since you are a kinsman-redeemer,"* she whispered, repeating the words Ruth had whispered to Boaz. "An' then he asked her to stay with him all the night."

"He's more a gentleman than Jefferson Canfield." Jeff moaned at her touch and turned to hold her and kiss her. "What do you want from me, gal?" He could hardly speak.

"I want you to quit workin' long enough so we two can get hitched. Tonight."

He held her face in his hands. *"Tonight?"*

"Old preacher's up to your place now. I told Willa-Mae I'm gonna sin for sure if we don't get on with it. She sent Hock for the old preacher. Big Hattie went for my mama and papa, too." She kissed him again. "Don't ask me to leave you, Jeff. It won't take no time for the preacher to say the words, an' then I can help you—stay by you when you wake, be your pillow when you sleep. Tomorrow is the Lord's Day. After church we can take the wood to Fort Smith. We'll have a whole day together if'n we get hitched tonight. Ain't gonna be another Lord's Day till *next week*. I don't want to wait. . . ." Her breath was soft against his neck as she spoke. "Come to the house."

Jefferson rested his head on her shoulder. He felt weak like a kitten and strong as a bull all at the same time. "I reckon I knows how ol' Samson felt. I'm licked, an' that's the truth of it." He glanced at the half-filled wagon. "Reckon the work'll wait till after I done right by you an' the Lord."

She let her fingers play on the back of his neck. "I reckon it'll wait."

Willa-Mae had already washed and pressed Jefferson's uniform and laid out his medals so he could put them on in the proper order. While Jefferson bathed and cooled himself off in the creek, Willa-Mae sent her daughters down to the little log cabin in the woods to sweep and clean and place the feather mattress and the brand-new Eiffel Tower quilt in front of the hearth.

The wedding itself took hardly any time at all. The words were said, the prayers were prayed, and everyone yawned and went on home to bed as Jefferson and Latisha walked slowly toward the golden windows of their little house.

Sunday morning would come early, after all. . . .

The small white frame house had only one bedroom, a front room, and a kitchen. It was called the Weaning House by all the Warne family. In this house newlyweds lived out the first months of marriage and thus weaned themselves from the big family. Children were forbidden to climb the trees or play around the Weaning House. It was a private place, a secluded island in the center of the larger boisterous family.

Tonight Ellis lay with Becky in his arms and listened to the peaceful sounds of night. He could remember being Julie's age when his oldest brother, Matthew, had married and brought his bride to this very house. Young Ellis and his cousins had slept in the hayloft on the summer nights that year and had looked far off across the field of corn to where the lights of the Weaning House glimmered, then winked off. They had wondered about what magic the little cottage held and talked quietly among themselves about why anyone grown-up enough to live off by themselves would want to go to bed so early. Each of them vowed that when they were old enough to be married, they would stay up very late and play gin rummy until dawn!

Ellis glanced at the clock. Nine-thirty. The lights of the Weaning House had been off for over an hour. Becky lay against him, her breath deep and even with peaceful sleep. He imagined his young nephews wide awake up in the hayloft, pondering the dark windows of this place. *"Why do you suppose Uncle Ellis was in such a hurry to get to bed?"*

It was a mystery, all right, to anyone who had never been in love and lived in the Weaning House. This thought made Ellis chuckle.

Becky stirred at his laughter. "What are you thinking?" She laid her cheek against his chest.

"About when I was a kid," he answered.

"And?" She sighed, and the sweetness of her breath brushed against his skin. Such a small thing to bring such great pleasure. Even her sighs were magic.

"And . . . I'm glad I'm not a kid anymore." He stroked her back.

"Anything you would change?"

"I would never leave you again. Never go to war. I would marry you the day I knew I loved you so that not one minute would be wasted." He kissed her.

"And since there is no changing the past, what about the future?"

Ellis had been thinking about the future a lot lately—about his impending surgery, his time in the hospital away from this place and from Becky's touch. He smiled into the darkness. "You know, when you touch me I can feel it clear down to my toes."

She exhaled another sweet contented sigh. "Me too."

"I mean both sets of my toes—even the ones that are back in France."

She laughed. "Hmmm. I didn't know I was so powerful."

He turned to face her. For a while he simply held her. Finally he said, "I don't want to give up any time, you see? Not a day or a week or a month away from you. Your hands are better than a surgeon's. You soothe away any pain I might feel in a day. When I walk and the ache comes, I think, 'Well, there is always tonight. Becky will touch my wounds, kiss me, and make it all better.'"

She kissed him gently and then with fire. "Like that?"

"Uh-huh."

"Then stay with me," she whispered.

"Yes. Let's stay here awhile. No hospital. We can . . . help Pop. The campaign."

"And every night I can kiss you and make everything all better."

A breeze rustled across the tall corn in the field—the first sigh of a great storm that was gathering on the horizon of their lives. But tonight it seemed a whisper of peace as they loved each other in the seclusion of the little house.

CHAPTER FORTY

Jeff's Field

Trudy sat quietly beside Scott in the buggy. The Mount Pisgah congregation was already in full swing as they passed by on their way to the little white church. Trudy felt a twinge of envy for the joy of the voices that radiated from the little building. Perhaps she looked too long at the open front door.

Scott slapped the lines down hard on the back of the carriage horse. "You are quiet this morning," he remarked as they turned onto the main road.

"Am I?" Trudy had not stopped thinking of all the things Little Nettie had said to her. But how could she ask Scott the truth of the matter? Would he not guess that the children at the school had been talking to her? If what Nettie said was true, Scott would resent her for telling. If the child's words were false, Scott would be furious about the gossip of "pickaninnies," as he called them.

"What's wrong?" he asked, leaning close to her. "Got the Sunday-wanna-play-hooky blues?"

"Something like that." She studied the cotton fields, white for the harvest. "I was thinking . . . how I hate to interrupt schooling for the picking time." In truth, she was thinking of the children of Billy Jones. When school resumed after the harvest, they would not be in class. Did Scott have something to do with that?

"They put them all to work; that's for sure." He glanced at her. "Even the little ones. Ever seen the harvest? Little children out there dragging a seven-foot sack of cotton along behind. This sharecropping system is a throwback to the last century. I've been telling my uncle there are better ways."

Trudy did not reply. His conversation was coming dangerously close to telling her the very thing she dreaded to hear. Perhaps what she had considered progressive about Scott was merely a different way to justify taking the land from people like Delpha Jean Jones and her children. And maybe that of others as well.

The leaves were beginning to turn on the high slopes of Mount Pisgah. Soon the hillsides would seem to be on fire with the colors of autumn. Trudy had looked forward to seeing the seasons change in this place she thought was paradise. But this morning, as she gazed across the little rock farms at the foot of the mountain, she felt a rising sense of dread. More was changing in this place than just the seasons. She glanced at Scott, who seemed to be examining a thin plume of smoke rising in the distance.

"What is it?" she asked.

"Nothing." Scott slapped the reins down hard, urging the horse to a faster trot. "Someone who thinks he's outsmarted the powers-that-be around here. That's all." He fell silent, staring solemnly ahead to the church steeple of his uncle's church.

The remaining smoke from the distant woodpile seemed to be the topic of conversation among the men surrounding old Mr. Howard and the overseer Folz this morning outside the church.

The Old Mister was laughing. Folz's face was cold, resentful. His look sharpened as Trudy and Scott approached the group.

"He's outsmarted you, Folz." Mr. Howard chuckled, clapping the tense man on the back. "That's all there is to it. Set fire to that woodpile! Why are you takin' it so hard? He's a smart one, that Jefferson Canfield."

Trudy's head snapped to attention. *What did Nettie say about the teacher's beau stealing her brother's wood?* She lowered her eyes in an attempt not to appear too interested in the male conversation, which was as much a Sunday-morning ritual as singing hymns.

"He ain't as smart as he thinks," Folz said. "There are ways."

Mr. Howard snapped his fingers at Folz. "I'll tell you right now; I don't like your ways of handling Nigras. Us Howards have our *own* ways! You do what you like somewhere else, but not on Howard land. That Jefferson's a good worker." The old man noticed Trudy. "He's gonna marry that Latisha who helps down at the school. She's bright, too."

Trudy nodded. "She is . . . special to me."

Folz snorted. "Special!"

"It's their breedin'. Latisha and Jefferson are gonna give us another generation of good workers," continued the old man. "My granddaddy said the Nigras were no different than breedin' good cattle. You buy the right stock and breed it right, and you can get both strong and smart. Ain't that so, Teacher?"

Trudy's anger began to rise from deep within.

Scott stepped in to her rescue. "Miss Meyer is no authority on cattle, Uncle."

She felt grateful to him for saving her from such a dreadful question.

"Sometimes smart ain't all that good in a Nigra, though," continued the old man. He gave a big laugh and gestured toward the smoke. "You take that Latisha. She was down in that field Jefferson is clearin' for me." He leaned in to Trudy, then looked up at Folz, who was squirming beneath his employer's ridicule. "You heard about this, Miz Meyer?"

"No," Trudy answered honestly. She did not add that she wasn't sure if she wanted to hear it.

"Well then." The Old Mister seemed pleased to tell it again.

Folz looked furious but said nothing.

"So," The Man explained, "there they are clearin' that wood from the field—it's gonna be Jefferson's field to farm when he's through, so this buck figures he's got a right to the wood. But Folz here tells him and Latisha different. 'That's Howard wood,' Folz says."

"That's the truth, too. Shifty thievin' nigger," Folz threw in.

Trudy glanced at Folz and then away. Part of this dreadful Sunday duty was listening to such garbage and keeping her mouth shut like every other docile female in the county—although Trudy had to admit that the women didn't talk much differently.

"So Latisha just couldn't keep from speakin' up. Scott here says those darkie eyes of hers were flashin'. Ain't that so, Scott?"

"She didn't like it," Scott joined in.

The old man turned his focus on Trudy. "Those darkie eyes. Sullen. Sometimes they flash, and a man really knows what they're thinkin'." Again he turned to Scott. "You'll see it more. When they get wind of you bringin' a tractor onto the Jones place, they're not gonna like it one bit. You gotta watch out for the sullen looks. You see that look come your way, and you better watch your back."

Folz nodded. "That's what I'm sayin'. You let him get away with takin' that wood on to Fort Smith to sell. You're payin' him a dollar a cord. That Jeff Canfield is gonna have no respect. That's what I'm sayin'."

Howard shrugged and soothed, "Well, now, Folz . . . he didn't outsmart me, did he? I would have handled him right off. Old Jeff figgers that's his field. *Jeff's field*, he's thinkin'—he can't see it any different."

Folz was staring at the smoke as though he heard no more of Mr. Howard's monologue. "Jeff's field," Folz muttered. "Jeff . . . Field . . ."

By now the men had clearly forgotten that Trudy was standing there. She backed up a step as she recognized the dreadful realization that made Folz's hands trembled. Deputy East had spoken the name of the black man Birch had been with on the train. *Jeff Field.* The warrant was sworn out for someone by that name.

Could it be? Trudy wondered. Trudy had never seen the brother of the Canfield girls. He had always been working somewhere when she had stopped by the house. *Jefferson Canfield. Jeff Field.* The connection was too close not to be dangerous for the man.

She studied Folz. A fire seemed to be burning behind his eyes as he glanced at his horse. Would he ride away from the church? But ride where? To tell whom? Had the search for East's fugitive spread even this far into the country?

Trudy touched Scott's arm. "I'm going in."

"You feeling all right?" he asked.

She nodded. He couldn't know that just being near him and knowing the truth made her feel ill. She hurried up the steps of the church building. A number of people had already slipped into their places. Family pews were jealously guarded with handbags and hymnals, reserving them against some stranger who might accidentally sit there.

Trudy scanned the half-empty sanctuary, then consulted her watch. Two hours yet to go. She slipped out the side door to the brand-new lavatory building with real flush toilets. Old Mr. Howard was so proud of it. She went to the ladies' side and locked the latch. Leaning against the door, she considered staying here for the next two hours. The church bells tolled, announcing that everyone who mattered had better be in their places.

Trudy waited another five minutes as she considered what she must do. Should she slip out and run across the cotton fields to find the older Canfield brother and warn him that his name was awfully close to the name of a fugitive wanted by the Missouri and Arkansas authorities? Should she mention how Folz's eyes had brightened at the mention of *Jeff's field*? And should she tell them all that Mr. Howard's nephew wore a gold chain and a fraternity pin and that he also had a tractor? Should she tell Billy Jones's widow that her little family was being pushed off their land by a handsome young college graduate who planned to start small and see how far he could develop this land?

Don't show them sullen eyes. They'll run you off if you show sullen eyes.

But the folks of Mount Pisgah knew that already. Even Little Nettie knew more than Trudy knew. Trudy was the one who was learning something new every day, who was surprised when the word *nigger* tumbled out of the mouths of men in their Sunday suits as they waited to worship the Lord of heaven! Was this not the same sort of hypocrisy that had driven her family from the old country in hopes of finding refuge in the Golden Land, America?

Every resident of Orchard Street had shared a similar history. They had not been allowed to own the land they farmed in Russia. In Poland. Throughout all of Europe, it had been the same!

Trudy's heart was beating fast. *What day is this? What year? What century? What nation?* Somehow she had stumbled into an ancient evil, dark and sinister and cruel as death to those forced to live within its shadow.

Yes, she must warn them!

"Trudy?" Scott's voice called her outside the lavatory even as the hymn began: " 'The Son of God goes forth to war. . . .' "

"Trudy? Are you okay in there?" Scott asked. His voice showed genuine concern. He had not changed in his demeanor toward her. Perhaps he could not imagine the insight that had struck her like a lightning bolt.

"I'm not feeling well," she said. Indeed, she felt terribly ill. He had found her. Too late for her to escape now. It was too late to slip away to Mount Pisgah Church and look into the eyes of the man called Jefferson Canfield to see if he truly was the Preacher!

"I'll take you home if you like."

"Yes, I . . . need . . . to . . . go. . . ."

✳ ✳ ✳

Folz and the store manager had ridden off together down the road just as Trudy climbed into Scott's buggy. There could be only one reason, Trudy thought as she watched them go. The one telephone in Mount Pisgah was located at the general store.

Trudy closed her eyes and rested her head on the support of the buggy top as they approached Mount Pisgah Church. Could she risk having Scott see what was in her eyes?

The strong deep voice of a man boomed out from the little church, calling to Trudy's heart. "This is what God Almighty says about His Son. . . ."

What followed was different than anything Trudy had ever heard in Mr. Howard's church.

> "He shall not judge after the sight of His eyes, neither reprove after the hearing of His ears: but with righteousness shall He judge the poor, and reprove with equity for the meek of the earth!"

Scott whipped the horse beyond the range of the voice.

Surely this is not the same God preached about in the other church, Trudy thought. Then she remembered how old Mr. Howard had declared that the Good Book was an effective method of keeping the slaves in line. Was there not also some warning in that book for men who had power over other men's lives?

She could not think of that now. She could only hope that the sermon would not be over before she got rid of Scott and slipped back to Mount Pisgah Church.

Even before Scott's buggy wheels clattered back down the lane from Trudy's cabin, she had slipped out of her pale blue Sunday dress and put on her gray hiking skirt and comfortable shoes. She paced impatiently, knowing that she must not go out until he was well out on the main road. She dared not risk Scott seeing her slip into the little church, yet every minute seemed precious. Over an hour had already fled past since she had known what she had to do.

At last she ran down the path and past her little schoolhouse. There had been no footprints in the dirt that first day, but these precious lives had left their mark on her heart.

"God of the needy," she prayed as she ran, "God of the poor, God of justice, help me not be too late!"

No breeze stirred to carry the message of the Preacher to Trudy as she ran. Only her own breath and the beating of her heart sounded in her ears.

The sun glinted on the closed windows of Mount Pisgah Church. She heard no voices raised in singing. Could they be gone so early? Trudy stopped in the middle of the dirt lane and hoped that they were only praying inside. That the silence did not mean they were gone.

She walked forward, straining to see inside the windows. The door was closed. The church was empty.

Trudy was too late!

Jefferson and Hock had finished loading the wagon before church had ever begun. Willa-Mae and Latisha had cooked up food enough for two days of travel. Church services had let out early so Jeff and Latisha could travel the road toward Fort Smith.

Latisha sat proudly beside her new husband on the bench seat of the wagon. She passed the Eiffel Tower marriage quilt to Willa-Mae for safe-keeping and received a stack of older quilts for when they camped down by the river.

"We're gonna be stopped early, I reckon." Jefferson looked up at the sun. "We'll camp down by the river, mebbe fish some. Then we jus' sit back like rich folks."

Latisha laughed and tucked her arm through Jefferson's. "Y'all see. He's spoiled already."

Jefferson closed his eyes and inhaled as if he were ready for a nap. "We're gonna sleep late, an' then when we feel like goin', we'll take the road to Fort Smith an' sell this here load."

Hock patted him on the back. "I took your mama up to the Poteau Mountains huntin' possum. We come back a week later, an' she was already in the family way with your oldest brother!"

"Hush your mouth, old man!" Willa-Mae scolded. "How you go on!"

Hock ignored his wife and pointed skyward. "There gonna be a full moon tonight, Son. Good moon for plantin'." He winked broadly, and Willa-Mae nudged him hard in the ribs until he said, *"Oof!"*

"Get outta here," Willa-Mae ordered Hock, who walked away strutting and humming a strain from "Bringing in the Sheaves." Willa-Mae shook her finger at Jefferson. "You be good now, boy, or I'll whup you for sure. Don't be workin' Tisha too hard."

Jefferson knew his mama had not meant that the way it sounded, but Hock cackled at her all the same and then ducked when she came flying after him.

Jefferson grinned and Tisha ducked her head shyly. She hid her face against his arm as he clucked the mules, and the wagon groaned and creaked out of the yard.

Mount Pisgah General Store, the sign read. It was Sunday, but the store appeared to be open. Two horses, a buckskin and a bay, were tied to the hitching rail outside the building, and the door stood ajar.

Birch considered this a blessing. He was hours later than he'd intended, and every farmhouse around the area was empty. He supposed that everyone in the community was in church. Perhaps Jefferson was in church, too, but Birch needed directions to find it. He intended to ask the way to the Canfield farm, as well.

The store was a false-front wooden building dating back at least a hundred years. Birch was greeted by the aromas of cheese, tobacco, and new leather harnesses. Hames and chains and handsaws hung from hooks. Shelves were stacked with overalls, denim shirts, and canned goods. Barrels of flour rested on the floor, and in the corner was an old wall telephone and a man speaking loudly into the mouthpiece as the store clerk looked on.

"I'm tellin' you, Philby! I think we got your man down here! Big buck nigger, name of Canfield. That's right! He's trouble all right! You'd best bring a bunch with you. It's gonna be like treein' a bear!"

Birch stepped back from the entrance to the store out of sight. He recognized the man on the telephone. Tall and lean and tough-looking as old bones, he was the same one Birch had seen at the campfire last night!

The urgent voice continued. "He is takin' a load of wood up the road your way. Yep . . . that's right. . . . Well, I wouldn't wait none. He's a smart one. . . ."

Birch had heard enough. He mounted his horse and cantered away before the lean man ever knew he had been overheard. Half a mile later, he pulled his horse to the side of the road and scanned the broad fields of cotton and stands of corn shocks in the fields.

In the distance a single dark plume of smoke rose, as though someone was burning brush. Clearing land. The scent of oak was in the air. Birch clucked his horse to a slow lope and headed for the smoke some miles distant.

It was like a nightmare. Trudy's legs felt weighted as she ran the last mile to the Canfield house. As she topped the rise, she could see Hock and Willa-Mae Canfield and their daughters sitting around a big table that had been moved out into the yard. They were eating dinner together. But where was their son? It was Sunday. Did Jefferson Canfield work in the fields on Sunday?

Willa-Mae shielded her eyes against the afternoon sun when Trudy waved to her. All heads pivoted toward Trudy, who strode down the hill toward the house. Her students stood obediently as she reached the gate, but they did not—would not—look at her when she called.

"Missus Canfield!"

Willa-Mae seemed embarrassed by her arrival. She looked at the food-laden table. It was only proper to invite the schoolteacher to sit down and have a bite to eat with the family. But it was clear the family did not welcome her.

"Won't you come in, Miz True?" Willa-Mae said stiffly. "Come set a spell and have a bite."

Trudy was breathless. Her lungs felt seared and legs ached. She scanned the fields wildly, then let her gaze linger on the bristling stacks of wood down in the lower field adjoining the cotton field. "Missus Canfield—" Trudy gasped and clutched the gate as though she might faint. "Where is your son?"

Willa-Mae exchanged a look with Hock. "Why you wantin' to know, Miz True?"

"Because—" she looked from one to the other—"I think . . . there may be some men hereabouts who think he is someone else . . . someone they would very much like to put in jail."

"Jefferson?" Hock exclaimed. "What anybody want with Jeff? He ain't done nothin' since the day he come home from the war, except work down there in that field clearin' and cuttin' wood."

Trudy put her hand to her head. What if she was mistaken? What if what she had seen on Folz's face was nothing more than anger over what had happened down there in the field?

"Well, I . . . I . . . there is a deputy in Fort Smith who is looking for someone named Jeff Field. Over something that happened across the border in Missouri."

"Jeff ain't been to Missouri," Willa-Mae said firmly. "But come on, now, and set a spell." She gave her girls a look that warned them to be polite. "You come all the way out here to warn us; that's right kind of you, Miz True." She swung back the gate and took Trudy by her elbow as though she feared Trudy would fall down. "You been runnin'?"

Trudy felt foolish. If Willa-Mae was unconcerned, perhaps this was only Trudy's imagination. But there were some things she knew she had not imagined. *The tractor. The Jones farm.*

"You know that terrible man, Folz," Trudy began.

A stunned silence fell over the group. "We knows the overseer," Willa-Mae said.

"He's angry." Trudy studied Little Nettie, whose eyes displayed resentment. "He's angry about the wood."

Hock laughed. "Figgered he would be. Ain't nothin' that man can do, because Jeff done talked to Old Mister about it. Got it all arranged. He's takin' the wood on in to Fort Smith to sell."

"Fort Smith?" Trudy croaked. Images of East rose to her mind. *What if East spots Jefferson? What if East—?* "When did he leave?"

"About two hours ago." Willa-Mae leaned in close. "You feelin' all right, Miz True?"

"I just wish he were here. You see, I was hoping to meet him. Wondering if we met before on the train, you see."

"Ain't likely. Jeff don't ride in the white folks' cars," Hock said. "Set your mind to rest now. Jeff is gone off with his new wife. You know Latisha."

"He and Latisha are gone together?" Trudy sighed and rested her head in her hands. Certainly she had been chasing around the countryside for nothing. She was the only one concerned.

"Yes'm," said Little Nettie. "Jeff done dressed up in his uniform, an' him an' Latisha got hitched last night. Slept down to the little cabin that we'uns cleaned up, too."

"I'm glad to hear it," Trudy said to the child, grateful that finally Nettie was speaking to her again. "And I have some news for you about your play-teacher and her play-chillens."

"Is that so?" Nettie stepped close to Trudy and stared right into her face.

"You were right about the play-teacher's beau, and she is all finished with him, Nettie. You hear me? You can bring her out to play again."

At that Nettie threw her spindly arms around Trudy and hugged her. "That's right nice. I been missin' her. Jeff brung her home to me from Paris. It were a shame to put her away." Then, "You want to see a picture of my brother Jefferson in his uniform, Miz True?"

Trudy nodded, and Pink and Nettie raced into the house to bring the Eiffel Tower quilt and three pictures of Jefferson Canfield.

"Ain't he big and handsome, Miz True?" asked Angel.

Trudy held the photographs in her hands and nodded. She could not make her voice work. *The Preacher!* Strong and tall in his uniform as the French general Pétain presented him with the Legion of Honor. He was a hero. But what had he come home to?

Trudy raised her tearful eyes to Willa-Mae. "I *have* met your son, Missus Canfield. On the train." Her tone was ominous. "We must stop him . . . warn him . . . before he reaches Fort Smith."

"What? What you sayin', Miz True?"

"They want to arrest him. Take him back to Missouri. *Please!* I would not have run here to tell you if I were not afraid for him."

Hock stood up and straightened his bent back. "Him and Tish got a two-hour start." He placed his hand on Willa-Mae's shoulder. "I'll hitch up the wagon. Y'all clean up dinner."

When Doc's Apperson chugged to a stop in front of Tad O'Brien's home, both O'Brien and his cousin Hugh Flannery were waiting out front on the porch. Doc was pleased that both men were present. He had hoped that the invitation to come to O'Brien's would have happened much sooner, but better late than never.

O'Brien and Flannery were wealthy leaders in the farming community. O'Brien ran an immense feed-and-grain business, and Flannery owned one of the largest dairies in the state. Like Doc, both men were of Protestant Irish stock. Because the two men were so influential, Doc was grateful that they had agreed to meet with him to discuss his campaign.

"Come in, Doc," greeted O'Brien heartily. "'Tis good to see you again." The three were soon seated in the study, and Doc prepared to discuss his campaign's needs.

"And how is your political ambition working out?" inquired Flannery.

"Much better than I was thinking it might," Doc said. "Seems a whole lot of people don't want to be buying what Hopewell has to sell."

Flannery and O'Brien exchanged looks that to Doc seemed very odd, as if the fact that his campaign was going well displeased them in some way. "Of course," he added hurriedly, "that's not to say that I do not stand in need of your help. You touch businessmen in the cities that I have not been able to reach. What I'm hoping is that you can get me their ears, if only briefly."

There it was again—that strangely unhappy glance. "It seems," O'Brien said, "that there is a misunderstanding here. We asked you to come out here today to suggest that you *withdraw* from the race."

Doc was stunned. Here were two men of his own generation who had seen what the terrors of racism could do to innocent people. Did they really want him to leave the election wide open for Hopewell?

"I am not understanding your meaning" was all Doc could manage.

"Why, it's very simple," remarked Flannery. "You are on the wrong side of the issue this time around. We are not wanting more immigration to this country, nor any foreign entanglements either. All our boys who died—including your own, Doc—what did they accomplish? Did they die to open this country to those who will take bread out of the mouths of their little brothers and sisters? No . . . the dead would not be thanking you, Doc."

O'Brien took up the argument. "We've been working to be accepted as good Americans all these many years, and we've come far. Would you be seeing that effort all undone for the sake of such as the ragged and dirty immigrants? Catholics, every one! Doc, you'd best be thinking of your own. Leave off this election nonsense. Besides," he added, "you'll not win anyway, I'm thinking."

"And where do you come by that information?" Doc asked.

"Plain as day!" spouted Flannery. "Would you not be knowing that

Hopewell has the support of the Klan? Five million they are in this country, and two hundred thousand in this very state. They won't let you win,
Doc! But worse, do you wish for them to be lumping us together with
those other Irish?"

Doc stood up. He towered over the other two men, and even though
he spoke softly, he controlled himself with difficulty. "And what other
Irish would you be meaning? Those who have no courage, perhaps?
Those who would turn informer to save their own worthless hides?"

"Now just you wait a minute, Doc Warne." Flannery started to rise.

Doc shoved him back down in the chair, almost pushing the chair
over backward. "Don't be standing until after I've gone, or I'll not be responsible for what may come of it. Now you will hear what *I* have to say.

"We, of all people, should know the evils of men who condemn others because of their race or religion. I, who saw my own father murdered,
have not forgotten, even if you have. Racism is surely the worst of all sins,
if such there be, because it teaches otherwise good men to do evil to others and call it just. Abuse, vile treatment, wicked dealings, even burnings
and hangings—things that no man would call right if directed at him or
his family—he justifies if they are aimed at another race, those he calls
inferior to his own."

"But surely it's natural—," O'Brien began to argue, then subsided at
the menace of Doc's bulk looming over him.

"Aye, natural as sin and death! From the mouth of hell it comes, to
set one sinner against another because of his religion or his language or
the color of his skin. But you are wrong about the Klan and others of
their slimy breed. They'll not be winning this time. America is not
Ireland."

With that, Doc stormed out of the house, slamming the door behind
him.

O'Brien flung open the door and yelled, "You'll be getting no support
from us!"

"I'll not be wanting anything from you," retorted Doc loudly as he
reached his car. "There are plenty of good people, including our president, who see things the same way I do."

"Have you not heard, then?" Flannery called. "Wilson has collapsed
on his speaking tour. They say he's had a breakdown because no one is
taking his side. He may even die. Then who will you have on your side?
Polacks and niggers, and that is all. Watch yourself, Doc Warne! Trouble
is hanging over your very head!"

CHAPTER FORTY-ONE

Last Night in Eden

The mules were hitched to the wagon. Willa-Mae gave strict instructions to Lula that she was to take all the young'uns down to the schoolhouse, just like Miz True said. They were to lock the doors and keep the lights out and not open those doors for anyone at all.

Trudy rode in the back of the wagon. Hock drove and Willa-Mae was at his side. The five Canfield sisters stood in a bunch and waved after them as they left. Little Nettie raised the arm of her porcelain teacher doll in farewell.

That had been an hour ago. Now Trudy fretted as the wagon jarred over every bump and seemed to creep slower than a walk. *Can't these mules go faster?* Hock had placed two shotguns in the back under a blanket. Trudy eyed the weapons as the blanket slipped, and the sunlight glinted on the worn stocks. Then she raised her eyes and gasped as the dust from a rider billowed up behind them on the road.

"Someone is coming!" Trudy spread her skirt over the weapons. The rider came on fast, his hat pushed back on his head, the way Scott wore his Stetson. Trudy peered through the dust behind the wagon. But it was not Scott. Tall and lean, the man carried himself with ease on his mount. His saddle was a heavy western one. His left shoulder tilted slightly up. Just like . . . could it be?

"Stop the wagon!" Trudy declared.

Willa-Mae swiveled toward her in astonishment. "What's wrong with you, Miz True?"

Trudy could see the questions in Willa-Mae's eyes. There was no time to lose, was there? *Stop the wagon?*

"It's *Birch*!" Trudy rose to her knees and waved to him. He took off his hat and waved back as the long-legged horse made up the distance between them.

Trudy had not realized she was crying until Willa-Mae handed her the corner of her apron. "You got dust all streakin' down your face."

"Oh, Missus Canfield!" Trudy said happily. "It's Birch! You see? He can go ahead. Find Jefferson and Latisha for us!"

Willa-Mae punched Hock. "Pull up them mules! You hear the lady!"

He obeyed, but Trudy noticed he didn't do it willingly. She could tell what he was thinking. *Who is this Birch fella? After all, Miz True had kept some doubtful company, hadn't she?*

Birch slowed his mount to a gentle lope. His face lit up when he saw Trudy. He rode to the side of the wagon and, his eyes full of her, sat aboard the prancing animal and simply gazed at her in silence. There was no time to talk of what had gone wrong, not a moment to think of such things.

Trudy wiped her tearstained face. "It is good . . . to see you again, Birch," she managed.

"The girls told me . . . Miz True Meyer, they said. The teacher gone with their mama and papa to find Jefferson." He glanced at Hock. "Your boy's in a heap of trouble, Mister Canfield. I'll go on ahead. How much time they got on us?"

"Over two hour now," Hock replied grimly. "Soon the sun be goin' down, too."

"Did he plan on goin' all the way to Fort Smith tonight?" Birch patted the lathered neck of the horse.

"No, sir," Willa-Mae said. "He and his bride gonna camp down by the river, he say, somewhere between here an' there. They has a big wagonload of firewood. You can't miss the tracks—they'll be deep, I reckon, where he pulls off the road."

If Birch could not miss the tracks, then Trudy imagined that it would not be difficult for others to follow as well.

"You got a gun, Mister Birch?" Hock Canfield asked.

"No gun."

"Miz True." Hock motioned for her to take out one of the old shotguns and a box of shells. "Reckon you might be needin' that."

Birch nodded and took the weapon. His eyes lingered on Trudy's face. "I thought I'd never see you again," he said quietly. "Almost gave up hopin'."

"Me too."

"Well then—" he touched his fingers to the brim of his hat—"we'll talk about it later."

At that, he spun his horse and galloped off down the road.

Hock watched him go. "What's one white man gonna do against that bunch?" he asked. Then he turned to Willa-Mae. "That horse of his is pert near give out. Reckon we need the Lord, Willa-Mae. Need the Lord to help us find Jeff before them other folks does."

The smell of the river drifted inland through the woods to cool the low places in the road to Fort Smith. The scent of moss and reeds mingled with the aroma of someone cooking Sunday supper far away.

Jefferson's stomach rumbled. He laid his big hand on Latisha's head. She lay sleeping on his lap. The sun scraped the pines, and the gravel road was all in shadow. There was a likely looking place to turn off the road ahead. A narrow, seldom-used wagon track wandered back from the main highway. It would take them part of the way to the riverbank, Jefferson thought. He pulled the lines a hard left, swinging the heads of the mules toward the cool of the river.

The wagon bumped and rocked over the slight berm before the iron-rimmed wheels found the grooves that kindred wheels had left behind, and the pulling became easy. Tisha slept on, not waking until Jefferson pulled back on the lines and the groaning journey ended at a lane that ran out into an unfenced pasture. Beyond the tall brittle grass of the autumn field lay a narrow strip of woods that sloped down to the very edge of the river. Through the trees, Jefferson could see the moving sparkle on the murky current of the wide Arkansas River. Sunlight broke through the trees, sending a shaft of light down on a place beneath a large hickory tree.

Latisha opened her eyes and looked up at Jefferson. "Why we stoppin' here, Jeff?"

He stroked her cheek. "I'm hungry." He gestured toward the river. "We can make camp here."

She lay motionless with her head on his thigh. "Listen." The wind made a peaceful rushing sound, like water through the trees. Birds phrased short songs and were answered by other birds singing farther off. "I never heard nothin' so pretty." She sighed and wrapped her fingers in his.

"Sounds just like woods always sounds."

"No, it don't. I never heard it before . . . never really heard it before last night. Now everything sound all different. Like the air singin' to my heart."

He hummed an answer, as if to say he heard it, too. They sat that way together for a long time, as though there were no measure of time, no circle of minutes or hours or days that could close around them and squeeze them from this timeless moment.

Maybe hours passed like that. Jefferson did not know. The mules flicked flies with their tails and jangled the harness, and after a time, Latisha sat up and stretched and Jefferson set to making camp.

It happened so quickly that for a minute Trudy could not comprehend why the wagon suddenly lurched to the side, rolling her from her place and sending Willa-Mae crashing into Hock.

The little man grasped his five-cent straw hat as it tumbled off his head. The mules instinctively halted at the first feel of the broken wheel scraping against the rocky road.

"Oh, Lord!" cried Willa-Mae. "Lord, have mercy!"

Hock and Willa-Mae climbed down as Trudy jumped from the sagging left corner of the wagon bed. The iron rim had broken free from the wooden wheel. Spokes pointed out like barbs from the ruptured hub.

Kicking the dirt, Hock shook his head. "Got no spare. Sent both spare wheels with Jefferson. Haulin' that wood, I figured he might have need with such a load."

"He have need," Willa-Mae said softly. "Oh, Jesus! He have need, but it ain't a wheel he needin'."

The mules swung their big heads around to try to see past the blinders as though to ask, *"Are we going on?"*

Trudy rested her arm on the bed. The shotgun caught her eye before the broad-rumped old jenny stamped her foot impatiently.

"Ain't nothin' for me to do," Hock said, shaking his head, "except to take one of these here mules an' follow after that feller."

Willa-Mae raised her hands and looked heavenward. "Oh no, Hock! If those men finds you on the road by yourself, I'm gonna lose me a husband today. Remember Billy! Oh, Hock! Don't forget what they done to Billy! With his wife an' chillens sittin' right there in the wagon, they take him out an'—"

Hock slammed his hand against the wagon. "That's all I been thinkin' about is Billy! You wasn't there, woman! I know what those men aim to do to my boy! I seen what they done to Billy, an' I can't stand back an' let them do the same to my son! Not without a fight!" He grabbed the shotgun.

"You can't go alone, Hock," Willa-Mae begged. "They ain't gonna hang you if you got Miz True ridin' in the back of your wagon, but—"

He kicked at the wheel. "I ain't got no wagon, now does I?"

Trudy touched his arm. "No. But you've got two mules. I can ride one."

Hock snorted. "No white gal gonna ride a mule bareback cross-country."

Trudy looked him in the eye. "You're not going on without me. Willa-Mae is right. There is the smell of blood in the air." She turned to Willa-Mae. "You go back to the schoolhouse. Stay with the girls. The men won't bother you if you meet them on the way. They aren't interested in hurting a woman." Then to Hock she said, "I'm going with you. They'll think twice if there is a schoolteacher there to witness everything they do and say."

Hock nodded. "They think twice when they see a white woman ridin' a mule along the road with an old black man to the side of her."

"We'll just tell them the truth. You were driving the schoolteacher to Fort Smith when the wagon broke down. Let me handle it." Trudy felt the minutes ticking past. "Please, Hock. Unhitch the mules. Let me carry the shotgun."

"You don't know nothin' 'bout no scattergun."

"I do," Trudy insisted, wresting it from his hands. "I learned to shoot by killing blackbirds for a penny apiece in an orchard near Fort Smith."

He reluctantly agreed as Willa-Mae prayed, laying her hands on Trudy's shoulders and then Hock's. "The Lord go with y'all." She was weeping as she said it. "It's okay to be scared, Miz True. But don't let 'em know you's afraid. Like any wildcat, they'll scratch you to pieces if they thinks you is scared of them. Be *brave*, gal. An' they'll turn tail and run, because they ain't nothin' but cowards theirselves, hidin' under white bedsheets an' swoopin' down in a bunch to kill folks who ain't done them no harm."

Hock stripped the mules of everything but collars and cut the lines back, tying them short for reins. He hefted Trudy onto the gentle gray jenny, then climbed aboard the black mule. "We'll make time now," he said, studying the sinking sun. Then his eyes locked on Willa-Mae's face, as though he might not see her again.

Willa-Mae pressed her cheek against his leg, "Bring our boy home again, Hock Canfield. The Lord is goin' with y'all now!"

The mules trotted side by side as though they still pulled the wagon. Hock scanned the road, pointing out the heavy tracks of Jefferson's load and then the tracks of what seemed to be dozens of horses. "Too many critters on the highway for Sunday," he muttered. Then he kicked his mule to a faster gait.

Trudy's jenny naturally matched the speed of its partner stride for stride as the afternoon shadows lengthened into the deep blue of twilight. They met no other riders coming or going in all that time. It seemed as though all the tracks were riding to converge at one unknown place for one single purpose.

Jefferson was content with the place they had chosen to stay for the night. As he built a lean-to, he talked about the nearness of night and how rocks in the road and washouts would have made it unsafe to travel farther. He and Latisha worked together, making a pleasant camp in the woods halfway between the river and the meadow. Jefferson judged the work and the location and said that even if it wasn't for the coming night and the washouts and the rocks, he would have wanted to stay here. And then he told Latisha that maybe they would not leave in the morning after all but stay on in this sweet Eden for a while before returning to the real world to peddle their wood.

As if to verify that thought, Latisha put one hand on Jeff's arm and a finger to her lips. He followed her gaze to where a doe stood watching them from the far side of the clearing. They remained motionless and silent and so did she, judging the creatures who had invaded her world. Jefferson slid his arm around Latisha, and with that movement the doe knew that somehow it was safe to graze. She moved forward cautiously into the tall grass, a fawn following after her. The doe lowered her head but kept her eyes on the man-couple.

Jefferson started to turn back to his work. Latisha plucked his elbow and nodded toward another shadow at the edge of the clearing. A large buck studied them before joining his mate in the meadow. Each couple regarded the other; then their attention turned back to themselves, as though no harm could come where there was love.

And there was love here in this place.

"It's like we's the only two people left in the world," Jefferson said. "An' the Lord put us here in Eden for a while. Them critters knows we ain't got a mind for hurtin' them tonight." He looked to the river. "But I expects them catfish in that river need to be caught and fried up to make this place perfect."

Doc slammed into his house, startling Julie's kitty out of its nap on the small braided rug that lay just inside the door. The cat made a clawing dash for the staircase, skidded into the banister, and charged up the steps three at a time.

"The blackguards," Doc muttered loudly. "Those evil-hearted, backstabbing—Molly!" he yelled, pushing into the kitchen. He almost ran her down, since she was already coming the other way.

"Doc," she said, almost breathless. "Doc!"

"Threaten us, will they?" Doc was scowling fiercely. "Backing of the Klan, has he?"

Molly grabbed both Doc's arms and shook them, pleading with him to look at her. "You . . . you've already heard?"

"Heard what?" Doc replied, finally noticing the look of fear and dread on his wife's face.

"The warning." She gasped. "The terrible threat! Julie found it on the door of the barn. Oh, Doc, it was not there two hours ago. Someone has been watching the house—they saw when you left, and they came here again!"

"Easy now, Molly darling," Doc said, sounding calmer than he felt. "What does this threat say?"

Big tears welled in Molly's eyes and rolled down her cheeks. "Oh, Doc," she finally managed, "it said, 'This is your last warning. Quit now, or what happened to the father will happen to the son!'"

CHAPTER FORTY-TWO

Night Fires

Bright moonlight penetrated the canvas of the lean-to. The woods resounded with the calls of night birds and animals that slipped from their nesting places to forage.

Latisha lay with her head resting on Jefferson's chest. He stroked her back.

Touching his mouth with her fingertips, she sighed. "What you smilin' about?"

"Thinkin' what my pappy said." He chuckled at the memory of their send-off. "I'd be right pleased, I think, if you'd be in the family way by the time we get home."

She raised her head to look at his face and kissed the cleft of his chin. "You know what my mama says about the moon an' young'uns?"

"No."

"She say that chillens made in the full of the moon gonna be gal-babies." She smiled into his eyes. "You want our firstborn to be a gal-baby?"

Jefferson hummed his thought as he took her face in his hands. "Long as she is as perty as her mama. I'll take a whole passel of gal-babies if you say they ain't gonna look nothin' like me."

"An' I was gonna say the same to you about havin' little boys. I want them all to look like you." Latisha squeezed his arm. It was so big around that she could not circle it with both hands.

"It's all that wood," he said. "Splittin' wood."

"An' I want all our boy-babies to be as big and strong as their daddy."

He touched her face. "There ain't nothin' in this world that matters to me like you do, Tish. All the while I was cuttin' the wood, I was thinkin' how life don't mean much if a man don't have a woman he can love an' work for. I reckon I'm like the wolf or the eagle—ain't but one mate in my life but you. When I said them words last night at the wedding, 'Till death do us part,' I didn't mean 'em. Not even death. You hear me, gal? There ain't never gonna be nobody but you for me. And if'n I should die—"

"Don't talk of such things." She put her hand to his lips to stop the thought from being spoken.

"No. I gots to. You know life ain't a certain thing. We like the grass, the Good Book says. Now, I want to tell you somethin'. Listen . . ." He fell silent. The rushing of the river and the wind blended into one voice. "You hear that river rushin' by?"

"I hear it, Jeff."

"Life is just like the river. It passes so quick an' carries a man away just like a little twig goin' into the sea. I seen men pass jus' like that. They wasn't hardly growed. They had no chance to know a woman like I knows you. But my life feels almost complete because of you. I got every blessin' the Lord can give any man, I reckon, an' I'm content. I want you to know that. Not even death can part my heart from yours."

"Then we'll take them words from the vows. 'Not even death!'" She burrowed her face into his neck. "An' if I go before you, or you go over yonder before me, we'll meet beside the Jordan. I'll be waitin' for you, Jeff—in a place like this with the air so sweet like pines an' the wind in the trees an' critters lookin' up unafraid when we walks past."

He rolled over, cradling her in his arms. "Yes," he whispered. "We make that our wedding vow. I can see the place now. Ain't no need to fear what come upon us. Heaven's a real place, an' as long as we be there together, I ain't feared of nothin' this old world gonna bring me." He kissed her gently. "The Lord's buildin' our house in just such a place beside the river. He promises us a mansion, an' I ain't gonna doubt His word on the matter."

They lay together as the fire and the moonlight cast moving shadows through the trees.

The breeze stirred the curtains at the head of the bed. The faintest sound of chimes floated in with it. *Wedding bells,* Ellis thought sleepily, *I can still hear them ringing the wedding bells.*

A few moments later, a second set of bells added its voice to the first, and almost immediately a third set joined in as well. Ellis flicked open his eyes and stared at the dark ceiling. Peal after peal rang out from the nearby Presbyterian church. Ellis jumped out of bed, alarming Becky. "What is it, Ellis? What's wrong?"

"I don't know," he said abruptly. "Must be a fire somewhere." He fumbled in the dark, trying to locate the harness for his wooden leg.

Becky lit a lamp and Ellis pulled on his denim work pants. By then, someone was hollering up at the window of the Weaning House. "Ellis!" the voice of his brother John demanded. "Ellis! Pop says hurry! He got a call from Jim McBride. The Catholic church is on fire!"

"I'll be right down," Ellis called back.

Becky was also dressing hurriedly. "You don't have to come, Becky," Ellis said, knowing that she would anyway.

"You and John take the buggy and hurry on," Doc ordered as they met him out in the yard. "I'll take the car and pick up the others."

Soon the little buggy was moving briskly up the road toward the church. Ellis and John filled up the seat while Becky and a wide-awake Julie clung to the cargo platform on the back.

The bells bounced from hillside to canyon and back until the entire Ohio countryside seemed to be clamoring for all its inhabitants to wake up. Over the rise, Ellis could see a glow in the night sky. It reminded him of the cross burning he and Becky had witnessed, only this time about half the circle of the horizon was illuminated with a fierce orange glow.

"Get moving, Ellis," John urged. "It looks like the whole thing is blazing already. How do you suppose it happened?"

Three Model T trucks roared past them, carrying more people to fight the fire. In the back of one, Ellis could see his mother and two of his brothers.

The bells in the steeple of St. Francis Church also joined in the alarm. Their clanging was a strange counterpoint to the roaring of the flames, now clearly audible from the top of the hill.

"Someone must be trapped inside!" Becky shouted. "Hurry, Ellis, hurry! They need help!"

The little cart horse was already giving his maximum effort, catching the wild alarm of the night. He shifted leads from left to right and back again, casting terrified looks over his shoulder as if a nameless terror were in close pursuit.

Nothing could have prepared Ellis for the view of the church from the top of the rise. The front half of the building was already engulfed in flames, and the ringing of the bells took on a frantic note. "How can anyone still be alive in there?"

A double line of men was passing buckets up from a pump in the yard. As Ellis watched, the man at the head of the row threw a bucket of water against the side of the church. The fire responded to the puny insult with a terrific burst of combustion that shattered the window right over the men's heads. They sprinted out of the way as a shower of hot glass shards rained down on them. It was clear that the battle to save the building was already lost.

A shaft of flame erupted up the steeple of the church like a volcanic explosion. Sparks spewed forth into the night sky, raining down on the firefighters as they looked on helplessly. The roar of the fiery air as it reverberated up the chimney formed by the steeple reminded Ellis of a blast furnace in a steel mill.

"Can't we save whoever's trapped inside?" pleaded Becky.

The bells were clanging wildly now, as each new torrent of scorching air rocked them back and forth. "It's all right, Becky girl," soothed Molly. She hugged Becky on one side and Julie on the other. "I said the same. 'Tisn't anyone inside, you see. It's just the old church building its own self calling for help, pleading for someone to save it."

Another blast of blistering air shot through the steeple, producing one more frantic peal from the bells. Then the roof over the bell tower caught fire, and flames leaped past the roof into a fountain of flaring destruction.

At the rear of the structure, some men were still trying to move some of the church's furnishings out to safety. Ellis moved to join the group that included his father and brothers, but he was stopped by Jim McBride. "Don't be trying to go in, lad," urged the neighbor. "The roof could go at any time, and the boys'll be needing to dash out to save their lives. Don't chance it for a few prayer books more."

Indeed, only a moment later the cry went up: "The roof! The roof is going! Everyone out now!"

"Get back!" Paul Mazurki urged. "It could go like a bomb!"

The circle of helpless onlookers scattered to a safe distance just as the roof sagged in the middle and swayed. From the steeple came a wrenching noise and a terrific crash as one of the huge bells, its supports burned away, fell into the interior of the church.

An audible groan went up from the throats of the crowd as the steeple gave up the fight at last and bent over sideways to fall into the middle of the flaming roof. There was a great whoosh as the remaining windows blew out in explosions of flame.

In seconds nothing recognizable remained . . . other than scattered heaps of burning rubble.

✳ ✳ ✳

Could it be the moonlight?

Nudging Jefferson from deep sleep, the brightness penetrated his consciousness. Tisha was curled up beside him. He sighed at the touch of her. Then the scent of kerosene jerked him wide-awake.

He opened his eyes. The brown canvas of the lean-to was glowing too much to be illuminated by mere moonlight. The peaceful sounds of the night birds were eclipsed by an ominous silence.

He sat up. Were the woods on fire? "Wake up, Tish!"

She sat up, blinking against the light that seemed almost like daylight, only it moved around the lean-to. Shadows swept across the canvas above them and behind them.

She cried out as the crunch of footsteps sounded outside. "Jeff!"

Jefferson leaped from the bed and scrambled out.

✳ ✳ ✳

Latisha covered her ears as cries and thuds resounded outside the lean-to. The laughter of what seemed like a thousand voices covered the rush of the current and the sigh of the wind.

"Jeff!" Tish screamed. The light became even brighter, as though flame would touch the canvas and devour it. "Jeff!"

He did not answer her. Instead, the flap of the lean-to was thrown back. A flaming torch was thrust into the space, and a man's voice whined, "Well, ain't that sweet! Lookie here what we got, fellers! We done ketched us a big buck nigger and his little whore!"

Latisha pulled the quilt around her and scooted against the back wall of the lean-to. Only the canvas separated her from other voices.

"What are we gonna do with her?"

"Why, she can watch what we do to uppity niggers! Watch us slice him open and hang him up from that there hickory tree!"

"Jeff! Jeff!" Latisha cried. "Lord! Oh, Lord! Help us, Jesus!"

The figure holding the torch stooped down and peered in. White and ghostly, the peaked hood of the Klan garb concealed his identity. His amused laughter stirred the cloth that covered his face. Eyes glinted from behind the slits. "Well, little nigger-gal, you comin' out?"

"What you done to Jeff? *Lord Jesus!* What happened to Jeff?"

"Jesus ain't the God of niggers," said the ghost cruelly. He reached in and grasped Latisha's leg, pulling her, kicking and screaming, from the shelter.

The entire camp was surrounded by a white circle of Klan members holding torches, guns, and clubs. Like a horseshoe with flaming nails, they moved in. Jefferson lay tangled in a thick rope net, unconscious. Latisha kicked the brute who held her and then crawled to Jefferson. She touched his head through the net. He was bleeding badly but still breathing.

The ring of phantoms closed in until she could see the boots of working men and the shoes of city men beneath the hems.

"Please don't hurt us. . . . Don't hurt Jeff," she pleaded, throwing herself over Jefferson.

The first phantom leaned down close until his white mask was inches from her face. He grabbed her by the hair and pulled her head back until her throat was exposed like a lamb for slaughter. He ran his finger across her neck, making a slow splitting sound. Those around him laughed the nervous laughter of anticipation.

He hissed, "That's what we're gonna do with your man, honey. You can watch if you want, or close your eyes. . . ." He gave another low chuckle, as if her terror delighted him. He jerked her hair until she cried out from the pain. "And after we're gone, you can cut him down from the tree. Take his black hide home and nail it on the barn door, if'n you like to."

"Please!" Latisha wailed. "Don't do this, mister! *Don't!*" She clasped her hands to beg him. He kicked her hard on the shoulder, sending her sprawling on her back.

He leaped up and raised his arm to point across the meadow. The wagonload of wood stood at the end of the lane. "Get that wagon, boys! This nigger likes big bonfires, I been told! Let's pull that wagon out in the meadow and light her up so we can have light to work by!"

Every other man broke from the circle and ran toward the wagon. Picking up the tongue of the wagon, they cheered one another on, rolling the load off the road and into the pasture.

Ellis stood by the buggy, next to Becky. He watched Doc walk away from the smoldering ruins of the church. On one side of Doc was Mazurki, his face blackened and his normally bristling eyebrows all but singed completely away. On Doc's right was their neighbor, Jim McBride. McBride's hands were burned, and he held them stretched out in front of him as if even brushing them against his pants leg would be too painful.

"Come over to the car," Doc was saying. "I've brought my bag. I'll give you some ointment for those burns and some pills you'll be wanting for later."

"I'm leaving this place," said Mazurki abruptly. "I won't live where this thing can happen."

McBride stopped suddenly. "No," he said grimly. "I'll be after hunting down the swine who did this. And when I find them, there'll be hell to pay."

"And hell will be collecting, too, I'm thinking," said Doc.

"Meaning what?" demanded McBride.

"Meaning that the old troubles will be starting all over again, and only the devil will be the winner if they do. We can't be running away," he said to Mazurki, "but we can't go after taking the law into our own hands either. Isn't that what you've been telling me that I must speak against?"

"Yes, but this breaks all bounds!" said McBride angrily.

"That it does," agreed Doc. "All the more reason that we must put the bounds back, stronger than before. Catch them, arrest them, and lock them up for the good of all. But, Jimmy—" he looked McBride squarely in the eyes—"take the root of revenge out of your heart before it grows up and crushes us all. Now, let me be looking after your hands."

"Take *your* hands off me, Doc Warne," said McBride fiercely. "You are no true friend of mine!" He stalked off toward his car, calling loudly for a drink and someone to drive him home.

"He don't mean it, Doc," offered Mazurki. "His hands . . . they hurt him. And his pride . . . he helped build that church."

"Ah." Doc sighed. "If you remember, Paul, so did I. But I hope you're right. Now, more than ever, we must surely all be pulling together. We'll whip these night-riding dogs yet."

"Come on, Pop," said Ellis. "Hop on. You're too tired to drive back. Let Becky and me give you a ride home."

"No, thank you both," Doc said. "Molly and I will be wanting to talk."

☆ ☆ ☆

Like a lantern, the full moon rose over the mountains to illuminate the tracks in the road. Hock followed the trail easily, pulling back on the mule as the trail branched down a wooded lane toward the river.

Beyond the treetops an eerie glow lit the night sky. The smell of burning oak wood was thick, and a plume snaked skyward from some enormous fire.

Hock moaned and rested his head in his hands. "My boy! My boy! We be too late, Miz True. Look there. That be a fire from Jeff's wood, I reckon, lightin' the world for a mile. That ain't no campfire! Lookit them tracks—gotta be at least a hundred of them varmints gone down that road! They got my Jefferson, an' we too late to stop 'em! Oh, Lord Jesus! Why life be so hard? Why ain't they hanged me instead of my boy?"

Trudy stared at the orange glow of the fire. It was not more than a mile off the main road. Was Birch there? Had he found Jeff and Latisha and tried to warn them? What had happened? "Maybe we're not too late," she said, fingering the trigger of the shotgun.

"What you sayin'? The only way we have of not bein' too late is if'n the Klan was here an' us an' Jeff was somewheres else."

"I'm going back there," she said, not waiting for an argument.

"Then I reckon I am, too. My heart done bust already. Don't matter if I die tonight."

Trudy whirled on him. "Yes, it matters! You are not coming, Hock Canfield! You want Willa-Mae and those girls of yours to get thrown out like Billy's family? Now stay back here! Hide yourself good until this is over!"

"You ain't goin' back there without me."

"Then you'll die, too! Don't be ridiculous! They won't hurt me. Latisha is my student. I won't sit back when they might . . . do unspeakable things to her!" Trudy kicked the mule hard, pulling away from Hock. "Now *think*! I'm tellin' you, Birch and I can handle this. You stay back, or I'll tell Willa-Mae you came on an' killed yourself out of despair!"

Hock's narrow shoulders hunched forward. He wept openly. "I ain't no kinda man. They kill me for sure, hurt Willa-Mae an' my babies if I goes. An' then what? Oh, Lord, what am I gonna do? They *make* me a nigger. I ain't nothin' at all."

"Get out of sight," Trudy hissed. Then she nudged the mule up the lane by the eerie light of the distant fire.

CHAPTER FORTY-THREE

Crossing Over

The Apperson clattered up the hill. Julie waved from the backseat, but neither Ellis nor Becky waved back. Only the tired and sleepy carriage horse nodded wearily in reply. The stump of Ellis's leg was aching, and he had shooting pains in the foot that was no longer there. "Nobody won," he muttered.

"What did you say?" Becky asked softly, rubbing the knotted muscles in the back of his neck.

"Nothing really," Ellis replied. "I was just remembering something a German officer and I talked about in the hospital in France."

The sound of a quavering *ah-ooh-gah* from the Apperson's horn reverberated through the autumn air like the dying cry of an immense bird. It was repeated again and again. "What's Pop up to?" Ellis wondered. "He must have engine trouble or something. Or else there's some old cow that refuses to get out of the road."

Becky shivered, even though the night was not chilly. She clutched Ellis's arm tightly. "Something's wrong," she said. "Drive faster, Ellis. Something is terribly wrong!"

The cart horse finally struggled to the top of the rise overlooking the valley of the Warne farm. Far below they could see the driving lamps of the Apperson, but their feeble glow was not what attracted attention. "They've set the corn on fire!" Ellis whipped the startled horse into a lope.

Pushed by the rising breeze and already acres in size, an ugly orange monster was devouring the fields of Warne grain. As the buggy bounced

and skidded downward along the rutted road, Becky and Ellis watched
with horror as the unsatisfied flames reached out glowing tentacles toward the barn and the house.

The Klan members had not bothered to conceal their vehicles. Trucks
and Model Ts were jammed in a line along the lane. Horses were tied to a
picket rope between two stout trees. Anyone who passed along the highway could have seen the distant fire, then walked a few hundred yards
back and found the transportation for the gathering.

"Y'all come! We gonna lynch us a nigger tonight!"

The Klansmen's voices rang through the woods, sending a chill of
dread and horror up Trudy's spine. Their laughter was shrill and de-
monic, as though the mouth of hell had opened and spilled out rejoicing spirits of darkness to dance a witches' sabbath around the bonfire.

She shuddered and remembered the words of Willa-Mae. *"Don't let
'em know you's afraid. . . ."* Trudy slipped off the mule, catching it by the
reins and leading it the last quarter mile through the woods. She tied the
jenny to the low limb of a tree and dropped down to creep fifty yards to
the edge of the clearing. Clutching the shotgun, she crouched behind a
stand of elderberry bushes to watch the ritual.

Jefferson Canfield was still alive! His hands were tied behind his
back, and he was on his knees beside the great flaming heap of wood in
the center of the field. A net covered him, as though he were some great
and terrible beast the white-robed priests of hatred had captured and
prepared to sacrifice to their hideous god. Half a dozen Klan members
ringed him. They were taking no chances. Rifles were all trained on his
body.

Twenty yards away, Latisha was also held at gunpoint. She, too, was
kneeling. Her hands were clasped, and she begged the faceless creatures
for mercy. They laughed and taunted her, shoving her back with their
boots and telling her they might spare Jefferson if only she would lick
the dust from their toes. She clasped the legs of the one who said this to
her. Trudy moaned as the girl licked his boots, only to be kicked back.

Latisha! Poor child!

These creatures had no intention of sparing the life of the Preacher.
No degradation would convince them. No heart-wrenching debasement
of human dignity could change the outcome of this human sacrifice!

Trudy turned her eyes to the flaming cross that blazed at the center of
the oak wood. The brilliant light cast pointed shadows like dark barbs
behind the men who gathered in the field. A rope was tossed over the

high limb of a hickory tree and tied off. The noose at the end made a swaying shadow across the Klan members who jeered up at it. Soon it would be too late! *Too late!*

Where was Birch? Did he watch from the safe ring of darkness, too? What could she do, one woman alone? *Lord God . . . the God of Jefferson Canfield, help me! Where is Birch?*

Hock trailed behind Trudy at a safe distance. Here were the vehicles that had carried the murderers of his son. He dismounted and tied the black mule at the end of the picket.

Walking around the last vehicle parked on the lane, he recognized the freight truck used by Mr. Moss, the manager of old Mr. Howard's store. So Moss was in on this! Hock scanned the picketed horses, easily finding the big buckskin gelding ridden by Folz. Beside that horse was the shorter bay, which the young Mr. Scott rode in his fancy riding boots and English saddle.

Hock shook his head in rage. These men had covered their bodies and faces in white robes of righteousness, but under those robes there could be no darker souls than their own! Had they killed Billy? With the murder of Billy Jones, had they managed to cancel the tenant contract? How many more men would they slaughter in these woods?

He leaned heavily against the fender of the freight truck. The back contained four one-gallon canisters of gasoline. Hock looked toward the glow of the Klan fire and then back at the gasoline cans.

He clenched his fists. *"I ain't a nigger!"*

By the time the buggy reached the bottom of the grade, the church bells were once more pealing the alarm. *"Turn out,"* they called. *"Evil has come upon us again!"*

The horse's legs pounded like the pistons of a steam engine as Ellis made the turn into the farm lane. A gust of wind swirled a hail of sparks across the road. The buggy swung wildly toward a ditch, then righted just in time as the animal shied from leaping flames along the fence row.

As they skidded to a stop, Ellis jumped off, unmindful of his wooden leg. He tumbled over on the ground, making Becky cry out. But he was on his feet at once, hobbling toward the house.

Molly was coming down the front steps, her arms loaded with photographs.

"Where's Pop?" Ellis shouted.

"Out in the barn, setting the animals loose," she told him. "Can you help him?"

Tongues of flame darted up from the cornfields, like blazing pitch-forks hurled into the air. The wind grew stronger, heading directly to-ward the house. A cloud of dense, dark smoke flooded the yard. The barn and the path leading to it disappeared in the murk. Ellis was seized with a fit of coughing, and his eyes burned and streamed with tears. He wished he had his gas mask back again.

When the smoke parted, the roof of the barn was already ablaze. Through the open doors Ellis could see his father furiously unlatching stall gates and shooing the animals out into the pasture. Ellis moved to help him, but his father waved him back. "That's the last!" he yelled.

At the well in the yard, Matt and John pumped furiously, and Luke was directing a stream of water onto the roof of the house. "Come on," Doc said. "We'll help your mother carry out her precious things."

"I can't move fast enough, Pop," Ellis said. "Let me stand under a window and you can pass things out to me."

A family Bible from the old country, a quilt made by Molly's great-grandmother, the wall clock that was the first thing Doc and Molly had purchased for their first home in America—all these things made the journey out through the window to Ellis's waiting arms, and then brother Mark transported them to the safety of the open yard.

Neighbors were arriving by the car- and truckload. Paul Mazurki climbed a ladder on the far side of the house to get onto the roof and beat out sparks with a wet burlap sack. Other friends took turns spelling the brothers at the pump. Jim McBride, his hands wrapped in bandages, stood in the center of the road and directed newcomers to useful places.

But none of their efforts could stem the overwhelming advance of the flames. When another wave of smoke broke over the crowd, Doc or-dered everyone to get back till they could breathe.

When they could see the house again, the roof was on fire. "Stay back!" Doc said. "We've done all we can do."

Resigned to watching her home burn, Molly stood surrounded by children and grandchildren in the midst of a heap of belongings. "Doc," Ellis heard her say, "do you think we should count heads to make sure we're all safe?"

Each little family totaled up its members and reported to Doc. "I guess that's it," he said. "Everyone is accounted for."

"Where's Julie?" Molly said nervously. "*Where's Julie!*"

Little Howie spoke up. "I told her she shouldn't do it."

"Do what, Howie?" asked Doc urgently.

"Julie said her kitty was up in the bedroom, and she had to go get it out."

All eyes turned toward the window of the third-story bedroom, just under the burning eaves. Becky screamed and pointed. Julie was framed in the opening!

"Help me!" the little girl called. "There's fire on the stairs! I can't get down!"

There was a rush for the house. Ellis stood by, feeling useless. He knew he could not dash up and down the stairs, could not do anything except stand and watch as others saved his little sister.

"Help me!" Julie sobbed. "Hurry!"

"What's taking so long?" Molly demanded. "Why don't they have her out yet?"

John staggered back out the front door. "Too much smoke." He gasped. "Fire on the stairs . . . nobody can breathe."

More neighbors ran into the burning home to drag out an unconscious Doc and lead the others, blinded and choking, to safety.

"Get a ladder!" someone yelled.

"Julie! Julie!" Molly begged. "Oh, God, help us!"

Ellis's eye lit on a coil of rope and an old horseshoe lying on the ground. Seizing them both, he yelled up to Julie, "Duck, Julie! Duck down!"

The one-legged man, who never expected to be the team's pitcher ever again, hurled the most important strike of his life as the horseshoe, trailing the rope behind it, sailed squarely through the center of the window.

"Tie it to your bed!" Ellis shouted to Julie. "Now I've got this end. Slide to me, Julie. You can do it!"

A moment later Julie was in Ellis's arms, hugging his neck. "Look," she said, unbuttoning her jacket. "You saved me, and I saved my kitty!"

The wide sweep of the Klan leader's arm pointed at Jefferson. It was time. The net was removed from the big man as gun barrels prodded him to his feet. Blood streamed down over his torn shirt, and for an instant Trudy envisioned him fighting as he had that afternoon in Missouri.

But tonight the Preacher did not fight. He turned his gaze on Latisha and called to her in a voice that resounded through the forest: "Raise your head, gal! Remember the promise—"

The fist of the leader came hard across his mouth, but Jefferson would not be silenced. "Remember the vow! I'll be waitin'! Tell Mama

I'll be waitin' over yonder with Widdie an' the other young'uns! Tell her, Tisha! Tell her I done gone to my Father's house! Tell Pappy I ain't afraid!"

Latisha pulled herself erect. She struggled to stand, only to be shoved back to the dirt. "Yes, Jeff! Yes, Jeff! I'll be lookin' for you, Jeff!" She was sobbing, choking on the words as they rushed from her throat in a torrent of grief.

Where is Birch? Trudy could not wait. Her hands trembled as she stood up from behind the brush. She checked the twin barrels of the scattergun.

No one even glanced her way. All eyes were wild with hysterical anticipation at this, the last act in a man's life. Hands clapped together in a rhythmic pounding, and the chant drowned out the last words between Jefferson and Latisha. *"Die, nigger, die! Die, nigger, die! DIE, NIGGER, DIE!"*

The leader turned to face his followers. He raised his hands to call them to order. "Fellow Klansmen! Brothers!"

Was there something familiar about his voice?

Trudy's heart was in her throat as she clenched her teeth and strode forward toward the wall of robed backs. She held the scattergun like a soldier's weapon, ready to use it.

Suddenly the leader, who stood beneath the rope, looked toward her. The peak of his hood tilted quizzically as though her march amused him.

Jefferson bowed his head as the rope was slipped around his neck.

The leader pointed his finger toward Trudy. "Miz Trudy Meyer! Hey, boys! We got us a Jew-gal come here to watch the hangin'!" He laughed as a hundred heads turned to gape at her.

She recognized the voice. "East! David East! Let him go!"

"What you intend to do when we don't?" East shouted back.

At the sight of Trudy marching toward her own destruction, Birch made his move. Clothed in the white Klan robes he had been using as his pillow for months, Birch stepped from behind the leader of the mob.

"What are you gonna do, East?" he asked in a quiet voice.

"The river is deep," Deputy East replied, turning just as Birch raised the shotgun and placed the barrel hard beneath East's chin.

"You don't say?" Birch was smiling behind his mask. "Deep enough for your headless body, I reckon," Birch threatened, ripping away the mask and grasping the leader in a strong headlock until he cried out.

Moments elapsed as East's followers gaped at Trudy, even stepping aside as she passed through them.

Latisha sat up and cried, "Oh, Miz True! Oh, Teacher! Praise God somebody come!"

Trudy rushed to Latisha's side.

"Let the buck go!" East commanded.

"Smart man," Birch menaced, jabbing the weapon tighter beneath East's neck.

"Smarter than you think, mister." East was trembling. "How do you and that gal figure on getting your niggers out of here? And where do you think you can run that we won't be there waitin' for you?"

Murmurs passed through the crowd as the noose was lifted from Jefferson's neck and the rope around his wrists was cut away.

Then, from the back of the circle, a single rifle raised above the head of Latisha Canfield, drawing a bead on Jefferson. Latisha leaped to her feet, throwing herself in front of the gun as the finger squeezed the trigger.

The explosion of the rifle fire echoed across the countryside, hurling Latisha backward by the force of the blast.

Another explosion ripped through the trees down the lane. Bits and pieces of an automobile and a truck were thrown skyward on a cloud of rolling fire.

"They're blowin' up the cars!" someone shouted, and the stampede began. Men ran wildly across the field toward the flaming rubble of their vehicles. The frantic neighing of horses turned loose increased the panic of the Klan. Tripping on their robes and on one another, they filled the night air with curses as Jefferson dashed across the meadow to gather Latisha in his arms.

"Ah, no," Birch moaned, giving East a shove. "Not the girl. Oh, Lord." He slammed the rifle hard against East's head, sending him reeling to the ground. Birch ripped off his mask and robe and threw them down to cover East. "I've called the federal marshal, East," he muttered to the unconscious man. "Looks like when you come to, you're going to be facin' several counts of murder." He kicked the Klan leader and then stepped over him.

The last of the Klansmen had disappeared into the woods. Hock Canfield ran from the far side of the clearing toward where Jefferson cradled Latisha in his arms as though she were a child and he were rocking her to sleep.

"I blowed up their things and let their horses go," Hock stammered. "Lord told me what to do." His eyes flitted to his son and to Latisha. "Oh, Jesus, *no*," he groaned.

Trudy was kneeling beside the couple. Latisha's eyes were still open. "We've got to get her to a doctor!"

"Tisha, oh, my Tisha," Jefferson whispered. "Don't leave me now! Please don't—"

"Got to, Jeff." Latisha's voice was barely audible. "Can't call back that river. That river carry me on to the sea, like you say."

"No, gal! Not yet! I can't live a whole life without you, gal!"

"It ain't so long, Jeff," she breathed. "You remember what we say? Look, Jeff . . . I'll meet you over yonder. I can see . . . see it clear . . . there's our house . . . *oh!*" The pain of dying coursed through her for an instant.

Jefferson wept with her as though his soul were being torn from him as well. "Don't leave me, Tish!"

"Be brave." Her hand raised to brush his cheek. "Get on, now. You go across the river. Live awhile, an' then . . ." Latisha's eyes flickered. She smiled gently as she looked past him. "There He is, Jeff. His hands out. I ain't afraid—look there—" The light left her eyes; she gasped once and was gone—a willow twig swirling on a strong current carried away to the sea.

Jefferson hung his head and wept. He did not let go of her.

Trudy touched his arm. Her eyes met his in mutual grief.

He rolled his eyes to Hock's face. "Oh, Pappy," he moaned. "The best thing I ever done for her is to let her go on while I gotta stay behind an' live in this old world!" The massive shoulders shook with sobs.

Birch stood over the Preacher. He had brought the big bay gelding from where the horse had been tied down by the river.

"Preacher," Birch said, his voice firm, "Preacher, listen to me! You can't stop here!"

"I can't leave my Tisha."

"You gotta get out of here, Preacher," Birch urged. "She knew—you gotta get across the state line to Oklahoma."

Jefferson raised his face to Birch, pleading.

Birch shook his head. "Listen. This East feller's got a warrant out for you from Missouri. I've got a federal marshal coming for East. He'll go to jail for this—"

"Moss and Folz and Young Mister Scott was in on it, too—I seen their horses," Hock volunteered

"But all the same," Birch warned, "you can't stay here now. That's not the whole tribe of monsters. These few might be hauled to the federal court, but there are plenty more who will remember. Chase you down!"

"Let them!" Jefferson let his tears fall on Latisha's face. "They do me a favor if'n they kills me now—"

Hock shot a glance toward Trudy as he knelt beside his son. "Don't talk so. A man can't kill himself from despair." He reached out for the body of Latisha.

Jefferson buried his face against her for a moment. He threw his head back and moaned again. "Don't take her, Pappy. I gotta hold her. See, she ain't cold yet, Pappy! Lemme hold her."

Little Hock put his hands on the big hands of his son. "I'll take care of her, just the same as you done for Billy. Let her go, Jeff. She's gone now. She's waitin' for you over yonder."

"Yessir," Jefferson said in a small voice. "I reckon." He passed the body of his young bride to Hock, who held her as he would hold a child. Hock smoothed back her hair, and his chin quivered.

"Take my horse," Birch instructed. "He's a good one, Preacher. This is an Oklahoma horse. He's been wantin' to get home since the first day I met him. He'll swim that river and take you right to the Choctaw Indian reservation. No need to touch the reins." He took Jefferson's hand in his own. "I'll come for you when we get your name cleared. Me and Trudy will come together for you and bring you home."

Jefferson nodded. He glanced toward the slowly moving current of the river, then mounted the big bay. He did not look back again as the horse sensed his willingness to cross the broad Arkansas.

Birch followed them on foot with Trudy at his side. Together they watched the horse and rider swimming hard against the endless flow until they at last emerged safely on the farther shore.

Epilogue

SPRING 1920

The wildflowers bloomed early that spring, covering the hills and fallow fields in a crazy quilt of color. A soft breeze blew across the land, changing the tints from bright to soft, then bright again. From the hilltop Willa-Mae thought all the land was a moving sea of violet and blue and orange and yellow. The drifting shadow of a cloud deepened the hues here, and there the sunlight made them glow again.

"I'm gonna miss this place, Lord," Willa-Mae whispered. "Ain't never know'd no place but this."

At her side, Little Nettie furrowed her brow. "What's it like up North, Mama?"

"Don't know for sure," Willa-Mae answered truthfully. "But I suppose the Lord is there, jus' like He's been here for us."

"Is He with Jefferson, too, Mama?"

"I know He is, chil'. That's why I keeps on livin'. We don't know 'bout Jefferson, but the Lord knows. He knows ever'thing."

"Mister Birch an' Miss Trudy say he never come to the Choctaw nation. Never brung that horse on home. Say he jus' kept on ridin' by, they reckon. What if Jefferson come home an' we ain't here no more, Mama?"

Willa-Mae had pondered such thing a thousand times since the Old Mister sent word that they had to leave. "I don't reckon Jefferson ever be comin' home to this place again, chil'."

"But if he do, Mama! He gonna find that no white man ever got arrested. Won't they kill him, Mama, for gettin' away?"

"The Lord done eased my mind, Little Nettie." Willa-Mae looked toward the west. "Jefferson ain't comin' back here no more. And if I never more see my boy on this side of the river, I know I got a big reunion up ahead of me." She scanned the row of ragged crosses marking the graves of her children and of Latisha.

Little Nettie read the letters on Latisha's cross.

LATISHA CANFIELD
Wife
Jefferson C.
In My Father's House

"Mama? Who's gonna come tend this here grave? And Widdie's grave? You know these ol' crosses gonna fade away if someone don't paint on 'em ever' year." Nettie cocked her head skyward. "Who's gonna come look after 'em?"

The question made Willa-Mae smile slightly. Maybe spring was the very best time to say good-bye. The flowers—the memory of these flowers would comfort her when she remembered. She picked a bunch from the grave of Widdie, and then from the grave of Latisha, and one each from her babies.

"I reckon they been planted in the Lord's garden," she said, holding a lupine out to Nettie. "Take it, chil'. Press it in the pages of the Good Book Jefferson left for you. Remember, the Lord Himself tends the restin' places of His chillens. He planted these flowers. Watered 'em. Made 'em perty."

She inhaled the sweet fragrance. Better than Paris perfume. "We done cried a sea of tears, Nettie, in this place. Can't change what was—what is. . . . But one day the Lord gonna make my chillen live again. Bloom again. Rise up outta this sea of sorrows all changed an' forever beautiful. An' He'll do justice to them who done wrong. He'll wipe away our tears forevermore."

Little Nettie cradled the flower as though it held some vision of that day. "Tisha's in this flower, Mama. And Widdie." Then to the bloom she said, "I'm takin' you with me for a promise. . . ." Her young eyes raised to sweep over the ever-changing landscape in farewell. "Good-bye ain't forever. . . ."

In My Father's House

"It ain't what I do in this world that makes me worth somethin'. It's what the Lord's already done that makes me worth somethin'."
—JEFFERSON CANFIELD (p. 309)

Have you ever felt unloved? unworthy? scared? desperate? bitter? alone? brokenhearted? Then you're not alone. Throughout *In My Father's House*, Birch, Ellis, Max, Trudy, Becky, and Irene face a barrage of these emotions.

Birch is overwhelmed with grief and loss as he thinks about the deaths of his loving mother and brother, Bobby—and about the mean drunk of a father left behind. Does he really have any home left to go to?

Ellis is scared and bitter. Life hasn't turned out like he expected. In fact, as far as he's concerned, his dreams are gone, along with half of his leg.

Max is trapped by the customs of his community, and the girl he loves is an outsider. He's desperate to escape his neighborhood—to make something of himself. But at what price?

Trudy had been sent east for schooling and to find a suitable mate. Instead she meets a man she never expected to become involved with—a man surrounded by scandal.

Becky is shocked when the man she loves returns home from war a different person, with a soul more disabled than his body. Will it be possible for them to regain their love? for her to prove to him that the loss of his leg does not mean the loss of her love?

Like Max, Irene is trapped by her love for a selfish man determined to have things *his* way and in *his* timing.

All these people long to be loved—for who they are. It's a longing that cannot be met merely by human connection, a longing that Birch's mama understood:

> *I loved you when you wasn't nothin' but a squalling, useless little runt. . . . Hear me now, boy . . . remember the Lord loves you even more than I ever could. And He's right there with you. . . . You just lay yourself in the Lord's arms like a baby, Birch. You don't need to be strong all the time. Let Him love you.* (p. 249-250)

It's this same kind of love the wise Preacher, Jefferson Canfield, says, that makes us "somethin'" instead of "nothin'."

"I don't need no medal to tell me I'm somethin'. Jesus already told me: 'Jefferson, you're worth My life. Jefferson, you're worth My sufferin'. Jefferson, the Son of God Almighty loves you. Your life and your soul are worth eternity! (p. 310)

Are you trying to be strong all the time? Or are you letting the Lord love you? Are you trusting Him as a baby would trust his mother? Or are you trying to do in your own power? As Jefferson says, "Babies ain't nothin' but squallin', messy, hungry little things! But, oh my, how they is *loved*! Not because of what they can do, but just *because*" (p. 310).

Jesus loves *you* just *because.* Not because of what you do. Not because of who you are. But because of who He is and what He has done for you.

Even if you believe this, difficult times will come. Such turmoil is inevitable in our human existence. But when difficulties come, why not lay in the Lord's arms and let Him love you? Put your trust in God—instead of in other humans, fate, or yourself. Let Him "teach you how to walk, how to talk, how to run and laugh and sing!" (p. 310).

As an African-American in the racially prejudicial America of 1919, Jefferson Canfield faced overwhelming odds. But he did not allow those odds to affect his spirit or his beliefs. Jefferson was secure in the knowledge that he would forever be in his Father's arms and that someday he would take his place in his Father's House.

We trust the following questions will help you dig deeper for answers to *your* daily dilemmas. You may wish to delve into these questions on your own or share them with a friend or a discussion group. Most of all we pray that you will "discover the Truth through fiction." For we are convinced that if you seek diligently, you will find the One who holds all the answers to the universe (1 Chronicles 28:9).

Bodie & Brock Thoene

SEEK . . .

Prologue

1. "Theo shook his head in amazement at how things had changed" (p. x). Twenty-two years earlier he and the father of David Meyer had been fighting on opposite sides of a war. And in this war, he and David Meyer fought on the same side. Have you ever been surprised how things can change in your life? Tell the story.

_____

_____

2. Do you know anyone who has fought in a war? If so, how has that experience changed that person?

_____

_____

PART I
Chapters 1–3

3. Max, Ellis, and Birch found themselves surprisingly cheering for an enemy as they watched the skillful aviator maneuver the skies over no-man's-land in France (see p. 6). If you were there and you'd just experienced the horrors of war, could you cheer for an enemy? go out of your way to help him, as the three Americans did? Why or why not?

_____

_____

4. If you were Molly and had lost three babies and two older sons, would you want to be able to see their granite memorials out your window every day (see p. 11)? Explain.

_____

_____

5. "Mrs. Fleischer always made it a practice to speak to Trudy in Yiddish just to point out how terrible it was that a girl like Trudy had been raised in a home that was practically not even Jewish anymore" (p. 18). Has anyone ever criticized your home, upbringing, or religious stance? How did you respond?

_____

_____

Chapters 4–5

6. For men at war, the name *Mother* and memories of ordinary life become all the more precious (see p. 25). When has a crisis made you reflect on home? When have "the mundane things of everyday life" (see p. 26) become important?

_____

_____

7. When the soldiers got letters, they always wondered: "should they eat first or read first?" (p. 33). When has "a note from home" or an e-mail from someone you love or admire made a difference in your life (whether good news or bad news)?

_____

_____

8. "Every man had his own private ache tonight" Birch realizes after he learns of the death of his mother and brother (p. 39). What is your private ache right now?

_____

_____

9. "Mama had been like a live oak tree, rooted in her love for the Lord and her desire to raise her sons to serve God and their fellow men. Pa, too, was made of oak, hard and irascible. But he was no live oak. He was more like a fence post, a barrier rooted deep to

keep things in and keep other things out, a line of taut barbed wire that crossed his heart and said, *Go no farther."* (p. 40). What person do you know who is like Birch's mama? who is like Birch's pa? Explain.

_____

_____

Chapters 6–8

10. Irene was compelled to share her soul with Trudy (see p. 45). Have you ever been on the giving end or the receiving end of a confession? How did it make you feel? Did making that confession change anything about your relationship with that person? If so, in what way(s)?

_____

_____

11. Have you ever lost a loved one (as Trudy lost Henny, and the Canfields lost Widdie)? How have you dealt with that grief? In what ways has it affected your faith?

_____

_____

12. Somehow Molly knew that "momentous things were taking place—things of which her boy Ellis was a part. . . . Ellis was in danger" (p. 57). Have you ever sensed that a loved one was in danger somehow? How did you respond to that inner sense?

_____

_____

Chapters 9–11

13. Trudy "wished she had another reason to celebrate the end of the war—someone special coming home to her. Just to her alone"

(p. 68). When have you wished for someone special? In what ways has that longing been fulfilled? not fulfilled?

_____

_____

14. When Birch agonizes over his friend Ellis losing his leg, he wonders if war is really worth it (see p. 78). Do you think war is worth it? Why or why not?

_____

_____

15. How were Jefferson Canfield and the other black soldiers treated by the Americans? the French (see p. 81–82)? Why do you think there is such a contrast?

_____

_____

Chapter 12

16. When Ellis looks at the place where his leg should have been, he wonders why the fighting had to take place man-to-man. It seems like such a waste. And he is left with bitterness and says, "I am the desert. . . . And I have no peace" (p. 91). Can you identify with Ellis? If so, how?

_____

_____

17. "Life is hard."

"Yes. And that is the truth of it. It always will be. You have lost your leg and the world is still a toilet. Your loss changes nothing, means nothing, unless it makes you a better man. This is why we suffer. Like a fire, it burns the filth of our souls away" (p. 91).

Do you agree with Theo's assessment of suffering? Why or why not?

_____

_____

18. Have you experienced a "sea-change" in your own life (see p. 91)? Or seen a sea-change in someone else's life? What happened?

_____

_____

PART II
Chapters 13–15

19. Ellis couldn't bring himself to tell his family about his wound (see p. 96). What "wound" do you carry that you don't feel comfortable revealing to others? Why?

_____

_____

20. To Rebecca Moniger "nothing else mattered but being at the end of that ramp when Ellis walked down. She had imagined it for months—through Christmas and Easter. Since the war had ended she had thought of nothing else" (p. 98). When have you experienced that kind of anticipation?

_____

_____

21. "Birch thought that Max was the luckiest man in the world" (p. 105). Whom do you consider to be the luckiest person? Why? What do you admire about that person?

_____

_____

22. Ellis treated his mother and Becky with a roughness that was unlike him when he returned home (see p. 114)—all because he had a wounded soul. When has a wounded soul caused someone to treat you roughly? or you to treat someone else roughly? Have you reconciled in any way? If so, how?

_____

_____

Chapters 16–18

23. Have you ever felt locked into a tight little world, as Max did upon his return to his neighborhood (see p. 122)? Have you felt like "a foreigner, trespassing in their sleeping world" as Birch did (p. 128)? Did you stay or leave? Why? What changed in your heart as a result?

_____

_____

24. What are some of Max's good qualities? his bad qualities? Is he the kind of person you would want to date and/or marry? Explain?

_____

_____

25. "A baby would have ruined her life. She would have had to drop out of school. . . . . You think I would want to . . . leave her with that sort of burden? I did what I did *for her*," Max tells Trudy (p. 132–133). Do you agree with Max's logic? Why or why not?

_____

_____

26. "It seems to me that love, real love, should not hurt like this," Trudy tells Irene. "Don't let him hurt you, Irene. It's hurting him, too, if you do. Just walk away—run away from him if you have

to—but don't let him ever hurt you like that again" (p. 140). Have you ever been in a position similar to Irene's? allowed someone you love to hurt you? If so, what can you do—or have you done— to regain respect for yourself?

_____

_____

Chapters 19–21

27. Put yourself in Birch's shoes. Not only does he provide Jefferson and the other black soldiers with sandwiches through a creative strategy, he also "did a remarkable thing" in Trudy's eyes. "He climbed the steps of the car reserved for coloreds. By choice. She knew what that meant and liked him for it" (p. 162). Would you put yourself on the line for a person you just met? a person obviously "different" from you? a "society outcast"? Explain.

_____

_____

28. "You're talking as if you're a cripple," Doc tells his son Ellis. Then he taps his index finger against his temple. "The only thing that can cripple a man is what's up here" (p. 172–73). Do you agree with Doc's statement? Why or why not?

_____

_____

29. Ellis "had thought it all out and was prepared to give up everything he had ever wanted. Now Doc was telling him he was wrong. He didn't much like it. It was much easier to be resigned to loss, wasn't it?" (p. 173). Is it easier to give up and to be resigned to loss—or to fight it? Why?

_____

_____

Chapters 22–25

30. "Some men were windows into the glory of heaven. So close! Others—many others—were like holes in a dam, and the darkness of hell poured through their lives and sucked folks down, drowning their souls in hatred," Jefferson realizes (see p. 182). Had you ever faced someone who looks nice on the outside, but is ugly on the inside, like Deputy East (see p. 203)? Or Hopewell (see p. 199)? Were you drawn in to the ugliness or not? What happened? Would you do anything differently the next time you face someone with an ugly soul?

   _____

   _____

31. Jefferson vowed to "tell stories about the little things that came into his head, and men would hear and want to know the Lord of Light" (see p. 182). Is this a goal in your life? If so, to what extent do you live out this goal before others?

   _____

   _____

32. Joseph and Sadie Meyer went beyond duty in their patriotic zeal in order to survive prejudice. Have you ever faced prejudice of any kind (racial, gender stereotypes, physical, such as Ellis faced in chapter 24 when "the cripple" played baseball, etc.)? How did you deal with that prejudice?

   _____

   _____

33. What do you think is the origin of prejudice? Fear? Ignorance? An unwillingness to change? Hate? Explain. How can keeping those "origins" in mind change *your* response to prejudice or your own prejudicial views toward others?

   _____

   _____

Chapters 26–28

34. When have you fought with someone you love and wished you hadn't (like Max and Irene in chapters 25 and 26)? What was the result of that fight? What did you learn?

_____

_____

35. Even though his sister Widdie is dead, Jefferson is not able to put her to rest in his mind until he comes home to Mount Pisgah. Then he sees her as she is now, walking through a flower garden (see p. 217). What do you believe happens after death? How does that view influence how you live your life now?

_____

_____

36. If you were Birch and someone you loved was a mean drunk, would you go back home to say "I love you" as Birch is determined to do (see p. 230)? Why or why not?

_____

_____

Chapter 29

37. "Have I told you lately how much I love our home, Molly? Isn't our life together something grand? . . . You have no thought that I could ever wish for more, do you now? For myself, I mean. We may still be ambitious for our children's success and happiness, but I feel no lack for me" (p. 239).

   As you look back on your life, would you view it with the same contentment and sentiment as Doc Warne? Or would there be things you wish you had done differently? And, if so, how?

_____

_____

38. Was Birch's "homecoming"—his meeting with his father—what you had expected (see p. 245–248)? Why or why not? Do you think there is anything Birch could have done differently? If you have to deal with a violent and/or angry person, what part of the relationship are you responsible for? What part of the relationship is not your responsibility?

_____

_____

39. "I'm in need of holdin', Jesus," Birch whispered as he lay on his back on the church pew. "In need of a Father tonight" (p. 250). Have you found yourself in a similar position? When?

_____

_____

PART III
Chapters 30–32

40. Did you ever, as a child, get in a fight because of a principle (as Julie did when she fought for her father's reputation in chapter 31)? What happened? What was the end result? Do you still find yourself fighting today—perhaps in different ways—for what is right? Explain.

_____

_____

41. Does it bother you when animals are mistreated (as it bothered Birch when the horse is mistreated by the foreman in chapter 31)? Have you ever acted on that feeling? If so, what was the result?

_____

_____

42. Were you ever penalized in some way because of false or ridiculous accusations, as Trudy was when she was let go from Belle Grove School in chapter 31? What has happened since then?

_____

_____

Chapters 33–35

43. Although Trudy has to quickly find another teaching position, she shows determination when she says to her father, "I will do more than manage. . . . I will educate them. . . . I am your child, after all, am I not?" (p. 284). In what ways have you shown determination in a difficult position? In what ways are you like or unlike your parents?

_____

_____

44. How does Trudy break the ice with the folks in Mount Pisgah (see chapters 33 and 34)? How could you break the ice with others when you're in a new situation?

_____

_____

45. Ellis, Becky, and little Julie come upon a circle of Ku Klux Klan members having a meeting at a church and singing "The Son of God Goes Forth to War," using that as their theme song for "cleansing" the nation of "accursed" people (see p. 302). Why do you think some people become so hateful?

_____

_____

Chapters 36–38

46. Have you ever wondered if you have done something so bad that God could never forgive it? If so, what is it?

_____

_____

Scripture promises: *As the heaven is high above the earth, so great is His mercy toward them that fear Him. As far as the east is from the west, so far hath He removed our transgressions from us* (Psalm 103:11-12). Why not let go of that "transgression" today and trust God's forgiveness?

As Jefferson Canfield says, "As far as east is from west. That's mighty far, sisters and brothers. A man can't walk that far. An eagle can't fly that far. No fish is gonna swim an ocean that wide! God put our sin that far from us! Jesus took it all away when He died for me" (p. 310).

47. Do you think that all people are created equal in the sight of God? Why or why not? Explain your answer.

_____

_____

48. "The day he had longed for—the day he had dreaded—had finally dawned" for Ellis . . . and he panicked (see p. 321). Can you relate to Ellis's cowardice (with a wedding, a career move, etc.)? What happened?

_____

_____

Chapters 39–42

49. Trudy is surprised by what she learns about Scott from Little Nettie (see p. 341–342). Doc Warne is surprised and angered by Flannery and O'Brien, who in the guise of friends try to convince him to withdraw from the political race (see p. 364). When have you been

surprised to learn about a person's character "below the surface," especially someone you thought you knew well?

_____

_____

50. "Ellis had been thinking about the future a lot lately—about his impending surgery, his time in the hospital away from this place and Becky's touch" (p. 352). What's on your list of things to think about for the future?

_____

_____

51. "Ain't no need to fear what come upon us, Tisha. Heaven's a real place, an' as long as we be there together, I ain't feared of nothin' this old world gonna bring me. . . . The Lord's buildin' our house," Jefferson tells his bride at the beginning of chapter 42. Shortly after that, the Klan arrives . . . and Latisha is killed. Does this event make Jefferson's words earlier null and void to you? Why or why not? Do you think heaven is a real place? Can you say you are not afraid of anything this world brings you? Why or why not?

_____

_____

52. Faced with the horror of what is happening to Latisha and Jefferson, Hock Canfield says in despair, "They *make* me a nigger. I ain't nothin' at all" (p. 380). Do you believe that others make you who you are? that you make yourself who you are? that God makes you who you are? or some combination? Explain.

_____

_____

Chapter 43—Epilogue

53. How did evil men try to wreak their vengeance on the Canfields and the Warnes? Did evil win, in your opinion? Why or why not?

_____

_____

54. "We don't know 'bout Jefferson, but the Lord knows. He knows ever'thin'," Willa-Mae tells Little Nettie. "We done cried a sea of tears, Nettie, in this place. Can't change what was—what is. . . . But one day the Lord gonna . . . do justice to them who done wrong. He'll wipe away our tears forevermore" (p. 391–392).

    Do you believe the Lord knows everything? that one day He'll bring justice to this earth? Why or why not? How does your view of "ultimate justice"—or the lack of it—affect the way you live today?

_____

_____

About the Authors

BODIE AND BROCK THOENE (pronounced *Tay-nee*) have written over 45 works of historical fiction. That these best sellers have sold more than 10 million copies and won eight ECPA Gold Medallion Awards affirms what millions of readers have already discovered—the Thoenes are not only master stylists but experts at capturing readers' minds and hearts.

In their timeless classic series about Israel (The Zion Chronicles, The Zion Covenant, and The Zion Legacy), the Thoenes' love for both story and research shines.

With the Shiloh Legacy series and *Shiloh Autumn*—poignant portrayals of the American Depression—and The Galway Chronicles, which dramatically tell of the 1840s famine in Ireland, as well as the twelve Legends of the West, the Thoenes have made their mark in modern history.

In the A.D. Chronicles, their most recent series, they step seamlessly into the world of Yerushalayim and Rome, in the days when Yeshua walked the earth and transformed lives with His touch.

Bodie began her writing career as a teen journalist for her local newspaper. Eventually her byline appeared in prestigious periodicals such as *U.S. News and World Report*, *The American West*, and *The Saturday Evening Post*. She also worked for John Wayne's Batjac Productions (she's best known as author of *The Fall Guy*) and ABC Circle Films as a writer and researcher. John Wayne described her as "a writer with talent that captures the people and the times!" She has degrees in journalism and communications.

Brock has often been described by Bodie as "an essential half of this writing team." With degrees in both history and education, Brock has, in his role as researcher and story-line consultant, added the vital dimension of historical accuracy. Due to such careful research, the Zion Covenant and the Zion Chronicles series are recognized by the American Library Association, as well as Zionist libraries around the world, as classic historical novels and are used to teach history in college classrooms.

Bodie and Brock have four grown children—Rachel, Jake, Luke, and Ellie—and five grandchildren. Their sons, Jake and Luke, are carrying on the Thoene family talent as the next generation of writers, and Luke produces the Thoene audiobooks. Bodie and Brock divide their time between London and Nevada.

For more information visit:
www.thoenebooks.com
www.familyaudiolibrary.com

THOENE FAMILY CLASSICS™

✪ ✪ ✪

THOENE FAMILY CLASSIC HISTORICALS
by Bodie and Brock Thoene
Gold Medallion Winners*

THE ZION COVENANT
Vienna Prelude*
Prague Counterpoint
Munich Signature
Jerusalem Interlude
Danzig Passage
Warsaw Requiem*
London Refrain
Paris Encore
Dunkirk Crescendo

THE ZION CHRONICLES
The Gates of Zion*
A Daughter of Zion
The Return to Zion
A Light in Zion
The Key to Zion*

THE SHILOH LEGACY
In My Father's House*
A Thousand Shall Fall
Say to This Mountain

SHILOH AUTUMN

THE GALWAY CHRONICLES
Only the River Runs Free*
Of Men and of Angels
Ashes of Remembrance*
All Rivers to the Sea

THE ZION LEGACY
Jerusalem Vigil
Thunder from Jerusalem
Jerusalem's Heart
Jerusalem Scrolls
Stones of Jerusalem
Jerusalem's Hope

A.D. CHRONICLES
First Light
Second Touch
Third Watch
Fourth Dawn
Fifth Seal
and more to come!

THOENE FAMILY CLASSICS™

✪ ✪ ✪

THOENE FAMILY CLASSIC AMERICAN LEGENDS

LEGENDS OF THE WEST
by Bodie and Brock Thoene

The Man from Shadow Ridge
Riders of the Silver Rim
Gold Rush Prodigal
Sequoia Scout
Cannons of the Comstock
Year of the Grizzly
Shooting Star
Legend of Storey County
Hope Valley War
Delta Passage
Hangtown Lawman
Cumberland Crossing

LEGENDS OF VALOR
by Luke Thoene
Sons of Valor
Brothers of Valor
Fathers of Valor

✪ ✪ ✪

THOENE CLASSIC NONFICTION
by Bodie and Brock Thoene

Writer-to-Writer

THOENE FAMILY CLASSIC SUSPENSE
by Jake Thoene

CHAPTER 16 SERIES
Shaiton's Fire
Firefly Blue
Fuel the Fire

✪ ✪ ✪

THOENE FAMILY CLASSICS FOR KIDS
by Jake and Luke Thoene

BAKER STREET DETECTIVES
The Mystery of the Yellow Hands
The Giant Rat of Sumatra
The Jeweled Peacock of Persia
The Thundering Underground

LAST CHANCE DETECTIVES
Mystery Lights of Navajo Mesa
Legend of the Desert Bigfoot

✪ ✪ ✪

THOENE FAMILY CLASSIC AUDIOBOOKS
Available from
www.thoenebooks.com or
www.familyaudiolibrary.com